MN

Also by Gina Frangello

My Sister's Continent
Slut Lullabies

A LIFE IN
MEN

~~~~~~~~~~~~~~~~~~~~~~

A NOVEL

Gina Frangello

ALGONQUIN BOOKS OF CHAPEL HILL   2014

Published by
ALGONQUIN BOOKS OF CHAPEL HILL
Post Office Box 2225
Chapel Hill, North Carolina 27515-2225

a division of
WORKMAN PUBLISHING
225 Varick Street
New York, New York 10014

This is a work of fiction. While, as in all fiction, the literary perceptions and insights are based on experience, all names, characters, places, and incidents either are products of the author's imagination or are used fictitiously.

LIBRARY OF CONGRESS CATALOGING-IN-PUBLICATION DATA
Frangello, Gina.
A Life in Men : a novel / by Gina Frangello.—First Edition.
pages cm
ISBN 978-1-61620-163-0
1. Female friendship—Fiction.   2. Life change events—Fiction.   3. Man-woman relationships—Fiction.   4. Voyages and travels—Fiction.   I. Title.
PS3606.R3757L54 2014
813'.6—dc23   2013024028

10 9 8 7 6 5 4 3 2 1
First Edition

For Sarah B., 1968–1998,
for inspiration.

And for Kathryn K., 1968–2011,
for those sad, sad times when life imitates art.
I miss you, girl.

In eternity this world will be Troy, I believe,
and all that has passed here will be the epic of the universe,
the ballad they sing in the streets.

—MARILYNNE ROBINSON, *Gilead*

◎ ◈ ◎

Maybe there is nothing, ever, that can equal
the recollection of having been young together.

—MICHAEL CUNNINGHAM, *The Hours*

A LIFE IN MEN

Where Are We Going, Where Have We Been?

(GREECE: ZORG)

Pretend I'm not already dead. That isn't important anyway. It's just that, from here, I can see everything.

There we are, see? Or should I say, *There they are?* Two girls sitting at a café off Taxi Square, eating anchovies lined up in a small puddle of oil on a white plate. Both girls are obsessed with salt. Since arriving in Mykonos, they have ordered anchovies every day, lunch and dinner. As a result, they are constantly thirsty. They carry large bottles of water with them everywhere, written on in Greek lettering, the blue caps peeking out the tops of their beach bags along with their rolled-up beach mats. The curly-haired blond girl, Mary, jokes to the straight-haired blond girl, Nix, that this influx of salt is going to be a turnoff should they pick up any hot men. Mary has cystic fibrosis, and sometimes one of the first clues parents get that their baby has CF is that the child's sweat is especially salty, so much so that the baby tastes salty on the parents' lips. Apparently Mary's parents (who are not her biological parents, so this is particularly strange) share her affinity for salt, because no one noticed that Mary was an odd-tasting baby, and for this reason, along with a variety of other factors, like her ability—unusual in CF patients—to digest her food, the disease was not diagnosed until she was seventeen. Today as they sit at the tiny sidewalk café, Mary places an anchovy on her long pink tongue and lets it lie there while she savors its taste.

Several postcards lie strewn on the tabletop between them, and Nix picks one up without looking at the photo on the front. Hand trembling slightly from her caffeine-and-nicotine buzz, she begins doodling idly, sketching a box inside another box. Inside the outer box, Nix writes:

Anonymously Tragic Story of Terminal Illness in Boring Midwest

Then, inside the smaller, inner box she scribbles in tiny lettering:

Glamorous Story of Young Women on Holiday in Sunny Greece
=
Story Suitable for Chick Flick

"Who are you writing to?" Mary asks, her hand reaching across the marble tabletop, but Nix withdraws the postcard quickly, abruptly aware that there is no one on earth to whom she *could* send such a card except, of course, to Mary herself. She knows that if she showed her doodle to Mary, Mary would laugh, and yet Nix finds herself tucking the card into the book inside her beach bag instead.

"Nobody," she says.

THE GIRLS LOITER at this café for quite some time. It is early still to hit the beach, and they have no particular agenda. Mary reads James Michener's novel *The Drifters,* which seems a weird choice to Nix, something their mothers might bring on holiday. Nix takes out her novel, too—*Couples* by John Updike—but instead of reading she stares at the picture on her hidden postcard, tucked between Updike's pages. She stares at the outer edges of the larger frame until its lines become shimmery and transparent, until its text begins to blur. Then she focuses on the inner frame, the one involving romantic outdoor cafés, bright sun amplified by azure water, beach mats, and banter. Next to their now-empty plate of anchovies, Nix's English cigarette box rests like a prop to signal that she is the "bad girl" of that narrative. Even Greece itself seems a prop for stories featuring nubile young blonds in sunny locales, generally involving sexual intrigue, female bonding, and madcap adventures. Nix sits, not reading Updike, content to wait for the next reel of this vacation movie to begin spinning. If the encroaching shadow of their usual story—the one involving Mary's shortened life span and Nix's thrashing inadequacy to its weight—nags at her, she is relieved to pretend otherwise, basking in the Grecian sun of reinvention.

She does not yet realize, of course, that neither movie frame scribbled on a postcard will prove large enough to contain them, or shatterproof against everything about to happen. How *could* she realize, after all? Let the living enjoy their illusions while they can.

MEANWHILE, THE IMAGINARY camera, abetted by the very real script, has established that Nix is the wilder of the two. What of it, though? Her weakly blinking pride in this fact is perpetually diminished by the chronic illness of the other, so that ordinary acts like going to Greece for two weeks before the start of their junior year of college take on—for Mary—a kind of heroism that all Nix's wild antics pale beside, as she is not sick, just nineteen and reckless and normal, with all the luxurious frustrations normalcy affords. In two weeks, Mary will return home to her parents' house in Kettering, Ohio, whereas Nix will spend the first semester of her junior year at Regent's College in London. Yet even though Nix has been away from home for two years, at Skidmore College in New York, and will not be in Ohio again until winter break, Mary was the one their parents—both mothers and Mary's father—clucked over when they said their good-byes at the airport, anxiety narrowing their eyes and raising their voices.

Such moments bring out the bitch in Nix, even though no one, not even Mary's own parents, could possibly want Mary to stay healthy more than she does. If anything bad happened to Mary on this trip, Nix would die not only of guilt but of misery. Mary is like her sister: a handpicked twin. Several of Nix's friends from Skidmore are already in London or traveling elsewhere in Europe right now, but Nix was overjoyed when Mary wanted to go to Greece, and so she canceled plans with other, more sophisticated friends so she could travel with

Mary. And yet. It is not easy, living in the shadow of someone's Tragic Illness, so that everything you do seems insubstantial by comparison. Other people in the world would have to agree that this is true.

Only Mary seems to find Nix's adventures—or "mistakes," as Nix's mother would say—worthwhile. "I can't believe how worldly you've gotten," Mary says, setting Michener aside and guilelessly taking Nix's hand across the table. "While I've been cloistered in Ohio spitting into Dixie cups, you've been, like, having affairs with rich East Coast men and jaunting off for weekends in Manhattan—now you're off to live in England like some modern-day E. M. Forster heroine, for God's sake! It's crazy—all the stuff we talked about when we were little, you're actually *doing* it!"

Nix carefully blows the smoke of her Silk Cut in the opposite direction of Mary's damaged lungs. Exactly half of her best friend's imagined scenario is true: indeed, Mary has spent the better part of her freshman and sophomore years of college consumed by learning to deal with her disease, since she'd never learned the ropes as a kid. The other half of the scenario goes more like this: while Mary has been spitting into Dixie cups, Nix has been sleeping with a married English professor who doesn't remotely love her and developing a coke habit she cannot economically afford.

Mary's grip on Nix's hand tightens. "What I need," Mary whispers urgently, "is an adventure."

Nix says, "Retard, we're in Greece. This *is* an adventure."

"You know what I mean."

"Ahhh," Nix drawls. "I see. We need to get you devirginized."

"For starters, hell yeah."

With calm certainty, Nix surveys the crazy white buildings of Mykonos, the glare of the midday sun off the water, thinking how the humidity complements Mary's curls and that, for a blond, Mary has an uncanny ability to tan instead of burn. At this moment, just to look at her, no one would ever know Mary was sick—though if they did, Nix figures, here in Greece it might only make her sexier, because men love damsels in distress as long as they don't have to actually rescue them.

"That won't be difficult," she promises.

THERE ARE MANY beginnings to any story. Maybe the real beginning was the day Nix—then still known as Nicole—bit Mary in kindergarten, during a dispute over a yellow crayon, and they were forced to sit in the Naughty Chair together. They emerged best friends. Maybe it was the night of high school graduation, when Nix assured Mary's continued virginity by allowing Mary's boyfriend, Bobby Kenner, to screw her, under the pretext of their shared grief over Mary's newly realized death sentence, this grief only gauzily covering more violent emotions like jealousy, anger, and fear. Maybe the beginning was Nix's phone call from Skidmore to Kettering, in which she first uttered the phrase "Greek Islands," like a siren call, into the ear of her isolated, lonely friend. Or maybe the beginning—on this bright August morning in 1988—has not even happened yet and is still to come, to result from one of the myriad miscalculations made by one or the other of the girls once Zorg and Titus make their entrance.

But all stories have to start somewhere, so for the sake of simplicity it shall begin here, in two girls' small pact made over a small café table on a small island, and it will prove to be the beginning of everything.

THEIR PLAN PROCEEDS smoothly enough. The girls meet two men precisely as such men are usually met: at a bar. Though Mykonos is full of tourists, this bar is predominantly Greek, and so two blond girls stand out as though illuminated by a spotlight. If it had not been these two men, it would have been another two, or another two after that. It is a bar where the likelihood of two blond American girls' entering alone is slim, but the chances of their exiting alone nonexistent. The girls call this kind of place "authentic."

The first two men to speak to them are dark haired and olive skinned, like every other man in the bar. There are, in fact, almost no women in the bar. In that way it is like one of those old-man bars at home in Kettering, where occasionally Nix and Mary and girls like them wander in to make change for a dollar to feed a parking meter, and see man after man on barstools and at the pool table, reeking of smoke and hopelessness. In Kettering, no girl would go to such a bar on purpose because in Ohio there is nothing glamorous about men drinking alone. In Mykonos, however, Nix and Mary feel a thrill at the lack of female presence.

The preponderance of men is *so* extreme, however, that Nix is about to poke Mary and quip that maybe they have come to a gay bar by mistake (it being Mykonos, after all). Before she can do so, two dark-haired men are standing in front of them, offering to buy them drinks. The men are both in their late twenties or early thirties and handsome— not just "all right" but certifiably hot. One is taller than the other and good looking enough to be a movie star, at least in the bar's dim light. Already Nix is thinking that as soon as possible they will have to excuse themselves to go to the bathroom and do rock, paper, scissors over which one of them gets this man.

Then abruptly she changes her mind. After all, she is off to England to fuck legions of Sting look-alikes who will say sexy things to her in their delicious accents. Therefore, why not give Mary this man, this Greek? The girls sip the wine the shorter man ordered for them, which is thick and sweet, like sherry. Nix thinks of the boy who devirginized her on her senior high school trip to the Bahamas, a boy with hips so slim she could have crushed them between her gymnast thighs, who had a pimple on his jawline, and how, when he thrust, the zit was exactly at her eye level because he kept flinging his head back. She did not have a movie-star Greek on hand to take *her* virginity, so she did things the usual way. But she is still near the beginning. She will have years of zitless men, British and otherwise, with whom to dilute that memory, whereas for Mary, the beginning and the end will be too close.

Nix drains her wine.

In foreign countries, time does not operate the way it does at home. Service in restaurants is slower, and falling into bed with a man is faster. Within minutes of awkward introductions, Mary and the movie star are already holding hands. Mary leans against the solid trunk of him as they listen to a Greek band. A mild buzz beginning to tingle her legs, Nix watches approvingly, smiling. The shorter man reaches for *her* hand, but she moves it away.

I mean, really: Just because she's given Mary the Adonis doesn't mean she plans to spread her legs for shorty over there. Jeez. Nix holds up her empty glass in a universal gesture, and the short Greek scurries off to get her more wine. This may prove to be a long night.

The House of Reinvention

(LONDON: YANK)

For those who are lost, there will always be cities that feel like home.
Places where lonely people can live in exile of their own lives—
far from anything that was ever imagined for them.
—SIMON VAN BOOY, *Everything Beautiful Began After*

Arthog House exists so far off the tourist grid it is not accessible by Tube. The fact that Mary ends up living there will later seem nothing short of implausible. Desperate for funds, she answers an ad run across in a transient newspaper, *TNT,* for a bartending job at the Latchmere Pub. Despite her lack of either a Blue Card or experience, she is hired on the spot, because who else would bother to come all this way, especially a blond American girl? At first she doesn't live in the same neighborhood as the pub, but then she does. Arthog House claims her as one of its own. It is not what she intended for herself when she came to London, but it is what happens. She will never even see Buckingham Palace. She will never take a single photograph of Big Ben.

The house—one step above a squat, in that it comes with electricity, crap furniture, and a hairy-eared landlord called Mr. D. who appears every Sunday to collect the rent—is located on a residential street just north of sprawling Battersea Park Road, but south of the Thames and even of the green park proper. It is a park where someday gentrification will give birth to quaint cafés lining the small lake, but during the fall of 1990 it boasts only derelicts kipping on benches. Like a backpacker's Tara, Arthog House bears a plaque proclaiming its name, embedded just to the left of the front door. If the two-story white stone building bears a clear identity, the small pocket of neighborhood in which it resides does not. According to residents of posh Chelsea to the north, anything south of the Chelsea Bridge falls within the domain of Battersea. To the on-the-dole islanders occupying the estates, however, Battersea begins on *their* street, Battersea Park Road. Mary's black pub customers deride their shabby white Lower Chelsea neighbors to the north: laborers, hairdressers, wantonly racist old ladies perpetually pushing shopping trolleys, a United Nations of drug dealers who revolve in and out by the season. Though the clientele of the Latchmere Pub is mostly white, fights regularly break out, its white underbelly majority not at true peace in Battersea, but clearly unfit for Chelsea.

Arthog House has four bedrooms, one bath, a basement kitchen, and a kitchenette on the upper floor in the sitting room. The three downstairs bedrooms are occupied by a constantly rotating parade of Kiwi males who all work as laborers at a nearby construction site. Every time one of them leaves for Mallorca or Turkey, another takes his place so quickly that Mary has found it pointless to endeavor to learn each new name. The Kiwis also dominate the basement kitchen, although they never seem to actually cook. Since they each share a bedroom with at least one other man, the kitchen, the only place for privacy, has been informally dubbed The Brothel, because it is where the Kiwis go when making it with some local girl, and so its door is usually closed.

Upstairs at Arthog House, four residents share one bedroom and a sitting room. Three of those four are male, too: a South African, a Dutchman, and an American southerner. Mary, then—the fourth—is the only female in the entire house, a Wendy among Lost Boys. Because she does not realize that here at Arthog House she holds no monopoly on the desire for reinvention, she plays her cards close to her chest. Or maybe that is not even her reason. The truth is, taken outside her habitual environs of the American Midwest, she

has little idea who she is. Unmoored from her history, she feels dangerously blank, like a hologram of herself walking around. The reason for
this is twofold. First, of course, is the universal principle of unformed
youth, which does not even occur to her because twenty-two-year-olds
do not *feel* as unformed as they are. The second reason is more individual, more unique, in that at home she had grown used to feeling
important, larger than life, because of the illness that has wormed its
way into her previously ordinary existence, bestowing what passes for
character on even the most banal of daily activities. Here in London,
however, without the manacle of her tragedies, divorced even from her
name, her identity feels so light it might simply float away.

Dearest Nix,
   The lie has grown beyond my control. Like a double agent, I am
asked to prove my identity daily, answering to your name even in bed.
Weirdly, this is proving much easier than it sounds . . .

Mary hears her lover's voice booming into the hallway pay phone
outside their bedroom. "Mum, Dad, I've joined the circus!" It is six-
something in the morning, London time. What time this makes it in
South Africa is beyond her ken. Joshua's voice is unnaturally loud,
as though he and his parents are speaking via tin cans on a string
from opposite sides of a playground. She envisions his parents (she
has no idea what they look like—Joshua has brought no photos) as
more elderly than befits their son: the mother with snow-white hair,
both parents pressing ears to one old-fashioned wall telephone, though
surely they have cordless in Johannesburg. "The flying trapeze," Joshua
cries, his jubilance belying the bruises on the backs of his knees. "No,
Dad, it's not really like that, there aren't any animals, not how you
think of the circus—not, like, fat ladies with beards or three-armed
midgets. No derelict drifter types either—practically everyone's an
ex-gymnast like me."

Mary muffles a laugh with her pillow. It's true enough. His circus,
composed mainly of Russian and Chinese acrobats who do not speak
much English, is a clean-cut, hardworking bunch. Which no doubt

accounts for why Joshua rarely *sees* them outside rehearsal, preferring the "derelict drifter types" of Arthog House.

"The last male trapeze artist got married and went back to China," Joshua is saying, "so the girl was looking for a new partner—she came by Covent Garden, and I just happened to be doing my act—" Silence. "I told you this already—" More quiet, the halls reverberating with the concentrated quiet of people trying to sleep. "Street performance isn't like that here," he says, voice dropping. "Loads of talented people do it, the tourists come round purposefully to watch—it's expected, they *want* it. It's not charity."

Mary rolls onto her side, pulls the chilly sheet over her skin. The bed across the room is empty; Yank must not have come home last night.

"I am an *ex*-gymnast," Joshua says louder, transforming himself with one sentence from a competitive athlete to a circus performer: *poof!* In her hazy half sleep, Mary imagines him with giant purple shoes, a bulbous nose, even though the circus in which he performs has no clowns either; it's not that sort of show. "Oh, that's a brilliant idea, Mum, why didn't I think of it? English girls are just queuing up round the corner to marry some foreigner whose been doing flips at Covent fucking Garden for spare change! Let's see, I've got a list of some right here, maybe you can help me narrow it down—would you prefer a blond or brunet daughter-in-law? Don't worry, I won't ask your preference for skin color, that's a fucking given!"

The phone slams into the receiver, so hard she can feel vibrations in the mattress.

In the times she's eavesdropped alone, Joshua has said the word "fuck" to his parents at least two dozen times. Other than that, his phone conversations are not so different from the ones she has with her parents back in Ohio. In essence, they follow the same pattern. The parents demand a return home, and their demand is met with increasingly strident refusal. Whereas his parents get angry, hers tend to cry. Phones are slammed. The routine has ceased to be inherently interesting.

For this reason, she does not immediately rush into the hallway to comfort her lover. And also, of course, because she is naked in a house full of men.

Joshua reenters the bedroom. Mary was sleeping when he left, so only now does she realize, peeking through shut eyes, that he, too, is nude—apparently having carried on the entire phone call with his bare ass facing the staircase leading downstairs. His body, darker skinned than most strawberry blonds, permanently colored by the African sun, is lean from his "poverty diet," but muscles still ripple like waves just beneath the surface of his skin. It strikes her, not for the first time, that only the utter dearth of women in this traveler's subculture could account for her having scored such a magnificent specimen with absolutely no effort: Joshua courted *her* at the Latchmere, coming in night after night while she was tending bar, offering to walk her back to her B & B across the Chelsea Bridge after her shift, until dire loneliness finally prompted her to go home with him instead, despite not having touched a male body since high school. The albatross of her held-too-long virginity had become stranglingly heavy, and she longed to be rid of it so fervently that Joshua's hotness barely factored in—she scarcely *noticed* it, even, until she was on the kitchen floor of Arthog House, crumbs stuck to her bare back, his serpentine penis striking with a jolt that switched on all her internal lights.

Joshua had no clue she was a virgin, and thus he felt no compulsion to be gentle. If anything, he fucked like a man running for his life, the electric-eel frenzy of him proving a wordless match to the puzzle of Mary's own desperate flight. Though they had barely conversed beyond light banter across the bar of the Latchmere, the very next morning she moved into Arthog House.

Now, returning from his phone call, he tiptoes so as not to wake her. Mary is conscious of telling herself he wouldn't want her to have overheard his family drama, but really she is afraid to open her eyes. His heightened emotional state might necessitate some response she has no ability to provide. They have been together two and a half months. The fact of their couplehood has seemed to her from the first unlikely, surreal, and temporary. A compilation of ingredients adding up to *safe*.

He flips back the sheet and climbs in beside her, their bodies immediately sinking into the middle of the bed. Thanks to their combined weight (and vigorous sex), the mattress collapsed in its center a while back, so that lying at either edge gives the precarious feeling of balancing on a ledge. The bed is uncomfortable for one person; for two it verges on ridiculous. Mary and Joshua fall together, arms and legs crowding, not fitting right. Wordlessly Joshua adjusts her limbs as a nurse might the pillows of a hospital bed, intertwining them with his own until they fit. He has an ease with bodies that no doubt comes from years of being prodded, poked, and spotted by his coach and teammates; though he is not a smooth talker, physically he lacks any of the self-consciousness typical in young men. This preternatural physical authority has become the touchstone of her London life. The smells of his skin — smoke, sex — reassure her, lull her back to a place where she can sleep again, anesthetized.

But if they make love, the drug will be even stronger.

Still not opening her eyes, Mary guides his callused hands over the swell of her ass — *You bent down to pick up a broken glass behind the bar, and I fell in love with your ass,* he has told her on a number of occasions. Then, not trusting even that, she moves his hand between her legs.

"My fucking mum, the stupid cow." His words come hot onto the back of her neck. "She wants to know why I don't just marry a British girl and get dual citizenship so I can join the Olympic team for England. She wants to know what I'm waiting for, I'm not getting any younger, you know." The venom in his voice seems to be traveling through his veins, his muscles, making his fingers rough. She tries to concentrate on the sensation, to not become derailed by individual words, though abruptly it occurs to her that Joshua's parents clearly have no idea she exists. This knowledge elicits no particular feelings, despite the fact that she, on the other hand, uses Joshua as a constant excuse to her parents. Staying in England for a man is a paradigm that might make sense to them. Her parents still send letters to her old B & B in Chelsea; she stops by regularly to pick up her mail. They know nothing of Arthog House or why she cannot risk their envelopes addressed to her sliding through its mail slot.

"I'm never going back there, Nicole," Joshua swears, fingers still moving, each stroke a morphine pump. "Never." But Mary already knows this. He is set to leave London on New Year's Day, departing for Amsterdam, the circus's home base and first stop on their world tour. "I'm writing my brother and telling him about the stash I buried in the yard—he might as well enjoy it."

Were she nursing any doubts about Joshua's sincerity, this would put them to rest: if he is voluntarily relinquishing his drugs, he must mean business.

He tosses her onto her back, his body poised over hers. When they make love, Mary often thinks of him shedding his skin, the essence of him remaining intact and whole beneath. Though he refuses, she sometimes begs him to discard the condom, fantasizing about the way his healthy semen would invade her insides, pumping her full of his youthful vitality like a golden, dirty petrol. The Super Athlete and the Dying Girl. That she keeps this irony to herself only increases its erotic power. Her body arches up to meet his; moans form in her throat despite the fact that Joshua's phone antics must have woken the entire house. Still, noise leaks from her mouth like smoke drifting out from under the cracks of their bedroom door: a warning, a dare.

Like everything else, the salve of him is running out of time.

When I walked into the Latchmere for the first time, every single person in the pub was male, from the owner to all the customers. Right away I thought of that old-man bar in Dayton where we went to make change before the Prince concert—do you remember the sad energy of that bar, how it looked like no one inside had seen a woman or sunlight in ages? I thought of the way you sashayed to the bar with your five-dollar bill sticking out between your fingers, your nails painted black and the polish chipping, but you could always carry that kind of thing off, you could wear tights with holes in them and make it look like art. And then of course I thought of Mykonos, and it was like the ground beneath me got wavy, and when they asked me my name I blurted out, "Nicole," without planning it. Just with that one word, though, right away everything felt different. Like you had opened up your skin for me

to step inside and I could be you, brave and sexy and free instead of
sick and scared. Of course I was still me, so for a moment I panicked,
thinking they would catch me in the lie, but nobody blinked. It
wasn't like I'd claimed my name was Diamond or Madonna, some
outrageous alias girls would run all the way to London to assume.
They pay me cash at this under-the-table job, so I could have told
them anything. I could have been anyone new, but instead I am
constantly reminded of you . . .

JOSHUA AND NICOLE are in the common room eating breakfast before any sane person is even awake—Yank cannot get the hell
away from them wherever he goes. Last night, when he came in around
3 a.m., they were already asleep in the room he once shared only with
Joshua, and Yank could tell they were naked under their flimsy sheet,
its floral pattern almost worn away from the years the sheet has no
doubt resided in Arthog House. Yank lay awake, pondering the sheet.
For the piddly twenty-seven pounds per week Mr. D. collects (from
everyone but Nicole, who never kicks in), he bet his ass the landlord
didn't *buy* the cutlery, sofas, refrigerators—everything must've been
here when he bought the joint. Yank wondered how often this old
sheet had been washed—how many people had shot their wads on
it over the years, how many tits it might have touched. He knew he'd
never sleep, then. He'd be up half the night, listening for movements,
for anything sharp or sudden enough to have bucked the sheet off
Nicole's body so he could get a look. Instead of playing that game,
he went to the common room to crash on the futon, across the room
from the sofa where the Flying Dutchfag was snoring.

He'd gotten maybe two hours' sleep, tops, when here the happy
couple was again, making tea and munching Weetabix cross-legged
on the dirty carpet like children playing picnic. Nicole, at least, is
dressed now, in the Harvard sweatshirt and ripped Levi's that've
been her uniform since the air turned cold. Joshua is already smoking a fatty, so Yank sits up in time for the kid to pass it his way. On
the other sofa, Sandor is still snoring, that crazy porkpie hat of his
over his eyes, revealing sunflower-colored stubble.

"You on at the Latchmere tonight?" Joshua asks Nicole.

"Not until seven. You guys coming in?"

"Wouldn't miss it," Joshua says. He nods at Yank. "Would we, mate?"

"Money to be made, kiddies," Yank says back.

"Don't go on your own," Joshua tells Nicole. "I'll be back from rehearsal by six—wait for me and I'll walk you over. After what happened to Yank . . ."

He is referring to Yank's recent mugging on Battersea Park Road. Some little shits from the estates tried to take his camera off him; when he wouldn't let it go, they kicked him a few times in the head. Since then, though he hasn't been dizzy like with the concussions he's had in the past, something's not quite right: he keeps walking into rooms and forgetting why he came, and his head's been hurting nearly nonstop for two weeks. He still has his camera, though.

"What've you got on today?" Joshua asks him.

Yank sniffs the air. "Hmm. Think I detect a whiff of baking for tonight's entrepreneurial endeavors."

Joshua laughs appreciatively. The hash cakes were Joshua's brainstorm, though he has scant time to bake them anymore. Joshua and Nicole even thought up a perfect slogan, "Pixie Dust Bars will make you fly," and made little flyers they distribute at the Latchmere's weekend after-parties, when at closing time the pub's owner chases out the prats who have wandered down from Chelsea, before locking in the regulars to party until dawn. Pixie Dust Bars are Yank's only foray into dealing these days—something about Nicole's cheerful involvement and bubble-lettered adverts diminishes the sense of risk. It doesn't even bring in much cash, but Yank likes the ritual of it: the measuring and mixing of batter and hash oil. It's the first time he's regularly used an oven in more than a decade.

"My bag's getting a mite heavy, too," he tells Joshua, holding up the duffel that bears all his worldly goods and shaking it for good measure so the loose coins inside clink. "Some of us ain't in the prime of our lives anymore. Maybe time for some coin-swap action so I can switch to bills and lighten my load."

Nicole starts bouncing up and down on her knees. "Oooh, I love coin swap!" she cries. "Can I come?"

Yank has to stop himself from barking at her to shut up. He's assumed the fact that she helps him out sometimes with his schemes to be an unspoken secret between them, not something she mentions to Joshua, though he cannot say why, and obviously he was mistaken. Joshua, though, chuckles. "How'd *this* happen, mate? My old lady's become your protégé for a life of crime." Before Yank can even answer, the kid has crushed out his hash cigarette and gulped the last of his tea and is kissing Nicole good-bye, quipping, "Have fun, you two outlaws." Then he's down the stairs. Everything else around here moves in slow-mo, but Joshua is so fast he could leave a trail of light behind him.

Nicole continues picking at her cereal, taking dainty sips of tea, like she's barely noticed his departure. Joshua is always running out of doors these days. He's got a real salary now, long hours of training. Not that swinging around on a flying trapeze is much of a proper job (though in travelers' London, it barely registers on the Richter scale of weird), and with the circus full of foreigners, who knows if it's even strictly legal? But it's not exactly *illegal,* which is more than Yank can say for anything he's done to make money since the mideighties.

"You're not leaving this minute, are you?" Nicole asks, eyes darting to the door of the common room. "I have some things I need to take care of first. I could go in about an hour—forty-five minutes if you're in a hurry."

Some things I need to take care of. Like the girl's got an appointment with the goddamn Queen. "Cool your jets, darlin'," Yank says. "I'm gonna crash a few more hours. We'll go when we go."

When he gets to their shared room, he closes the door hard. If the rickety old thing had a lock, he'd use it.

After my diagnosis (A.D., my parents have taken to calling it),
sure, I was still encouraged on the surface to do the things a normal

middle-class girl should do. Finish college, get a job, even date. But the unpredictable, wilder possibilities of life instantly disappeared, got shoved to another side of a wall and categorized as "too risky" for me. I was to follow the simple, linear trajectory of the terminally ill. No wasted time, nothing that would tax me too much (ah, the mantra of the education major: "Short days, summers off!"). Maybe, if any man would have me, knowing I was damaged goods, I could someday leave my parents' house for my husband's. But that was as big as any of us dared to dream for me. The safest route, the life not quite lived.

The one time I got anywhere close to real adventure, in Greece, you aborted our mission, sent me home like a child who had lost her way in a dangerous woods. But look, Nix, look—here I still am.

MARY'S FLUTTER DEVICE is in the bedroom. Yank's slammed the door, and even though Mary lives in there, too—Yank and Joshua have crammed their scant clothing into the dresser drawers and given her the entire wardrobe—Mary pauses at the threshold, intimidated, an intruder in her own home. An intruder in their home. She stands in the hallway, near the foot of the staircase across from the pay phone, waiting.

In a little while, when Yank has fallen asleep, maybe she can sneak in and get her giant purple rucksack without looking like she is *following* him or something. Already she's embarrassed about having invited herself on his outing. She should have held her tongue; then he might have asked her, as he sometimes has lately. She hears jazz playing on the other side of the door, and she knows there's no reason she can't just open it, but she stands frozen. She needs to get her rucksack to the toilet like she does every morning after Joshua leaves. Over the running of the bath, she will sit on the floor and blow into her Flutter device, her coughing muffled by the sound of the gushing tap. Most days, she doesn't stop until the tub is almost overflowing.

Before arriving in London in August, she'd completed three chest physiotherapies daily to loosen her stubborn mucus, lying half-upside-down while her mother played percussion on her chest and back with a practiced cupping motion, handing her Dixie cups to spit into.

black bowler. This head gear, combined with his extreme paleness
and height, gives him a menacing, neofascist look that his Dutch accent only exacerbates, so that during the early weeks of their acquain-
tance, Mary was constantly expecting him to utter some phrase such
as, *Damn, I hate the Jews.* In fact, he has become her closest friend
in London, confiding in her things he would never disclose to the
men, such as the way his father savagely beat him after discovering
him—aged thirteen—with his mouth around his best friend's cock
("We were literally inside the closet, as they say!"), prompting his
parents' divorce. Such as his regrets over dropping out of art school in
Amsterdam, and the corresponding fact that he is now, slowly and he
believes without a trace, embezzling funds from the art reproduction
company for which he works, all in the hopes of going back to school.
Last night, Sandor slept in his leather pants, and between that and the
morning joint Joshua and Yank smoked in his "bedroom," he smells
like he's emerged from a nest of testosterone and hash chips. He pads
barefoot down the stairs to the toilet, which sits between the first and
second stories of the house, and blithely shuts the door behind him.

Just fucking great. Now even if Mary does retrieve her Flutter, she'll
have to wait to use it. Sandor can soak in a tub for hours, using all the
hot water they'll have that day. But at least the common room is empty
now. Mary dashes back to its kitchenette, searching for something carbonated. Brits love carbonation; even their lemonade is bubbly, and she
usually stocks the minifridge with it. Carbonation will start loosening
her mucus, a preliminary to her eventual PT. She flings back the fridge
door. Bare. Nothing but the empty box of milk she and Joshua used on
their cereal and some cases of film Yank can't afford to get developed.

Shit, shit. She kicks the minifridge, hurting her toes. Nothing lasts
a minute in this place. Tears of frustration prickle in her eyes, irrational because Joshua will not let her contribute one penny toward
rent—she does not even buy groceries, other than the one time she
made eggplant parmesan for Sandor's birthday—so how could she
possibly explain to these men that their casually consuming her lemonade feels like grand theft? Desperation mounting, she races downstairs to the real kitchen. Owing to some tic of British architects, it,

like the kitchen in her old B & B, is on the lower level. This room technically belongs to everyone in the house, but protocol has established that she, Yank, Joshua, and Sandor use the common room kitchenette exclusively. As quietly as possible, she pries open the door of the refrigerator and peers inside.

Predictably, it is full of beer. Although beer is indeed carbonated, she detests it. Never mind: Mary pulls out a can of Foster's and pops the tab, chugging. She remembers when one beer used to rush to her head like a row of tequila shots, but these days she is a bartender whose customers buy her drinks as "tips"; these days she lives in a house over which a perpetual hash fog dwells; these days she makes it her business to be numb as much as possible.

Eventually she hears Sandor's combat-booted feet stampeding down the stairs. "Parting is such sweet sorrow!" he singsongs loudly from the front door. This is their morning routine: He always bids her an elaborate farewell, ignoring Yank as he departs. She is supposed to continue the game by rushing to the front door and kissing his cheek, like a 1950s housewife. Today, though, she cannot see the front door, and doesn't answer, lest he peer downstairs to find her downing Foster's before 9 a.m. Somehow her beer seems less acceptable than the fact that Joshua and Yank were smoking hash an hour ago. Sandor of the deranged fashion aesthetic, a semicloseted homosexual and secret embezzler, is clearly in no position to judge her alcohol intake, but when she hears the front door close she exhales relief.

If she doesn't complete her PT before Yank's ready to leave, she shouldn't go with him. She should take advantage of her privacy and stay back, do a morning treatment and then another a few hours later to make up for lost time. The pollution of London and the smoke inside Arthog House have collaborated so that her mucus has darkened— a sign of a serious infection, though she doesn't feel ill. Still, the thought of all those meandering, silent hours alone terrifies her more than being busted with beer by Sandor, even more than going into the room to find Yank awake and perhaps in some state of undress, looking at her like he knows she's a liar. She marches back to the second floor and opens the door, not timidly but with purpose.

Yank is dead to the world. The ratty blanket pulled up as protection from the weak London sunlight barely reveals hair already graying—unlike Joshua and Sandor, still in their early to mid twenties, Yank is past thirty-five. Too old to be *here* without it implying something more shady, pathetic, and irrevocable than it does for the rest of them, who are really just kids. Yank's long legs hang off the edge of his bed, which of course is nothing more than a mattress on the floor. Heat rushes to Mary's face. *This*—this sad, aging man—is what she found so intimidating? A jazz tape is still playing, and she presses "stop" to see if he'll stir, but he doesn't. She takes the tape out and holds it for a moment in her hand. Jack Teagarden, another artist she's never heard of. She puts it back where she found it, though she does not press "play" again, merely grabs her rucksack and hurries once more out the door.

There are so many things I forgot to ask you at the Athens Airport. Like how much of being a woman is synonymous with having to lie. Like why adulthood is a house of mirrors, and every time I turn another corner, collect another experience, the walls just seem to multiply with more versions of me, more secret passageways I don't understand. Like why I crossed an ocean to meet the man you loved, but haven't had even half the nerve to look for him now that I'm here. Like why, once today becomes important, "the future" is automatically fucked.

EARL'S COURT ISN'T one of Yank's favorite Tube stations because it tends to be crowded and well manned, which increases his chance of getting busted. On days when Nicole runs the coin scam with him, though, they've got to hit bigger stations, ones with more than one ticket machine, so today they'll start out here—at least the machines are close to the exit, in case they have to run. At the stations he usually haunts, where sometimes no one's even on duty and he can stand for half an hour at one ticket machine, milking it until it runs out of change, he and Nicole couldn't tag-team. Theoretically they can make twice the money between them, and the girl hands all the cash over to him anyway, so why not use her? Of course in truth, since they have to spend time moving around from big station to big station, Yank suspects the bottom-line earnings are a wash.

He has to admit, though, Nicole's great at prep. Her delicate fingers move quick and efficient as a child's in a sweatshop, wrapping and unwrapping the coins, preparing them for the swap. With Joshua rarely around anymore, sometimes Yank just gets the scale out first thing after he wakes, and he and Nicole pass hours that way: diligently wrapping ten-pence coins in aluminum foil, then weighing the coins and unwrapping or wrapping more accordingly, until each ten pence weighs *exactly* the same as a fifty-pence piece on the scale. Yank's always prepared now, keeping the coins jammed in his duffel bag wherever he goes. Even if he trusted everyone at Arthog House not to steal the coins (which he certainly does not), there is no way to know when he may have to make a break for it, so anything important Yank keeps on him, in what Nicole calls his "bag of tricks."

The swapping today proceeds routinely, as Yank drops the first carefully wrapped ten-pence coin into a ticket machine, presses "cancel," and watches a shiny new fifty-pence piece fall into the coin-return slot.

Repeat.

At a return of forty pence a shot, doing this a hundred times a day, he's made a forty-pound profit—a neat two hundred a week *with* weekends off. More than enough money for basics like food, drink, tobacco, and hash, with a tidy sum left over for luxuries like rent.

Not heroin.

It goes without saying that he could make a better living if he went back to dealing, but for over a year he's steered clear. Most of that time he was on the run, keeping out of London altogether until a particular police investigation died down, and on the lam he found creative ways to put food in his belly if not always a roof over his head. He killed time in Marseille, bummed his way up to Paris and around Belgium, before judging it safe to return to London, so long as he keeps a low profile and steers clear of his old haunts. It isn't just the cops, but some former associates, too, who might still like to fry his ass for him. Dealing is no longer safe.

Earl's Court is proving easier than Yank expected. Still, he nudges Nicole—you've got to fold your hand at the peak of luck, before things turn sour—and gestures toward the back of the station, where they quickly swipe their Tube passes in the turnstiles and disappear into the crowd of commuters, jumping onto an approaching train.

"So I think our resident faggot's making off with my jazz tapes," Yank announces conversationally, lingering near the door despite plenty of open seats. "They're disappearing one every couple of weeks, like I'm not gonna notice. He took my Stan Robinson the other day. Cheap little fucker—he oughta be paying more rent, since he's got his own room."

"But it's a *common* room," Nicole protests. "You and Joshua practically ash your cigarettes on poor Sandor while he's sleeping on the couch."

"Still," Yank says, hoping to send the girl a message, "he can afford more, he's got a *job*." Then he chuckles to himself. "Least he says he does. I don't know about you, but I never heard of door-to-door art salesmen where I come from. You ask me, the Flying Dutchfag's just a few blocks over from where we're standing right now, in some public toilet with a dick up his ass, calling it commission." He snorts. "*Art salesman*. Art of bending over, more like it."

"Can we go to West Kensington?" Nicole asks, interrupting.

They're on the District line anyway.

"What for?"

"What do you mean, 'what for'?" she says back. "For the same thing we're going to be doing all day."

He knows she can be this way: bristly and smart assed. She's not a big talker, which suits him fine, but unlike most quiet girls she seems to keep her mouth shut not out of docility but out of an intense secretiveness. She's also better at keeping her guard up than most of those who actually *should*, probably because she's not high all the time—or maybe because her secrets aren't that interesting.

"Whatever, Kemo Sabe," Yank says, rising to get off at the West Ken stop.

They stand there on the platform. He's been here before: it's a sleepy station, often unmanned. Today, though, there's a guy on duty. It's not the kind of place you can operate out in plain sight—since they're the only ones here, the guy's got nothing else to look at but them. Yank turns to Nicole and says, "Well, better move on."

She says, "I just want to look around."

To say this seems crazy would be an understatement. Look at *what?* Even if she were one of those London history buffs, he's not aware of this station's having any kind of interesting history. He gives her a look: She is wasting his time. Doing some kind of female thing, acting out with inexplicable petulance to sabotage his agenda. Without another word, she disappears into the station, wandering out toward the road, out of his range of vision. Yank walks back toward the platform. Whatever. Not his problem.

The next train is approaching by the time Nicole comes running back. "Yank, wait!" she calls, and his eyes dart around automatically to see if anyone's paying attention, feels for the hundredth time like kicking himself for failing to make up a new alias when he met Joshua and Sandor. "Come on," Nicole pleads, catching up with him and tugging his arm. "There's a pub next door—we should toast to the Pilgrims! Yesterday was Thanksgiving at home, you know."

Home. Her use of the word doesn't sit right.

"Fuck the Pilgrims," he says. "This isn't a social outing, girl. I don't want a goddamn drink."

Though, of course, he does. Every day without H is a complex juggling act of filling his body with substitute substances to quell the craving just *enough* to make it to the day after that. Alcohol is crucial to the mix: so necessary and so absolutely the lesser of two evils that it has not really dawned on Yank that he has become a drunk.

"I'll buy," she offers.

He sighs. "What," he says, following her back into the station, out onto the road, "you two-timing Joshua with some bartender from the pub next door or something? I'm not coming along to play your beard if you're trying to pick up some guy."

"Oh, for God's sake," she snaps. "Why are you acting like such a lunatic? What's wrong with you?"

He blinks. This may be a fair question. He is not sure what's wrong with him.

The pub is called the Three Kings, and it's the kind of overly boisterous, studenty joint he hates. Since Nicole is his regular bartender, she knows what he drinks and goes to the bar and orders them both bourbons. At Arthog House, they always drink Southern Comfort and soda. It's a habit he, Joshua, and Sandor already had before Nicole came around. Sandor had a bottle of the shit when the three of them met, all stowing away on the same ferry from Amsterdam. After they found themselves cheap digs to share in Battersea, Southern Comfort became "their" drink. They never buy anything else at the off-license, except that one time when Nicole and Joshua got it into their heads to try sherry, which had a creamy, nausea-provoking quality none of them could stomach. At bars, though, no matter where he's lived, Yank drinks bourbon like he did in Atlanta—like Will taught him to—even if after all his years in London he still can't get over how meticulously small the pours are, which means he always has to spring for a double.

Nicole slams back her drink. Her hands are shaky, her face slightly red. Maybe the guy she's looking for snubbed her. Maybe she's going to have some attack from whatever's wrong with her that makes her take so many pills and hide in the bathroom every morning to cough her lungs out. She claims she's got asthma, and that would explain the inhaler she carries everywhere, but Yank's known other people with asthma. Even though he lives in a virtual cave now, that doesn't mean he always has; it doesn't mean he doesn't know shit about anything. Asthma doesn't cover it.

She stands up abruptly, her drink gone, his still half in his glass. "Okay," she says. "We can leave now."

"Honey," he tells her, "you are acting pretty damn loony yourself."

"I know," she says. "I know."

They walk out of the pub.

THEY'VE GOT TO go all the way to Victoria Station so they can catch a real train back to Battersea, since Nicole balked at having to walk across the Chelsea Bridge in a little rain. Turns out not to have been such a bad move, though: Right outside a Victoria Station newsstand, Yank sees a sealed box marked *Evening Standard* sitting unattended. He just has this *feeling* about it, so he picks it up and carries it onto their train. Once seated, he opens the box with his knife while Nicole half watches.

It's full of currency cards. "Whoa," he mutters under his breath. These sweepstakes pay big, maybe ten grand, to whoever picks the winning number for the next day. Unlike in a lottery, the numbers are not random: the *Standard* lists clues along with the winning numbers from the past few days, almost like a serialized mystery novel. Americans, Yank has learned, prefer blind luck, whereas Brits like to *solve* shit.

"All we need to do," he explains to Nicole, who is looking out the window now instead of at the cards, "is spread these babies out in numerical order and figure out the pattern. We better get a newspaper, to check out the most recent clues."

She says, "Do you ever get tired of the way, everywhere you go, people look at you suspiciously like you might kill them?"

Yank feels his legs twitch. Maybe the girl got some speed off Joshua and ate it this morning while he was crashing? She is in rare form.

"How do *you* know who's looking? You're staring out that window in a trance."

"The window's like a mirror." She meets his eyes in the glass.

He averts his gaze. He goes quiet, flips through the cards.

Nicole rests her head against the glass, water dripping from her wet hair. She looks different wet. Generally, despite his natural urge to see her naked since she sleeps in his goddamn room, Yank finds her appearance uninspiring. He was surprised when Joshua took such an interest in her—even more so when he moved her in after one lay. She looks pretty much like a small-town American cheerleader, which he guesses is exactly what she was at home. Since Joshua—with his mismatched clothing and patches sewn onto his jeans, his straggly hair and onyx earring, and his inability to go ten minutes after waking without lighting a hash cigarette—is the type any American cheerleader's mother always warned her about, Yank knows he ought to feel at least a mild pleasure at seeing these two shacking up together, thumbing their noses at society. He can't manage it, though. He knew plenty of Suburban Princesses like Nicole once upon a time; he even married one when he was a young Rebel Without a Clue like Joshua. He thought Hillary could balance him, tame him, all those old jokes. Even after Will came home from Nam junked up and twitchy and mean, still he thought he could have both worlds, follow Will's fire wherever it led, the way he had since they were boys, and then Hillary would put out the flames with cool pitchers of sweet tea, her hands on her hips with expectation, her belly swollen with their child.

That turned out real well.

Albeit Hillary was never like this one in bed. Yank's been privy to quite the show, waiting it out night after night in the common room for the fucking to die down so he can crawl into his own bed instead of bunking with the Flying Dutchfag. Though you wouldn't think it to look at her, Nicole's the kind who moans "fuck me" things, who begs for it, then yells like she's being beaten or transported to heaven. Listening to her in Sandor's company has robbed the experience of considerable luster, but when Sandor's not around (where does he go?), sure, Yank's gotten off good a few times. Once or twice he's even been roused from sleep by her gasps, sharp with each of Joshua's thrusts, their furtive, urgent sex six feet away on the next mattress. But by morning, the girl's drinking tea again in the common room, wearing some cashmere cardigan with pearly buttons, and he barely registers her presence: it wasn't *her* he was jerking off to, just a universal sound in the darkness.

That wild hair is definitely her best feature. When it's plastered flat, her face is more angular than befits a girl her age. In the train's window, her profile reflects back at him, sharp and bony without the volume of her curls, mascara runny under her eyes. In Joshua's too-big biker jacket, she seems a drowned waif. She is, he decides, not even *that* pretty.

Yet for the first time, she looks like something he recognizes: something raw and hollowed out enough to match her nocturnal sounds.

"So they must've taught you some math at Harvard, huh?"

She looks at him at last, but her eyes are glassy like an addict's, blank. It takes a moment before she seems able to connect to herself what he's said.

"I didn't go to Harvard," she says edgily, and she turns back to the window, nothing but the blackness of a tunnel outside.

He snorts. "Figures."

He watches her lips move in the glass. "This sweatshirt belonged to some random guy I met in Greece. I never lied about going there—I can't help it if you made assumptions."

"You don't have to explain yourself to me, baby."

"They teach math at other colleges, too," she snaps, twisting to face him head-on.

"Really?" Yank says. "I wouldn't have known that."

The rolling of the train. From the corner of his eye, Yank sees the people in their car watching him with caution. Obviously the girl's all too aware that their stares are not meant for *her*. No, she's got some-where else to go, someone else to be anytime she wants, a college degree even if it's not from the Ivy League, parents, a home—and though he had those things, too, once upon a time, he could smack her face for it and feel no remorse. She's just slumming here with them, a fraud like the damn Harvard sweatshirt.

She coughs, a small hack at first, and then it seizes her body so that her tiny frame jerks back and forth, banging into him as she shakes with the spasms. Like someone living near a Tube station that drives him crazy at first, Yank barely notices the rumble of her anymore. But now he turns to look at her and smiles a little, the smile tight on his face like something new he is trying out. "Bet you start doing that every time poor Joshua tries to put his dick in your mouth, don't you?" He laughs.

She shoots him a dirty look, the lower half of her face buried in the leather elbow of the jacket. The cough has subsided, and she inches toward the window, away from the places where their limbs have been in contact. He is aware of her suddenly not knowing what to do with her skin, the way girls act when they've gotten close to a man without considering the implications. He suspects that if she were not wedged between him and the window, she would jump up and move to another seat to avoid touching him. In his lap he still holds the box of currency cards; in his hand he still wields the blade.

Fuck her.

All at once, her back shakes in a violent convulsion that wracks her body deep as her hand fumbles blindly in her purse for that inhaler— he sees her skinny wrist flicking back and forth to prime it. But when the next cough takes hold, rather than bringing her hand to her mouth so she can suck the medicine in, she gropes in the air like somebody who's drowning. Her head snaps up as her fingers search madly to stick the mouthpiece of the inhaler where it's supposed to go. Yank's eyes travel with the hand and then he sees it.

Blood.

Running down her chin, spotting the fragile white of the palm that peeks out from under her leather sleeves. Not more than a few seconds have passed but she is fucking *covered* in blood all down the front of her body. Yank notices, from the corner of his eye, a woman about his age dressed in office attire jumping to her feet in alarm; hears several passengers gasp. Nicole, too, gasps breaths of blood. "Oh God, oh God," she sputters in between the bursts, and no one, *no one* approaches, no one moves forward to help her, because of *him*, because of Joshua's jacket, because of his goddamn knife.

She's slumped forward, fetal, closing in on herself. He pulls the lapels of her jacket toward him to get her body upright, and the look in her eyes is like that of an animal just shot, not yet dead: hopeless and mad with fear, whites visible above the top of her irises, bugging from strain. He whispers, "Holy shit, girl. What's going on?" but nothing— she doesn't even seem to see him. Around them, passengers murmur to one another and a man calls out, "You'd best get her to hospital!" but from a good distance. Blood is dangerous. They look like a couple of killers, a couple of junkies. She could have AIDS.

It may be the first time in the history of the world that fate has been on his side. The train wheezes to their stop, its doors creaking open in a puff of movement. Jumping to his feet, he grabs Nicole under one arm, the box of currency cards under the other. But in the throes of her cough she's writhing, can't walk normally. The box of cards thuds out of his grasp, hitting him in the knee and crashing onto his boots, so that he has to kick it away, cursing, and half drag Nicole to the door fast before it closes. The *Evening Standard* box rides off with the train, his get-rich-quick dreams with it.

And then they are on the platform, not captive on a *Twilight Zone* train car of blood and suspicious stares. Beside him, she coughs and gulps air, blood gushing from her mouth in sporadic spurts like water from a fountain. Battersea is a sleepy station, a "nobody who lives here goes anywhere" kind of place, just the kind of gateway to invisibility and anonymity Yank was looking for when he returned to London. They are on the platform alone, her slumped on the ground. His heart races like a bullet.

"Nicole." Higher than his usual voice. "What do you need? An ambulance?"

She waves her arm at him in agitation, and he doesn't know if she's dismissing the idea, if she's even trying to communicate with him or just flailing around. Who knows how long an ambulance might take to arrive anyway? She could bleed out before it got here, if that's what's happening—what the fuck *is* happening? Another cough overtakes her and she spews a fresh, dark handful. He feels his body inch back involuntarily, like a kid recoiling from a bug, and when she looks up, her expression is venomous, transforming her more profoundly than did the rain. Though he has heard her climax, though he has seen her bare limbs in the dark thrashing out from under Joshua's duvet, though he has her blood on his hands, he has never *seen* her before this moment.

"Go," she commands, no geyser following the words. "Fuck off, leave me alone."

And he turns. Not the answer he was expecting, but yeah, in his vast experience with bodies spewing blood, *leaving* is always the best course of action. He can call an ambulance from the pay phone in the hallway at Arthog House, and if no Good Samaritan has come along by the time it arrives, the medics will take care of it. Take care of her. He pictures himself explaining to Joshua—not that he owes the kid any explanations, not that Joshua will be around much longer anyway—how he came home to make the call, to get help. That Nicole told him to go.

Already she is no longer looking at him. Her head rests on her knees, so that he cannot see her eyes, only the pale, tender zigzag of the part separating thickets of her hair. Through the rips in her jeans, blood dots the rough skin of her knees like Rorschach splotches. A breeze starts up—could be another oncoming train, more passengers to help her out, or could just be the onslaught of winter. He goes to her, pulls her resistant body up under the arms, and picks her up like a baby, starts carrying her toward the exit though she resists, pushes at his chest.

"Cut that the fuck out," he says low. His hands shake. And remarkably her arms, crackly in the leather on which her blood is drying cold, encircle his neck, holding on.

When the gene for cystic fibrosis was finally isolated last year, the form of the disease I have was classified as a "mild" genetic mutation. I guess that accounts, among other things, for my functioning pancreas, that Holy Grail among CF patients, an organ that, by failing to fail, kept me from being diagnosed for so long. Even before I came here, when my mom was freaking out about how I shouldn't travel alone, Dr. Narayan kept telling her that my lungs were in "remarkably good shape" for someone who'd gone seventeen years with no treatment. He said I was "entitled to sow some wild oats" and that she should let me go, not that she could have stopped me. He told me to enjoy myself.

See, mild, get it?

MARY HAS LOST track of time. Forever, it seems, she and Yank have been on this street, heading back from the train station, as though Battersea Park Road is a treadmill that never ends. At first, Yank tried to put her down to walk on her own, muttering, "My back hasn't been the same since those goddamn park benches in Marseille," but her legs felt floppy and her steps so tentative and frightened that he scooped her up again, taking long strides like a short-distance runner who knows he'll give out soon and is trying to cover as much ground as possible, fast. Sometimes she's conscious of his grip on her—leather on leather—but other times he recedes so that she's only floating, dizzy, the sky spinning above. Every now and then the blood sets off in a violent spurt, metallic and hot in her mouth, and if she panics and tries to inhale too fast after the cough's grip loosens, she breathes the blood straight back in, and it feels like drowning. Even when no blood comes out, she and Yank jerk at each isolated hack like shell-shocked vets starting at distant fire.

Outside the front door, he finally sets her down on her feet, leaning into her with his hip as though expecting her to crumple. Mary thinks of her mother balancing grocery bags while searching for house keys in her purse. This, then, is what the body comes to: an inanimate object to be balanced between stone and hip. Yank flings back the door, catching her fast before she can topple into the foyer. The place is a ghost town by day, no sound. The staircase beckons menacingly as Yank guides her, one hand under her armpit. Her hands, gripping the wall for balance, leave bloody fingerprints behind them.

Then here they are. In the room they share, though they are strangers. Already her mind is reeling, calculating the damage. Joshua's jacket, which thank God is leather and can be wiped clean—she can run it under the tap if she has to, claim the jacket got drenched in the rain. The stains on the stairwell can be removed simply enough. She shrugs the jacket off, voice ruined, rasping, "Hold this," and once Yank takes hold of the jacket, the imperative of hiding the evidence seizes her, sends a jolt of energy through her muscles even though she's still seeing stars. Recklessly she pulls her sweatshirt off, turns it inside out so that the blood is still visible but less wet, and lays the inside-out garment on the carpet like a tarp. She tries to strip off her jeans, too, before she dares to sit on her bed, but she loses her balance, falls backward in her underpants and bloodstained bra, legs flying skyward, still tangled in the pants. Yank is staring at her with naked confusion. She jerks her legs in his direction, less dizzy now that she's horizontal, mumbles, "Help," and he steps forward and pulls the tangled Levi's off her feet along with her boots.

Underneath, her socks remain remarkably free of blood, still tan and pristine. She dares not touch the bed with her hands.

"We've got to get rid of this," she orders, aware of the hysteria creeping through her hoarseness. It is on the tip of her tongue to beg him to find a trash bag in the Kiwi kitchen and just dispose of her blood-stained clothing, but then she remembers the sweatshirt. The fucking Harvard sweatshirt. Her hands lower to her face. "Oh God," she whispers. "I've got to get to a launderette."

Yank crouches down on his haunches, at her level now.

"I hate to break it to you," he says, almost cautious, "but you ain't *going* anywhere. Listen, girl, you think this joint's never seen a little blood? Calm the fuck down—you oughta keep still."

As if on cue, she bolts up in a cough, blood flowing both out of her mouth and down her throat at once, choking her. Too late, the fresh spurt spills down her fingers onto Joshua's faded floral sheets. And then tears are running down her face, sobs wracking her back, even though they're lubricating everything and making it worse—she can't calm down, can't stop.

"Okay," Yank says, loud. "I get it. You don't want Joshua to see all this—whatever *this* is. But listen to me—" When she doesn't look up, doesn't respond, he takes her chin and lifts it to him. "Baby, you gotta get a grip. *First*, we stop the blood. Is there some way—you say you don't want a hospital, but if you don't want to go bleeding all over your boyfriend's bed, maybe the ER would've been a better—"

"My bag," she says, gesturing toward the wardrobe with only her wrist, afraid to move again, afraid to breathe. Yank releases her chin, goes to the wardrobe. Above her purple rucksack, her clothing hangs, clean and orderly on hangers, like the clothes of a normal person. Yank pays them no mind, pulls the pack out roughly, and tosses it at her feet. She holds up her bloody hands, and he moves forward again, and with one motion he unzips the main compartment. She watches his eyes take in the minihospital inside, and slowly he begins to extract the contents. Her Flutter device. Albuterol inhaler, locked and loaded. A plastic bowl, like one that might be used to pour water over a baby in a tub. A stash of antibiotics in their orange prescription bottles, endless vitamins. Dr. Narayan's typed certification of Mary R. Grace's fitness to fly, though she notes with relief that Yank's not taking time to inspect the fine print. His eyebrows arch questioningly, though, as he holds up a plethora of Dixie cups, as if when she packed she thought cups were unobtainable in England . . .

Then finally, what she is looking for. She grasps it with greedy red fingers: a large container of codeine cough syrup.

Yank whistles low. "Damn. That looks like the kind of wicked shit I'd like to get my hands on under better circumstances."

Her fingers shake; she can't get the childproof cap off the bottle. Yank opens it for her and hands it over, but even then she can't swallow, coughs the sticky red-orange liquid and more of her own blood all over his hands. He is *covered* in her blood, of course. He's long since stopped recoiling from it the way he did at the Battersea train station, though she hadn't noticed until just now how he's not even flinching as it hits him, how he's treating it like water. Wordlessly he holds the bottle to steady it and puts his other hand on the back of her head to keep her still, too, and in this way they manage to dump some of the liquid down her throat.

Twice more, each swallow bigger than a whole recommended dosage.

She closes her eyes. Though it's too soon for anything to have taken effect, her lungs already feel less spastic, less desperate to contract. Minutes pass, the world receding behind her shut lids, and when she opens them again she is for the first time conscious of sitting there in her underwear, conscous of Yank's hand still tangled in the back of her hair. Almost violently, she jerks her head, flicking off his hand. He stays crouched, still watching her with those ice-blue, serial-killer eyes.

She should stand up to dress now while she still can, but what's the point? The jig is up. Already the cough syrup is at work to sedate her, rendering a rapid cleanup of her bodily crime scene ever more out of reach. *You should've seen it*, Yank will say when Joshua and Sandor get home. *She was like that scene from* Carrie, *man, a goddamn bloodbath*. And Sandor, who is something of a pussy, will pucker his face in disdainful concern, while Joshua, kind and at ease with bodies, will want to help, will say, *Why didn't you tell me?* But to any extent that illness can be romantic in concept, at the end of the day mucus and blood are the opposite of sexy. Joshua will pity her now, not desire her—will be repulsed that he has been making love to a walking corpse. Balancing the baby-bath bowl on her knees, Mary gives up, coughs some blood and phlegm inside.

Yank says, "What do we do now?"

But she only clamps her eyes shut against him once more, longing for the reprieve. For the codeine oblivion that can take her outside the grotesque mess of herself—far, far away from here.

IT TAKES YANK five minutes to walk to the estates, which are closer than the Latchmere or he'd go there. The black kids loitering outside could be the same little shits who kicked him in the head and tried to steal his camera, but for this kind of transaction that doesn't matter; in this kind of transaction, enemies are friends. They don't have anything on them, so they point him to one of the flats. Her blood's cold and stiff on his shirt and jacket, his movements jerky like the Tin Man in need of an oilcan. He sees one of the younger boys gaping at the sight of him, but nobody asks. Who'd want to be an accomplice to the things of which he is obviously capable? The cat who opens the door he knocks on is white, a mild surprise, though he's got dreads and is wearing a Rastafarian-colored shoelace tied around his throat like a necklace, a dirty feather sticking out of the knot. He takes one look at Yank and gets down to business, barks at his old lady and a couple of café-au-lait-tinted little girls to let them alone. No offers to taste the shit together, or talk mishaps and music to kill some time: today they want him out as fast as he wants to leave. It's why he didn't wash her blood off in the first place. In a cool twenty minutes he's back turning his key in the door.

Back to where he left her half-naked, clothes in a pile on the carpet, head lolling onto her red-tinged knees. For just one moment before he opens the door to his and Joshua's room, fear grips him: What the hell was he thinking, leaving her alone? Who knows what might have transpired while he was gone? Then he opens the door and sees her, still slouched against the wall. She *could* be dead, but no, at his weight on the mattress she opens her eyes, and all her earlier faces — the venomous woman of the train station, the dying animal of their long walk home — are gone. She smiles like a child at a father, serene.

"We're going on a little trip together, darlin'," he tells her.

"Where?" she asks foggily. She more topples over than lies down, her tiny body curled fetal on its side. She's trembling from a drop in blood pressure, a loss of blood, the aftershocks of trauma — who knows? Yank shrugs his crusty jacket off, clumsily maneuvers the bloody sheet out from under Nicole to cover her up, his knees pressed against her abdomen in the thoughtless way their bodies first touched on the train. He hasn't forgotten she's there yet — hasn't forgotten the jut of her clavicle, the curve of her ribs, the shadow of darker hair through her flimsy panties — but she's no longer the thing he wants most in the room. He's pretty sure that's not why he's doing this, but he wouldn't bet his life on it.

He's pretty sure the matter was decided in the broken way her head recoiled from his hand, the harshness with which she spat into her little plastic bowl, the hopeless turning away of her bloodshot eyes. In those gestures he understood all he needs to about her body's betrayals. And though he's got little to offer her or anyone, the one thing he could think to do was to say without words, *I'll take your shame and raise you one. At least whatever's wrong with you isn't your own damn fault.*

He has been carrying his paraphernalia around since his exodus from London a year and a half ago, just like she carries hers — the way an agnostic might still carry his grandmother's rosary, just in case. His hands shaky, too, from the energy of shifting one desire into another, Yank pulls his old spoon from his bag of tricks and clicks it against the orange bottle of her cough syrup.

He toasts, "To the Pilgrims," loads the spoon, and begins to cook.

She watches him heat the heroin, her eyes as innocently curious as his son's on the rare occasions he bothered to give Hillary a break and warm the baby's bottle. This girl watches him this same way, as though when he's achieved the right temperature he may spoon-feed the dose right into her mouth. Instead, when the tourniquet goes around his biceps, he sees her eyes flick down to her own puny girl-arm, no veins even visible, and then her fingers reach out to touch the strong, ropy veins that pop from his skin, throbbing with ugly, beautiful life. Her fingers are cold, and he notices her teeth chattering, too. Just before the needle's pierce, he lets himself lower down next to her, his longer body pressed against her smaller one, and from somewhere far away, he feels her trembling cease.

Then he doesn't give a shit anymore about being a reminder of how low she could go, who else she could be — he didn't do this for anyone but himself, this one perfect moment, sliding once more down his own rabbit hole, soaring through his own private sky, riding his own long-lost wave. Never as good as the first time, but he'll take it, thank you, God, you evil fucker, he'll take it.

His skin's gone fuzzy, he can't say if he's touching her or anything. Time does not exist. Air buzzes around them, electric.

"My name is Mary. Mary Rebecca Grace."

Her breath rattles like a baby's with croup — like his son's that end-less night before Hillary finally reached the doctor on the phone. The boy was fine in a few days, yet déjà vu knocks the wind out of Yank like a punch so that for a moment he doesn't comprehend her words.

"I have cystic fibrosis. I'm less than a year away from the typical life expectancy for people with my disease."

And then he does give a shit.

He turns onto his side, lifts her limp hand from the mattress, and shakes it with one soft jerk. "My name is Kenneth Blair," he says. "I'm wanted for the murder of a dealer named Shane O'Leary. I didn't kill the bastard, I just dumped his useless body in the Thames. He was my best friend. If I were a better man, I would've killed him, but I'm not."

To his surprise, the fucking girl smiles. "Excellent," she drawls, pulling her knees farther in against her ribs. "Stick around and maybe you can do that for me, too." Her finger wags aimlessly, like maybe she's parodying her mother back in Ohio. "The walking dead should never travel without someone who knows how to hide a body, you know." She giggles, but it fades fast into something mirthless, airless. "*Poof.*"

Hard not to kiss her then, except that he might suffocate her. Hard not to put every part of him inside her, except that they've got work to do.

It's hard to focus when she's quiet, too. Yank holds his body immobile as a statue, still straining to hear his boy's fragile breath, but pretty soon he has to roll his ankle—three, four times compulsively—waiting to hear a crack. At the sound, he's a little jarred to notice her still there next to him, head lolling, eyes closed, dried blood coating her pale skin. And all of a sudden he can't *stop* looking. Even when she opens her eyes and watches him, shame doesn't matter anymore; he can't remember this high up why it ever did. He shifts her knees off his ribs, sits up, and fumbles for his camera.

"You mind if I take some pictures of you, baby?" But he's already clicking a test shot, not waiting for her answer, shifting a little so that the thin light from the filmy window won't overexpose and dilute the color of her blood. She throws her head back trying maybe for a laugh but loses track of it, flops onto her back, nodding like she's the one who just shot up instead of him.

"Whatever floats your boat, Desperado." Voice croaky. Already tears are sliding a river into her hairline, leaving weak tracks in the red. Yank knows the tears are not about him, even if he wishes they were. His heart hammers in time with the shots, *fast, fast, fast,* trying to catch her trail of tears, but soon she's zoning too far in her own narcotic stupor to make them anymore. Even when she's asleep he keeps clicking; at one point he rearranges her limbs so she's fetal again and still she doesn't stir. It's only once the light shifts—a sign that the others may soon return—that he makes himself chuck the camera back under some clothes. Time will be running out.

"Someone to hide the body, huh?" He laughs louder than when anyone can hear. "Who knew you were such a freaky little bitch?" But he's only talking to himself, like the born-again junkie he is. Soon enough—though not before taking a slug—he will cap her orange syrup and put it back into her rucksack. He will bring her baby bowl to the toilet and rinse it in the sink, watching the red insides of her swirl down the drain until it's white, then zip that into her bag, too, placing everything back in the wardrobe under her neatly hung clothes. Soon enough he will open up his duffel bag and shove all her ruined clothes inside, noting a faint tinge of red on the carpet where they once rested but deciding that you'd have to be looking for it and that in this place—in places like this—no one ever is. He will soak a facecloth and, after that proves insufficient, a dish towel, methodically wiping the dried blood from her face and hands, though he will not be able to remove it fully from her fingernails or the tips of her curls; he will debate, then decide against, trying to get it off her bra, underneath which her nipples are stiff from water drying cool on her skin. He will contort her cleansed body inside Joshua's Led Zeppelin T-shirt, though when he strips the sheets, there will be no new set to replace them with, so he'll just leave Joshua's mattress raw and unexplained. As he works, his body will hum productively, the lactic acid that burned his arms earlier from carrying her now forgotten, so that he feels young and without pain, though he was never really young enough that pain wasn't involved.

This will come later, though. For now, camera securely hidden, he reclines on the island of their mattress, listening to her breath more carefully than he ever has to any jazz riff. She rattles like a broken space heater, no trace of his son anywhere now. She's merely a car engine that won't turn over, some failing machine. In any merciful world, there would be a way he could simply reach out and flick the switch to off.

It's so easy to hide things from people who don't want to know anyway. Joshua and Sandor came home, and Yank gave them some tale about how I was sick from our first batch of Pixie Dust Bars, how I threw up on my bed and he stripped the sheets and sent my "useless ass" to crash. I heard his flat, lying voice and closed my eyes again and imagined his story into being. The smell of burning hash oil permeated the house. Sandor clucked concern but I wasn't sure if it was over me or the cakes.

Finally Joshua came in and sat on the side of our bed, smoothing back my hair like a mother, and though I have been nurtured before, too many times, something rose in my throat so I almost told him everything then. Instead, he pushed up the Led Zeppelin T-shirt Yank had dressed me in and lowered my underwear around my knees like a snare. Maybe in case I planned to throw up again, he turned me onto all fours, and without a word, with Sandor and Yank still talking low in the common room, rode me so hard my head hit the wall. I started coughing into the pillow, but thank God no blood came up. Still, when I began to moan, Joshua covered my mouth and whispered, "Control," and slid a sock (whose?) between my teeth to bite down on, continuing his frenzy. I knew I should be pissed. I knew that somehow he'd figured out there was more to Yank's story even if he couldn't fathom what, and he was punishing me, just like you were on the ferry when you made me swallow that gross bath-cube candy. But I wasn't angry. I thought of Yank on the other side of the wall, taking in the pounding, and I knew Joshua and I were both screwing for him in a sense. That all over the world, men and women are fucking for people not even in the room, and I bit into the sock and coughed and cried a little, and as soon as he came, Joshua stood and zipped his pants, then left to sell cakes at the Latchmere. I thought Yank would stay behind but he went.

What if he had stayed behind? Or maybe that is only a story I'm telling myself.

Lately Joshua has taken to regaling me with South African fables. When he returned from the pub, drunk and smelling of a world of men, he twined his body around mine on our sunken mattress and whispered, "In South Africa, this bed could be dangerous." Then told me the legend of the Takoloshe, a demon some superstitious blacks in his country think sneaks into homes at night to steal souls. In reality, he said, the deaths are caused by gas leaks in faulty, old-fashioned stoves, which is why believers say the demon is tiny. His eyes were bright as he explained, his hand trailing circles on my stomach. Yank had not returned to the flat with him, though I heard Sandor puttering around next door. Joshua kissed my neck over and over again, and I knew he was apologizing even though he didn't need to. He whispered to me as if telling me an urgent secret, "The ones who die are always those closest to the ground."

But Nix, I already know that is a lie.

IT HAS BECOME a matter of now or never. Clutching *London A to Z* (zed!), Mary rides the Tube to West Kensington and disembarks, an excited dizziness overtaking her the way it might a devotee of Virginia Woolf upon arriving at Bloomsbury Square. Turning left out of the station, she walks the few blocks to one of the places she crossed an ocean to see. Ten Archel Road, the flat where Nix lived for four short months. The building is white stone, not so different from Arthog House, unremarkable. Mary cannot go in because she has no key, but she stands outside imagining Nix rushing up and down its steps on crisp fall nights, buzzed and smelling of pub smoke, perpetually searching for her keys. Nix being Nix, in high-heeled boots and her swingy camel coat, hair flattened by London rain.

Mary sits on the steps. There should be more to do here, but what? She avoided coming for so long that the coming itself has taken all her reserves, leaving nothing for gesture or ceremony. Through her tights, the December cement is cold on the backs of her thighs. She gets up.

Around the corner she looks for the Indian restaurant, and there it is. There it is! She expected a takeaway joint (Nix mentioned getting her meals to go), but no, the place is upscale if also gaudy, decorated in heavy reds and golds. Through the window, the woman at the hostess stand is unexpectedly beautiful, elegant, serene. She can see the woman returning her stare, so she nervously rushes inside.

"Hi!" The word comes out too loudly and the woman jumps, as though Mary may be concealing a gun. "Is Hasnain around?"

The woman's sphinx face is blank. "No."

"Oh! Well, I'm a friend of his—can you tell me when he'll be working?"

The woman says, "There is no Hasnain who works here."

By the way the woman has said it, it is clear what she means, but Mary cannot let the smile of anticipation off her face. She cannot admit what she is hearing. If it is not *this* Indian restaurant, then which one can it be? There are hundreds in London, and this one is around the corner from Nix's flat, just as Nix specified in her letters. She says brightly, "Hasnain doesn't work here anymore? Do you know where he works or how I can get in touch with him?"

The woman looks very young, really, no more than her early thirties. Suddenly Mary realizes how delusional she was when she walked in—she had assumed herself face-to-face with Hasnain's mother. There is no way this woman could be the mother of someone older than Nix. She feels unhinged. The woman is right not to trust her.

The woman says, "There is no Hasnain." She has not spoken slowly, but Mary hears her as though through underwater.

Later there will be no memory of leaving the restaurant. She will ride the Tube, transferring at Earl's Court and heading to the Baker Street Station, then veering right (past the shop where Nix purchased cappuccino every morning on her way to class?) until she reaches Regent's College, inside the majestic Regent's Park. There is a zoo in here somewhere, but Mary does not see it. She watches swans wandering around, wondering if they are the same swans Nix mentioned in her first letter describing the school. *Ah, the magic of London!* Nix wrote with the irony of a traveler more experienced than she really was. Once, Nix climbed a fence into the college grounds after hours, when the gate was locked. Mary is not sure what Nix was doing that for; she cannot remember if she ever knew. She was with her flatmates, girls who have graduated by now and are home with their own memories of Nix—of *Nicole*—and no memories of Mary, whom they have never met.

Mary is exhausted. Since her "major hemoptysis" (as Dr. Narayan called it on the phone), there has been no more blood in her sputum. Still, she does not feel the same. All week she's been afraid to use her inhalers, to thin anything out lest she start bleeding again. She found herself making excuses to Dr. Narayan: how smoggy London was, how smoky the air of Arthog House and the Latchmere. At last, she ended up blurting out, as if to a priest in a confessional, "I've been skipping my PTs—the house where I live is so crowded, it's just hard to find the privacy to do them." She pronounced "privacy" the English way. Silence expanded on the other end of the line, and her cheeks burned. Dr. Narayan sighed. "I thought you were smarter than this," he said, his clipped accent not unlike the mysterious woman's in the Indian restaurant. "I thought you understood there is no way we can help you unless you're willing to help yourself."

Until the night of blood, Mary had not felt truly *ill* since the infection that led to her diagnosis at seventeen. Now, heading back to the Baker Street Station from Regent's Park, her ragged breath and clammy skin shame her, her body revealing its ugly truth. Waiting for the Tube, she leans against a wall, trying to stay out of the way of flextime commuters, when an announcement comes on the PA system that the Bakerloo line has been delayed owing to a "body on the tracks." Mary looks around in disbelief, but no one else seems to have registered the news. Londoners calmly read newspapers or munch a Cadbury. Soon the train comes anyway, the body no doubt having been unceremoniously removed.

Next to her in the crowded car is a trendy boy, hair dipping deeply over his left eye, jaw sharp as a knife beneath the curtain. "Does this happen often?" she asks him. "Delays because of . . . uh, bodies on the tracks?"

The boy laughs, one short bark. His breath smells of smoke, and momentarily Mary imagines burying her face in his chest. "You have no idea!" he proclaims, almost proudly.

Apparently, all over London, commuters are hurling themselves to be electrocuted and run over, but nobody minds. It would be in bad form to make a fuss.

She changes trains at Earl's Court, rides back to West Kensington. Outside, the sky is dark now. She needs to go back to the Indian restaurant to ask the *real* questions. Were there former owners? Has Hasnain died? Moved away? She has to find him.

Outside the station, the Three Kings pub dwarfs one corner, beckoning as it did the day she rode here with Yank. Nix would have seen this pub every time she went to and from the Tube, which would mean—though none of the letters mention it—that she went there at least occasionally or, let's face it, probably a lot. The Three Kings is the antithesis of the Latchmere, the crowd well heeled, sparkling clean. Girls drink wine and half pints of cider. Guys are loud but in a good-natured way, so familiar in their bland good looks that Mary doesn't feel strange entering alone. The pub is gigantic; nobody will notice her amid the commotion. If people look her way at all, they will think her friends are at the bar getting drinks; they will think she is waiting for a date. She sits at a table with her cider.

She is on her second drink, wishing cider were more carbonated so that it might help break up the mucus in her plugged chest, when the bartender makes an announcement. "We've had a bit of a bomb threat," he explains, laughing. "Er, better evacuate, yeh?"

Mary jumps up as though her seat is on fire. Again, though, it is as though she imagined the words. Brits sit at their tables casually finishing drinks. Some laugh. The roar of the pub makes individual sounds indistinguishable. A few people head lackadaisically to the door. This, Mary realizes, is their idea of "evacuation." She races for the exit. Only a handful of the vigilant—probably American students—cluster on the sidewalk.

She heads back in the direction of the Indian restaurant, but the moment she sees the mouth of the Tube station gaping at her, yawning its smell of train exhaust and escape, she runs in and swipes her pass, bolting down the steps. As if fated, the train is waiting, doors slung open, a clipped British voice reminding commuters to "mind the gap." In the car, Mary grips the silver pole in front of her, hands slick against its surface.

On the wall is a sign warning passengers not to open or touch any unattended parcels, but to notify the Underground staff immediately and leave the train car.

In Kettering, Ohio, if you find an unattended handbag or parcel, you are taught to open it, looking for a wallet with ID. In Kettering, you would call the owner up and offer to drive over with the lost items. Perhaps in New York City, you look for the wallet intending to *steal* it, but you open the parcel just the same! It is 1990. Nowhere in America would anyone think an unattended package might contain a bomb.

During her time in London, Nix sent exactly four letters. In none did she mention that the city was dangerous, littered with bodies on the tracks, bombs on the Underground, pubs on the verge of explosion. She wrote only that she could walk alone at night without fear. Nix bragged, like recent expats are wont to do of their new environs, that nobody owned a gun.

As though everyone they knew in Kettering possessed firearms!

Nix's last letter was different from the others, which had an impersonal quality, like a travelogue. The final installment, by contrast, was breathless and giddy, if paradoxically the briefest. In it, she announced that she was in love. Though her mother had no idea, she was not returning to Skidmore for the spring semester but coming back to London immediately after the New Year. She had "big news" to share, which Mary feared might be her engagement to the mysterious Hasnain, whose surname Mary never learned. Nix wrote, *I'm sorry for how I've acted*, though it had felt impossible, during the anxious months before, to pinpoint precisely *how* Nix was acting—exactly what seemed off. *I can't wait to see you again*, she ended, signing that final letter in their childhood code, *BFA,* for "best friends always," which the other letters had mysteriously withheld, employing the far more impersonal sign-off, *Love.*

Mary holds her face into her *A to Z,* hot tears darkening and buckling its pages. The vibrations of the train make her heaving shoulders shake unevenly. Her mother was right. Though she initially came to London like a detective to follow a trail, after two years, whatever she hoped to find has evaporated. Nix is gone.

And all around her, London is burning, but nobody else has noticed. Even Nix.

Four months doesn't sound like a long time, but for me it has been another world. In this world, I've been to the Tate after eating a slice of hash cake, where I listened to Yank and Sandor argue over Dalí

for hours. I've made love with Joshua on the sloping concrete of an
underpass where part of Pink Floyd's The Wall was filmed, where
they now hold drag races. I've been to a reggae pub in Lambeth
where Yank had his pocket picked by a tattooed prostitute who gives
him freebies sometimes but must have decided she wanted back pay.
I've danced on the Latchmere bar during "afters" so wildly that I
fell, giving myself a bruise on my thigh the size of a grapefruit, while
the regulars cheered. I've watched fireworks for the Queen Mum's
birthday and braved the notorious Notting Hill Carnival (no riots
this year!), and I've come to understand that British toilet tissue is
too rough for use after sex and the myriad things this implies about
England. I've attended parties where the guests were from at least
eight different countries but basically everyone was a dealer, and
when an old geezer from the West Indies asked, "Love, what are you
doing here, who's looking after you?" I was set to protest that I am
an independent American woman who requires no looking after, but
Joshua came forward and said, "Thank you, umkhulu, I'm keeping
her safe," and I realized all at once that I don't know the first real
thing about him. It's too much work being you, Nix, but maybe I am
not quite me anymore either. I've done nothing I came here to do, met
no one I came here to meet, and still I've become someone new.

YANK AND JOSHUA are on the floor of the sitting room passing a hash cigarette back and forth. Tomorrow is opening night. For
the first time, Joshua will do his trapeze act in public; he has gotten
them free tickets, and after the show there will be a party for the
circus members' family and friends, though most have no people in
London. Yank was not particularly hot to attend, but Joshua pleaded,
"You'll dig it, high-wire acts and the Chinese swing—just your speed,
all high risk," until he shrugged his helpless consent. Lately he feels
weirdly connected to Joshua, a strange sense of responsibility for the
kid. He always *liked* him fine—better than he liked most people—
but there's more to it now. Like he and Nicole are conspiring somehow to protect him.

Joshua inhales, holds.

Yank says, "Buddy, this here's an intervention. You're gonna drop that flying Chink on her head, you keep this shit up."

Joshua laughs appreciatively. "Oh, plenty of people at the circus smoke," he says, as though Yank were alluding to the health of his lungs. "Just like gymnasts."

"You ever afraid you'll fall?" Seriously this time: he really wants to know.

Joshua chokes on his next drag. "Fuck, yeah! I'm always scared shitless on my way to work. I think, *What the hell am I doing, eh?* Gymnasts are constantly injuring themselves—everyone has surgery all the time, we're all scarred and stitched up like Frankenstein. But I was never worried. I've been doing it since I was small; it's like riding a bicycle to me. But the trapeze, bloody hell! The thing is, though, once I'm up there I can't focus on anything but what I'm doing, what comes next. It's the same as gymnastics that way—there's no room for fear. Like, nothing else exists."

Yank ticks off things in his life that have ever offered such primacy of experience. Taking photos when he was younger, in New Orleans, New Mexico, California. The kind of fucking that comes after a hot-and-heavy pursuit. In other words, not a damn thing he's done lately, except heroin. Even now, his heart is not in the passing of this joint. He would like to go into the toilet and shoot up, but he has to wait until Joshua fucks off to the Latchmere to pick Nicole up from her shift. Other than *her,* no one here knows he is using again. Even among circus freaks and skinheads, a junkie is a liability, and who knows, he might be asked to leave. So he hides his habit, though like the girl with her disease he no doubt leaves clues; no doubt the others suspect. He pulls the hash into his lungs hard, but it will never do enough.

"I'm going to ask Nicole to come with me," Joshua says, grinning behind the smoke. "You'll have the room to yourself in a month. Cheers for putting up with us, mate; I know we've been a pain in your ass."

This, then, may be the last of the man he has been: his past put on notice. Since he started using again, he's been telling himself daily to split, just disappear, but his body won't obey. When Nicole and Joshua leave London, though, whatever it is that's holding him here will be broken, and he can leave, too. *Yank* will at last recede into travelers' subculture lore: who knows whatever happened to that cat, a hard-ass dealer up Camden Town way who was thought to have snuffed his best mate? One more month to keep hiding his habit in the bathroom. Another month more to listen to the sounds of their lovemaking from the other side of the wall.

"You take good care of her out there on the road," he tells Joshua. It is not all he wants to say, yet even this much is a transgression in his world: telling another man how to treat his woman. But no, Joshua's not that kind, not the type to rankle.

"I lost the first girl I ever loved because of my own careless stupidity," Joshua says solemnly. "Believe me, I won't make that mistake again."

The cigarette is dying, just smoke between Joshua's fingers. Yank takes a deep swig of Southern Comfort. What a fucking name. There is not one damn thing he can remember that was comforting about the South.

"In my country," Joshua continues, "relationships between blacks and whites are illegal, you know. Of course it's only the blacks who actually get arrested. Which is, like, pretty much a euphemism for killed, everyone with a brain knows that. Except fucking me."

On the tape player, "Ramble On" blares. Yank looks at Joshua, at his fresh, unlined skin, and realizes to his surprise that he *knows* this story already, though he has never heard it before. This story has been the subtext every time Joshua looks at Nicole with such singular devotion, with a gratitude that belies his age and chick-magnet physique. This story has hovered in the shadows every time Joshua mixes Nicole's Southern Comfort and soda before his own; every time he has served her a larger portion of vegetables and rice than she can truly eat and waited until she pushes it away before finishing her food himself. Somehow, this story has even been implicit in the freaky way Joshua addresses the old, strung-out, toothless geezers from the estates with respectful Zulu greetings, as though they know what the fuck he is saying—as though he is atoning for something, proving something wrong in the absence of the thing itself, as though those black faces have anything to do with him. Already—all along—Yank has imagined Joshua's youthful body twined around the willowy, darker limbs of that *other* girl. He can see that girl in his mind right now, and he wants the needle even more than before.

Still he asks: "They *killed* her, man? She's dead?"

"Nah, she got off lucky." Joshua looks down. "She just lost an eye." He stares at the cigarette burning into his fingers. "I'd known her forever, like, since we were fifteen—my coach's maid. Who knows, once she could walk again she might even have gone back to work, if he still wanted her with the eye and all. He was fucking her, too, but that was all right, see, because she didn't *want* to fuck him. Rape is perfectly acceptable. Just not love."

"I hear you," Yank says simply. "The year you were born, what, sixty-eight, sixty-nine, I was a teenager in goddamn Georgia. It ain't South Africa, but I remember those days, too."

And absurdly it strikes him that this is the most he's said about his own past in years—that this whole conversation is a transgression of sorts. Because the men of his worldwide pack have come here (wherever *here* is—Taos, Marseille, London) devoid of pasts, searching for new lovers, siblings, and comrades, all at once. If they ever strike anything, it is only fool's gold. *He who cannot learn from the past is condemned to repeat it,* or some such shit. He waits, afraid of what may come out of his mouth next.

Joshua, though, is nodding fiercely. "The guys who did it, they were my teammates. Our coach was like our god. It was like I'd broken God's windows and pissed on his bed. *I* did that to her, you understand— it was my carelessness, my ego. I thought I could trespass on God, and they taught me a lesson."

"Buddy," Yank says, or maybe he is not Yank anymore, "you ever tell Nicole this story?"

To his surprise, Joshua laughs; the sound makes Yank jump. "Fuck, no," Joshua breathes. "Some romantic story, eh? What girl wants to hear a story like that?"

Once, a couple of months back, Yank walked in on Joshua and Nicole jumping up and down on their shitty mattress chanting, "Ah-so, jump!" over and over again, giggling and holding hands. Nicole seemed embarrassed, but Joshua had cheerfully explained that they were wondering whether, if the entire country of China jumped simultaneously, the earth would move. It was late, but still Yank had stormed to the common room, growling, "You better tone it down or I'm gonna kick both your dumb asses," slamming the door hard. How could *anyone* be so damn young they'd never even seen a cheesy kung fu flick, didn't know the saying was from Japan, not China? These kids were too young to know jack shit about anything. "Grouch!" they called after him, undeterred. "Scrooge! Cranky old man!"

And he has just been too long without a woman is all. He has been too long on the run, even when he stays in one place. It has simply been too damn long since he's made jokes holding someone's hand, since he laughed into the night instead of getting up fast and putting on his pants — too long since he's made anything but war, since anyone on this earth was truly *his*.

"Nicole's not just any girl," he tells Joshua. "I think she might surprise you."

But the joint is no longer smoking, has died out right against Joshua's skin, become ash. "I came here to start fresh," Joshua says vehemently. "Me and Nicole, we can go anywhere we want. We'll be moving from country to country, so that shit about having to go home after six months won't apply. We can see the whole world, and someday, when I get too old for the circus, we'll just pick the place we liked best, someplace quiet where we can have a garden."

Yank says, "That's some plan."

Joshua's shoulders shake. His breath comes shuddery. "Yeah," he says. "Yeah."

"I really hope you get it." Yank stands.

Because this is a case of mistaken identity. He is just a man who leaves rooms, closes doors. Every pivotal moment in his life, in fact, has ended just this way: him poised at a doorway, set to run. Hell, if you think about it, right now doesn't even qualify. *This* was someone else's moment all along. He is only around for the ride.

AND SO FINALLY there is this: the way her body tenses when Joshua first grabs hold of the metal bar and ascends, the trapeze beginning to move as if by magic, without any visible sign of a struggle as he swings through the air. The way the kid who, getting high first thing in the morning in his jeans with those clashing floral and plaid patches, is just another dime-a-dozen hippie, up *there* becomes something else: something animal and pure, possessing absolute authority. He wields his body like a knife. When Yank pulls his eyes away and looks at Nicole, she is visibly holding her breath as Joshua, hanging upside down in a unitard, extends his arms toward a black-haired girl who does not speak his language, and the girl—some crazy fucking chick who never learned there's nothing in the whole damn world *that* worthy of trust—lets go and soars into nothingness, catching his hands. They swing, they fly. Her leg touching Yank's on the bleachers, Nicole exhales loudly enough for it to pass for a sob.

"Kak!" Sandor exclaims, on Nicole's other side as he always seems to be—Christ, what if he's not even a queer at all and is in love with her, too?—"I thought maybe he would fall, my heart goes too fast!" He places Nicole's hand on his chest.

"Oh, Sandor! To think when I first met you"—she giggles, and something in her tone, in the phrasing, is already nostalgic—"I thought you were a Nazi."

"Oh, I *am* the big Nazi," Sandor says agreeably. "In Holland, we are all Nazis, this is just how it is, no offense. Nazis who decriminalize drugs and prostitution—it is a very fun country, you must come visit!" He falls against her and they chortle, clutching each other's arms, Sandor's hat falling to reveal his shockingly yellow stubble.

Joshua is no longer on the stage. Nicole has turned to watch a Russian man swallowing fire, her eyes alight and riveted, but Yank takes her by the upper arm and says, "I need to talk to you. Come on, girl. Now."

She looks over at Sandor apologetically. "We'll be right back," she tells him, and Sandor's mouth opens slightly, but they are already moving through the stands as Sandor calls out, "Hey! Bring back more beer!"

Yank leads her under the bleachers. There's no big top here; it's just a gymnasium where sports events are held, reinvented for the circus, visually transformed. He hears the clamoring of feet overhead, dramatic music piped in to heighten the danger of the performance, and he backs her slowly—his limbs moving with the mindless fluidity of a trapeze—against a pole and kisses her with the kamikaze force of his own confession.

Her body seems taken utterly by surprise. She loses her balance, topples against the pole, so that he has to catch her, her arms darting out to steady herself like a high-wire acrobat. He kisses her again, and this time she does not stumble, does not resist, though she does not quite kiss him back either. He's had to bend over to reach her—she's almost a foot shorter than he is—and he stands back up to his full height, his body not touching hers anymore. He lays one hand up lightly against her throat. Says, "If I pulled your skirt up right now and fucked your brains out against that pole, would you try to stop me?"

And she says, "No."

It's not enough. "Because you think you owe me?" he persists. "Or 'cause you're collecting experiences and it's one more way to slum before you go home and forget us?"

"I don't know." Then, with genuine surprise, "I'm not going to forget you!"

He laughs. Her eyes still look wild, but he suspects it might be the trapeze—her fear that Joshua would break his neck—and not him at all. "No," he says, "it's all right. Forget me. You don't owe me anything."

"That's what you dragged me down here to say? Okay. In that case, you buy Sandor's pint." It's on the tip of his tongue to retort that he's not buying that cheap ass a beer, especially since Sandor's been rifling through his bag again and stealing his tapes, though he's not sure where they could be hidden, because all Sandor's stuff is out in the open. It's in his throat to pretend that the girl isn't leaving at all, that they can still banter this way about slumming, pretending nothing is a matter of life and death, that nothing's going to change.

But *everything* changes, and though Yank doesn't know it yet, just before Christmas he will wake to a phone call asking if he knows where
Sandor may have fled to after embezzling four thousand pounds' worth
of sales revenue from his employer, an art reproduction company in
Reading, and Yank will mutter that (although Sandor's been "gone" for
a couple of days) he didn't realize he had moved *out*—that he doesn't
even know the guy's last name, though they have lived together for six
months. When the voice on the other end of the phone tells him that
the police have been notified of Sandor's crime and may be coming
around, Yank will go back upstairs and pick up his bag of tricks and
walk straight out the door into a bleak December rain, never to return,
so that Joshua and Nicole, who were supposed to be the first to take
off come January, will ironically end up the last ones standing upstairs
at Arthog House.

   Now he says simply, "Joshua already ask you to go with him on his
big world tour? 'Cause he's gonna, girl, so you better get your answer
ready."

   She shakes her head slowly no, but says, "Yeah, I thought he might."

   "There's worse ways I can think of to kill a year. Who knows—"
The music from above has heightened—something big must be going on. "I think you two have more in common than either of you was
banking on. I don't know if that's a good thing or a bad thing, but
maybe you oughta give it a roll and find out."

   She smiles. It is the kind of smile his mother used to give, the kind
only women know how to dole out: sad and generous at once. She
puts her hand over his, which is still around her neck, and her fingers
are soft, as if she's never worked a day, never known pain, though he
knows that isn't true and wishes he could still think it was.

   "I bought a ticket on British Air the morning after all that blood. I
wanted to see Joshua's opening night, but I leave tomorrow." She is still
smiling. "My parents, my doctors, are waiting for me. Joshua's sweet,
but we both know he doesn't even know me—we both know I'm not
what he bargained for. I'm heading to Heathrow so early no one will
even be awake to hear the door."

   It's not clear what he feels. A roiling in his gut, insides jumping from the touch of her fingers. And under that a powerful wash of relief through his veins, numbing him like he just shot up. *She's gone. It doesn't matter anymore. After tonight, she's gone.* Now that he knows this, he could do it. Push her against the pole again, grab her under the thighs to hoist her in the air, shoving her girlie underwear out of his way, and slide her down on his cock, ramming into her until those "fuck me" things she screams would all be for him. She's leaving; he's safe. All the better then if she throws some "fuck you" things in as a parting shot—hey, he likes it that way, too.

A stampede of footsteps shakes the stairs above their heads. Yank drops his hand, feeling her heartbeat still strumming on his palm. Without warning, his head fills—like lining up a shot in the lens of his mind's eye—with the image, again, of the coach's maid, the star gymnast's lover, that girl he will never see, never know. Just another girl in the body count of men, like the many he himself has stepped over to get to nowhere. Where are those women now? Instead there is only one girl in front of him, only Nicole, who is not even really *Nicole,* but though she's not what he thought, she is still whole enough that she would never sneak out on her lover under cover of night if she understood the full weight of Joshua's stake—of their goddamn shared stake and how much holding fast to each other might matter to both of them, in a way so little in the world matters to anybody. With every electric fiber of his body, Yank believes that he *needs* this girl to disappear—that he wants never, ever to see her again way more than he wants to help Joshua—yet still he finds his body leaning in close one last time. Her eyes transform at his approach, her lips parting slightly, this time anticipating the kiss. But the circus is over, they've missed the finale, the house lights are on, and instead Yank finds his lips grazing only her ear as he whispers, "It ain't morning yet, darlin'. Let me tell you a story."

Where Are We Going,
Where Have We Been?

The girls wake up hung over from sweet wine. Even with the shutters drawn, Nix notices Mary's lips, swollen and red from kissing her movie star, an airline pilot named Zorg. Zorg isn't Greek after all, as Nix originally assumed amid boisterous bar noises that drowned out the nuances of his accent, but a Spaniard, here on holiday, too, visiting his fellow pilot, the shorter Titus, a certifiable Greek who owns a villa in Mykonos. In the clarity of morning, Nix is embarrassed by the absurdity of the language associated with their evening: *Zorg, Titus, villa.* Who has names like Zorg and Titus? Who refers to their house as a "villa"? It is as though she has wandered by mistake into a romance novel, the cover featuring Zorg shirtless, his tanned, muscular arms encircling petite Mary. She rolls her eyes in the semidarkness. This eye-rolling is all for her own benefit, of course, since Mary—who would normally be laughing with her (they might repeat, "*Zorg, Zorg!*" in increasingly freaky tones until they were hysterical)—is so horny she has lost her sense of humor.

Nix's lips are not swollen, because she did not kiss Titus, but her breath and stomach are sour and her skin is sensitive from the sun and her hangover. Mary keeps barking at her to "get ready" or "they'll think we're not coming," so she drags herself to the shower in the dinky bathroom adjoining the bedroom she and Mary have rented in a private home. No sooner has she shampooed her hair, however, than the water backs up, brown and smelly. She tries to outrace it, rinsing her hair quickly, but the backup soon overtakes the short lip of the shower stall and the room begins to flood. Mary, already dressed, scurries to get the woman who rented them the room, while Nix sits on her mussed twin bed, white towel matching white bedspread matching white walls, shampoo drying on her hair. On Mary's return, the woman hollers at them in Greek for a good five minutes before roughly gesturing at Nix to get dressed. Nix puts her bikini on under her cutoffs, figuring her morning will now entail having to finish rinsing her hair at the beach once they've been evicted; however, the Greek woman only leads them around the corner and down the block, into another room furnished almost identically to the first. There—though not before demonstrating how to turn the shower faucet on and off several times—she takes her leave of them.

"They'll think we blew them off!" Mary whines again, so Nix hurries through her hair-rinsing in the new, unflooded bathroom, skips applying makeup, and dresses again in the clothes she hastily threw on moments before. She knows she looks unfit for the cover of Mary's romance novel, but this suits her just fine.

Although the girls are more than forty minutes late, Zorg and Titus are still waiting in Taxi Square, calmly sipping espresso, which Greeks simply call "coffee." By night, their olive skin and dark eyes had seemed nocturnal ("like melted pools of chocolate," Mary drunkenly rhapsodized), but in the daylight, their suave European handsomeness looks shiny and conspicuous, as though it has been painted on and scrubbed with a brush. Even Titus is considerably better looking than Nix took him for in the bar. The moment they see the girls approach, the men stand, Titus scattering some coins on the table. In quick succession, Mary and Nix have their cheeks kissed, one-two, one-two, and for a brief, frozen moment, Nix sees herself for exactly what she is: a terribly young midwestern girl who has grossly mistaken Skidmore for sophistication. For the first time, she begins to feel giddy: today is just the beginning, the prelude to her semester in London, the onset of her Education. Zorg has a rental car, but

Titus mounts his scooter, and Nix is happy to climb on behind him while Mary has to get into the boring old car, which looks like the one Mary's father drove when they were in grade school.

Nix's hair dries quickly on the winding road to Plati Yialos, a resort area a couple of miles away from Mykonos proper. By the time she dismounts the scooter, she has forgotten she is not wearing lipstick or mascara; she has forgotten her tomboyish jean shorts; she feels infused with the sun and breeze of the scooter ride, as though her limbs and hair and skin are all aglow. Plati Yialos is *nothing* like Paradise Beach in Mykonos, where the girls went yesterday, which was like a trip to the zoo: full of naked, hairy, drunken animals, some splendid and some just annoying. Tranquil and romantic, Plati Yialos is a curved golden beach with hazy hills in the background and a plethora of tavernas in which pretty, civilized people drink coffees and chat and read. Although Zorg and Titus have already had coffee, the girls have only had a flood in the bathroom, so they stop and join the strangers at a sheltered taverna for their morning caffeine. Zorg and Titus are fully dressed in pleated linen pants and button-down cotton shirts that are miraculously unwrinkled. They sit with their legs crossed at the knee like a parody of European style and worldliness, smoking cigarettes and sipping from their tiny cups. Nix watches Mary, who has on a tie-dyed miniskirt and string bikini top, her wild hair wound tightly into two coiled knots on the side of her head so that she looks like a messy Princess Leia, and finds to her astonishment that her best friend appears not at all out of place amid the glamour of the morning, despite her goofily informal attire. Mary is pretty. Mary is blond. Mary is young. This triad of powerful currency radiates from her, a passport to anywhere. Nix feels tingly — she, too, is in possession of this passport. When she catches Mary's eyes, they are shining.

The day is looking up.

For some reason, however, they do not remain at this tropical paradise but, as soon as the coffee has been ingested, pile back onto scooter and into car and take off once more. Nix is not sure where they are headed. The road has grown higher now, snaking around sharp cliffs that plunge downward alarmingly to the blue sea. Wind whips

Nix's hair, tangling it; neither she nor Titus is sporting a helmet. Her heart beats fast, like the exuberant Greek music pouring from the open window of Zorg's car.

Then she sees it: A secluded cove of a beach below. Zorg and Titus slow the vehicles, easing them off to the side of the road. Though Nix has never considered the fact before, this is the first time she has ever seen an entirely empty beach and the desolation feels magical. Her body is overrun with an electric joy. It is all she can do not to run madly down the sand hills and plunge into the water. How can it be that anyone in the world lives in Kettering—even in Manhattan—when there are places like *this* on the planet? How can this beach be empty? Why isn't everyone alive as excited about it as she is, and why are they not all here?

Nix silently thanks her mother's Catholic God—in whom she herself stopped believing the day her father walked out the door—that everyone else is apparently brain-dead, thereby granting her the grace of this beach, empty but for her surrogate sister and two unwrinkled, straight-from-the-pages-of-a-resort-catalog men.

SHE HAS ONLY just arranged her straw mat and towel neatly on the pristine golden sand, slathered sunscreen onto her already tender back, and reclined artfully on her arrangement, when Titus flops like a fish from his own towel, sand splattering everywhere, to rest his gelled head on her shoulders.

The weight knocks her off her elbows, her chin hitting her towel. Uh . . . what is he *doing*? Until this moment, other than her clutching his waist tightly on the scooter, they have had no physical contact. When Nix goes to the beach with her friends, even the longest-term couples don't lie on top of each other in the sand. It is common sense to know that sand is messy. It is common sense to know that's a man's large, gelled head on your shoulder for an undetermined period of time is likely to result in an uneven tan. Titus's warm head, bearing down on her, makes her feel she can't breathe.

"Hey," she says, "you're blocking my sun."

Titus contorts his face to look at her, confused. Really, he *is* a pretty specimen. If she had met him at Skidmore, she would be all over him. She thinks again of the boy she lost her virginity to, and how after the sex she worked herself up to believing she liked him, simply because he immediately seemed to have lost all interest in her. Back home in Kettering, she drove by his house at night with her girlfriends, giggling and squealing if his bedroom light was on. Mary was not on those endless car rides; she was in the hospital by then, on IV anti-biotics and steroids, having just been diagnosed with CF. Nix did not know what to do. When she visited the hospital, Mary's mother was always there, on her face an expression of frozen cheer that Nix kept expecting to melt away into Munch's *The Scream*. Outside the hospi-tal, there were keg parties and fake IDs and bands playing in Dayton's Oregon District, and foreign films at the Neon, and thrashing around to Siouxsie and the Banshees on precarious platforms at dance clubs. There was Bobby Kenner, the cute guy Mary used to lifeguard with at the country club and had been dating since the previous summer, who kept turning up at parties and crying on Nix's shoulder, saying how sad he was and how much he loved Mary, though Nix knew Bobby barely called Mary anymore. Nix had always been the "impulsive" one, but the complicated, toxic alchemy of why her impulses led her to fuck Bobby Kenner's brains out at one such party, on somebody's parents' bed, still feels elusive to her. That night, she wept theatrically into her pillow until she couldn't breathe, worked herself up until she wondered whether *this,* this gasping, was what Mary felt like when she was in the hospital coughing, though she knew deep down that it was not, that she was just a hysterical teenage girl trying to understand a situation too big and too sad for her to grasp.

Her best friend was terminally ill. They had, since kindergarten, loved each other with the symbiotic, if sometimes competitive, feroc-ity of two only children who did not have sisters of their own onto whom they could project all their desires and fears. Their relationship was balanced on constantly shifting scales. Nix was slightly prettier, infinitely bolder, more popular among their shared girlfriends for her bawdy humor and sense of adventure, and for years it had seemed undisputed that she was their leader, Mary her faithful sidekick.

Mary, though, had the better family: a reliable dad who would never abandon his daughter; a mom who taught at their old grade school and was loved by her students. Though the Grace family was hardly rich, they were more comfortable than Nix and her divorcée mother, who could not have continued living in affluent Kettering at all had their mortgage not already been paid off. And somehow, in late high school the balance started to shift in Mary's favor, so that she had become the kind of girl guys fell for without her having to *do* anything, even lose her precious virginity.

Mary's parents were among a new pro-adoption generation, the kind who, instead of treating Mary's adopted status as a dark secret, wore it as a badge of pride, calling her their "chosen" child, saying she was "special." Nix's very *existence*, in contrast, was an accident, her mother having gotten knocked up in college, her father graduating literally days before her birth while his dropout new bride stayed home to elevate her swollen ankles. True to these beginnings, Mary's staid, engineer dad doted on her, whereas Nix's charismatic, restless father had loved his music career (and, Nix's mother said, other women and booze) more; Mary had grown into "serious girlfriend" material, while Nix had become the kind of girl who drove past the houses of guys who weren't calling her, who was starting to rack up one-night stands at the dance clubs, who fought with her often-depressed mother nonstop over broken curfews and coming home drunk. Now Mary was ill, and Nix was terrified of losing her. But amid it all was a horrible, creeping jealousy, as though Mary's dramatic disease and the grief it inspired actually *verified* her virtue, her preeminence over whatever slutty irrelevance Nix possessed. Once Nix slept with Bobby Kenner, he stopped calling Mary altogether and started calling Nix, but only for sex. They would meet in secret, after Bobby had been out with his friends, and by midsummer Nix heard he was going out with a girl from another school, but still when he called she snuck out to meet him. "Nobody's going to want me now," Mary, out of the hospital now, would say during the long summer days while they lounged on chairs in Mary's yard. "Look how Bobby disappeared the minute he found out — like I was contagious." And

Nix would say, "He's just a pussy, he couldn't deal with it, not everyone will be that way, he's nothing, he's no great loss, I promise you that."

Though Nix had long aspired to go to Oberlin, as her father had, which would also have kept her in reasonable proximity to Mary, at the last minute she accepted a place at Skidmore, a small East Coast school, fleeing Ohio like her house was on fire. She resigned herself to the fact that Mary could be dead before they reached college graduation—that she was abandoning her best friend even if Mary was secretly better off without her. On that first winter break from Skidmore, when Nix reread her journal from the previous summer (*It's like she's the virginal, tragic heroine of a Victorian novel, and I'm just an expendable ho in a B horror flick*), she was so consumed with shame she burned the entire book in the fireplace one day while her mother was out, its plastic-and-calico cover stinking up the house.

Next to Zorg's overwhelming good looks, even next to Titus's swarthy masculinity, Bobby Kenner, with his ruddy cheeks and the shaved legs of a competitive swimmer, would look like a joke.

Yet Nix flips her shoulder hard, trying to toss off Titus's heavy head.

Meanwhile, Mary and Zorg are frolicking in the water. Mary was on the swim team in high school, so these water scenes, à la 1950s movies about young love, become her. She has broad swimmer's shoulders, incompatible with the rest of her tiny frame, though complemented by a curvy bottom the boys have always liked. Mary is, you might say, *known* for her ass, though few have ever seen it without covering. Nix has a pretty fine ass, too, if she does say so herself. This is one of the ways in which the two girls look alike, in addition to their blond hair, their similar height. Back home, people often asked if they were sisters. *The ass sisters.* Nix laughs to herself. Mary is topless here on this secluded beach, her small breasts pale in the sun. She and Nix both went topless on Paradise Beach, and Mary is planning to lose her virginity to Zorg tonight or tomorrow night, before leaving Mykonos for Ios, so why not show her boobs as a preview? Nix, however, has left her bikini top on. Her breasts are larger and rounder than Mary's; they've been known to attract attention. But today she is playing the part of the spinster friend in whatever 1950s movie would feature Mary and Zorg splashing each other in the surreal blue waves. Or better yet, the ugly, older sister in that Joyce Carol Oates story, "Where Are You Going, Where Have You Been?" which she read at Skidmore and loved so much she xeroxed it and sent it home to Mary. For once, Mary gets to be Connie, the hot-to-trot one, and she will be the plain, responsible older sister whose name she cannot recall. She owes Mary that much, though Mary does not know it. That much and far more.

Poor Titus has his head on his own towel now. He gestures up at the tranquil taverna high above the beach with his hairy hand and says, "They have the nice fish. We eat later the fish at there."

Jesus Christ. Nix stands, shaking her mat out again, movements terse with memories of her past shittiness. A smattering of sand flies in Titus's face. From behind her sunglasses she watches him swipe at his eyes foolishly, those thick knuckles surely only further grinding in the sand.

But girls are capricious. Only two hours later, in a complete twist of moods, Nix sits at the tavern thinking, *This is what life is all about.* Yes: the beautiful and the terrible intermingled. This thatched awning, whistling in the wind over this tiny restaurant—a heavy storm would pound it down to nothing, scatter its sticks to the sea. The rickety wooden legs of the chair sway under her slight weight, while below the looming cliffs lie rocks like so many sharp teeth that could tear a body apart. And wine. Three bottles of crisp white, nothing like the syrupy red of the night before, a slightly acidic cold bite that chases away the heat of midday with each sip. Ah. Yes. All days should be like this.

They have eaten a fresh fish they selected from a tank while it still lived. A thrill of murder swims in them. The fish was served still wearing its head, delicious, in a puddle of oil, like nearly everything Nix and Mary have eaten here in Greece. They dipped fresh bread into the oil once the fish was gone. Nix is wearing her top now (Mary, so impatient to get naked altogether, forgot to bring one), and it billows, a thin yellow cotton, in the wind. Titus's head is where it belongs, atop his shoulders, atop his torso, with his ass resting in his own chair. *Hallelujah,* Nix thinks. "Pass the wine," she says. Oblig-ingly, Titus tries, but the bottle is empty.

It seems Mary and Zorg are bickering, though Nix is gazing at the horizon and not really paying attention. Zorg's English is pretty good, and since Titus's is so inferior, the burden of conversation is not on Nix; she need only smile now and then. Mary and Zorg have been talk-ing intently about politics, a subject about which Nix is certain Mary knows little and cares less, but Nix has been in college long enough to know that sexy men bring out political opinions in otherwise disin-terested girls, so she does not question this shift. The horizon is like an endless, glowing light saber, Nix thinks, and dissolves into giggles, happily drunk.

Mary's voice snaps. "At least everyone in America doesn't live with their parents until they're thirty-five! At least we go to college and get real jobs instead of having a twenty-five percent unemployment rate like Barcelona!"

What? Did Mary really say that? How on earth would *she* know?

Zorg, however, seems nonplussed. He leans back in his rickety chair, waving a cigarette as if to shoo off Mary's words like flies. "You are so isolated," he says. "Barcelona is not Spain. It is where silly girls like you go to see Europe on your backs with the Catalan men."

"I've never even been to Spain!" Mary shouts back.

Zorg shrugs. "Barcelona, Mykonos, it is the same. Americans are so ignorant."

Nix has not been to Barcelona either but is pretty certain it is not indistinguishable from a Greek party island, so she's not sure she's following Zorg's argument. She looks at Titus for his take, but he, too, shrugs and says, "What I can say? He is right. American women, they are whores. What one can do?"

It is the best grammatical showing he has made all day. Nix gasps.

Mary straightens, composing her face. She is a well-mannered girl. The kind whose well-mannered mother passed along to her daughter the knowledge that you catch more flies with honey than with vinegar, something Nix is not sure she will ever learn. Mary says calmly, "Well, that's a generalization, Titus. Not all American women are promiscuous, though I can see where if you only meet them on vacation you might get that impression. There are all kinds of people everywhere—every place is the same when you get down to it. Nation is just an illusion anyway, but it doesn't stop people from believing in their own country."

Nation is just an illusion? What has Mary been *doing* while Nix has been at Skidmore snorting coke and coaxing the temperamental dick of her fortysomething professor?

Zorg, however, is unimpressed. "You do not have to believe in your imperialist country!" he shouts, banging his fist on the table, so that droplets of oil scatter. "You choose to be like the sheep!" Aggressively he throws back his head, his neck thick with tendons, like a horse's. "Baaa!" he shouts. "American sheep!"

"Well, okay," Mary says tentatively. "I'm not sure I even *do* believe in my country . . . you know, that strongly. But it's been a pretty good place to live, and I was raised there, so what else am I supposed to believe in?"

"You should believe in *my* country! And you will!"

Nix titters awkwardly. (*What the . . . ?*) But before she can jokingly ask whether Zorg plans to hypnotize them using the leftover fish carcass, Mary lurches forward and grabs her wrist, causing Nix to bang into the table, so that her breasts skim the oily surface of her empty plate. When she gets to her feet, she has two grease nipples staining her yellow shirt. *Fish and tits*, she thinks, trying to remember to remember the joke to repeat for some occasion in London.

"Come on!" Mary shouts, jerking her arm again. "We're going to the bathroom!"

The toilets are around the corner, behind small wooden doors in a rocky wall. Nix is surprised to find Mary crying, her breath rising and falling in crescendos. "He's crazy," she hisses into Nix's ear. "Holy shit. We've got to get out of here."

Nix is buzzing, a glorious afternoon-in-the-sun kind of drunk. "Chill out," she says in her best "I know all about men" drawl.

"European guys are all machismo, big deal. Don't worry about him. If you don't like him anymore, we can find you someone better to lose your virginity to—plenty of tourists in town."

Mary swats Nix in the head. "No, lush, I mean it—he's out of his freaking mind. He told me in the water that he's bringing me back to Spain! I thought he was just trying to be romantic, you know, woo me and make me think he was into me or whatever, so I was all, *Oh, that'd be great except I can't really do that because I go to college at home,* and he stopped dead still in the water and looked at me"—she grabs Nix's face for emphasis, by the jaw—"like this, he looked at me like this, and he goes, *You will come to Spain with me, or I will come to America and I will find you and I will kill you.* And you heard him just now! He said I *will* believe in Spain! He's planning to kidnap me!"

"Oh, he was just being melodramatic." Nix laughs. "Don't be such a gullible American. He was probably kidding."

"He was *not* kidding! He has no sense of humor."

"Fine, whatever," Nix says, letting the cool stone chill her sweaty back. "They're planning to abduct us, they just figured they'd spend a lot of money on fish and wine first and be seen in public with us in as many cafés as possible." She sighs.

Mary crosses her arms tight across her small breasts, creating the illusion of cleavage. "I have to get out of here," she insists. "You need to tell them you have a huge headache and want to leave, okay? Say your headache's too bad for the scooter and you want to lie down on the backseat of Zorg's car on the way home—I can't be alone with that psycho."

"Great," Nix says dully. She liked the *Splendor in the Grass* scenario much better, even if she *was* the spinster friend. This is quickly turning into a buzz kill.

AND SO IT comes to pass that two girls end up climbing— each sullen for a different reason—into a rental car with a Spanish man they have known for less than twenty-four hours, who may or may not be an airline pilot, whose last name they have not learned and will never learn. So it comes to pass that the man called Zorg guns the engine and takes off, not even bothering to wait for his friend Titus, still starting up his scooter. So it happens that the threesome in the car swerve together, at the speed of agitation, around the winding cliffs of Mykonos, the girls both too drunk and bothered to even realize they are not heading back in the direction of Plati Yialos, but onward.

MARY SITS UP front, impervious as a queen. In the backseat, like a naughty child who has eaten (drunk) too much, Nix reclines, head resting in the crook of her arm. The treacherous curves, around tightly wound cliff roads, feel like bed spins. Zorg is driving too fast. In the scenario they no doubt all envisioned, there would have been hours at the beach still for the three bottles of consumed wine to wear off. Instead, Zorg is pink in the face from climbing all the way down to the beach to retrieve their things, just to turn around and climb back up to the car at the insistence of Nix, who has claimed a "killer headache." Only now, as she grows dizzy from the car's lurching, has it occurred to Nix that it might not be the best idea to drive some of Greece's most hairpin turns with a drunken, pissed-off man at the wheel.

Well, okay, to be honest, she and Mary drank most of the wine. They are good for that, even at home. Not just the Ass sisters but the Lush sisters, too. Probably Zorg, who weighs almost as much as she and Mary combined, is not even *that* drunk. No doubt it will occur to him any moment that he should slow down—he is an airline pilot, after all. Nix closes her eyes, tries to sleep.

But no. Instead of settling into the rhythm of the road, Zorg seems to be only accelerating. When Nix sits up, she sees that his jaw is set, the muscles in his right thigh twitching, his broad hands clutching the wheel. The car rims the curves of the road like a darting tongue, teasing. Somewhere below, the restaurants, discos, hotels of Mykonos wait nestled at sea level, the rest of the island straining upward; they are caught in an elevated web of cliffs.

A lump rises in Nix's esophagus, signaling danger. Beneath her legs, the car's seat trembles, unsteady; she pitches to the other side of the car at each turn, clings tight to the door handle to keep herself still, as if clutching the rails of a roller coaster. Her hands are slick with sweat. She thinks of having to powder them before gripping the parallel bars, and even though she is not on a gymnastics team at Skidmore—has not done gymnastics since leaving Kettering more than two years ago—she is gripped by a terror that she will never touch a parallel bar again, a fear that this seat is the last thing she will ever hold before they plunge off a cliff to certain death below. She cannot imagine . . . oh, but yes, she finds she *can* imagine it: the weightlessness before her body begins to fly upward against the car's roof, the pitching in her stomach, so that she might vomit before she hits earth. It is in our DNA to be able to feel such scenarios in our bodies, like archetypes of fear: possible ways the human body can meet its end. With scraps of yellow hair, white and red flesh, torn to bits by the very teeth of the jagged cliffs she'd mused on earlier in her foolish, drunken rhapsody.

From what she can tell, Mary is utterly immune to Zorg's efforts to kill them. Serenely, Mary gazes out the window, impassive as though she wouldn't jump if someone tossed a snake in her lap. The tires hit a bump, perhaps no more than a stone in the road, but Nix's head bounces against the car's ceiling. Zorg doesn't slow the car. Dry dirt and rocks crunch and scatter beneath the wheels. Nix tastes blood, realizes she must have been biting her lip when her head hit the roof. How long before Zorg misjudges, one tire, one flick of the wrist, one crumbling piece of earth too far? Or maybe it is what he sincerely *intends,* only wants to make them suffer first for being American whores, for embarrassing him in front of his friend. Nix kicks the back of Mary's seat. Hard, in hopes of eliciting a response. Mary does not look back.

Shit, bitch, just because your life is cheap doesn't mean mine is! Then, *No, please, I don't mean that, Mary, Mary, we have to get out of this.* She kicks Mary's seat again, hard enough so that her toes feel damaged, tears welling in her eyes. This is it. *Oh god, oh Mom, hold on, we're going to die . . .*

"Zorg, honey." It is Mary's voice and not Mary's voice, all at once.

"I'm really sorry I acted so badly at the restaurant. Do you think you can ever forgive me?"

And in a split second, the speed of the car has reduced by at least half, and Zorg's large, meaty paw is on Mary's tanned, slim thigh. "Now, now," he says, the grandmotherly Americanism strange from his lips. "There is nothing to forgive."

The relief flooding Nix, the tears leaking from her eyes, are invisible to the two in the front seat, locked in their private dance. Nix finds that her hands are shaking uncontrollably; she sits on them, afraid that if Zorg catches on to her fear, he will catch on, too, to Mary's ploy to calm him. Mary has not turned to catch Nix's eye, but it no longer matters. In this car, they have already shared the instant of their deaths and then, in the same instant, been granted a reprieve.

"So, we go to Titus's villa, sí?" Zorg says, his voice a mask, too, he and Mary speaking from behind layers of masks. "We will give to your friend some headache medicine there."

"Zorg," Mary ventures, her voice so meek that Nix closes her eyes and wishes there were some way she could avoid the raw intimacy of witnessing Mary's fear. "It's been a long day. We've had a lot of sun and a lot of wine. I would really like to rest."

"You may rest at the villa," Zorg says, nodding, and Nix finds herself praying that Mary will not react, will not refuse, lest they be doomed once more to possible death on the rocks. Already the speed of the car has increased slightly—a test? If she were Mary, would *she* protest? Nix's mind reels; objectively, there is no way that venturing farther from town, farther from the public eye, can be a wise idea. There is only one thing that any man, in any language, wants from any girl at a Greek villa. The smarter thing, Nix knows, would be to call Zorg's bluff: to insist on being taken back to their rented room right now, to dare him to kamikaze himself off the winding cliffs, to hold his life as cheaply as one girl's rejection. Because once they get behind closed doors with him, Zorg will no longer be in any danger himself; the danger will all be Mary's. Still Nix finds, to her shock, that her body cannot process her mind's logic—that her body would do *anything* to survive this car ride, anything to postpone risk just one more minute. Mary has not responded, but her shoulders bear a dangerous stiffness, the body language of refusal. And all at once, Nix lunges forward, puts a hand on Zorg's shoulder, his shirt wrinkled now and stained with tanning oil, the heat of his skin radiating through the fabric. He jerks slightly, as though even in discussing her imaginary headache, he had forgotten Nix was there.

"Thank you for the offer," Nix says, and her voice sounds normal, not fake like Mary's and Zorg's. Her voice sounds utterly convincing. "Of course we'd be happy to go to the villa. That would be fine."

In the Month of Jacaranda

(KENYA: JOSHUA)

You can't hide.

    Here you are, under that burning sun, exposed. You realize that all you can rely on now is your body. Nothing you have learned in school, from television, from your clever friends, from the books you have read, will help you here.

    —FRANCESCA MARCIANO, *Rules of the Wild*

The drive from Nairobi to Maasai Mara is always the roughest. The Mara has no paved roads, or any roads at all, just tire tracks worn into the ground, a brand the intrepid have finally imprinted into the earth. Like a foxhound on the hunt, Joshua stalks these tracks. Mary's head leans against the window, knocking into the glass with each bounce, so she rolls her sweater into a protective cushion. Sometimes, when the vibrations lull her into a stupor, Yank's words play in her ears like a beating drum: *Darlin'. Let me tell you a story. Darlin'.* It's approximately ninety kilometers between the end of the proper road and the better lodges of the Maasai Mara National Reserve. Joshua slows and swerves constantly so as to avoid boulders, craters, dips. In no time, everyone is nauseated. The ground is so dusty that the clients slide their windows closed despite the heat, and Mary finds herself gulping air out of a narrow crack in the passenger's side window, coughing conspicuously until she has to field questions from the clients as to whether she's "getting sick."

It takes three hours to traverse ninety kilometers, bouncing violently all the way. She imagines it's like driving on the surface of the moon.

When they finally arrive at the Keekorok Lodge, Mary and Joshua have two hours before the clients' first game drive at 4 p.m. No matter how weary clients are, they are *always* raring to go on that first excursion of their safari, cameras blazing, fresh deodorant applied. Joshua's simple guide quarters await, but Mary cocks her head to the side and says, "Bar, baby, bar." Two double G&Ts later, her stomach settling from the false comfort of alcohol, the clients — parents Walt and Kathleen, and children Fiona and Liam — can be seen trotting down the path from their room. At their approach, Mary stands from the large cushioned seat she's been sharing with Joshua; his hand slides down her back gently in parting. And for a moment she sees herself as these American clients must: leading some *National Geographic* fantasy life, tooling around with her accented boyfriend, the two of them making a sexy picture amid the lodge's romantically African decor.

She has been doing this a lot lately. Drifting away from her body to survey the image of herself as if from above. The picture looks so much as she had *hoped* it would that she can scarcely believe it. Sometimes she feels she is being followed by an invisible camera crew, is tempted to turn and wink at the audience to say, *Can you fucking believe this?* The audience would consist of her anxious parents; of Bobby Kenner; of all those fair-weather high school friends who quietly removed themselves following her diagnosis; of Yank, as she lives the life he all but orchestrated when he urged her to reconsider spending her remaining time in Dullsville, Ohio, and to instead let Joshua show her the world. But mostly her audience would be Nix, always Nix: speechless, shocked, proud.

THEY ARRIVED IN Kenya from Japan — perhaps its polar cultural opposite — where Joshua's circus was making an extended appearance, and Mary was fresh off two weeks in the hospital in Osaka. Joshua's cousin Gavin had written from Nairobi to say he'd started a safari company and would give Joshua a job, and just like that, presto, their circus life was over, after nine months on the move and nearly a dozen European cities that had dazzled Mary with their beauty and promise initially, but that she'd wandered through alone, increasingly frustrated as Joshua spent his days in rehearsals and his nights performing the same show she'd seen twenty, fifty, seventy times, until near the end she'd spent most of Austria and Germany in dinky hotel rooms reading novels about other people, other places, not even bothering to see the sites, numb with living out of a suitcase and with northern Europe's relentless rain.

In contrast to her few months at Arthog House, to the strange intimacy she had forged with both Yank and Sandor, she and Joshua managed to spend the better part of a year in the company of his fellow circus performers without making any close friends. For starters, he was the only native English speaker in the show, but somehow it wasn't only that. When Mary wrote letters home to her mother, she was aware of her life's sounding eccentric and glamorous — a traveling circus! — but in practice she was often bored, a hanger-on like the unnecessary mascot of a single-minded sports team. Japan had been a relief. They would set up shop for a year, or so the plan went. Long enough to have some kind of life. Mary had even gotten a job teaching English and purchased a bicycle on which to ride to school. But her hospital stay derailed all that, frightening even the usually fearless Joshua with the language barrier and strange customs: family members washing the patients' laundry on the roof of the hospital; food served family-style in communal rooms, with stronger patients pouring the weaker patients' tea. Joshua had to bring Mary's nightclothes and towels, since such things weren't provided, and he'd missed performances while tending to her, and they were both still mortified at not having realized that, on Mary's release, they were supposed to leave her doctor a *tip*. Her legs so swollen from IVs of antibiotics that she couldn't even fit into her own shoes, they'd been back with the circus for only a few days when the letter from Gavin arrived. Like a sign.

JOSHUA IS LOST. How easy this is to hide from clients never ceases to amaze Mary, but she's learned to read the signs. He's scanning, using his binoculars, but instead of game she knows he's searching for other safari vehicles. Heedlessly he whizzes past the zebras that dot the landscape more plentifully than cows do the American Midwest, ignoring cries of glee from four-year-old Liam, on the bench seat in the back, who has missed most of the earlier zebras while poring over pictures of birds in Joshua's wildlife book. Smoothly claiming to be on the lookout for a lion, Joshua doesn't slow the truck, not even for a herd of gracefully loping giraffes, not even when Walt and Kathleen stand up in the moving vehicle to photograph receding wildlife as their cameras bob up and down from the rocky earth, whacking them rudely in the eyes.

Gavin has offered to throw some money at a local Maasai to sit shotgun in the truck until Joshua gets the lay of the Mara down pat, but Joshua repeatedly refuses because then Mary would have to sit in the back with the clients instead of beside him. Getting lost is no problem, he assures Gavin—the clients get excited when you seem to be looking wildly for something anyway. Just claim you've seen tracks of a lion stalking an impala, and they're near orgasm while you race around trying to figure out where the hell you are. And the beauty of it is that the lie is without consequence, because in the Mara you never leave clients high and dry. Of the Big Five, three practically hurtle themselves at you here. Leopards are always most elusive, and black rhino are more plentiful elsewhere, but on the Mara, elephants, buffalo, and even lions are simply everywhere, in addition to all the "lesser" (Mary often thinks "more beautiful") game. The challenge would be to spend a day *without* spotting at least a few lionesses dozing in the shade, or a lone lion king surveying his kingdom, poetically staring off across the plains.

On their first few safaris, Mary's heart would race when Joshua lost his bearings. She pictured them driving until they ran out of petrol, never encountering another human being, rationing the clients' Hobnobs and bad potato crisps, big cats circling as the pitch-black African night fell. But of course this never happened. Tourism has exploded in Kenya. Though at one moment they can seem alone in the wild, nothing else visible on any horizon, in truth, almost as with the animals, they never have to travel *that* far before seeing a cluster of safari vehicles parked, khaki-clothed travelers inside with cameras covering their faces, the sound of snapshots firing louder than the inexplicably silent footfalls of the elephants being photographed. In the beginning, Joshua (talking a blue streak about birds, for distraction) would sometimes end up trailing another guide—some *actual* Kenyan, usually Kikuyu—as he ferried his charges back to the Keekorok. Now, though, it never takes nearly that long. One glimpse of the river, one particular rock formation or cluster of trees, one memory of the way the tire tracks diverge near the overhang where they first saw the two lion brothers even Mary has come to recognize after repeated sightings, and Joshua is on his own again, trying harder and harder to keep *apart* from the fray.

"And there he is," Joshua says smoothly, pulling up alongside a straggling river, navigating the tires cleanly through knee-deep water to park on the other side. Around everyone's craned necks, Walt and Kathleen standing, the children on top of their seats, Mary sees what he is talking about: a hippo, its chocolate-gray skin still shiny with life, lying dead at the water's edge just under a small overhang of grassy earth. The hippo is on its side, fresh molten-pink scratches crisscrossing its hide, part of its head caved in, missing. Over the whirling in her ears, Mary hears the clients' oohs and aahs, their intakes of breath, their cameras maniacally clicking, and suddenly she glimpses the lion dozing on the overhang, his mane a darker brown than the dry grass, guarding his kill.

"A lion!" Liam shouts. "My favorite!"

His sister, Fiona, imperiously elbows him, half knocking him off the perch of his seat. "Shut up, do you want it to forget about that hippo and come eat you?"

Liam—Mary can't tell if he's hamming it up or sincere—begins to cry, shrieking, "*Eat* me? Eat me!" until Kathleen looks away from the hippo and takes her son in her arms, and Walt shoots Fiona a dirty look from behind his camera lens and mutters, "You want that phone in your room? Then knock it off."

Dearest Nix,

Here is what I know so far. Death is cheap in Africa. People come here for one of two reasons: (1) to recognize, even celebrate their own insignificance amid the heartless, beautiful vastness, or (2) to convince themselves of their mastery of Africa's majesty and malevolence by taking its picture, pinning it down on a page, assuring themselves it is something wholly separate from them.

Sometimes, a person who arrives in Africa for one of these two reasons ends up remaining for the other reason entirely. Africa can change your mind, and whatever you thought you knew of life and death can easily be switched around. You cannot choose whether this land will inhabit you, change everything you thought you knew. You can only arrive and do your best to keep an open mind.

The problem is, everything Africa has to teach involves a body count. All roads here lead to something dead. So, if you were hoping not to think of Death at all, not to let him learn your address, not to enter into either friendship or battle with his forces but, rather, to trick him into not recognizing your name, then you are in the wrong place entirely. You should have stayed home.

JOSHUA PARKS ON a hilltop so the family can photograph the Serengeti, the invisible dividing line between Kenya and Tanzania, and obediently Walt, Kathleen, and Fiona rise, snapping where he points. Mary watches Liam kicking the chair in front of him, bored. It's weird, she thinks, for Walt and Kathleen to have brought him along. Most of the English- and American-based safari companies don't even permit children under ten, or seven, or something like that, nor will the treetop lodges on Mount Kenya or the more exclusive tented camps. Gavin's company, however, has opted for *quantity* by keeping to the more mainstream lodges (lots of African kids stay at Keekorok, too: school groups and middle-class Kikuyu families). These lodges provide amenities like indoor showers and swimming pools but cater to big crowds, favor lukewarm buffets, and cannot be called truly "luxurious." Fiona is technically of an acceptable safari age at twelve—with breasts already bigger than Mary's—but just because she's allowed to be here doesn't mean she's mature enough to appreciate it. On the whole, this family seems the sort Mary traveled across the world to avoid; she would bet money that, at home in Saint Paul, they have matching "Kiss me, I'm Irish" T-shirts, and are prone to attend parades.

It doesn't matter, though. Mary has been here only since early fall, but already, just shy of Christmas, the clients are becoming a bit of a blur with their identical questions, their cocktail-party small talk. "Think of yourself as the social director of a cruise ship," Gavin told Mary the first time she accompanied Joshua on safari. "They think they're here for a walk on the wild side, but in reality the minute they see a blond American girl, they'll almost piss themselves with relief. If you like the circuit—if you don't tire of the endless smell of lion piss—I'll start paying you to go along, to chat them up, reassure them." He offered this while they drank Tuskers around the swimming pool outside his swank cottage in the rich—and overwhelmingly white—suburb of Karen, the picturesque stone wall surrounding his idyllic home topped with far less picturesque razor wire intended to keep out the "natives" who might aspire to steal his possessions or slit his throat. His leggy Swedish wife (or maybe they were not married) smiled a cocaine-numb smile, her eyes shielded by dark Chanel glasses. Her English was impeccable, yet she and Mary rarely spoke. She could not have been more than five or six years Mary's senior, but she seemed a whole separate breed. *What assholes,* Mary thought. She could hardly believe that Gavin, with his pleated linen pants and sharkish politician's smile, was related to Joshua. She felt disinclined to take his advice on anything.

It turns out, however, that he was right. No sooner do the clients depart—back to the States, to England, to Canada, to Italy—than she has already forgotten their names.

THE SKY IS darkening fast, Liam asleep with his head on Kathleen's lap, when Walt booms, "Hey, before we head back, let's check on our hippo one more time!"

Our hippo. Mary knew this was coming. If Walt hadn't mentioned it, Joshua would have, and she has spent the past two hours trying to come up with some plausible excuse to deter him. Her stomach lurches. Fiona moans, "Eew, gross," but without conviction, and already Joshua is grinning, turning the truck toward the river. He tosses a look over his shoulder, and in that moment he appears no older than Fiona, a trickster elf somehow entrusted with the safety of an entire upper-middle-class American family. "I should've brought some nose plugs, eh?" he says. "Our hippo friend will be getting ripe."

Mary closes her eyes, resolving to skip tomorrow's 7 a.m. game drive. No doubt they'll all be hot to return bright and early to watch the vultures and hyenas war over the hippo's stenchy remains. She pictures herself instead cocooned under the mosquito net, curtains drawn against the vigilant morning sun, Keekorok waiters bringing her a little metal pot of Nescafé and hot milk, since despite the international fame of "Kenyan coffee," nobody in the actual nation of Kenya seems to consume anything except crappy instant. *She* will spend her morning reading at the pool, wearing only a little black bikini, confident that even if she is not exactly a "guest," nobody will care, since her young, shapely body makes for a fine poolside ornament. No, she will not trot around at the crack of dawn, trailing Joshua like a faithful dog. Not this time.

True to Joshua's prediction, they smell the hippo before they see it. At times on safari, the air seems like something you could touch: so thick with animal urine or decomposing flesh that it's hard to believe such a scent carries no shape, no *color* to mark its presence. The scratches on the hippo's hide are already losing their pink rawness, browning in the heat and sun. There, at its mammoth belly, are the lion brothers Mary and Joshua have come to know, one (the larger, with his darker mane) feasting on the hippo's tough flesh, his younger brother lying insouciantly behind.

"Oh my God," Kathleen mutters. "I can't believe this! We've hit the jackpot on our very first drive!"

"Shut up, Mom," Fiona snaps. "The guidebook says we're supposed to be quiet around the animals."

"Your mother doesn't know how to be quiet," Walt says, barking a laugh.

"Dad," Fiona pleads nervously, "you're making it worse!"

The feeding lion does not even look up at their nasally twangs. The lounging brother stares at them, but with the kind of disinterest with which an infant surveys his own reflection in a mirror.

Joshua moves in closer. Mary is amazed, almost dumbfounded, by what a natural he is: Before they arrived in Nairobi, she had never even seen him pet a dog or drive a car. He was an urbanite, of Johannesburg and London, a peddler of hash cakes, a street performer. Now it turns out that in Johannesburg Joshua's father owns a drive-away business, and Joshua spent his entire youth—when not training at the gym—working with cars. While their truck has never broken down entirely, they have twice blown tires Joshua switched without batting an eye, and they once got stuck in a flash flood so that the vehicle floated downstream, and Joshua and two African guides who'd seen the mishap literally *pushed* the car against the river tide back onto the gravelly bank, where Joshua then did mysterious things under the hood until the waterlogged truck started again.

As close to the lion as they can get without hitting the hippo with their tires, Joshua kills the engine. This is his seventh solo safari, but Mary knows that on his fiftieth his eyes will have lost none of their rapture. He lives more in the moment than anyone she will ever meet, a chameleon in his ability to change colors and inhabit, fully and utterly, the role in which he has suddenly found himself. You can learn the lay of the Kenyan land, but you cannot learn *this,* this lack of being anywhere other than where you are in a given instant; this complete surrender to watching a lion eat a hippo; this absence of wanting or wondering about anything except the spectacularly commonplace miracle before your eyes.

Kathleen and Walt and Fiona click their cameras—they each have one!—at the speed of light, hungry for documentation. But Joshua, Mary suddenly realizes, has never taken a photo on safari. *She* owns a camera—she is an American, after all—and has brought it with her on their trips, and at first she was no different than Kathleen and Walt, taking forty-seven pictures of the same giraffe, mystified and half-afraid she was dreaming, desperate to prove she had really been here, really seen that. By now she knows that photos of animals lose their power in the retelling; it is looking back on the photo of Joshua and the guides pushing their floating truck, or of Joshua asleep in the morning light on their first morning in Samburu, that gives her pleasure. A photo of a lion loses its magic once you yourself are no longer in the scene, because a lion is supposed to be on the Mara, supposed to be eating a hippo—it is *you* who were never meant to be here.

"Sawa sawa," Walt says after a while, lowering the camera that, for this generation of safarigoers, has replaced the guns of old. Joshua has taught the family this Swahili term, which in this context means "I'm ready to go" or "It's all good" or "Cool," and signals a waning fascination with a given sight. But Joshua does not immediately start the car, and Mary notices that he is not looking at the lion and hippo anymore but at Liam, awake now and wide-eyed, rapt. Liam, who does not own a camera. Liam, who is not speaking anymore, not tormenting his sister, not eating his brought-from-home granola bar, but watching the animals with reverence, spellbound.

Joshua turns to her, eyes inscrutable. "He won't even remember this trip," he whispers. "Sawa sawa," Fiona says, and her father chuckles at how she is catching on.

No sooner had Gavin's letter arrived than Joshua began to wax rhapsodic about the African sky. He had grown up "going to the bush," and despite the enormity of the African continent—the geographic, political, and cultural gulfs between South Africa and Kenya—the move was clearly a homecoming to him. South Africa had made itself unlivable, but here was Kenya, with a kinder and gentler residual colonialism, with a smiling African population that had never been exactly enslaved, even with a spanking-new plan for democracy through multiparty elections, some ploy Moi had pulled out of his ass at the eleventh hour to appease the international community. Kenya, with the same endless sky and nearly red earth as Joshua's homeland. From the first it was clear that he felt more at home amid its landscape than he ever could have in the cities of Europe.

It had never occurred to Mary *not* to accompany him. If in Japan she had developed an obsessive taste for sushi, so she had also found a budding awareness that she could not rely on her health to per-mit stable breadwinning—that her life, no matter how she sliced it, would have to involve either protracted reliance on her parents or a long-term liaison with a man. Someone who cared enough whether she lived or died to put his money where his mouth was. Via a bad connection from Dayton to Osaka, Dr. Narayan had insisted that she needed a regular, English-speaking physician, not random doctors on the run. She *needed,* Dr. Narayan said, a cystic fibrosis center, and while Nairobi didn't have one, the city offered plenty of private pulmonary specialists for those who could pay. "Don't worry, dar-ling," Gavin quipped on another long-distance phone call. "England's left its mark here. Nairobi serves up Western-style medicine to its expats along with their high tea." His safari company was raking in the Kenyan shillings, the pounds, the American dollars. The movie *Out of Africa* was still fresh in everyone's mind; the Cold War was newly over; Americans were booking safaris year-round, even in the rainy season. And so Mary and Joshua packed alarmingly scant bags and boarded more than a day's worth of flights, and Joshua, who had been toting hash on his circus world tour inside deodorant containers to mask the smell, finally threw away his stash entirely, assured that Gavin would help him procure a new dealer in Nairobi along with a doctor for Mary, and made the flights stone-cold straight, as if to symbolize their new life.

Joshua even has short hair now, so as not to worry the clients. The shearing of her lover has made an almost uncanny difference in his appearance, and for the first time Mary can imagine the boy he was in South Africa, the serious athlete whose equally serious devotion to pot somehow failed to diminish his clean-cut charm. He's lost the underfed, shaggy vibe he gave off in London, and though Mary never aspired to date a hippie—never even *met* one before Arthog House—she misses the desperate, rebellious, hungry version of him more than she would have expected. This Joshua, close cropped and filled out, suntanned muscles rippling freely and nourished by goat *nyama choma* and piles of heavily salted *ugali,* seems strangely foreign to her, though she suspects that 99 percent of women would say he looks "better" now.

ON THE WAY out of the Mara, heading for one night at Lake Nakuru, Fiona and Liam throw up in tandem. Literally the moment Liam starts to barf, Fiona takes one look at him and starts spewing, too. They gush like geysers, stench filling the car. Kathleen shoves a plastic bag under Liam's mouth, and the flow of him continues, his puke hitting whatever cookie wrappings or melted Cadbury bars litter the bottom of the bag. Fiona, no longer in an active state of throwing up but mouth stained with vomit, barks at her mother, "Gee, thanks, Mom! Give *him* the bag. He doesn't care about his clothes anyway— what about me?"

Joshua has stopped the truck. He looks at Mary pointedly, but she realizes she isn't sure what he's signaling. Amusement? Irritation? He goes round to the trunk and flips it open.

"Okay, kids, out," Walt says sharply. "Let's get you changed."

Liam whines, "Fiona says we can't go outside—the lions will eat us!"

Walt snaps, "Do you see any lions?"

"Maybe we *should* change him inside the truck." Kathleen is picking at Liam's clothing, pulling his shirt over his head daintily, trying to keep from actually touching the puke, which is futile. By the time she's gotten his T-shirt off, gooey chunks of vomit dot Liam's hair.

"It really is safe," Mary says, though she has no idea if it is safe or not. "If you saw any animals, you could get right back in."

Fiona starts crying, a kind of smoldering rage bubbling over into tears. "I'm not taking my clothes off out in the open! Can't we wait until we get to a restroom?"

"Are you kidding?" Walt barks. "That's an hour away! We'll asphyxiate from the smell!

Liam is trying to climb Kathleen's body, but she holds him at arm's length, leading him gingerly out into the sun. Fiona crosses her arms over her chest in irritation, but her shirt is covered with barf, and Mary sees her give up and flop her arms down to her sides as she skulks after them, disappearing round the back of the truck to rummage through their bags for fresh clothes.

Mary sits shotgun, surveying the scene in the back. The seats where Liam was lying with his head on his mother's lap, and where Fiona antisocially listened to her Walkman, are both soiled. Joshua keeps napkins in their cooler, so Mary opens it—thinks about flipping the top off a Tusker for fortification—and climbs into the back to start wiping up the vomit. This kind of thing would be part of her job if she were a waitress, a flight attendant . . . a mother. She scrapes the lumps of puke into the already warm and heavy plastic bag, feeling something like penance or gratitude, thinking of the night Yank cleaned her, of Joshua scrubbing her dirty bedsheets and nightclothes on the hospital roof in Osaka. It is not often she gets to play nurse instead of patient, and the turnabout is oddly reassuring. This is the truth of the matter: they are all a mass of bodily fluids, of stenches, just like the rotting hippo. Fiona and Liam just don't know it yet.

She has the bag tied up at the top, the seats visually—if not olfactorily—clean by the time Joshua wanders over to the open door, where Walt, too, is waiting while Fiona changes clothes.

"Here," she says, holding out the bag.

"We'll keep that until we reach the gate," Joshua says. "Remember, we stopped at the toilets there on the way in—they've rubbish bins, too, and the kids can clean up."

Walt takes the plastic bag. "We don't want this inside with us," he says, and faster than Mary would have guessed possible, he winds his arm back and tosses the bag. He must have been a pitcher in high school; it arcs into the air like a rocket, off toward distant acacia trees.

Joshua gapes at Walt. He is, in this moment, extremely easy to read. "You can't just throw plastic onto the reserve!" He isn't shouting, but Walt looks taken aback. "This is a national reserve. You're not permitted to litter here."

Walt's face recovers quickly. He smiles mildly back at Joshua. "We weren't going to drive in a stuffy truck full of vomit," he says calmly.

He must be twenty years older than Joshua. He is a gangly man, paradoxically paunchy in the middle, losing his hair. He is not so much ugly as utterly nondescript, in the exact midwestern way of Mary's father. Joshua could put him down with one punch, though Mary has never known Joshua to hit anyone. Walt seems to fear Joshua not at all, seems entirely clear on the fact that he is the one paying Joshua and confident this payment covers his right to litter the Mara if he so chooses. Kathleen, Fiona, and Liam climb back into the truck, and despite Mary's best efforts to clean up, they all avoid the vomit seats, cramming together on the bench in the back. Walt enters after them, sitting on a clean seat up front, his legs casually splayed with masculine authority. Joshua stares after the bag, though they can no longer see it. It would be physically impossible to navigate the truck up in that direction, across that rough terrain, but Mary knows Joshua is thinking of making the journey by foot—of making them all wait in the truck while he goes to retrieve the bag.

"Let it go," she tells him. It occurs to her that Joshua, who according to Yank saw his first love almost killed and had no power to retaliate, may have "let go" enough things to last a lifetime—that his quotient may be prematurely expired. If he chases after the bag, they could be waiting here an hour, baking in the greenhouse heat of the truck. Plus, there is the chance he will happen on an animal who does not welcome his presence. Theirs is a *driving* safari, and Joshua does not carry a gun.

"Please," Mary begs. "For me. Let it go for me."

Joshua climbs back into the driver's seat, his eyes still off in the distance. He revs the motor and they jolt forward with a lurch. Mary puts her hand on Joshua's leg, which vibrates from the bumps, shaking her off. In the back, she hears Fiona saying, "Like I'm ever going to wear that shirt again. You should have just stuck it in the trash bag." Mary wipes her hands on her sundress, trying to remove invisible germs that may be a danger to her lungs. She is meant to avoid things like sick people, like rotting onions; she is not supposed to wipe up vomit and traipse around the third world. She is meant to believe that caution *matters*, but she has come to believe that the things meant to save you—like the barbed-wire fence intended to keep wealthy expats shielded from poor Africans—can often kill you, too.

THE NIGHT MARY agreed to travel with Joshua and the circus, she took out her medical equipment and laid it out for him on their dilapidated mattress. "I have asthma, like I told you," she said, "but it's almost just a side effect of another, more serious condition called cystic fibrosis. It's not a terminal illness, exactly, but it's progressive, and I don't have a normal life expectancy. Eventually I'll be on oxygen all the time, and either I'll get an infection they can't get rid of, or I'll pretty much drown on my own mucus and die that way." She didn't look at him but fiddled with the equipment on the bed, conscious of the fact that Yank had once touched it. "Do you still want me to come?"

He said only, "Nobody knows what the future holds, right? I could fall off the trapeze tomorrow and become a quadriplegic or get a brain injury and end up daft and eating through a straw. Does that mean you don't want to be with me now?"

"Of course not," she said.

"Right, then," he said, and he kissed her. "So you're coming."

Mary might easily have told him everything then. Instead she continued the unpacking of her rucksack until she could pass him her passport in silence and watch his face absorb the shock. Then she offered, "When I came to London, I changed my name, almost like a joke—but we ended up living together, and it stuck longer than I ever meant it to. It was just . . . a game, I guess. I know it'll be weird, but once we leave here, you shouldn't call me Nicole anymore."

"Why would you lie to me all this time?" he asked, childish confusion on his face, the pitch of his voice more distraught than at the revelation of her illness. "You were having a laugh? I don't understand. We . . . *I* was some kind of joke to you?"

There were many ways to address this, she knew. She could throw her arms around him and claim to be madly in love with him, but she was afraid he would see through that, that such a claim would undermine her real—if gentler—feelings for him. So she said, "It had nothing to do with you. It was all about me, always being the sick girl, wanting to escape that for a while." She peered into his face, the water-paleness of his eyes. "Haven't you ever wanted to get away from yourself? Haven't you ever wanted to become someone else?"

"Yeah," he said quietly, "I have," though he did not speak of the girl Yank told her about, just as she did not speak of Nix. The very day they left Arthog House, he began to call her Mary with surprisingly little effort. They never spoke of her deception again.

IN AFRICA, YOU *oscillate like a schizophrenic,* she scribbles in her Nix notebook by lantern light. *If you have come here on a journey to "find yourself," good luck. Here, you vary with the landscape . . .*

In Nairobi, your lover will buy a cheap Jeep and get carjacked before he has owned it a week. When you ask why he did not call for help, he will explain that if you shout "thief" in Nairobi, a mob is likely to beat your assailant to death right there in the street, so if you don't want blood on your hands, just hand over your wallet, just get out of the car. Though your city apartment complex will be considerably shabbier than Gavin's suburban home, it will be equally surrounded by barbed wire. You will be warned repeatedly not to exit the complex by foot after nightfall. To never, ever venture farther than River Road.

There are other stories of Nairobi that Mary cannot tell. Though she is not aware of it, in late 1991 the torture chambers in the basement of Nayoyo House are still operational. As she struggles with her daily resentment at not being able to roam freely, meanwhile prisoners, including journalists, are being whipped, burned, held underwater, molested, and not infrequently killed right in the city center. Likewise, there is a sophisticated, cosmopolitan side to Nairobi: a rising, educated African middle class and a decadent expat community still playing a glamorous game of *White Mischief* make-believe. But Mary and Joshua are alien to the former and too broke to buy entry into the latter, and so to these complex societies they are not privy. During the months Mary makes this mile-high city her home base, she will know only that its air is thin and that she is quickly winded even from a simple trip to buy groceries. That her yellow hair assures her of constantly being harassed by black Kenyans aiming to sell her things, so that she is perpetually fending off street vendors and small-time hustlers. That when she wants to go shopping, she is urged by Gavin—and Joshua, too—to frequent bland ("safe") malls that look like they could be in Los Angeles. She knows only that, while the Indian food in Nairobi surpasses even that in London, here in this city she will entertain more than one discussion with her pacifist lover about whether they should purchase a gun.

Approaching Lake Nakuru just days before Christmas, driving through the city's tree-lined boulevards, you are bombarded by the purple splendor of jacaranda. These trees bloom for only one month, forming vibrant, arched awnings over the road as you whiz by a gaggle of young boys, shoeless and rolling a tire alongside them as they run. When you finally reach the lake itself, a blanket of flamingos covers the water in pink motion, feathers rolling like waves, the sky alive with wings. Here, you dance with wildly gyrating hips alongside the local dance troupe that entertains tourists at the lodge. Here, instead of cursing the constant power outages in Nairobi, you are grateful for small mercies when the lodge permits your room additional hours of electricity for your medical devices while the rest of the rooms are temporarily powerless, to conserve energy. Here, your body entwining with your lover's beneath the romantic mosquito net can make up for any inconvenience of this country's unbelievably slow restaurant service, for the way everyone from the plumber to the hotel laundry service to the freaking police runs a perpetual hour (if not several days!) behind on "Kenya time." In the morning you are ravenous, pile your plate with mango slices, and drink several small glasses of passion juice, resolve to begin anew, still refusing to acknowledge that your moods here change with the extremity of Kenya's terrain. That all your resolutions are useless before this land.

WHEN HE CLIMBS into the truck for their Christmas Eve game drive, Liam hands Mary a sheet of paper. On it, he has written *Heart of Love* in dark ink, smeary from being colored over with a pink crayon. *Dear Mary*, the back of the paper says, *Mary Christmas I love you! Love Liam.*

Mary does not expect to burst into tears, but before she even registers it, Kathleen is cooing, "How sweet! Aren't you lovely! Look, Liam, Mary is crying because she likes your card so much!" Kathleen even wraps her arms around Mary, exhibiting less hesitance than she did when touching her puke-stained son. Mary wipes her nose on the sleeve of her peasant blouse, tries to extract herself from Kathleen's perfumed, bony embrace without appearing rude.

"Thank you," she says to Liam. "It's a beautiful card."

Fiona rolls her eyes, smirking. "Yeah," she says sarcastically. "He made one just like it for the lady who sat behind us on the airplane, and the maid who cleaned our room in Mombasa."

Mary bites her lip. She touches Liam on the head, his blond curls wispier, less substantial than her own: the hair of a human being not fully formed. He smiles wildly, half bangs his head into her stomach so that she can hug him, and though she believes she has lost the heart for it, she goes ahead with the embrace because Kathleen, Fiona, and Walt are all watching. His body is warm and pliant, and though she felt pressured into the hug, it is hard to force her arms to let go.

IN THE FILM *Out of Africa*, Meryl Streep's voice-over as Baroness Karen Blixen—known in the literary world as Isak Dinesen—says of her lover, Denys Finch Hatton, "I've written about all the others, not because I loved them less, but because they were clearer." In time, Mary will come to wonder if this lack of clarity is elemental to all love affairs in Kenya, at least among such expats as Blixen and Finch Hatton—as herself and Joshua. Those presumptuous enough to imagine their lives writ large, to pit their paltry individuality against a land they can never hope to understand or call their own.

HE WAKES HER on Christmas morning, though they do not have a game drive this day. "Come," he says, breath warm against her ear, the smell of sleep still on him, not yet overtaken by cigarettes, coffee, weed. The air is chilly and she takes with her the tasseled wrap they bought together at a market in Granada, winding it around her body as they step together outside their tent.

The sun, just beginning to rise above the peak of Mount Kenya, halos the rock of the mountain, creating a holographic effect. She stares into its golden-gray glow, blinking as if to adjust double vision. She thinks, *This might be my last Christmas.* She thinks, *There could not be anywhere better to spend it.* She thinks, *If I were to die tomorrow, I have had enough, it would be all right.*

Then she remembers Liam's card. Instantly she is blinking again, but this time the tears spill over. Here, then, is how it strikes: the sudden and devastating longing for a child of one's own. Mary is fully aware that *nobody*—no educated, world-traveling girl like herself—has a baby at twenty-three anymore. Yet there it is, the desire to fill her arms with baby, slithering around her body like an invisible snake and strangling her with wanting. Nearby, close enough that she and Joshua could reach it within a minute's sprint, a giraffe strolls awkwardly in the pale light. It is a strange sight at this hour, but animals separated from their herds are unpredictable: it may be hungry; it may be sick. It does not look troubled, however, from here. From a distance, it gives the impression of beauty, of perfection. *Like us,* Mary muses. *Like me.*

"I was thinking," she begins. Joshua's arm around her shoulders feels impeccably strong, and she uses it to bolster herself. In all this time, though she is anything but a convenient partner, he has never mentioned the possibility of their separating, has never been anything but surprisingly responsible, loyal, adventurous, brave. "Maybe—maybe we should get married."

Joshua barks a short laugh. "What would we do something like that for?"

She stares at his face, guileless, even innocent. Despite his perpetual tan, the skin around his eyes, which live behind habitual sunglasses, remains pink like that of a white mouse. It is the one space on his body that is vulnerable. The sun breaks free of the mountain, and Mary has to shield her own eyes from its sudden glare. Joshua lets out a contented sigh, kisses her hair.

"We don't have to play by those old rules," he tells her. "Marriage is the death of romance. We're writing our own story—the things they think we aren't allowed to do can't touch us here."

Water pools in her eyes again. "I feel that, too," she admits. "I mean, I think about it all the time—what people don't think I can do because I'm sick. What nobody thought I was capable of. But Joshua . . ." She isn't sure why she can't find her voice—why his words fall so completely in line with her own beliefs, and yet they scrape inside rather than caressing. She wants to say, *I'm not sure that proving "them" wrong is the best impetus for a life.* She wants to say, *Who are "they" anyway? Your "they" and my "they" don't even know one another.* Instead, she watches the giraffe bobble in the distance, its small head and sloping neck mimicking the curve of the mountain, nature in perpetual tandem. She tries, "Yank told me about your old girlfriend in South Africa. About what happened to her. You never talk about it. I don't even know her name."

For a moment, Joshua looks disoriented. He looks as though he may be trying to remember who Yank is. They have not spoken his name between them in months, though at times Mary has, irrationally, found herself wondering what it would be like to be here in Kenya with him instead of Joshua, imagining the different nature of their conversations in the still darkness of their tent. "I don't see what she's got to do with marriage," Joshua says at last. "Her name was Kaya, but I'm not still in love with her, if that's what you're worried about."

"No . . . that's not what I meant at all. It would be *okay* with me if you were, actually. That's not why I brought up marriage—because I was jealous. I . . . I just want to know you."

He laughs again. "Know me? Don't be daft. You've spent every day with me going on two years. We barely even talk to anyone save each other."

Mary shakes her head. "That's not true," she says. "We talk to *everyone* else. Circus people. Travelers. Clients. Our lives are full of random strangers."

For the first time since she has known him, the irritation that clouds his eyes is directed at her. "You're clearly upset about something," he says, "but I don't know what it is. I *did* love Kaya, all right? Maybe, if things had worked out differently, I could have seen a life with her. But as it turns out, that was just a delusional mistake. She could have run off with me—I had the money. It's not Communist Russia, for fuck's sake, you can leave the godforsaken shithole country if you like, if you can afford it. I told her to come, but she was too afraid. She said that we'd never be accepted no matter where we went, that we'd always be in danger. You can see for yourself that isn't true—you're American, you know London, you saw Europe, even *here,* for God's sake, there are people who do it. But she preferred to go back to work for a man who'd been raping her since she was a girl, some cult leader whose followers nearly killed her. She lost her eye, did Yank tell you that part? . . . Fuck it, I'm sure he did. If I'd have known he was nothing but an old grandmother gossiping on the front lawn, I'd have kept my fucking mouth shut. I'd have stayed with Kaya even if she had no eye, no education, I didn't care what anyone said, I wanted to run away together but she wouldn't. What else do you want me to say about that, Mary?" He narrows his eyes at her. "*Nicole.* When I asked you to come with me, you said yes. It turned out you were a liar, but at least you had courage. There's nothing to understand about me. My past is over. I'm here with you, now."

Mary blinks in the sun. She is openly crying, but this seems to frustrate him more. He paces, kicking the short brown grass.

"You want me to marry you to prove that I love you? Do you think I give a shit about some official piece of paper? It won't change anything. All I care about is what's between us in the moment—the church and the government can kiss my ass."

"But what if we wanted to have a baby?" she blurts out. "It's good to be married, for legal reasons, for that."

"A *baby*?" he mutters incredulously. "How could we have a fucking baby?" But instantly his pacing slows, and when he turns to her, his eyes are softer, pitying, and Mary's tears stop falling with something like shock, something like shame. "You're not well," he reminds her softly. "Wouldn't that be selfish of us? You're the one—I'm not trying to be cruel. You're the one who says you might not have long to live.

What about the child, then? What about *me*? I'd be saddled the rest of my life — I couldn't bring a baby on safari, could I? Or to circus rehearsal, or a gym if I were coaching? How would I be meant to handle a baby if you were gone?"

"I don't know," she admits.

"Can you even *do* that?" he persists, and though his voice is gentle, quiet, it feels relentless, as though he is slapping her. "Could your body handle a pregnancy?"

She shakes her head numbly. "I'm not sure. Women with cystic fibrosis . . . a lot of times there are fertility problems, and not everyone lives long enough to try. I think it's . . . maybe it's discouraged. But people have *done* it. Women have had children. Some adults with CF live way longer than the norm, into their forties, and my lung functioning is still really high for someone my age. If I were to have a baby young, like this — our child could be a teenager by the time I died. Even older."

He puts his hands on her arms. She wants, desperately, to go back inside the tent, to forget everything she started in her fit of half-awake madness, but his grasp holds her steady. "That's quite a game of roulette," he says, smiling like a father. "Those stakes are pretty high."

"You're the one who said Kaya wouldn't take a chance," she fires back. "You're the one who said you chose me because I wasn't afraid!"

"Fair enough." He drops his hands but still she does not move. "Here's the truth, then. After I found out you'd lied to me — I was angry, yeah. But in another way it confirmed that we were right for each other. I figured this kind of shit, this middle-aged settling-down-and-having-a-family business wouldn't apply. That it wasn't our fate, and that was fine with me. It still is."

"If it were left to fate, I'd still be in Ohio — you'd still be in South Africa!"

He nods, his calm infuriating. "You're right. And there was nothing I saw there that made me want to bring more life into the world. Every day growing up, I saw human cruelty, mindless conformity, people pushing one another down. You can say South Africa's fucked up, and that's true, but look at it here, too. Moi torturing people, animals

driving the wounded members out of the herd, giraffe mothers forgetting and rejecting their own offspring if they're separated for
twelve days. It's not just South Africa that's brutal, it's *nature*. And
now you want to have a baby when you could die before it's even
old enough to remember you? Fuck, woman! I'm just trying to live
without hurting anyone, trying to find some scraps of beauty under
all this shit and have a bit of fun. Why would anyone bring a child
into this sick world just to set it up for more pain than usual—that
sounds obscene, don't you see?"

"Obscene," she whispers. "My wanting a baby is obscene."

"I'm sorry." He takes her into his arms, radiating heat already in
the sun, though Mary's teeth are chattering, knocking against one
another nakedly. "Look, I'm not trying to hurt you. If you really want
to get married—I think it's bullshit, Mary, but if it's honestly important to you, then we'll do it, all right? You think it over, and if you
still want to, maybe we can manage it in Nairobi over the New Year,
before I've got to go out again—I'm sure Gavin would set something
up."

"Oh, excellent." Her voice is acidic against his chest, though she
doesn't mean it to be, though she knows that between them he is
the ethical one, and she is a selfish woman who would saddle Joshua
with a burden he never wanted, all so she can fill her desperate arms.
She pushes off against his solid chest, flings her body as far away as
she can get. "Then you and Gavin can both have your imported white
wives, but no children to get in the way of your good time."

The flash of rage sparks in him like lightning. He pulls back his
hand as if to strike her, and she flinches, though all he does is wave
his arm futilely in the air for a moment, confused, a look almost of
fear on his face before he, too, begins to cry. They stand opposite
each other, not making eye contact, weeping in the blazing morning
sun beneath Mount Kenya, their audience of one giraffe disappearing on the horizon.

"You said you wanted me to tell you about Kaya," he says through
his tears, "just so you could throw it in my face that I should marry a
black woman on *principle*? But no, wait—let me get this straight—I

should have a baby with *you* first? What's the matter with you? I don't know what you're talking about! I don't even know who you are!"

When he reenters the tent, he zips the flap up behind him, closing her out. Mary spins round dizzily, hands over her eyes, fighting the impulse to sit down on the grass, willing her body to move in some direction away from the tent—perhaps to the main house, where guests take their meals, where she can find coffee to clear her head. She staggers a few inches forward, coughing from the phlegm in her throat, which tears always summon, humiliated to think that Joshua, on the other side of the zipped flap, may believe she is hacking for sympathy. Forcibly, she lowers her hands, swallows furiously, stares out into the brightness, longing for her sunglasses. Turns toward the path.

It is only then that she sees Kathleen, sitting on the canvas chair outside her own tent, smoking a cigarette, though Mary has never seen her smoke before. She wears only a white robe, her tanned, skinny legs poking out beneath the plush fabric like a young girl's. She stares at Mary unabashed, in a way that strikes Mary as distinctly un-American, lacking politeness and discretion. For a moment their eyes lock across the empty African land, across the dehydrated grass, across the gulf of their separate womanhoods. Then Kathleen smiles slowly, less with kindness or comfort than with simple recognition, before she stands and disappears back through the flap of her own tent, to her children and her man, leaving Mary on the path.

The problem of Africa is one of trash.

On CNN, you hear about the AIDS crisis, genocides, starvation. In politically correct novels by award-winning American writers, you can find out all you ever wanted to know about clitorectomies. But when you live in Africa, when you drive its roads for a living or sit day after day in the rumbling passenger's seat of a man who does, when you are not a war hack or an NGO worker but just an unheroic woman whose mucus and earwax happen to turn green and then black when surrounded by dirt and pollution, Africa's singular, most defining characteristic will come to be its piles of uncollected trash. By the side of the road. Piled into hills atop which donkeys graze and barefoot

children play. Under the wobbly heels of sadly beautiful young women
walking home from church.

Of course, your antilittering, nature-loving lover will claim
not to notice, to take no offense. He will shrug, smoke his hand-
rolled cigarette, and tell you South Africa was this way, too. It is all
pretention anyway, he will say: to feign that civilization can eradicate
trash when in fact the opposite is true. In the United States and
Europe, the government tries to pretend that life isn't dirty, but in
Africa, ugliness is in your face along with splendor.

The Maasai, however, and all those who practice the old ways,
bury their garbage, with or without the government's help. Their
villages may lack running water or electricity or hospitals or schools,
but they are pristine, as clean as the dry, white animal bones lying in
neatly stacked piles for reuse . . .

"I HEARD A lion growling outside our tent last night!" Kathleen gushes too loudly as they drive around the Ol Pejeta black
rhino conservancy. "Everyone else was asleep, and at first I thought
I was dreaming, but I heard it at least six or seven times. At one
point I literally got up to feel the canvas of the tent, to see if it was
strong enough to withstand an attack. I was terrified to go back to
sleep—what if the kids woke up and left the tent, and it was still
out there?"

"Yep," says Fiona. "Liam and I usually get up in the middle of
the night and wander around in the pitch dark in, like, Africa. That
makes total sense, Mom. That's a completely rational fear."

"Oh, don't worry," Joshua says, ignoring Fiona. "It couldn't have
been a lion—they've got an electric fence around the camp."

"Well, you know, there *were* three power outages last night," Walt
drawls in a smooth, mocking tone. "*I* didn't hear any lion, mind you,
but apparently one *could* have been lying in wait until the moment
the electric fence was on the fritz so it could storm the joint."

"I'm not crazy," Kathleen says, voice wounded. "I'm not making
this up. I heard it."

"I've heard big cats at night around here," Mary says quietly. It is true. She heard one last night also. It's just that she has stopped finding it noteworthy by now. It's just that she has stopped getting up in the dark to check the thickness of the canvas. "That fence is in a shallow trench—almost any animal out here could jump it. It's more for keeping the tourists in than for keeping the animals out, frankly. We've found tracks before, right outside our tent, haven't we, Joshua?"

She sees Walt roll his eyes toward Joshua, some attempt at male camaraderie, but Joshua doesn't take the bait, doesn't answer anyone. His pale eyes, shielded once more by his usual dark glasses, stay firmly on the road, both hands on the steering wheel while Mary's leg, usually sweaty under the palm of his left hand, rests free in the hot breeze, alone.

Without him, you are a woman alone in the African bush. Without him, you have the equivalent of a couple of hundred American bucks, sent by your parents for your twenty-third birthday. Without him, you have no vehicle to get back to Nairobi, and though you are the sort of woman and he the sort of man who would understand your shared apartment to be "yours" were you to separate, within a month you couldn't pay the rent.

This is the life you have wrought in Africa. For more than a year you have followed a man. To Europe, to Japan, to Nairobi, where you cannot even sit still but traipse after him on safari after safari, trailing his adventures without bothering to stake anything of your own beyond him. You are a middle-class American with a BA in education, supportive parents, health still stable enough to withstand nonstop travel in rough terrain, and scant excuse to have not held a stable job since London. How have you become this woman?

Before you met him, you were a frightened girl. In his athletic arms, under his competent hands, with his miraculous electric eel of a cock, you became someone else, someone traversing the world. But you have traveled this world on your back, on hands and knees, on rugs and floors and mattresses and beds, under mosquito nets, and against the walls of hotel showers. You have seen the world via rumpled sheets and the peeling paint of ceilings and the dust under beds.

Kenya is approximately the size of Texas, yet within its perimeter exist mountain peaks, the second-largest slum on the African continent, Muslim villages on the Indian Ocean where everyone still travels by donkey, majestic waterfalls, sprawling bush, five-star resorts, tin-shanty food stalls, tea plantations of fluorescent green, icons of world literature, missionaries, more than sixty spoken languages. In an hour's drive, you can go from a landscape as lush as Ireland's to earth so hot and dry you could not survive a few hours without the roof of your truck to shield you.

I've gotta say, Nix, this diverse and primal land is as good a place as any to die.

It is building a life here that's proving more difficult.

THE NIGHT AFTER Christmas, when Mary slides her body around Joshua's, whispers, "Please don't be mad, please," his arms encircle her right away, but his dick is temperamental. Even after she's blown him for a while, he still doesn't have his usual perpetual hard-on. "I chewed some *miraa* earlier," he finally confesses, though she's not sure she believes him. She didn't *see* him do it, and usually he'll try to share it with her, though *miraa* makes her feel like she's sucked down an entire canister of albuterol, heart hammering inside her chest, mind manic, the exact opposite of the cloak of beautiful numbness she's felt on hash cakes or gulps of cough syrup. "Why didn't you tell me?" she asks, and Joshua shrugs his naked, rippling shoulders, says simply, "I was pissed off," so Mary goes back down on him, but there's something ugly in it now. She has to perform tricks to finally get him hard, and her heart isn't in it; she doesn't feel the pitching in her gut that used to come with his raw, uncovered skin. If she wants him inside her, it is only as a survival tactic, only so their Christmas drama can be *over*, not because she wants her body fucked. She keeps gliding her mouth until Joshua's body responds.

"Shit," he moans, "you're so good, you feel so great, baby." He laughs, throws his head back. "Remember the time I ate speed in London? I was so wired you had to work on me till, like, five in the morning, then we rutted like animals with poor Yank right in the next bed—Christ, we were such assholes." Strong fingers twirling through her tangle of hair, he doesn't know she wants to disappear, he doesn't know anything about her, she has opened her body so wide for him that her entire self has disappeared and he doesn't know she's missing. His prick hard as a biceps now, one more muscle. "I couldn't keep my hands off you, I couldn't help myself."

He's getting on top. Around them, the poetic mosquito net shimmers in the twilight, which usually gets her going, but not now. She thinks of Yank in the next bed. She thinks of Joshua and the magic of their lovemaking in the days before Osaka, before her hospital stay, before his scrubbing bedsheets stained with the blood of her IVs, before the weeks upon weeks when sex was nothing she could want, when all she craved was air, when mere kissing winded her even before her fever finally shot up. By the time it was all over, the bubble of constant, infatuated fucking had burst. Now, like so many couples, they often just fall asleep companionably. If she is his whore, his traveling geisha, then she sure is a shitty, inconvenient one. Neither Gavin's glamorous Swede nor the decadent expat beauties of Hemingway stories, she is just a sick former virgin, a woman who used to want her lover's body with the intensity of religion but now wants a baby, wants to be able to walk on a public street past nightfall without the threat of murder and plunder, wants to be able to rely on the bloody electricity, wants her mother. London feels mythic in memory: Yank in the next bed, listening to them, wanting her. She doesn't know if that's true, but she thinks it is; she wants it to be. Yank's body against hers the night of the circus, the way he kissed her, the way his hands trembled against her throat—though that may have been the drugs, not her. Joshua's dick inside her now could be his. Outside their guide quarters at the Samburu Lodge, alligators swim in the shallow river. Lately geography has been her aphrodisiac. In new places, the first night in a new lodge or in their tent staked in front of a fresh, intoxicating view, her libido shoots up almost as though she could fuck the land and Joshua is its conduit. Or maybe that is a story she tells herself. He feels better inside her than she wants him to. She wants to be in control, using her body to get back into his good graces, manipulating him, but it's not like that. There are monkeys in the trees outside, even on the front porches of the guests' rooms, monkeys running on the roof, alligators in the river. Joshua's dick, Yank's dick, could split her body open, her soul flying right up through her mouth. She is screaming for him now. "Harder," she screams, "harder," and his body is built for pushing beyond limits, in gymnastics, on the trapeze, he can always obey, he can fuck her so hard lights flash in her head. No shame. Flipping her over on hands and knees, his fingers working her clit like a gear shift. No control. She's just a machine, her body, *Fuck me, fuck me, fuck me.*

After, they lie on the bed side by side and she's not angry at him anymore. He is just Joshua. Not a river, not Yank, not any kind of villain or pimp. He has never meant her any harm. Her anger is at herself. He wasn't lying; he must have really chewed *miraa* earlier, otherwise he would be dead asleep after sex and he's not.

"I'm sorry for the things I said." He doesn't sit up, doesn't look at her, but his voice is louder than usual. "It was stupid of me to talk about marriage that way. I was an idiot. I've loved you from practically the minute I saw you at the Latchmere, and . . ." Now he does sit up, gazes down on her, and she has to fight the urge to look away, to cover her body with the sheets. "I'm honored that you want to spend your time with me. I would be honored to marry you. We don't have to do it straightaway, like I said—we don't have to involve Gavin, I know you don't like him. We can invite your parents. We could even do it in the States once we can afford tickets, maybe by spring. A woman should never have to ask her man to marry her. I wasn't acting like a proper man. I'll try to do better, Mary, I promise."

Sometimes, things simply happen too late. Sometimes, beautiful things are simply not what we want, no matter how badly we want to want them.

She knows he takes the tears in her eyes for *yes*. Why wouldn't he? She proposed the day before. She has followed him all over the world. Her yes is implicit.

"What do you say we go to the bar and have a drink to celebrate?" He prods her under her ass with his foot, bouncing on the bed a bit with excitement. No, he has never meant her one bit of harm. He is just a boy, really—a muscular, damaged, beautiful boy with an almost ridiculous prowess in bed, and a tender, ricocheting heart. She sits up, strokes the pale skin around his eyes, trying to memorize it.

"I'm exhausted," she pleads. "I don't think I'm up to the bar."

He kisses her cheek. "Do you mind if I go, then? Maybe some of the other guides are there. I'm still a bit wired."

"It's fine," she says. "I'll be asleep before my head hits the pillow."

He pulls on his discarded clothes, a beautiful boy on his way to make an announcement of his engagement to an assortment of half-drunk Kikuyu guides, who like him as everyone seems to like Joshua, who have embraced him as a kind of white kid brother/mascot and will probably buy him drinks and toast his pretty blond fiancée and tell him horror stories about their demanding wives to frighten him in a good-natured way.

As soon as he is out the door, Mary stands, too, and begins to dress.

SHE ISN'T SURE why she thought Kathleen would be on the front porch of their family bungalow smoking again, as though she smokes every minute of the day, when in truth they have spent six days now in each other's company and Mary has witnessed her smoking only that one cigarette, possibly bummed from a member of the staff at the last lodge. Still, Mary approaches the bungalow, dark but for a lantern, and sits on one of the chairs on the porch. The Samburu Lodge has more wildlife on the premises than most of the lodges, and hotel staff tends to patrol the main pathway well into the night, bearing torches and chasing off any wayward animals that have come up from the river. Mary sits on the dark porch, waiting. After some time, the man with the torch comes by, dressed in his Samburu garb and carrying no weapon other than a large walking stick. He and Mary nod at each other. Possibly he was walking this path while she was screaming her stupid head off for Joshua to fuck her harder, and for a second her heart races, but no, she is sitting on Kathleen's porch, wearing her white skin and yellow hair, and she has learned enough in just a few months of safaris—the way Joshua's clients already blend in to one another, their features and names indistinct—to know that this

Samburu man has seen too many of "her" to care about *her*. She is all the same to him. Mary waits long enough so that he comes back again, and still she is sitting on the porch. He says, "Lady, you like me to bring you a drink while you look at the stars?" and she says, "No, *asante.*" Joshua has not come back yet from the bar. There is only one main path, and when he finally does he will see her sitting here and she is not sure what she will say. But for now, he has not come, and so she waits.

The man has walked by with his torch three times by the time the door to the bungalow opens and Kathleen steps out, again in her robe, a cigarette and lighter in her hand. When she sees Mary on the porch, she jumps, yells, "Holy shit," the lighter scattering to the stone steps.

Mary says, "I just came by to see if you were out here. I figured I'd wait."

Kathleen's fine strawberry-blond hair is up in a loose ponytail atop her head. In the dark, the lines around her eyes and mouth less visible than in the intense sun, she could be Mary's age. She bends to pick up the lighter and Mary sees a glimpse of her small breasts inside the robe, taut and close to her chest, not what Mary imagined the breasts of a woman who has borne two children would be. Kathleen leans against the doorframe and lights her cigarette, inhaling greedily. "Okay," she says. "That's a little weird, but all right. Uh. How long have you been here?"

She sounds different without her children, without Walt. Her voice is less loud, but stronger, almost rude, the way her stare was on Christmas morning. Mary isn't sure why, but she prefers this version of Kathleen, even though she suspects Kathleen thinks she's crazy.

"Joshua is in the bar telling everyone we just got engaged," Mary says.

"Great," says Kathleen. "Congratulations."

"Thanks. We're not really engaged, though. He just thinks we are."

Kathleen narrows her eyes, and now Mary can see them, the lines. "Why would he think that?"

"Because I proposed to him yesterday." Mary laughs, shrill to her own ears. "But it was just a mistake. I think I'm going home soon, actually."

"Oh, well, I don't blame you," Kathleen says. "You'll probably regret it, though." Mary nods. She wishes she could ask for a cigarette, but that is out of the question.

"You have a beautiful family. My best friend back in Ohio, Nix—she used to act just like Fiona when we were twelve or thirteen. She pretended like everything her mother said was the dumbest thing she'd ever heard. She had an attitude a mile long. She was an amazing person, though. It was just a stage, I mean. You probably already know that . . . Fiona is your daughter, I'm probably not telling you anything you don't know."

"Honey," Kathleen says. She blows smoke at Mary's face. "Honey, do you need to get out of here? Do you need help getting back to Nairobi? Do you need to borrow money?"

Mary coughs. "No, no—it's nothing like that. I just . . . I haven't talked to a woman in a long time. I hardly even know any." And there it is. The end of a certain road, right here at Kathleen's door, though Mary did not know until this moment that *this* was why she came. She had believed herself here to make excuses for her embarrassing Christmas morning behavior, had believed herself here to ask an older woman's advice about Joshua. Had believed herself here, even, for a drag of Kathleen's cigarette: anything, anything but this.

Kathleen is so silent that Mary can hear her own raggy breath. She closes her eyes.

"My friend Nix died in 1988. She was killed on Pan Am Flight 103—the Lockerbie disaster. Libyan terrorists did it, they say. A whole bunch of American college students were killed, trying to come home for Christmas break. She was one of them."

"That's awful," Kathleen says, though of course Mary realizes it is no more awful to her than anything you can hear on the news any night of the week. "I'm sorry."

"It was supposed to be me."

Now Kathleen's eyes flare with alarm. "Honey, don't say that!" she reprimands. "That's crazy—why would you be supposed to explode in a plane? Your friend wouldn't want that! You didn't do anything wrong. Those terrorists are lunatics, they hate everybody—*you* have nothing to feel guilty about."

Mary nods, feels her head bobbing senselessly. There is no energy left to explain: How Nix, the bravest girl she ever knew, had a whole life stretched out before her, whereas Mary was already doomed to debility and an early death. How in any "fair" world, Mary should have been able to take one for their team of two and sacrifice her own, less valuable life for Nix's rich, exciting future. How now, through some perverse twist of fate, *she* is the one left standing, compelled to live for both of them, to pick up where Nix left off and conquer the world in her best friend's stead, even though she is clearly not up to the task. She chews on her lower lip until Kathleen comes closer and embraces Mary's head with her free, cigaretteless arm, holding it to her stomach, since Mary is sitting in the chair and can't be properly hugged.

"Some of them were still alive when they hit the ground," she says into Kathleen's robe. "This report I read, it explained how there were about fifteen seconds inside the plane when all the passengers must have known something was wrong—before the explosion. I don't really understand how they could estimate that, but sometimes I just start counting, to see how long she was afraid." She removes herself from Kathleen's body—nothing like Mom's, too narrow, too hard—and starts swiping at her eyes before realizing there are no tears left. "The lucky ones died from the blast. But some people only passed out from the altitude, and as the air got *thicker* they woke up. Woke up falling. They found people in the fields—friends holding hands. Somebody was clutching a patch of grass. Mothers with babies still in their arms."

She hears a sob in Kathleen's throat. Even that is not for Nix, Mary suspects, but for Fiona and Liam—for Kathleen imagining herself trying against all hope to shield her children with her body as they plummet through a Scottish sky. Somehow, though, it is enough.

"Liam's so cute," Mary says, trying to smile. "I want to have a baby.

But I guess going home and leaving the guy who wants to marry me isn't going to help me get pregnant, huh?"

Kathleen snorts. "Well, if you're looking for advice on pregnancy," she says, her voice brassy with relief at being back on stable ground, "I'm the wrong person to ask. By the time I was your age, I'd had three abortions. Once I married Walt, my body was done. I couldn't get pregnant if they dipped me upside down in a vat full of sperm."

Now it is Mary's turn to act speechless. In the past two years, she has lived surrounded by junkies, dealers, thieves, and circus freaks, yet it is entirely possible that she has never been so shocked. Kathleen starts giggling, first a delicate snorting and then, when Mary looks down, embarrassed, a full on cackle, like a witch. She covers her mouth to keep in the sound, and the smoke from her cigarette wafts into her eyes; Mary watches her wave it away, her wide blue eyes tearing. "Oh, Jesus," Kathleen gasps. "That was priceless. The look on your face. You must be more straight-laced than I took you for—sorry."

"It's not that," Mary manages.

And then Kathleen isn't laughing anymore. She shuffles her manicured feet. "Oh, I know," she says, sighing. "I know what it's because of."

"But wait," Mary says. "You mean Fiona and Liam aren't your children?" The minute the words are out of her mouth, at the expression on Kathleen's face, she understands. It is what everyone asked her constantly in grade school, in high school: *What happened to your real parents?* When Mary would come home crying, her mother would smooth back her hair. *You tell them that the people who raise you are your real parents,* Mom said. *You tell them that anybody can make a baby with their body, but your parents are the ones who take care of you forever.* But when Mary tried that at school, her friends rolled their eyes. *No,* they explained, as if she were special needs, *your real mother is the one whose stomach you grew in, and if everyone could make a baby with their body, your adopted mom would have made one of her own—obviously she couldn't and that's why they bought you.* Only Nix never talked this way. Nix's father left when she was seven or eight—Mary can't remember exactly—and years later Nix would say, *I wish I'd been adopted so I wouldn't have been here for my father to leave us and my mother to hate me for it—I wish somebody better had come along when I was born and taken me away.*

"I'm adopted, too!" she blurts to Kathleen. "I didn't mean it that way. I was adopted when I was, like, a couple weeks old. My parents were awesome—they *are* awesome, I mean."

Kathleen stubs her cigarette out on the wall of the bungalow, tosses it far from the porch, where—Mary suspects—Walt will not see it. "When I was your age," she says, "I was a Studio 54 girl. Do you even know what that is? Do kids still know about Studio 54 and Andy Warhol?"

"Uh," Mary says. "Campbell's soup and stuff."

"Mmm, and stuff all right," Kathleen says. "I was a model. Not a very successful one—I wasn't tall enough for the runway, so I had to mainly do catalogs. I did a few album covers, too. When I met Walt, I was so coke-addled that I'd started having seizures . . . I'd gone to look at an apartment to rent because the guy I lived with had broken my jaw, and while I was there I had a seizure and fell down a flight of stairs. The law student showing me the place had to call an ambulance. That was Walt." She shrugs. "I still had a couple stints of rehab even after we moved to Minneapolis. Then we adopted Fiona, and that was that."

Mary settles on, "Wow. He must have really loved you. It sounds like you were a bad bet—no offense."

"None taken. I was no kind of bet. I don't know what the hell he was thinking."

"He saved you, though."

Kathleen's fingers work the spot on the wall where she's left a smudge of ash, wiping the stain away. "You're a lot of different people over the course of a lifetime. Sometimes, who you need to be at a given moment intersects with what somebody else needs. There are no princes on white horses. Nobody saves anyone from any-thing." And suddenly she smooths back Mary's hair with her ashy fingers—later, in the mirror, Mary will see the smudge on her fore-head. "You couldn't save your friend, honey. You need to live your own life. You need to let her go."

But Mary finds she can't talk about Nix anymore; she has exhausted her reserves and feels cleaner, lighter, yet aware that if she dips her foot back in, she will fall into something deeper and messier, beyond Kathleen's powers of purification. Instead she says, "You don't regret it, do you? Moving to the *Midwest,* settling down? Do you ever miss New York and all that adventure?"

Kathleen rummages inside the pockets of her robe, maybe for another cigarette, but her pale, fluttery hands come up empty. "I got my jaw broken. I got my insides vacuumed out. I wasn't having a whole lot of fun. My kids are my life now. I'm president of the PTA. I bake cookies. I go to church and get down on my knees and thank God I'm still alive." She sighs, looks at the door to the bungalow, stares at it hard as if she's trying to figure out if it belongs to her, though Mary knows she'll open it soon. She says, "I miss it every day."

So, Nix, this is it. You are dead, and I am the one who is now 23. So what am I doing still alive? How long will my luck hold? What if it holds another ten years, another twenty? Is this how I want to live, or only how I wanted to die, pretty and poetic among the wildlife, a flash of glory moving too fast to catch, like you? What if, after everything, I am permitted an actual adulthood? What if I actually have to get a life?

AT THE SAMBURU village where Walt and Kathleen pay the village elder for a tour, Liam crawls into one of the many huts too short for Joshua or Walt to stand inside, scoots his body onto the animal skin rugs that cover the dirt floor of the sleeping area, the entire hut otherwise empty except for a fire pit, and rests from the heat of the sun. While the Samburu warriors hand Walt a spear and make him dance with them; while Fiona, laughing, takes a video; while the three older members of the family and Mary listen to the Samburu children — heads shaved in the fashion of this tribe, and most of those under five not wearing pants or underwear — reciting their numbers in English and French, their "chalkboard" nothing but the smooth side of a long strip of tree bark, their teacher hitting them upside the head with a long stick if they seem not to be paying attention, Liam naps. As

Kathleen and Fiona try to navigate the makeshift open-air market the Samburu women have set up for their arrival, struggling to figure out which mama to buy a beaded necklace or carved impala from, when every woman's goods are nearly identical, Liam begins to run around, pantomiming a game of chase with the nearby Samburu children, waving his arms until a few, first staring at him warily behind their dusty eyelids, begin to giggle and join in. As Fiona passes out to the children the cookies that she bought from their own village elder for five times what they would cost at the grocery store in town, Mary wanders back to the truck to sit with Joshua, who never bothered to get out to begin with.

If there is any truth to Africa, it is this: when you witness a demonstration of two warriors making fire, afterward they will try to sell you the sticks they used to strike the spark. *These sticks are special,* they will tell you. *We go all the way to the mountains to get them.* Africa is yours for a price. If authenticity is defined by a lack of economic exchange, forget it. You are a consumer and Africa is your photo op.

Afterward Kathleen and Fiona sit close together in the truck, knees touching, giant, beaded collars around their necks, admiring the amateurishly constructed jewelry and carvings they've acquired. Despite perpetually wearing sun hats, they are both tan by now, radiant. "That was the best thing we've done!" Fiona gushes to Joshua. "That was so cool!" Mary simmers in a stew of contradictory emotions. Who is she, of all people, to put a price tag on "experience"? The Samburu village is not a scam—it is not taken down and replaced with modern brick buildings and television screens the moment the tourists depart. It is *real,* it exists with or without anyone to pay admission. Who is anyone to judge Fiona for being moved by it, to judge the Samburus for benefiting from money they truly need? Liam sleeps again, his head against the windowpane. To him, Africa could be downtown Minneapolis, could be a playdate, could be his new house. He is the only one among them able to experience this place purely, and he is the one who will not remember it.

I have been writing to you about Africa, but the truth is that I am
speaking from one small spot on the globe, one tiny hotel room, one
finite body. I cannot pin down a continent. I have been talking to you
about what this land can do to you, but here is the simple truth of what
it can do to you: anything you let it.

This is not about Africa. This is about the scraps of me lost along
the way, left behind in the wardrobe of Arthog House, in the hostel
shower in Paris, under the low wooden bed in Osaka, along the Kenyan
roadside like discarded trash. It's not about sex either. If anything, that
primal language of bodies has been the one space where Joshua and I
have needed no translator, where we have always met as equals. It's the
rest of the time that we struggle with a language barrier, though we both
speak English. It's the rest of the time that I have been waiting around
to be defined by him, by Kenya and Japan and Europe and London, by
your death, by my illness. And still I don't know who I am.

WHEN YOU LEAVE the Samburu National Reserve, the el-
ephants always appear, as if to say good-bye. Here, it is nothing to find
your vehicle surrounded by twenty, forty of them, going about their
silent, peaceful business as you ferry your charges out of the park.
Joshua, who knows elephants from home, says that they have tempers,
that sometimes they charge, but Mary has never seen the Kenyan
elephants be anything but gentle. Their eyes are huge compared to a
person's, but look minuscule set into those mammoth gray heads, the
way stars look small in the vast sky. There are several calves among
them, one baby so small it cannot be more than a few weeks old.
"Elephants make excellent mothers," Joshua tells his family of human
charges, whom he will soon never see again. "They're not like giraffes.
They'll take in a calf, even from another herd, if it's lost—and they'll
never forget their own child. Elephants are highly intelligent and compassionate." Walt begins to take a battery of photos, but Kathleen,
Fiona, and Liam merely look out the open top, quiet as the elephants,
watching. They have enough photos, and maybe they have seen enough
elephants and no longer care. Or maybe they have seen enough elephants that they can finally see.

"How would you describe me?" Mary asked Joshua the night before, under their net. "When I'm gone, how will you remember me?"

"Gone?" he said. "I don't want to think about that. Look at the way I smoke—my lungs could give out before yours. There are no guarantees." But she knew that for all his words about living in the moment, the fact of her death was imprinted on him. Otherwise there would have been children, where now there will be none.

"Humor me," she begged. "When you think of me, what do you see?"

Joshua grinned. "You've got a sexy ass. How's that?"

"Good. What else?"

"You're a great dancer. You're the only white woman I've ever seen dance with African people and not look like a prat. You're a strong swimmer. You don't look strong, but you are."

"More," Mary murmured, her head on his lap. "More."

"You make that little huffing noise with your nose. Like a small bull. When your sinuses act up."

She bolted up to face him. "I make a huffing noise with my nose? That sounds disgusting!"

"No," he said seriously. "It's cute. Oh—and you never brush your hair but it always looks amazing. Your skin tastes like pretzels, but down here"—he touched her not for the last time, she reminded herself, not the last time yet—"you taste like orange squash."

On the long drive back to Nairobi, where their safari will come to an end, they stop at the Nanyuki Children's Home. This is something Kathleen set up from home, in Minneapolis, on the phone with Gavin, who must have had to scramble to find something to satisfy her, who left to his own devices would surely know nothing about an orphanage off the main road in an untouristed city. Kathleen, Walt, and Fiona spend two hours in a tiny grocery store buying supplies to bring as a gift. The store is the size of a small apartment in downtown Dayton and seems to have all of three people working at it; it is not remotely equipped to sell enough diapers, tampons, rice, sugar, notebooks, shoe polish, toothpaste, to supply eighty orphans for a month. Joshua plays ball with Liam in the parking lot, chases away peddlers who come with their shoddy metal bracelets, their postcards, trying to show Liam toys, thinking Joshua is his father and will buy their loot if his little boy whines. Joshua dismisses them in his pidgin Swahili with the unintentional but unmistakable authority of one who spent his formative years assured that those with black skin would do his bidding, even if he drinks with them now. He casually tosses the ball back to Liam, who cannot catch but tries, squealing, and every now and then, he yanks the boy by his shirt to keep him away from cars pulling in and out. It takes an extra truck—the store has one—to load all the goods Walt and Kathleen have purchased. Kathleen leans against Mary for a moment, watching the workers load sacks of flour. "This whole thing," she says, "cost about what it would to buy three weeks of groceries for a family of four in Minneapolis."

"Everything you're saying is physical," Mary told Joshua. "My ass, my hair, my taste. That's not me."

"Who says?" He swatted her ass, tickled her until she laughed despite herself. "You feel that, don't you? Maybe the separation between body and mind is just girly rubbish."

"But body isn't everything," she insisted. "Do I believe in God? What do I think about my mother?" It was on the tip of her tongue to ask, Who was my best friend in childhood? but that would be a trick question because she had purposely never mentioned Nix and so what he knew of her was absolutely nothing. "What's my favorite book?"

"What's my favorite book?" he countered.

She opened her mouth, but there was nothing. "I've never seen you read a book," she said at last.

"It's Cry, the Beloved Country." He sighed. "I've read it a half-dozen times. I used to take it with me into the bath at Arthog House even, when Sandor wasn't hogging the tub—I lost my copy, though, a while back." He flung his head back violently against the pillow. They had spent so long on the road in hotels that every conversation they'd ever had, it seemed to Mary, had taken place in a bed. "That's the only book that ever spoke to me, the only one I bought on my own since I left school, so fine, I don't read much, maybe it was a stupid question. So what? We have the rest of our lives to learn all these things about each other. That's the whole point."

After the truck is unloaded, the orphanage director calls the children out. She is a pretty woman, smartly dressed, urbane and educated, clearly from somewhere other than here. While Walt stands by with his camera, giant zoom lens protruding, the director arranges the orphans around their donated supplies: another photo op. One of the children is in a wheelchair, so they simply wheel him close to the sacks of rice and gesture to the others to cluster around. None of the children are smiling, despite all the goods. They are cleaner than the children at the Samburu village—they all have underpants—but they are even more somber in the face of tourists in their house. Unlike the Samburus, they are not proud of their traditions, cannot charge a fee; they are simply charity. Joshua helped the workers unload the truck, but now he is waiting in the driver's seat of Gavin's truck, sunglasses on, ready to roll. They are more than an hour behind schedule, thanks to the time spent in the grocery store, and it will be nightfall by the time they reach Nairobi. He is impatient, foot bobbing up and down, the muscles of his thigh visible through his pants; he runs his fingers through his hair the way he once did in London when his hair was long and straggly, only now there is nothing to fiddle with, so his hands come back to his lap, restless.

Mary wanders away from where all the orphans have gathered with the family, their white faces beaming as Walt snaps a picture. She heads deeper into the orphanage complex, hoping to find a toilet, since she desperately has to pee. Soon enough she locates it, past the girls' and boys' dorms, just a little wooden outhouse with two doors, segregated by gender. The stench inside would be overpowering except that she has been in Africa for nearly four months. A hole in the ground, though there is toilet paper at least. She squats, she wipes, she tosses in her squares, she tries not to breathe. Roughly forty girls, sharing this hole. Does the smartly dressed director use it, too, or does she have her own accommodations somewhere hidden? Mary wanders onward, toward an open door in the back through which she sees a crib.

As she enters the room, more cribs emerge into sight, like a flower slowly blooming: there must be ten or twelve in all. Inside most, children sleep, though a few are empty, their occupants perhaps with the other kids outside. It must be nap time for the babies. On the wall, several roaches crawl freely. Nanyuki isn't tropical, not like Lamu or Mombasa, where the roaches are the size of small rodents; these are normal, American-style roaches, and Mary knows she would be a fool to think that children's homes in American cities aren't riddled with them, too. Still, she feels like screaming with something akin to impotent rage. Under a web of netting, one infant sleeps; she cannot be more than three months old, her worn-out Onesie pink. The other babies do not have nets over their cribs, but the staff must be making some effort to shield this one, owing to age or illness.

"Are these the babies with no mommies?"

Mary whirls around. It is Liam, jumping at the doorway, obviously having broken free of the photo shoot. "Where did their mommies go?"

"They're waiting for them," Mary says around the lump in her throat. "Their mommies just haven't come yet."

"I waited for my mommy," Liam proclaims loudly. "I waited in Romania. I waited and waited, but my mommy was late."

He is *Romanian*? Christ, who knew?

Filthy plastic toys are piled underneath a crib in the corner, a blanket tossed over them. Liam takes one look and hits the cruddy floor, crawling around, pulling off the blanket. Mary holds her breath, anticipating what he may find under there, but no, it is just the ridiculous cluster of toys: broken stuff it would not seem anyone on earth would want to touch much less play with, except that this curious little American (Romanian?) boy—who no doubt has an entire playroom full of the latest gadgets back home—apparently does. He bangs on some crusty red button, which yields a weak squeak. Delighted, he bangs some more.

Inside one of the cribs, a small girl—maybe two years old—stares at Mary, wordless. Most of the children in Kenya speak Swahili; even though the older ones learn English at school, Mary rarely hears them use it. She goes to the little girl, the toddler's face a sharp triangle, eyes huge, and holds out her arms. The girl, amazingly or not so amazingly, reaches back, so Mary picks her up. Her bottom is soaked with urine, although Mary can feel a thick, squishy diaper under her clothes. Her thin legs circle Mary's rib cage. How long has she been lying here?

Liam continues to bang and push around the toys. "This is ridiculous, you know," Mary says to him, though he doesn't even look up. "I'm supposed to be clean, like the girl in the plastic bubble. I'm supposed to avoid germs and rotten onions. I'm not supposed to be here, in Africa, holding a baby covered in pee. If I want to live long enough to have a baby of my own, I'm not allowed to do this." She laughs out loud, buries her face in the little girl's head, crying now, although Liam doesn't seem to notice. If she were somebody else—if she were Nix—maybe she would march right outside to the director and volunteer to stay here, to work, to care for the children. Maybe she would forge her own life in Africa, independent of Joshua. But her illness demands narcissism, demands more care than she has granted it, and she is just being stupidy sentimental anyway—Nix didn't even like kids. No, if she were Nix, she would march out to the truck and bum one of Joshua's cigarettes; she would blow smoke in his face and say, *You're beautiful, but I'm leaving.* She would say, *I love you, but not enough for it to be all my life means.* And so Mary carefully files this under the list she is starting to tally, the list of who she is: *I confuse cowardice with kindness.*

Instead she will wait until he departs for his next safari. Just past the New Year, while he believes they are saving up for tickets to America, where they will have a wedding. Instead she will leave behind nothing but a new copy of *Cry, the Beloved Country,* with an inscription that reads, *Thank you,* because that is all it makes sense to say. She will wait at Jomo Kenyatta International Airport, the only white woman at the tiny, overcrowded café, but long enough in Kenya to no longer be bothered by the lack of space between bodies, to have stopped noticing her own deficiency of pigment. She will drink a coffee to quell the scraping in her stomach, to soothe the knowledge that she will never again touch him. Finally a woman alone in Africa, she will marvel at just how much fragile hope it takes to hurtle your body into the sky and across the ocean, back to a place called Home, when you no longer remember what waits for you on the other side.

Where Are We Going, Where Have We Been?

(GREECE: ZORG)

Two blond girls stand on the balcony of a beautiful cliffside Greek villa. They are perched too high above the winding road to escape by jumping, and any passerby would probably not understand English if they shouted, *Help!* Nix and Mary would appear simply to be admiring the pretty view—which is exactly what they are pretending to do while Titus and Zorg mix cocktails in the kitchen. The two men are evidently unconcerned about leaving them alone, confident that there is no means of escape.

Nix feels as though she has landed in the middle of a play, one of those old-fashioned ones in which the characters are all in disguise and are saying things that don't mean what they seem to mean. Zorg is playing the part of cohost, smiling and mixing drinks as though he has not brought two women here against their will. For their part, the girls are acting like gracious guests, oohing and aahing at the view, asking for drinks they do not want so that they can have a moment alone together. Only Titus, who actually *lives* here in this ultramodern, hiply gorgeous abode indeed worthy of being called a villa, seems unsure of his role, wandering around with a look of resigned tolerance on his face. Is his resignation to the fact that Nix has shown him no affection, and that in addition to footing the bill at lunch he is now forking over his alcohol to a girl who doesn't plan to give him any? Or is he resigned to some more ominous plan of Zorg's? Nix keeps a smile plastered on her face, heart hammering.

What seems clear to her above all else is that if one side or the other gives up the pretense of Nix and Mary being willing guests, things will quickly descend to a place to which none of the four really wishes to venture, and so they pretend, though Mary keeps pulling her inhaler out of her beach bag to forestall an asthma attack and an unraveled look has crept into her eyes.

"Okay, so I have to get Titus alone." Nix hears her voice like some leader in a heist film, all strategy and verve. "He didn't see what Zorg was like in the car. Titus doesn't seem deranged—he seems like a normal guy. He's not going to want his friend to fucking hold us hostage at his house! I have to ask him to talk to Zorg and calm him down. Titus doesn't really understand what's happening. Once he does, everything will be fine."

"Or," Mary says, starting to cry, so that she has to turn her back to the balcony door, "once he tells Zorg that we said he kidnapped us, Zorg will become even more furious and rape me for your freaking viewing pleasure."

"Jesus Christ! You're not being helpful."

"That's because you're going to get us killed!"

Nix and Mary gape at each other. The alarm on Mary's face is so intense that Nix immediately whips out her camera, says loudly, "Smile!" and starts clicking it in Mary's direction. Mary glares at her, not smiling, not playing along, but at least irritation has replaced the terror in her expression. Through her peripheral vision, Nix sees Zorg and Titus fashionably arranged on the sofa just on the other side of the balcony's glass door. She whispers into Mary's ear, "You *need* to hold it together. Don't let them see you crying. We don't want them to know we're upset. I'm serious—now laugh like I just said something funny."

Mary spins around and performs as instructed, though her teeth look bared. Nix laughs back. Ha-ha-ha-ha-ha. They throw their heads back, necks exposed. Girls laughing. See?

"We have to go back in," Nix says. "I want you to listen to me,

Mary. I'm going to get us out of this, okay? Please just keep your mouth shut. If you have to be with Zorg when I'm not around, just cough a lot, cough something up! Use your inhaler. Freak him out a little."

Mary nods. Nix doesn't trust her—she has an awful suspicion that Mary wouldn't dream of lowering herself—but to her relief, Mary says, "Fine, I'll spit mucus at his feet if I have to," and Nix can breathe again. Then Mary's eyes narrow. "But," she begins, "if you aren't with me and Zorg, where would you *be*?"

TIME IN FOREIGN countries doesn't work the way it does at home. Service in restaurants is slower, and world-changing decisions are faster. Mary and Nix will probably remain on that balcony for another fifty seconds at most, before Nix slides open the balcony door and leads the way inside. In that time, this is approximately what transpires:

Where would you be? Nix considers the question. She has never known a moment of truth, so sure, maybe this is one of them. One of those moments when you have to decide *who* you are, *who* you will be.

And Nix: *Who has she been?* A cute midwestern girl, an abandoned daughter, a spelling-bee champion, a betrayer of friends, a lazy student at a boutique college, a professor's mistress. *Who will she become?* A traveler, she hopes, Greece and London just the beginning. Okay, but beyond that? Will her legacy be one series of self-gratifications followed by another, just another American life, another female life on humanity's swarming anthill? Of course. Yes, of course it will; she knows that already, though she is not sure how any more than she knows how Mary knew unemployment statistics from Barcelona, or how her body instinctively understood what it would feel like to go off a cliff. She is not an Immortal. Her pretty American face will not launch a thousand ships; men will not (thank God!) wage war over her. She is neither Mother Teresa nor Gandhi, nor even, on the smaller scale, a selfless Peace Corps volunteer who can live with mice nesting in her pillow. She is an English-lit major with no real skills. This world is enormous and she is a small speck on it, awed by her own anonymity and insignificance, yet knowing that inside her, life positively pulses and surges like an exposed wire, bursting to get out, to spark.

She thinks again of Connie from "Where Are You Going, Where Have You Been?" She and Mary are just Connies, after all, only Mary has been elevated in meaning by having a fucking death sentence on her head, and Nix realizes, perhaps fully for the first time, how mind-bendingly happy she is *not* to be the Tragic Heroine of their story. To be able to wonder who she will be at forty, at sixty-five, even at ninety-three like her maternal grandmother. Will she travel the world collecting lovers, like Anaïs Nin? Will her journals be published someday, her life an exotic inspiration to other women? Or will she eventually marry, even if she does not desire it now? Will love render her weak as a newborn kitten, longing for domestication? Will her hard, flat stomach someday swell and then deflate, bringing forth children—God's wildest and most daring creation? *Is* there a God, and does it matter, when he will not save them now?

In the story, Connie opens the door and goes out to Arnold Friend to prevent the murder of her entire family upon their return from some boring barbecue. Connie is just an ordinary, superficial girl, an airhead full of boys and the drive-in and judgments at her fat, staid sister, with a smart mouth and a nowhere town clinging to her skin. But in that moment of swinging open the door and walking toward her own abduction and possible death, she is a hero, too, and it occurs to Nix that this brand of heroism—a practical, "what else can you do?" heroism—comes naturally to her. She will let Titus inside her because, in doing so, she can gain his trust and get him to call off Zorg. She simply cannot let Mary be raped, Mary who has borne enough, including Nix's own treason. She will wrap her arms around Titus and whisper, *My friend has a terminal disease, she's a virgin, you can't let him take advantage of her, please, talk to him—do it for me.* Yes, but Mary, a good girl who gets flies with honey, would never approve—would turn to vinegar before ever permitting herself to become a whore. For a moment Nix's heart somersaults and she falters, unsure. But fear is an essential ingredient of heroism, isn't it? A lack of fear leads not to nobility but to indifference. Okay then:

she will moan just right, she will say the things a courtesan would say if she were just an ordinary girl from Kettering. Every courtesan has been just an ordinary girl from somewhere. Every hero is a speck on a giant, uncaring planet, just like Nix.

"Do not *do* anything," she says to Mary with the urgency of a suitor's promise, and she slides open the glass door, smiling at her waiting drink.

WAIT, CAN WE back up here? Can we make it all turn out differently? As it turns out, not even the dead can accomplish that.

It is a mere three and a half hours later when they drive away from the villa and back down to Mykonos proper, to a small disco just opening for the night. Look. In walk four people: two smartly dressed, dark-haired men, and two young blond women in inappropriately beachy garb. They have their choice of tables, but the men select a dark one in the corner. A round of tequila sunrises is ordered. Here, take a long gulp for fortification. All right. Let us proceed.

To Mary's dismay, they are the only ones in the disco. It's not the same, all-Greek bar of their first evening, but out of the way enough not to be popular with tourists, especially so early in the evening. Titus tells the waitress to run a tab, beaming and confident like a man who has gotten a raise. Nix, next to him, seems cowed, Titus's arm slung around her sometimes, then at other times withdrawn disdainfully. Mary keeps trying to meet Nix's eyes, to communicate in some wordless fashion, but Nix won't cooperate, looks elsewhere, mainly down at her lap. Mary has never seen Nix wear this body language. It is as though some alien force has inhabited her friend's skin, and although Nix's big blue eyes appear the same as ever, some other being lurks behind them.

Mary, however, cannot help feeling giddy. She was so skeptical about Nix's mysterious plan, but look, it *worked*! Here they are, down from the menacing hills, out of that isolated villa, and in a disco with a waitress, a bartender, a DJ—other actual human beings! Sure, maybe they are Greek humans who don't understand English, and maybe there are not that many of them, but still, halle-fucking-lujah. Who knew how long Titus and Zorg might have kept them prisoner? Titus could have gone out for provisions for days—forever!—without anyone being the wiser. They could have been turned into sex slaves; they could have been tortured and murdered.

But no, here they are sitting at a small table, drinking with strobe lights pulsing and American pop music pounding. Here they are, very much alive.

THINGS HAD BEEN tricky for a while, back at the villa. Nix had strutted inside from the balcony and whispered something to Titus, resting her small palm against his chest as she leaned toward his ear, and just like that they were gone, disappearing down a hallway toward what Mary guessed was Titus's bedroom, leaving *her* alone with the crazy one. Some plan! Zorg, his eyes already narrowing with drink, patted the white sofa until Mary obligingly sat down; then he placed his hand on her thigh just as he'd done in the car. Mary's body pulsed with wanting to jump up and run, but to what end? Zorg's hand, which had seemed so debonair when holding his tiny espresso cup in Taxi Square or smoking at Plati Yialos, now looked meaty and animalistic, rubbing hot circles onto her thigh, his thick fingers slipping under the fringy bottom of her tie-dyed skirt. Oh God. For the first time in her life, Mary began to cough on purpose, violently pounding her chest and hocking up mucus on cue. She spit the phlegm into the already wet napkin under her cocktail. The instant revulsion in Zorg's eyes simultaneously gave her strength and made her want to hide.

"You are coughing all day—what, you are sick?"

Mary hacked again, vigorous enough to make her throat scrape. "I'm afraid it's pneumonia," she said, then worried she was not supposed to speak—Nix had told her to say nothing, and what if pneumonia contradicted what Nix was telling Titus? Then, rebellion surged: if Nix wanted to write her lines, *she* should have stayed here with the weirdo. "I get pneumonia sometimes, from my asthma," she elaborated. "I might be contagious. I hope I didn't get you sick last night, at the bar."

Zorg flung his legs out in front of him in an agitated fashion, making a clicking noise. "I am supposed to fly in three days," he said. "You run around putting your mouth on people when you should be in a hospital? You better not have made me sick. I have other things to do, real work, not just running around fucking like the rich little American girls. You understand, little girl? You think I should fly a plane while I spit this shit up on my lap, like you?" He made a noise again at the back of his throat, a hiss. "Disgusting. *Morí*, what is the matter with you?"

"I'm sorry," she muttered. "I didn't realize yesterday that I was so sick. You'd better stay away from me, I don't want to infect you."

He took a long swig of his drink. "It is too late for that. Last night you are all over me. Any germ you have, I already have. Now, I just don't kiss you." He laughed an angry laugh. "Eh, but your *mouni* doesn't cough, sí?" Before she could even wonder what the word meant, his hand was there, wedging its way between her thighs to cup her vagina. This time she did jump to her feet, but she stumbled across his arm, yelped as she tripped and fell into the glass coffee table, and then cried out when its round edge slammed hard into her shin. On the sofa, Zorg watched with bemusement, his eyes nearly slits. Terror and pain pulsed in Mary like twin amphetamines; her body felt like it was charged with voltage; it was all she could do to remind herself that the superhuman strength she felt was illusory, that there was no way she could win against Zorg in a physical struggle. She thought of advice her PE teacher had given back in seventh grade when the girls were separated from the boys to talk about sex. She couldn't recall the specifics of the sex talk, but she remembered her gym teacher saying, "If any man ever tries to rape you, pee on him. Vomit, do something disgusting, crap your pants if you have to." The gym teacher was a soft-spoken woman with a pockmarked face. Mary and her peers were embarrassed and shocked; they began to titter behind their hands. Now, all at once, Mary remembered the look the woman had given their laughter: a gaze so withering Mary could still feel its sting. Would she have to resort to literally pissing in her pants, or on Zorg if it came to that? *Could* she? She looked at the balcony outside, beckoning, and thought of simply sliding open the door and jumping with a running leap, but her legs kept still.

Footsteps jarred her, and when she spun around she expected to find Zorg right behind her. But Zorg was still on the sofa, a plush white throw rug under his feet; the sound had come from Titus, who stood on the hardwood floor across the room. As she gaped at him, he quickly approached Zorg and began whispering in animated Spanish. From the zeal of Titus's tone, Mary expected that Titus must be lecturing him. Nix had gotten through to Titus, and he had come away from their . . . conversation? . . . tryst? . . . to intervene. Then the two men laughed and Mary's heart dropped with fear that she had misunderstood—why, if Titus were reprimanding Zorg, would they be chuckling together? Tears congested her sinuses. She stared at the balcony again.

Suddenly Zorg stood. From his greater height, he looked down at Mary with a soft look in his slitted eyes. Mary mistook the softness for an attempt at seduction, and bile rose in her throat as though she might vomit involuntarily after all. But instead Zorg pointed to the other hallway, away from where Titus and Nix had gone. He said gently, "Why don't you go to lie down? There is a bedroom for guests down this hall. Maybe you feel better after some sleep, and later, we can go to town for drinks and dinner."

Her exhalation came so fast and hard she gagged on it. Then, understanding overcame her, and she composed herself, embarrassed. *Of course.* Nix had gotten Titus alone so that she could tell him about Mary's disease—so she could turn Mary into a pitiable object without being overheard by the object herself. In the end, even an asshole doesn't want to molest the terminally ill. Sweat broke out all over Mary's body but cooled instantly from the excessive air-conditioning of the villa. She turned to retreat, eager to get away from Zorg and even Titus now, to take her pathetic, unfuckable body away from them, to remind herself to feel grateful rather than humiliated. But where was Nix? Taking her own nap in Titus's bed? More likely now that Titus had proved himself a decent guy, Nix was going to fool around with him after all, as a reward. Nix, the beautiful one, the healthy one, who had only to take off her clothes and the world bent to her will. Mary's heart vibrated like a wild bird from the extra doses of albuterol she'd sucked in for show. She scurried down the hall to the first bedroom she saw, closed the door, and hurled herself onto the fluffy white duvet. In contrast to the surge of energy she'd felt in the living room, her body now was exhausted, to the point of panting.

Dizzy from booze and hours of fear, she fell instantly asleep.

WHEN MARY WOKE, the sky was darkening. Zorg and Titus were in the living room, still drinking as though no time had elapsed. When they saw her, Titus went to retrieve Nix, and they all climbed into the car within mere minutes, as though everyone had been waiting for Mary, her slumber delaying their departure. Now here they are: Nix and her magic turned sour, a bad taste left (perhaps literally) in her mouth. Did she get *any* enjoyment from Titus? Mary can't help wondering. Sex still looms like a distant island, half-shrouded in mist and lapped by dark water. Until Zorg's unwelcome grope, she hadn't even felt a guy's hand between her legs since Bobby Kenner. Bobby, that coward. Yet another thing Nix was right about.

Well, this time Mary's not going to make Nix think of everything — she has her own plan. Titus, with his new bravado, keeps talking as though after "dinner" (there's no food in this bar, but who knows where he next plans to abscond with them), Nix will be spending the night at his villa. Mary is uncertain where this leaves *her* — dropped off back in their rented room, or dragged along for the ride — but either way she requires no eye contact with Nix to know neither of them is ever going back to that hillside hellhouse, and if Nix isn't speaking up for herself, it's up to Mary to get them out of this. The only problem is that her plan requires something of a crowd, and this early in the evening the disco is not providing it. But patience is a virtue, and so she will wait.

"You are hungry now," Titus says. "You like to eat?"

"Oh, not yet!" Mary cries. She knows she is supposed to have pneumonia, but her objective is to avoid getting back in the rental car at all costs, and she can't think of another way to achieve this, so she jumps to her feet and cries, with exaggerated animation, "Order another round of drinks—I feel like dancing!" She flashes her eyes at Nix, signaling, *Come with me*, but Nix only averts her gaze. Mary rushes out to the dance floor alone. Zorg and Titus do not dance—she learned this the first night they met at the all-Greek bar. Flushed with wine and the enthusiasm of going native, Mary and Nix had whirled around that bar, which had no dedicated dance floor, but Zorg and Titus never joined in, just smoked and drank, stationary at the bar. At the time, their aloofness had seemed sophisticated, but now, as Mary shimmies around the empty disco, they seem instead two guarding sentries. To her frustration, Nix remains at the table with them, one foot out of her sandal and kicking aimlessly at the table's wobbly center leg. Abruptly Zorg puts a hand on Nix's knee to still her. His hand rests too long; a chill pricks down Mary's back, so that her body involuntarily shivers like a bad dance move. No, there is no way in hell Mary is getting back in that car. She will run for it if she has to, but if it comes to that she will have to somehow give Nix a sign.

All at once, people enter the bar. Four guys! Their Harvard sweatshirts and baseball caps shine under the ricocheting strobes. There is something so awesomely American about them, in their unfashionable garb, with their too-short hair, that Mary nearly starts to weep with relief. Of the four, only one is good looking, as muscular and dark as a Greek, whereas the others exhibit various degrees of wimpy shoulders and visible freckles, with dumb white sneakers on their feet. Oh, joy! The makeup Mary applied this morning has all been rubbed off by sunscreen and seawater and her face's pressing against Titus's cool guest-room pillowcase; she has lipstick in her beach bag but is afraid that if she were to scurry to the bathroom to put some on, these men would be gone by the time she returned. So instead she does what she can. Her hair has been wound in its usual beach do: two tightly coiled knots on the sides of her head. Until now, it has not occurred to her to release her hair from its trap, but all at once she does so . . .

The impact on the Harvard boys is akin to that of Rapunzel letting down her long mane. Perhaps this is because she is the only woman in the disco—aside from the sullen, slumping Nix, half-hidden by Titus's bulky form—but still Mary feels buoyed by their gawking. Fuck it—she may be a clueless virgin, her lungs damaged goods, but her *hair* is something to behold, curly and thick, flowing wildly past her shoulders and down her tanned back. She is still dressed in a skimpy bikini top, since she didn't bring a shirt to Plati Yialos, and is thus doomed to live out the rest of this drama in a powder-blue bikini with red strawberries littering it like so many miniature nipples. Never mind—lack of lipstick and silly strawberries be damned! The American boys elbow one another, forming low whistles under their breath.

(For the boys, this bar is suddenly looking better than they thought it would. If only there were three more of her, one for each. But then, the sport of competition is fun, too. Who will take her home for the night? The choice might appear obvious, but that is the beauty of these situations: in a mysterious bar on a Greek island, who can tell which man a bikini-top-clad woman dancing alone on a dance floor may go for? Clearly she is nothing like the girls at Harvard! For all they know, she may even be foreign: Swedish or some other blond race known for their sexual liberation. They take a table nearest the dance floor, send the most nebbishy among them to get the beers. As for the other three: game on.)

For the rest of her life, Mary will think of Mykonos as having a sound track, and the first song on the sound track goes like this: "Boom, boom, boom, let's go back to my room." This song is blaring now, and without even looking at one another or conferring, all at once the three men not getting the drinks are out on the dance floor, boogying it up the way she remembers the boys in middle school dancing, when *Saturday Night Fever* was all the rage. It would be fair to say that she has never seen three men trying so hard. They move steadily closer to her, and it strikes her that if she were at home in Kettering, and three men began to stalk her around a dance floor with the clear intention of simultaneously putting on the moves, she would feel invaded, indignant at their presumption and aggressiveness. Here, however, she remembers Zorg's meaty hand grasping her crotch and lingering on Nix's knee, and instantly her arms float over her head, swaying provocatively. She swings her hips in a slow circle. She is Guinevere; she is Maid Marian; she is that actress in the stylishly tattered clothes from *Against All Odds*; and these men are her saviors. They just don't know it yet.

The handsome one reaches her first. It is a shame because of the three, she trusts him least. But he is clearly their leader, and she needs this to be a team effort. He dances around her and says, with such an astounding lack of originality that she almost fears he does not possess the intellect to complete this arduous mission, "Hey."

To which she responds, "I want you to listen very carefully." She speaks with a smile on her face, not looking at him directly. "I am an American and I have been kidnapped by those two men in the corner. Don't look! You need to pretend that you know me from home. Do not leave me. If you do, I could end up dead."

The guy stops dancing. "Jesus Christ. Do you want me to go say something to them? Wait—are you messing with me?"

Mary shouts, "Jeff!" and throws her arms around the man while his comrades stand, mouths agape. Swiftly Zorg and Titus jump to their feet at their table on the other end of the bar. Nix begins to bite her lip, something like hope visibly rising in her vacant eyes. Mary pulls away and stands clutching the man's warm, solid arms as she exclaims, "How's Lisa? What are you doing here? Why didn't she tell me you were coming?" She waves maniacally toward Zorg and Titus's table, crying out, "Nix! Look who's here! It's Jeff, from Ohio!"

AND JUST LIKE that, the world begins to spin madly off its axis. The Harvard man's knees buckle at this strange girl's words; he almost collapses right out of her grasp. His body could easily be hurtled right off the earth's surface into deep space. For you see, his name *is* Geoffrey, and his younger sister's name is Lisa, and although

In the Company of Fathers

(QUERÉTARO: DANIEL)

Come back again,
come to the edge of the garden
and look into the flesh and bone
of this house where you can't come in.
—SANDRA M. GILBERT, "Invocation"

She's a little drunk when she first notices the letter.

The blue envelope stands out amid the stack of white-enveloped bills in Mary's tiny foyer. She picks it up, the return address in Mexico, a city she's never heard of called Querétaro. She knows no one in Mexico, has never been there—it makes no sense. It makes no sense, and she has downed a bottle of cheap red wine, alone, in her cheap furnished studio, so for a moment the only logical possibility seems to be that the letter must be from Nix. Nix, somehow not dead after six long years, but hiding out in colonial Mexico like war criminals once did in Buenos Aires. Mary clutches the blue envelope and bursts into tears. Tori Amos rasps on the CD player—"so you can make me cum,/that doesn't make you Jesus," she screams. If Mary were any more of a cliché, slamming wine alone and listening to a sexed-up, pissed-off female vocalist, she'd need three cats curled up on her lap and a pint of Häagen-Dazs. The handwriting on the envelope doesn't even resemble Nix's, looks male and vaguely illegible, and then at once it hits her: Yank. She rips open the envelope, hands shaking. Yellow legal paper falls out, and this jibes so closely with the movie reel turning in her head that for a moment she does not understand the salutation. *Dear Daughter.* She has to read it again. *Oh God, oh my fucking God.* Mary jumps to her feet, runs around her glass-topped coffee table, reading words she cannot comprehend in her excitement. And then—then she sees it, there at the very end of the letter. *Your biological father.* His signature: *Daniel Becker.*

It is not her dead friend back from the grave. It is not even Yank. Most of all, it is not her birth mother—no, just the bozo who fucked her birth mother more than a quarter century ago. Mary stares down again at the messily scrawled page. *What* is she supposed to do with this?

PEOPLE TO CALL:

Mom. But Mom will freak. Mom does not even know Mary put her name on the adoption registry; it's been languishing there for nearly three years. Mom will cry, though she may try to hide it. Mom will say, *I don't understand why we aren't enough for you,* even throw in, *Is this why you spent years running all over the world and neglecting your health, because you don't think of us as your real family?* No, there simply isn't a polite way to explain how some stranger could justify Mary's existence in a way her parents—who have made every sacrifice for her—cannot. There is no "gratitude" in her feeling like an unmoored boat, wanting to lay down anchors of heredity. Okay, so she won't call Mom.

Eli. Her boss, also her lover. She could call him. Except for the small matter that, right now, Eli is home with his wife, Diane, and their three kids, which if she is perfectly honest is probably why Mary was listening to Tori Amos and drinking alone and hallucinating letters from Nix and thinking of Yank. Except that if Mary were to call Eli, she would be treading into *Fatal Attraction* territory, and it is bad enough that her sheets smell like his semen and that she puts her face against them and inhales deeply, even though she does not remotely love the motherfucker. No, definitely not Eli.

Joshua. *Oh, Joshua.* If the number worked anymore, she'd use it. If in truth they could never quite talk to each other, even in person, Mary has forgotten that part, and why the hell shouldn't she? She dials, knowing in advance the futility, but this time quits midattempt, hangs up.

It always comes to this. Mary goes to her Nix notebook, on the bookshelf next to her photo albums from her travels. It always ends this way, Mary and her imaginary friend, her dead confidante. Mary, alone, talking to the ether.

Back when I put myself on the registry, I was just bursting with plans of action, wasn't I? I can just see you looking down on me and laughing at my naive idealism (oh, Nix, do you "look down," do you look anywhere?). Fresh back from Kenya and chomping at the bit to pursue my new and perfect life. Sorting out where I'd come from was only part of that picture—I'd also get a job where I could make a difference, and whip my health into the best possible shape so that when the time came I could withstand fertility drugs and pregnancy without my health going to hell. Oh, yeah, and of course I would meet a man. A stable guy who had never been a circus performer or drug dealer or safari leader or Olympic hopeful, just a regular person with whom I would fall in regular love. In my fantasies, most of these things would already be in place by the time my biological mother materialized like a final puzzle piece, and when she and I looked into each other's faces, we would recognize everything. For the first time, I would be able to place myself in both a mirror and the wider world. My birth mother and my baby would both be my history, so that even when I was gone, parts of me would remain—I'd have contributed to a circle of life that is valuable without requiring justification, like art for art's sake.

Three years, though, and no one came sniffing around, until Mary felt vindicated about not working her parents up for naught. Three years, and until tonight, that had seemed to be that.

Meanwhile, Mary spent those years watching her other goals of marriage and family chase each other down the tubes. What is there to say about a woman's hoping to find love and failing? It is the oldest story of the contemporary world. Her friends from high school either had left Ohio or were already immersed in domestic bubbles that did not include her. Her new colleagues at Columbus State were interesting, but mainly older and married, though a few were single women who liked to barhop after class. Unlike the traveler's subculture of London, however, Columbus bars boast young, blond, corn-fed beauties galore. Competition was stiff for a prize that seemed depressingly less appealing than it had from faraway Kenya, and when push came to shove, Mary could not seem to meet a man in Ohio who evoked any passionate impulses. She seldom met a guy who had traveled farther than Fort Lauderdale for spring break, who had more serious aims than getting laid at the end of the evening and someday buying a luxury loft condo with a Euro kitchen. It was *normal*, she knew; they were the normal ones, and she the freak. Why should a man in his twenties be fixated on marriage and children? Why should mere boys understand matters of life and death? How could she hold never having lived in Kenya or Japan against anyone?

Soon enough, she had gone twenty months without sex.

Enter Eli the Married Man.

WHEN HIS YOUNG lover shows him the letter, what Eli says is, "This is bullshit. Jews don't put their kids up for adoption. It's some kind of hoax."

Mary snorts. Dressed in her XL Harvard sweatshirt (she didn't go to Harvard), she looks like she could be all of thirteen. "Right," she drawls. "Because I'm Princess Diana and everyone wants to be related to me. Because I'm an heiress, and this guy's trying to scam me by claiming to be my biological father." She turns away from him derisively, shifting toward the edge of the bed. "A hoax," she says, almost pityingly.

She has no panties on under her oversize getup, and he sees her ass, so he doesn't say what pops into his mind next: that maybe she wrote the letter *herself,* because she wanted to appear to be at the center of the kind of tumult some of their students have been going through.

Their Somali students are particularly dramatic, shell-shocked with tales of medieval rape and pillage, of biblical stonings set against modern-age bombs. This past year, the Somalis have arrived in Columbus by the thousands, and Mary has taken a special interest in them, devising an ESL class geared toward Muslim women and girls. She even wrote a grant to get funding for outreach to Somali immigrants, who, as Mary wrote, are "without a sense of community or representation." If the grant is approved, it will bring a nice chunk of money into the American Languages Department, which would give Eli an excuse to offer her a real adjunct position, a step up from the nondegree evening classes she teaches now. Mary's firm ass cheeks nudge his hip, and even though he doesn't exactly want to fuck anymore, he keeps his mouth shut.

"Jewish," she says, and her delicate little fingers rush up to feel her nose, as though expecting it to have morphed into Barbra Streisand's. "Do I look Jewish to you?"

Eli sighs. "Judaism's a religion, not a race. If some Jews share physical characteristics, that has to do with having similar ethnic ancestry, but there are Jews all over the world, with different physical traits. It's impossible to tell if someone has Jews in their lineage by looking at them."

"Okay," Mary says. "But if it's not a race, then how can it be passed down genetically? This guy says I'm Jewish because my birth mother was a Jew. Religion is a matter of practice, not biology." She turns to face him. "Anyway, I must be the first Jewish girl in the world named *Mary*."

"Actually, you'd be at least the second," Eli says. Then he closes his eyes, a pounding beginning in his temples.

BY THE TIME Eli gets home, he's decided out that he's never going to see Mary again. Well, he'll see her at work, of course, although truth be told, he doesn't have to be around much at night when she's teaching; he's just gotten in the habit of working late so that they can screw in his office, the halls empty and spooky, Mary bent over his desk like a naughty schoolgirl—no, he won't think about that now. When he enters the kitchen, his wife kisses him hello and he feels himself recoil, has to backtrack by claiming he's getting a fever and she should keep her distance. This gets him sent straight to bed so he won't infect the kids, and it's only minutes before he's flipping through channels on the TV, unable to focus, kicking himself because he wanted to get back to Mary's little studio apartment.

Confusion floods his throat like bile. Already he knew he was more attached to Mary than to his usual flings. She is the ideal mistress: completely discreet, demanding only in a sexual way. She lives in her own universe, that girl—he doesn't know what she's thinking about most of the time and he doesn't ask. Not that they don't talk—they talk all the time. About the plight of the Somalis, about all the places they used to live. Mainly it's their shared nostalgia for travel that drew them together. Daily, during the ten months of their affair, Eli has wondered when Mary will figure out that *she* doesn't have three kids or a spouse she's been with for more than twenty years; that she can take off anytime she wants, ditch her Somali grant and the Spanish classes she takes to better communicate with her Mexican students, ditch Eli's forty-five-year-old ass, and get on a plane. It's only a matter of time, and this knowledge of her impending departure heightens his desire. The perfect mistress is one who is sure to leave you before you tire of her. Sometimes Eli grows nauseated with the knowledge that Mary will loom even larger in his erotic memory than she does in the flesh. Not all men get so lucky.

The next morning, claiming a full recovery and making his escape to Mary's, he is able to read the letter again, this time more slowly, looking for proof. Of what, he is not precisely sure. Only that somewhere the guy must have tripped up, revealed his true intentions, which are surely seedy. On paper, Eli already doesn't like the letter writer.

Dear Daughter,

I can't bring myself to call you Mary, though this is what I understand they named you. During the eight days I cared for you after your mother was no longer with us, I called you Rebecca, which was your mother's name. She wanted to name you something else, Linda or Lisa, I think it was, but I refused for reasons I no longer remember. Since they named you Mary, I wonder if they have told you that you are Jewish. I don't even know if they knew. In Judaism, it is the mother's religion that counts, and your mother was a Jew like me. What should I say? Congratulations? Sorry? Surprise?

You have an older brother, a half brother by my first wife. His name is Leo and he lives in New York, where you were born, as you have probably been told (though maybe not). He was already old enough to be somewhat self-sufficient after your mother was gone, and I raised him the best I could. I was in no shape for a baby. A friend of my father's was a lawyer, and he was able to help arrange for your adoption without ever telling my parents you'd been born. That was pretty easy, since they were not speaking to me at that time, or at most times. The lawyer was a good man, and he helped me even though I hadn't seen him in years and had always been rude to him when we'd known each other in the past. The people he found for you were not people he knew but a couple someone he knew had heard about, and it was all done privately and quickly. That's how it was done in those days. Sometimes the kid was never told. I'm glad this was not the case with you. I'm not trying to do anything wrong here. If anything, I'm trying to atone, because life has been good to me even though I never deserved it.

The father who gave you up was a basket case. He was shooting heroin and couldn't work and lived like an animal. Your brother lived through the worst of those years, and he doesn't think well of me for them now. Because you were spared my bullshit, I'm hoping you will give me a chance. I've been clean now for eighteen years. After my parents passed away and I unexpectedly came into some money, I headed down to Mexico, to San Miguel de Allende, when it was hip for artistic types to do that (I believed myself a writer back then). Here, I fell in love with a Mexican woman and we made a life together. We live now in the city of Querétaro. I helped her raise her four children, but I never had any more children of my own.

I would like to know you. I don't want to infringe or make assumptions. But after the PI I hired to locate you told me you had actually already put yourself on the adoption registry hoping to be found, I got the courage to make contact. If you would like to see where you come from, you will always be welcome in our home.

With sincerity,

Your biological father, Daniel Becker

With sincerity, his ass.

As Eli rereads the letter for the fifth time, Mary jabbers on the phone to her adoptive mother in Kettering. Usually he and Mary don't talk to people from their real lives when they're together, but today Mary seems to have forgotten he's in the room. Eli's hoping the mother will forbid Mary's going to Mexico, get hysterical, and guilt-trip Mary into burning the letter, but no, from what Eli can follow, her mother seems to be *encouraging* her crazy daughter. "No!" Eli hears Mary squeak with sudden alarm. "I mean, thanks for offering, you're being *really* cool about this, Mom, I totally appreciate it—but I think it'd be too awkward if you guys came . . . don't you?"

The mother doesn't seem to agree, so they debate while Eli feigns great interest in his coffee, picked up on the way over, since Mary has an appalling ineptitude with regard to any domestic task whatsoever. This, too, is part of why Eli likes her, if *like* is quite the right word for his feelings, and if *feelings* ever had much to do with his behavior. Still, if it is only his dick that's involved, why is he thinking about going to Mexico with her, since she won't let her father accompany her? Why, if it is only that he wants to bang her young, undomestic brains out, is he already plotting what he will tell his wife so he can get on the plane?

I HAVE TO GO *check this Daniel guy out, even though part of me is afraid of being disappointed. At least something is finally happening, right? Otherwise, what are my options? Just more of the same. Yeah, this is what I left Joshua and his marriage proposal for. A married man nearly twenty years my senior. A lover I can't even pretend offers me a future. This is what I got instead of the majesty of Kenya: a studio in fucking Columbus, Ohio. A job that I believe in but that doesn't*

*pay even enough for me to afford car payments without my parents'
help—that doesn't offer health insurance, so that my dad has to pay
extra to keep me on his company's policy. Three years past my median
life expectancy, and here is where I am: underemployed in the frigid
midwestern winter, balling a balding father of three because he is the
first man I've met since I landed in Ohio who can actually carry on a
conversation, and that level of desperation can make any ridiculous
moral error feel like love. Too often, having downed more than my
share of wine alone in my studio, I've called my old phone number in
Nairobi, hoping to hear Joshua's voice, but nobody ever picks up and
it's ridiculous to imagine he would live there after all this time. If I
really wanted to reach him I would have to call Gavin's company, but
it's a longing without purpose: what would I say? I don't even want to
rush back to him, exactly; it's more that he's the only one who might
understand my pathetic, misguided arrogance in assuming I could so
easily find a "better" life. It's only that I have come to realize that a
dying woman, least of all, should ever treat love as a disposable fruit
that grows on every tree. It's only that, however much I believe in my
Somali grant or starting my master's in education in the fall, there is
no substitute for having someone who puts you first, who does not put
his pants back on at ten thirty and head home to his wife.*

*So now. Daniel Becker, this father who went looking for me
without even knowing I was on the registry. An expat himself, who is
welcoming me into his home. I should be thrilled. It should be what
I have been waiting for and craving . . . but Nix, I'm not sure, really,
that it isn't just "something to do."*

THE ADDRESS IS 18 Hidalgo. Eli has it on a scrap of paper, though he and Mary are both more than well versed enough
in Spanish to communicate successfully with the cab driver. It is
night. They drive a long stretch of highway from the airport, past the
kind of billboards and tufts of dying grass that could be anywhere,
before things go all colonial, before the streets narrow into the kind
of Mexico Eli recognizes. They drive past a square lit up with Christmas decorations, and Mary grows animated, begins interrogating the

cab driver about the holiday festivities, which seem to boil down to about 150 different parades and performances put on by the various churches—all Catholic, of course—outdoors, where it is still a temperate sixty degrees at night in late December. Eli can only thank God they skipped Christmas by a day, or probably the girl would have dragged him to Mass. In this moment, he would like to smack her. She's just *passing*—doesn't she know that? Then he feels like an idiot. He is an atheist, for God's sake, or at least agnostic. Where is all this righteous Jewish indignation coming from? He married a Jew largely by accident, because he was a radical—or posing as one—and so many other radicals were Jews. He and Diane have never been inside a synagogue together unless it involved somebody's wedding or funeral. If anyone's the fraud inside this cab, it's him.

This square, though, is something else. The cab driver stops on a corner so that Mary can ooh and aah over it. There is a life-size Garden of Eden, with papier-mâché mannequins of Adam and Eve, in sultry fig-leaf fashion, and another section Eli assumes must signify Christ's descent into Hell, as it's populated by devils that flash red lights, carry pitchforks, and leer menacingly. Another area of the square boasts an elephant with a moving trunk; Eli has no idea where the elephant fits into the Jesus story. And of course, the crèche. Baby Jesus and the Holy Family, who in this setting look appropriately Mexican. In the distance, Eli can see three guys dressed up like the Wise Men, one in full blackface, posing with children for a photographer, for money of course. The camera's flash is just another bolt of light in the extravagantly illuminated square.

"He says on New Year's Eve the women from the town set up booths and cook in this square, and it's a big party," Mary says breathlessly, as though he doesn't speak Spanish better than she does. "There's a local drink—*ponche*—he says we have to try."

"I've had *ponche* before," Eli says in his best jaded older man. "It tastes like Sprite with cinnamon floating on top. It sucks."

Mary falls silent and Eli feels stupidly glad. She leans back into the seat of the taxi. Her blond hair stands out so sharply against the night sky that it is almost as though she glows. Her body is small and

disappointment in her voice, as though she, too, would like to escape to some anonymous, margarita-doling hotel. "I hear something."

And then the door swings back. The woman standing inside is a knockout, Eli can't help thinking, despite *her* short stature, largish nose, curly hair. She wears a man's robe, the belt wrapped around her waist twice. Her feet are bare. She is maybe forty years old, but could be fifty. Her eyes are lined, and there is a telltale cord of skin stretched between her neck and her chin that Eli remembers not seeing on Diane until she reached forty, but the symmetry of the woman's features achieves a kind of Sophia Loren agelessness, and her breasts, clearly braless under the robe, seem unnervingly high and firm. She is smiling hugely: she knows who they are. They are not in the wrong place. She begins to jabber in Spanish, and for a moment Eli is so dazed by her that he forgets he knows the language. Then it becomes clear what she is saying. Daniel is upstairs. Daniel is waiting for them. No, not *them* — her *you* is singular. She has no idea who Eli is. He looks at Mary, and next to the dazzling woman at the door she appears wan and insubstantial, her youth taking on a characterless blandness that seems to scream, *I have not lived!* It isn't true, Eli realizes: Mary is not your usual sheltered punk. Still, he wants to take her wan-ness under his wing and protect it. She seems something that, for lack of belonging to anything else in the picture, must belong to him.

Then the woman moves aside to let them in. They step together into the dark stone foyer, move forward to get inside the building. And then, they *see*. The small foyer opens up like the mouth of a cave into an enormous dome: a stone courtyard itself as large as one of the mansions in Bloomington, Indiana, where Eli was raised. The house seems to explode into monstrous proportions — yes, Eli realizes abruptly, this is not an apartment building but a *house,* owned by the letter writer! The courtyard is chilly, an indoor-outdoor space with some strange kind of plastic ceiling so high above them that Eli can barely see it. And all around the courtyard are rooms shut off from view by elaborate antique wooden doors. He cannot count them from where he stands, but there are at least ten rooms on the first floor alone, part of which is taken up by a wide stone staircase shielded by a wrought-iron gate and by this foyer. Upstairs, there may be almost twice as many rooms overlooking the courtyard, and Eli knows from his Central American days that inside these rooms will be passages, connections to other hidden quarters. He and Mary stand gaping.

The woman, who has introduced herself as Gabriella, moves toward the stairway, presumably to take them to Daniel. But Mary stops in the middle of the courtyard, at a fountain encircled with mosaic tiles. She stands, one hand over her mouth, and begins to laugh.

FIRST, GABRIELLA GIVES Mary the grand tour, Eli trailing after them — though it had not occurred to her before, Mary is suddenly unsure how to explain his presence. Each room possesses a chandelier the size of a king-size bed, as well as vintage furniture the likes of which she has never seen except in photographs. Velvet settees, elaborate canopy beds, marble-topped dressers, a dining room table that seats perhaps twenty with the chairs well spaced. Mary thinks of her parents' dining room table in Kettering, which seats six, and how they would drag kitchen chairs and cram them around to get ten people at the table when extra guests came. Gabriella chatters like a guide, a mix of Spanish and English, talking about how "we" had to get the furniture out of storage, "we" spent years antique hunting, and "we" bargained with the previous owner about the chandeliers, which were not meant to come with the home until Daniel walked away from the negotiating table, and the real-estate agent called and said the chandeliers could stay. Still, "we had to spend months restoring them," Gabriella says. "They were not in good condition." The house, she explains, "came with count papers" — a title for Daniel. No title for her, apparently, or if there is one, she doesn't mention it. Mary's legs feel leaden. Her father. *Count Daniel*. She feels like a character in a teen movie who turns out to be royalty.

When they finally meet Daniel, it is in hidden quarters on the first floor, near the very back of the house. First they pass through a media room with a large TV and new couches that — unlike the antiques — actually look comfortable; this room then leads to a bedroom, the only lived-in one, with a larger, less formal bed. Finally, heavy wooden doors swing back to reveal an office, and at the desk a man has fallen asleep on a stack of papers, with several books open and balanced precariously on top of one another. Gabriella moves toward the man, her feet making no noise on the mosaic tiles of the floor, and touches his shoulder, so that he jolts upright with a small cry of alarm. The left side of his face is creased from the edge of the paper stack pressing into it. His hair, near black without any visible gray, is thick and disheveled like a lion's mane. His face is thin, body sinewy and compact as a high school boy's. He wears a sweatshirt too large for him, with an Irish cable-knit cardigan over it. His pants are quasi army fatigue, with a missing pocket that looks like it was ripped off, perhaps by a dog. Like the woman's, his feet are bare. Despite the disarray and lack of dignity of his various parts, the whole picture is one of handsomeness. With a bookish virility, his nose slightly hooked, his smile startled and wolfishly charming, he looks nothing like a count. He also looks nothing like Mary's *father*.

He comes to her. He does not seem to see Eli. His arms are outstretched, but he does not embrace her, rather takes her by the shoulders and holds her at arm's length, studying her until she begins to blush.

"You look," he says, "exactly like your mother."

Then he leans forward, kisses her quickly on the hairline, and whispers into her ear, "If you'd told me you were going to bring your pops, I'd have put on a better shirt."

THAT NIGHT, MARY tosses and turns in an elaborate four-poster bed, listening to Eli snore. Only once before have they spent an entire night together, when his wife and children were visiting Diane's parents on Long Island. That night, Mary had been so happy to finally not be alone in her chilly bed that she dropped to sleep instantly in Eli's arms, immune to any sounds of the night. Now, her head feels like it is vibrating off the pillow. Despite his rumbling-thunder sound, Mary has been huddled close to Eli's body for warmth, and when she flips back the bedspread, she shivers before she can pull his sweater over her gooseflesh and find her Nix notebook among her luggage.

Jesus Christ, where am I, girl? What am I doing here? Nothing feels like it should. This weirdly sexy, disheveled old guy in his freakishly gigantic house doesn't feel like my father. *And Eli's only making things worse by serving as an audience to this whole absurdist play. In no reunion scenario I ever imagined would there have been a role for my "married lover," masquerading to Daniel and Gabriella as merely my "inappropriately old boyfriend." This is not how it was supposed to be. This is not how it was supposed to turn out.*

The moonlight illuminates the courtyard from above, but the temperature has dropped, and Mary has to huddle, knees under the sweater. She can see the white of the notebook's pages but can't make out her own words once written, as though already they've been enveloped by the night. In her mind she frames a picture of herself, a lost girl in a giant house writing invisible letters to a ghost. But lately, imagining herself from the outside, conjuring a poetic picture, doesn't offer the comfort it once did, and instead the hollow space under her ribs seems to widen. As she slides back under the bedspread next to Eli, finally not alone in a bed and at last in a house owned by her actual kin, tears run onto her pillow at how *badly* she wanted Daniel to be a woman. The realization pains her: yet another betrayal of Mom, whom Mary has already put through so much. But although she barely knows Daniel, already she understands that what she is looking for is nothing he can offer, that what she needs could only have come with a woman's skin.

Nix, she whispers, urgent, futile. *Nix, I wish you were here with me, in this crazy-ass house. I wish it could be you and not just another fucking man.*

Eventually her pillow is wet and she flips it over. Eventually she falls under the house's quiet, black spell.

IN THIS ENTIRE palace, there is somehow nowhere to hide to do PTs. For the first full day of their stay, Mary and Eli obligingly follow Daniel and Gabriella from town square to town square, drinking ceaseless *cafés con leche* at endless cafés until their hands shake, then return home to mellow out with Napoleon cognac swilled in the elaborate sitting room, its French doors open to the balcony, noise from the street below drifting in. Mary is a mass of anxiety and phlegm, plotting how to sneak away. They have walked all over the city "centro," listening to Daniel and Gabriella talk about Querétaro's history, about their courtship, about the wonders of San Miguel de Allende, an expat haven and artist colony they will visit during their stay. Mary waits patiently for them to stop talking and go to bed, but despite being the youngest, she is the first in the group to tire and escape to the bedroom. Of course, Eli retires immediately after, so that even in the privacy of their room she cannot be alone, and finally falls into another agitated sleep, PT undone.

The next day, Daniel has to work (he describes himself as "a kind of grief counselor"), and he leaves them to their own devices. Crazily, despite her subtle suggestions that she'd like to just hang out in the majestic house and read quietly—*alone*—Eli trails her like a stalker. She has no idea what to make of him. In Columbus she often feels herself to be clingy and servile, begging him to come over to her place, imploring him to stay one extra hour. At the meetings for the American Languages Department's part-time faculty, it takes all her power to act as though everything is normal in front of their colleagues—to not stare shamelessly at Eli as he runs the meetings, to not laugh too raucously at his jokes, to not find some excuse to steal a drink from his coffee cup, just to feel her lips where his have been. Somehow, here, everything has been reversed.

She has never done a PT in front of Eli—he does not even have a clue that she has CF. As usual, she has admitted to her asthma, has even used her inhaler in front him, and has a few times pressed him not to smoke in her presence when she's "having a bad day." But truthfully, in the time they have known each other, Mary has been almost freakishly healthy. Living alone, she has plenty of time to do three PTs a day; she works only at night, and her days are mainly spent lying around in sweatpants practicing Spanish tapes, then going to swim at the YMCA pool. Once, shortly after she and Eli first slept together, she had to go on antibiotics for a PA infection, but like a miracle the drugs cleared things right up and she never landed in the hospital. She missed only two classes. Eli came over with chicken soup, and though she was coughing continually, he seemed to think nothing of it.

This dementedly large house, this castle owned by her birth father the count, has a *chapel* in it, of all things. The chapel, Daniel and Gabriella explained, came with the house. Gabriella is, of course, Catholic. "We were going to nix the graphic crucifix," Daniel joked to Eli that first night, "but when Gabriella's family drop by, it cheers them up to see Jesus watching over our house to make sure she's not going to hell for living with a Jew." Eli, who has been doing a good impression of a humorless stiff, did not laugh. At home, nobody can tell a Jewish joke as well as Eli, yet here he didn't even crack a smile. Later he told Mary, "I can't believe he has a crucifix on his wall!" Mary swears that in the past forty-eight hours, whenever Daniel has said anything of which Eli disapproves, she's heard Eli mutter, "Oy."

And so it is in the chapel where she finally hides, late in the afternoon on their second full day. Sitting on the floor next to the altar laden with unlit candles, she uses her Flutter device to expel the mucus from her chest for as long as she can, listening to Eli, spurred on by the sound of her coughs, roaming the halls calling her name. The Flutter makes for a quieter therapy than the chest-pounding, spitting, and gagging sessions of her teen years, but it still is loud. Eli would never look for her in the chapel, though, so even when his footsteps approach, she only quiets down and gulps back her coughs until she hears his voice growing farther away. He does not know that Mary was once an altar girl at her family's progressive Catholic church and used to stand below Father Corbo holding the heavy, ornate Bible open on her head while he read from it during funerals. This was before funerals started to freak her out. This was when she believed, like all children, that she would never be dead.

THAT EVENING, WHEN they return from dinner in the biblical square, Mary rushes back to the chapel to do her evening PT under the pretext of suffering from Montezuma's revenge and having to use the toilet, where at least Eli will not follow. Once the heavy doors shut behind her, she reclines on the chapel's cold floor without bothering to turn on the lights and begins to breathe into the device, watching the little ball rise, noting with a boulder of dread that her breath is weaker already just from one skipped day, or maybe from the stress of being here, or maybe from the constant cigarette smoke Daniel and Gabriella have been blowing in her face. She breathes, trying to calm herself, running the Lord's Prayer through her head like a mantra, but the prayer itself makes her nervous instead of calming her as it did as a girl. If Eli heard her, he would not like it.

Of course, why should she have to please Eli? But the rage she wants to feel, just like the breath she cannot summon, fails her. Eli is someone who came with her to Mexico. He is someone who spoons her body, at least when he can sneak away to do so. He is someone who understands a life of perpetual movement, of living hard and fast, and of the gaping, escape-shaped hole left in a life once that motion has stopped. He is someone who doesn't judge her for sleeping with a married man, since he is the married man in question, so she does not have to explain that morality is something she simply has run out of *time* for: her body needs what it needs while it can get it.

The door jerks, knocks, swings open. Mary bolts upright in the dark room like a teenager caught with her pants around her ankles in her boyfriend's bedroom, tossing the Flutter device randomly, so that it clanks into one of the candlesticks on the altar and knocks it over, and she listens with horror as they all begin to topple like dominoes. She jumps to her feet, blinking at the light.

It is not Eli, however, but Daniel. His eyes are narrowed, confused. He says, "Um. What are you up to in here?"

And she says, "What are *you* up to? I thought you were Jewish!" She has said it in a tone like a snotty teenager's that she instantly thinks he must be glad to have gotten rid of her and spared himself this nastiness on a daily basis.

He stares back at her incredulously. "Don't tell me you were praying."

"No. I just . . . wanted to be alone."

"I heard you coughing. Are you sick?"

Are you sick? Here it is: the simple opportunity to tell the truth. Mary can feel her parents sitting on her shoulders like a cartoon parody of her conscience, whispering in her ear, urging her to *tell* him, to ask where this mutant gene came from, to find out at what age the various afflicted members of his family dropped dead. It has not escaped Mary that it seems to have *entirely* escaped her parents that the CF gene needs to be contributed by both birth parents, and that it is therefore likely that no one in Daniel's family even knows it exists, and she will be the one to break this cheery news of his legacy. She gropes frantically behind her for her Flutter device, which she cannot see beneath the clutter.

Daniel steps forward, like a father or a highly competent museum tour guide, and ushers her by the shoulder out of the room.

THE PORCELAIN DOLL is cracked. His daughter doesn't seem, to Daniel, like the type of woman who collected dolls as a little girl, but it is all he has left of Rebecca, his ex, Mary's mother, and he cannot help thinking that all he really has to offer her—Mary—is this relic. It was the only thing Rebecca didn't take with her when she packed her bags and left the baby and Daniel's son, Leo, alone in the apartment while Daniel was at the police station being roughed up for having smashed the window of his own car in a lunatic, drug-fueled rage, and for generally disturbing the peace of Greenwich Village circa 1968. As if any such peace existed, with or without Daniel to disturb it.

He says to their daughter now, "I kept it all these years. I always knew I'd track you down, once you were old enough to understand." He is aware that he sounds like a parody of the Father Who Gave Up His Child and does not know how to infuse the words with any essence of *himself.* He says again, now sounding like the Pathetic Has-Been Still Carrying a Torch for the Woman Who Left Him, "I can't get over how much you look like your mother."

His daughter clutches the doll. Mary's eyes have the look of fever, of someone who has glimpsed something she didn't know she wanted or needed and now cannot live without. She has an unquenchable thirst about her, a madness Daniel recognizes as more his own than Rebecca's. He doesn't like it, this infusion of himself into her features.

"Where is she now? Rebecca?" He notices she does not say *my mother*. Of course. She already *has* a mother—a father, too. What is the matter with him, using language like that? He wants to bang his head into the wall, but his daughter is looking at him with naked expectation. What would that imaginary self-help book call for in such a situation? Is he about to say the wrong thing? If so, what the hell should he say instead?

Your mother left you alone in a shithole apartment in a crap neighborhood, with an unstable older brother. Your mother left you in an open dresser drawer and ran for her life, away from me, because that was the kind of asshole I was, and nobody on earth could blame her— nobody except you. Your mother didn't like the way you cried and coughed and didn't latch onto her tit properly; your mother could have taken you with her, back to her respectable parents on Long Island, but she didn't, and apparently they were all glad as hell 'cause none of them ever came back sniffing around looking for you—believe me, I waited eight long days expecting them to show up in their snazzy black car; I waited for Rebecca's frigid mother to stand imperiously in the doorway with her ice-queen arms open for the baby; I waited to toss you into those arms and be rid of you and dared to hope they'd buy me off with a bit of cash not to come around, and I wondered how much they'd offer and how much smack I could score with it. But the knock on the door never came, they all forgot you, they went on with their Long Island lives, and I was the only one who did you any favors by calling my father's lawyer buddy and letting him take you off my incompetent, junked-up hands. Where is she, your mother, with her sexy ass and that wild hair and the way she used to stare at me like I was something? Fuck if I know, honey, fuck if I know where that bitch is now. Not waiting for you to call, that's for sure. Hey, here's something I kept because I must be God's biggest loser—who knows why I kept it, who the hell knows—hey, here's a broken fucking doll!

"She's dead," Daniel says. "She died only about a week after you were born. It was an infection she caught in the hospital. They tried to save her but they couldn't. The antibiotics didn't work. After she died, no one on her side of the family ever talked to me anymore. They didn't like me. I had a drug problem, like I said, and they held me responsible. I got her pregnant when I had no way of supporting a child. But we were *happy*. We were happy while it lasted. She loved being pregnant. She told her parents to go screw themselves. We had a good thing going, for what it was. You have to understand, the drugs, our problems — that shit was common for the time period. It's not an excuse. Or maybe it is an excuse. We weren't so bad. At least we weren't over there raping village girls in Vietnam. Your mother was a real looker. You look just like her."

His daughter's eyes pool over. Her mother is dead. No, her *mother* is back in Ohio, but the owner of this doll (which Daniel knows Rebecca didn't even buy, though he's not sure where it came from) is dead, and this makes his daughter sad. She stares at him, and the longer it lasts, the more he sees himself — Leo, too — in her. *This is it*, he thinks, *this is the moment*. He did not have twenty-six years with her; he does not have much to carry forward into his old age, but he has this: his daughter standing in woolly socks on these cold, formidable tiles, clutching a doll to her chest and crying for the loss of her mother. This is the moment he will remember whenever he thinks of her from here on out. In the remaining years before his death, he will never think of his daughter again without conjuring this image in his mind. Soon enough — within the next twenty-four hours — the memory will be tainted by the discovery of its falseness. Still, it will remain a moment frozen in time, and as such it is beautiful; it is perfect. Her grief for his tall tale. Her resemblance to Rebecca, who was always too good for him and finally figured that out. And to *him*, reflecting back out to the world like a piece of history, like the living, breathing pages of a book. Like something that will carry into the future.

• • •

He does not yet know that he will outlive her. Why would he know this? She is duplicitous, like the woman who bore her, and she has not yet told him.

He does not know, either, that out of his bullshit tale she has constructed one of her own. *An infection.* Yes, she has had plenty of these. The antibiotics didn't work, and no, of course they didn't, for this, too, is what will happen to her someday; it is what happens to almost all of them in the end, as the bacteria in their lungs grows ever more aggressive and drug resistant. She knows that of course women with CF are generally advised against having children because of what it can do to their health, the stress on an already broken system. Of course her mother's family would have blamed Daniel for knocking her up — her very life was at stake! And she — she *killed* her own mother! Tears roll down her face, and Daniel stands wrapped in his touching moment which is already becoming a memory, and she cannot speak, cannot break the news to him: that she is sick, too, that her life is equally doomed. She cannot tell him that her mother died for nothing.

And so they stand, cold footed and lying and both lost in their own beautiful myths. Daniel watches the emotion on his daughter's face, and he feels *love* and swells with pride at himself, with the thrill of watching himself from the outside as he watches his poetically weeping daughter and experiences love for her. If he had never given her up, she would probably be a ridiculous crack whore by now. Instead, he has this moment, this shimmery moment to cherish forever. It is transcendent.

ELI COULD GET used to this. Every morning, no matter what time he rises, Gabriella has empanadas laid out on the tiled kitchen counter and coffee brewing in the percolator. She is like a hotter Latina version of Diane. Eli can understand the attraction, why a man like Daniel — only seven years older than he is — would chuck everything and move to Mexico (not exactly a hardship with this house!) for a babe like that. He grudgingly has to admit that Daniel is a pretty decent-looking old guy, no hair loss, no sign of a gut, Jewy in that feral way women find sexy instead of in the nebbishy way that plagued Eli's youth. Plus, Daniel has money and a taste for the good life.

Eli shares that taste. He loves shit like this. Drinking coffee with a group—coffee should be legally mandated as a group activity, as should smoking weed. It's just not as pleasurable alone. In a rocking chair on the back patio, surrounded by pots filled with exuberantly blooming purple flowers, he and Gabriella and Daniel smoke cigarettes while Mary sits, one leg tucked under her, in her robe, the sinews of her bare foot breathtaking as she uses that one foot to push off the ground again and again, rocking. He stares at that foot and feels blood rush to his head, like a stroke coming on. She has some crazy magnetic beads wound around her ankle several times like an African princess. The bones of her foot stand out; her blackberry toenail polish is beginning to chip. Oh, the pleasure! Who are these people, Gabriella and Daniel and even Mary? Why should it feel so perfect here at one moment, at a moment like this, and so foreign the next?

Gabriella has family obligations on their fourth day, so Daniel is taking them alone to San Miguel de Allende. In freaky expat logic, although he is a count and lives in a virtual castle, the man has no car, so they take a taxi to the bus station (replete with shrine to the Virgin Mary next to the ticket booths) and eat knockoff Ritz crackers while they wait to pile onto a crowded bus, stifling hot and full of squalling babies and backed-up exhaust fumes. Somehow Mary falls asleep, like the near child that she is, then wakes in a coughing fit, grabbing that asthma inhaler out of her cheap bag and shaking it with a bony, floppy wrist, sucking its fumes down like a bong hit. It makes Eli stiff just watching her suck on that little apparatus, her silver-ringed fingers clutching it like she might a lover's prick. If the exhaust fumes weren't nauseating him, he'd try to slip his hand under her skirt when her father wasn't looking.

San Miguel de Allende looks like a painting. All terra-cotta and cathedral spires and old men peddling cartoon-character-shaped balloons and beggars hiding small, weary children under their shawls and Americans everywhere, tanned, trendily dressed American twentysomethings and older artist types, old bohos who look like Daniel, that hiply rumpled look Eli can never quite achieve, even though he's an old boho if anyone is. Eli would like to wander the shops and galleries, maybe pick up some Day of the Dead art for Diane, who is into skeletons and Frida Kahlo and all feminine dead things. Except how could he pass off some handmade dead figurines in a brightly painted wooden box as something he picked up in Longboat Key? Diane is not a part of this day's agenda. He's never—in two decades—spent this long in the company of another woman; usually he can barely stand to spend an hour with a mistress after sex without rushing back to familiar, smart Diane, who can talk politics with the big boys, who can still blow him with the best of them, even if her breasts sag some with wear and tear. Yeah, being with Diane isn't so rough. But—forgetting the kids for a minute—he can, maybe for the first time in his life, imagine what it might be to lead a life *without* Diane. There are Dianes everywhere; look at Gabriella. You could lead a life, a comfortable life with coffee and warm bread and good sex and love—yes, love—anywhere, couldn't you? You could lead it with Mary. Something about her is harder to place, though, less dime-a-dozen in both good ways and bad, and this makes her less reliable. He can imagine staying here, staying with *her,* traveling around Central America all summer with his kids instead of wasting his dad hours chauffeuring them all over bland Columbus, going to Little League and soccer games. Who can say the quality of their relationship would be less if he gave them something like that to remember instead of just being the body behind the wheel of a minivan? But if he did anything that rash, who can say how long it would be before he woke one day to find Mary gone?

Daniel ushers them right away to a café. It's on the main square, and Eli suspects they'll charge too much, but what the hell, a margarita will do everybody good. They sit at a small purple table on a shaded terrace, and Eli thinks that they make a glamorous enough entourage of three, that Mary's young presence adds an air of illicit mystery. He feels like a spy, and this sensation, mixed with the tequila, is pleasing. They fend off vendors selling foam-rubber puzzles and cheaply strung necklaces with waves of their hands and "No, gracias," but hand pesos to a few ragged children who seem numb and not at all grateful. It is strange that solicitors are permitted on the actual terrace, but that's what they get for eating on the main square. They order another round of margaritas.

Suddenly a pretty woman is approaching. She might be Mexican, but Eli can't tell. She's got long, dark hair, but she's tall and her skin is fair, and she's dressed in couture (it may be imitation) like a woman in a magazine, as if she's striding toward them with a photographer following her, though she's too old to be a model, thirty-five, maybe thirty-nine. There is such a purpose in her stride that it never occurs to Eli she is not headed for their table. Mary, of course, is oblivious to her. Soon enough, though, the knockout leans over, kisses Daniel on the cheek twice, Spanish-style, and sits down at the table's fourth chair, beaming. Eli feels almost dizzy. What's with all these gorgeous women? As if his luck in having a lover half his age weren't enough, there's Gabriella waiting on him at the castle and now *this*, sitting here at his table, cleavage beckoning. Who the hell is she?

"This might be awkward," Daniel begins, standing up for some reason as though giving a wedding toast. "Or maybe not. This is Esther. She's a wonderful artist. We've been together for seven years. She lives here, in San Miguel. We have a five-year-old son—actually, he's Esther's sister's baby, but her sister was unable to care for him, so Esther adopted him. We're raising him together—you'll meet him later today."

Eli chokes on a long swig of margarita. The sour properties of the drink suddenly seem overwhelming and burn his throat in a mad tickle. He coughs maniacally. Mary, sensitive to fits of coughing given her asthma, pounds him on the back.

"I'm so happy to meet you," Esther says, looking at Mary as though Eli is invisible. The accent, yes, is Spanish. "I've been telling Daniel for years to write to you! He never does what I say. I'm so happy that for once, he listens!"

Eli does not know what to make of the look on Mary's face. Her hand drops from his back with a clunk. She gazes at Daniel, and something about the devastation of her expression . . . he is speaking before he knows it.

"I don't mean to be offensive," he blurts out, like somebody about to say something offensive, "but does Gabriella know about this?"

"Gabriella and I are not married," Daniel says smoothly. "We're all free agents."

Eli snorts so loudly that Mary must think he is coughing again, and she turns to pound him on the back. He shrugs her off. His own agitation surprises him, but there it is; he's on a roll. "Look—" He gestures clumsily at Esther, nearly knocking over his margarita. "You seem like a nice person. I realize I'm acting like a prick. But for Christ's sake, Daniel, why would you bring your *daughter* to meet your . . . whatever the hell she is? Haven't you ever heard of *discretion*?"

Esther draws herself up tall in her seat, flipping her curtain of dark hair over her shoulder. "I do not dignify this with response," she says. And to Daniel, "Who is this man? You tell me your daughter is visiting, and I come with an open heart. You did not say she brings an old man with her who will yell at us about things that are not his business. He is, what, her other father?"

Eli stands. His (apparently old) face burns. "This is bullshit. I'm out of here."

To his surprise, Mary stands, too. He is not sure what she's doing. He's made a complete asshole of himself, and even if Daniel and Esther don't know him for the utter hypocrite he is, Mary certainly does. Maybe she's standing for a better angle from which to toss her margarita in his face? But shockingly she puts her hand on his wrist, exerts the mildest of pressures to pull him backward, away from the table. She turns to Daniel and says apologetically, "You're right, you're absolutely correct, if you and Gabriella aren't married—even if you were—what goes on between you is your own concern. Eli and I are in no position to judge anyone. But it makes us uncomfortable, after Gabriella brought us into her home and has been waiting on us hand and foot, to be party to something that may be being kept from her, that could be hurtful to her. We would rather you not have involved us. This isn't personal against you, Esther. We don't know you. I would like to meet your son and see your artwork. But not like this. I'm sorry."

The corners of Daniel's mouth twitch with bemusement. If Eli knew how to hit him over the head in a way that would knock him unconscious without killing him, he would do it, even if it landed his own philandering ass in a Mexican jail. Daniel puts his hand on Mary's, so that they form a near circle: Daniel, Mary, Eli, all holding hands. Other patrons stare.

"Look," Daniel says, "you two have the wrong idea. Gabriella knows! She's well aware. How do you think I spend almost half my time in San Miguel with Esther and my son? Do you think she's blind and retarded and doesn't notice I'm gone? I pay her the respect of not talking about Esther at length in her presence—did you expect me to tell anecdotes about my other family over dinner with Gabriella sitting right there? You've made a mountain out of a molehill! We have a situation that works for everybody, including both Gabriella's and Esther's families, whom, incidentally, I support. If you two want to sit here and vilify me, knock yourselves out, but you're just showing how American you both are, and how little you understand of the complexities of human relationships. Now, I'd like you to stay, but not if you're going to insult Esther and treat her like my *concubine* or something. Esther is a successful artist—she's an educated woman! She's made her own choices that work for her and I won't sit here and have her demeaned."

Two months later, when Daniel tells this story to his artist friends in San Miguel, he will transpose the facts so that it was *Eli* who called Esther Daniel's concubine, and Esther, standing by, flushed with wine, will not contradict him as everyone laughs. Six years later, when Mary tells the story to Sandor over an Indonesian *rijst-tafel*, she will say that it occurred to her only later that maybe Daniel was lying and Gabriella *was* completely in the dark—there was no way, after all, that either she or Eli would go up to her and ask or ever mention Esther's name. Thirty years later, when Diane is at last succumbing to an epic, two-decade battle with cancer and Eli is unburdening his soul, he will tell the story in such a way that it was his own guilt talking—that Gabriella, beautiful, loyal, and kind Gabriella, had reminded him of Diane, and that he realized in that moment of Daniel's smug, self-entitled treachery what a fool he himself had been and how he needed to make it up to his wife for his lies. He will not mention that in the five years following the end of his affair with Mary, he had two other lovers, one a seventeen-year-old student, before developing prostate troubles that changed his body's virility, and that finally at fifty, extramarital sex began to seem like more trouble than it was worth. When Esther, that night on the phone, tells the story to her twenty-year-old sister, her son's birth mother, in Spain, she will say only, "It was horrible. They never considered that maybe *I* was the wronged party! That witch Gabriella, who has never worked a day in her life, gets the big house, and everyone considers her his wife. They stood up to defend her territory as though I were a common whore!"

In the moment, though, Eli and Mary are cowed like children following a tantrum. Without looking at each other, they sit back in their seats. Eli immediately downs the last of his margarita, comforted by the dizzy spin of the terrace brought on by tequila mixed with an hour of inhaled bus exhaust fumes. He says, "Hey. Let's start over! We just got off on the wrong foot. Esther, you should show us your work—we love art!" He is aware that making art sound like a homogeneous thing one can love in an indiscriminate, all-encompassing way makes him sound even more of an unsophisticated American buffoon, but he has given up, settled into his role as the inappropriate jester of the day. He searches for the waitress so he can order another drink.

IT IS NEARLY 10 p.m. by the time they get back to Querétaro. Eli is already hungover from the earlier onslaught of alcohol, and Mary is coughing furiously and seems to be running a low-grade fever, though she denies it, like all young people who think they're invincible. Eli's starting to feel acutely homesick, though it's sure as hell not Columbus he wants but his wife, and his sons wrestling each other, and his quietly moody daughter practicing her guitar with her door closed. He wants *family*, in all its normal imperfections, and not this swinger's melodrama from a fricking Updike novel!

Daniel, on the other hand, seems none the worse for wear, and spent the bus ride chatting boisterously about his budding side career as a shaman. At first Eli thought he'd heard him wrong—Daniel and Mary were sitting next to each other, and Eli was behind them— but no, there he was, regaling Mary with how he and Esther were considering opening their own healing center in San Miguel, where, according to Daniel, people were coming from all over the world to "detoxify." Eli could not see the expression on Mary's face as he listened to her father detailing how he first realized he was a "channeler" for "voices of the other world" while at Esther's art studio, watching her work on a series of paintings of her dead relatives. "They just started talking to me," he said. "I was able to give her a message her aunt had for her mother, something she'd never said in life that finally gave the family peace." Eli felt his mouth gape and wanted to kick the back of Mary's chair. He heard only her coughing in response.

Now, at the bus station, he whispers to her, "A *shaman*! The guy's a crackpot! Here we were, worked up over the fact that he was lying to a nice dame like Gabriella, when the truth is he's out of his fucking mind!" But Mary's feverish hand only holds his wanly, with the air of someone who does not care anymore.

"You should see a doctor," Eli says in the cab, loudly enough for Daniel to hear. "You don't sound well. We have to leave day after tomorrow—you don't want to travel sick." He jabs Daniel in the shoulder, since Daniel is sitting in the taxi's front seat. "Hey, there must be a doctor in this town, right?"

"Tomorrow's Sunday," Daniel says indifferently. "Nothing's open."

"It's all right," Mary says in an exhausted voice. "I have some antibiotics with me. I'll start them as soon as I get home."

"Great," Daniel says, but Eli narrows his eyes.

"Why are you carrying antibiotics around?" he asks. "Where'd you get them?"

Mary sighs. "They're not three-year-old black market antibiotics from Africa or something, Eli—I got them from my doctor. I get lung infections sometimes, because of my asthma. I never travel without antibiotics."

"Oh," Eli says, cowed again.

The street is dark when they reach Hidalgo. Daniel fumbles in his pockets for a key. He swings back the giant door to reveal the dungeon-like foyer and the majesty of the courtyard, all dark, too, and they step inside. Their voices bounce off the plastic ceiling forty feet above; the closing door echoes in Eli's chest like a punch. From the house's rooftop you can count churches in every direction. He's wanted to take Mary up there and bend her over the edge, to slam into her doggie-style while her wild hair blows over the side of the building into the nothingness, but they haven't managed it yet. Getting to the roof involves opening a small door near the back of the house and creeping up an impossibly narrow, spiral stone staircase. At the top of the stairs, just before the door they must push open to enter the roof, is a small pile of cat shit. Gabriella has three cats, all of whom seem to be named Mami. Gabriella is afraid of heights, so she never goes on the roof or up the stairs to clean away the shit. Daniel claims to like to sit on the roof and read, but obviously he does not mind stepping over fossilizing feces to do so.

All the lights in the house seem to be snapping on at once. Eli hears Gabriella cry, "They're back!" Caught in the cavernous courtyard, Eli, Mary, and Daniel look up. Gabriella rushes from the direction of the kitchen, a man—obviously American and about Daniel's age—following. Maybe Daniel has a gay lover, too, whom they are about to meet? Eli chortles a little under his breath at the thought. Then Mary cries out, "Dad!"

DANIEL THINKS HE may have a heart attack. Already the whole way home he's been having palpitations, panicking that this joker Eli, who is at least twenty years older than Daniel's daughter, might tell Gabriella about Esther, just for the malicious hell of it. Now, here in the courtyard is this white-bread, middle-aged man rushing down the wide stairway with Gabriella. Daniel knows he's in for it for sure. His daughter is shouting, "Dad!" with such a clear relief that it sounds like she's just been sprung from prison.

And suddenly Daniel just wants out of this whole comedy of errors. Fuck Esther; he should never have written the letter. He *can't* have a heart attack now, though. It's late Saturday night, and as he told his daughter, no good doctors ever work on Sundays.

"I'm sorry to just show up this way," the interloper tells him. "Your wife was kind enough to let me in. I don't speak any Spanish, I'm afraid, but we were able to communicate just fine. Her English is great!"

Like anybody asked you, farmer.

"Daddy," Mary whines like a six-year-old. "I told Mom not to let you come!"

"I know, honey, I know," says Mary's dad—*Dad II, Dad Squared*, Daniel thinks, and he almost laughs, despite the stabbing in his chest. "But this is such a valuable opportunity. Mom and I, we never expected a chance like this." He looks at Daniel then, as though beseeching validation. "A health history," he says simply, "might mean a lot."

"It doesn't," Mary says between clenched teeth that spring from nowhere, "mean *anything*."

"You don't know that, sweetheart."

"Yes," she hisses. "Yes, I do."

Dad puts his hands up in mock surrender. His every gesture is full of a folksy hokiness. *This*? Daniel thinks. He and Rebecca gave up their daughter, their flesh and blood, to *this*? "I knew she'd say that," Dad says to Daniel, like one good old boy to another, over the head of the little woman. "That's why, you see—why I *had* to come."

It's around this time that Daniel notices Eli is trying to disappear right into the floor. *Yeah, how do you like it when the shoe's on the other foot, asshole? Who's the big, bad sexual perpetrator now, old man?*

"Uh," Daniel says, forcing himself to stop gripping his chest like a grandma and striding over to shake Dad's hand. "It's great that you've come. One big happy family, right?" Then, at the alarm on Dad's face, he amends, "I mean, it's good to see that my . . . that Mary's been cared for, that her father loves her and is concerned about her. That's what anyone who has to give up a baby hopes for. For your child to be loved." And then, ready to shoot himself in the head, he adds simply, "Welcome." He darts a desperate look at Gabriella, whose smile is frozen on her face in the way it gets when she's not following everything being said. Where, for fuck's sake, is the cognac when you need it? Why didn't Gabriella lubricate Dad with some good booze?

"I, um, don't want to interrupt any reunions," Dad says. "I can stay at a hotel, I just—do you think we could sit down somewhere?" He glances around the courtyard as though mystified. "And have a nice talk before I'm on my way?"

No, Daniel's heart will not have the good grace to give out on him just now. Instead he's going to have to sit down and answer questions asked by Mary's good cop and Dad's bad, just like in his old radical-junkie interrogation-room days. He gestures with his head at Gabriella, who somehow miraculously seems to understand that this is a plea for alcohol and scurries away toward the kitchen. It's then that he sees Eli backing slowly away.

Daniel throws his arms open, does a half-mad dance around the courtyard while Mary and Dad stand stupefied, and finally arrives at his target—Eli—and clamps his hand on his arm, patting him with naked, jocular aggression on the back. "Absolutely!" he booms. "Let's all go for a good chat, shall we? Gabriella will bring us some drinks. Let's go to the sitting room." He smiles widely at Dad, a smile he hopes doesn't come off as a smirk. "It's right next to the chapel!"

IT'S LIKE ROCKET science, getting everyone in one room at the same time. First, Mary rushes off to take her antibiotics, which seems to alarm Dad, who rushes off after her but returns—solo—a couple of minutes later. Then Gabriella appears with small, heavy cognac glasses on a tray, only to be told, "I'm not much of a drinker, but I wouldn't say no to a beer," by Dad, and she glides from the room again. Finally Mary returns, downing her cognac in a single sip, Daniel notices. And eventually Gabriella, who may wisely have paused to pop a Valium on the way, produces Dad's beer and stands next to the loveseat where Daniel is sitting, until Eli, who has been dragged to the seat by Daniel like a hostage in a robbery, hops up and moves as far away from Daniel as possible, allowing Gabriella to take his place. And then things get off to the best possible start, all stars aligning in Daniel's favor. Dad looks at Eli square in the face and says, all folksiness gone from his preacher's voice, "So who exactly are you?"

"This is Eli." Mary's words are rushed. "We work together in Columbus."

"I see," Dad says, not even glancing at Mary. "Ohio's a long way from here."

"I . . . uh . . ." Eli seems to be weighing his words carefully. "I didn't think Mary should come alone."

"Oh, you didn't, did you?" Dad says, his voice flat, innocuously menacing. "You two dating, are you?"

"Um," Mary says, "Dad. Yes. Sort of."

"Oh!" Dad cries, with a glance at Daniel, who obligingly raises an eyebrow. "Sort of!" Dad spreads his paws wide in exaggerated confusion. "You'll have to enlighten me — I'm just a simple, old-fashioned man. Back when I was dating, we didn't have a kind called 'sort of.'"

Sure you did, Daniel thinks. *You just didn't get out enough.*

"Dad," Mary says again, warning. "There's no need to be rude. Eli and I aren't seriously involved, is what I meant. We're friends. We sometimes date. He came to help me. He didn't think I should come alone, that's all."

"Yep, so he tells me. That's real considerate of you — Eli. So . . . Eli. How old are you, Eli, if you don't mind my asking?"

"Believe me," Eli says, almost meek, "I get your concern. Mary and I are aware of the large age discrepancy between us. That's why our relationship — that's why we aren't . . ." *Yeah, no good way to put 'That's why I'm just fucking her and not marrying her,' is there, Casanova?* "I care about Mary. I didn't think it was wise for her to come on such an emotional trip alone."

"I seem to remember offering to come on the trip myself," Dad says, looking at Mary for the first time. "And — bingo — here I am."

"I appreciate it, Dad," Mary says, another meek lamb just like Eli. *Where were all these meek lambs when these two were eating Esther for breakfast?* Daniel wonders, less amused now.

But then, to Daniel's chagrin, something shifts. Dad's eyes soften as he looks at their daughter, and he turns to Eli and out of nowhere there are tears in his eyes. "Thank you," he says. "I'm not saying that I approve of my daughter being involved with a man so much older than herself. For the record, I don't. But her mother and I worry about her to no end, running around the world alone, and it's good to know somebody cares about her enough to accompany her, so that if she were to get sick"—he gives Mary a stern, forbidding look—"yes, Mary, if you were to have an incident, hemoptysis or worse, even on the airplane before you got here—you can't stop Mom and me from worrying about that, you can't forbid us to care about you. It's good to know there was a competent adult with you, in case anything went wrong."

Daniel isn't sure he wants to know, yet his mouth says, "What the hell's a *hemo*—?"

"Hemoptysis is the medical term for coughing up blood," Dad says smoothly, over the small noise of terror Mary makes in her throat, like the early warnings of a growl from a dog. "It's not uncommon for people with cystic fibrosis, though when it happens to Mary it tends to be a *lot* of blood—a massive hemoptysis, they call it. She hasn't had an episode like that in over a year that I know of—but she hides things from us. She tries not to worry us and doesn't understand that her omissions make us worry more."

Daniel gapes at Mary, dimly aware of Eli's doing the same. "You have cystic fibrosis?"

Dad shakes his head, a pantomime of disappointment. "Well, sweetheart, I see why you didn't want me to come. You had no intention of getting your birth family's health history from this man, did you? Here we've been given the opportunity of a lifetime, and you came all this way . . . all this way"—his voice cracks—"without even telling him you're sick."

"I don't know what you want from me!" Mary cries, jumping to her feet. "You're being stupid and unrealistic. It takes a gene from *each* parent—he probably didn't even know he was a carrier, for God's sake! We're not the royal family, where there's been inbreeding for generations and everyone in the family would have the same genetic makeup that I do, Dad! Daniel's fiftysomething years old, *look* at him—he's perfectly healthy! It's my *mother* who's dead! It was her family where CF had already appeared—she died of an infection in the hospital just after I was born. I probably *killed* her. Should I have told him *that,* too? There, are you happy now?"

"Honey," Dad gasps. "Honey, you didn't kill anyone!"

"She should never have had a baby!" Mary screams. "Not that she'd have lived much longer, with or without me. She was twenty—she probably only had a couple years left if she was lucky. And so *what* if Daniel's family has it, too, Dad, then *what*? Do you think he's concocted some secret cure here in Mexico? What *difference* does it make? What the hell difference does it make to me, when I'll be dead in a few years no matter what anyone does—no matter what *you* do?"

Daniel watches Mary's father as he holds his hands over his eyes. With his slightly protruding ears and chimp-like comb-over, he makes a great model for See No Evil. The sight is painful.

"Mary," Eli says, his voice one of quiet authority, "stop yelling at your father. His concern is perfectly appropriate. You're acting like a complete brat. Shut up and sit down."

Daniel thinks, for a brief moment, that she will do it. But she whirls on her heels and pushes Eli square in the chest. She shouts, "You traitor," and storms from the room.

Daniel lowers his head into his hands. Something in him that felt vibrant and brimming with life just this morning is broken. Gabriella's hand is still there on his knee, but he finds that he can barely feel it—that even *she* does not feel like a haven anymore from all that he's wrought.

"She's not dead," he mutters. "Rebecca Channing, Mary's biological mother—they'd changed their name from Chenowitz. As far as I know, she's still alive and well and living on Long Island, or someplace like Long Island. She ditched us. I just didn't know how to tell Mary. It seemed so harsh. I didn't know the stakes." He cannot look at Mary's father, cannot peer into that fun-house mirror. "For the record, Rebecca was healthy as a horse. But she had a sister who died

young and she talked about it all the time—she was obsessed with her
dead sister. She died of a breathing problem. Her name was Linda."
He shakes his head, suddenly clearer. "No. No, it wasn't. It was Susan.
She was eleven or twelve, and their parents took all her pictures down.
That's the kind of people they were. They were monsters."

Mary's father looks at him then, his eyes stripped down to something Daniel will try, years from now, to write about, in yet another
novel he will never finish—after he has left Gabriella and gone with
Esther to Santa Fe to exist as a shaman, dwelling in a simple but luxurious adobe compound frequented by his followers. He will describe
the look as *that of a human body peeled of its skin to show its painful, hideous essence,* and Esther, who patiently reads all his work, will
write in the margins, *What the hell!?* but Daniel will keep the phrase
stubbornly in place until the half-completed manuscript is found in
the compound with him when his body is discovered, naked and shot
through the heart, murdered by the husband of one of his followers,
with whom he had been having an affair, with Esther's permission, of
course.

Now, however, the engineer father explains simply, "Watching your
child die could turn anyone into a monster. If you're lucky, you figure
out how to become just monstrous enough to survive it."

MARY'S BODY IS rigid when Eli enters the bed, her back to
him. She is still too warm, he thinks, though maybe less so than on
the bus. Her bottle of antibiotics and her inhaler are on the bedside
table, along with her chunky silver thumb ring, the only of her rings
that she takes off to sleep. It occurs to him that her father will never
let her get on that plane with him the day after tomorrow—that he
will whisk the feverish Mary away to the airport come morning and
bring her home. Eli senses that somehow he will never see her again.

He does not know what is in his mind and body. His emotions
have been in such flux these past few days that if he feels anything
it is a thin layer of resentment over a bottomless pond of numb. Just
over a week ago, he was a lucky stiff sleeping with a pretty young col-
league behind his wife's back, a wife he had no particular problems

with — not counting the lack of density in her skin, the loss of her collagen to age, the fact that she sometimes acts like his mother (well, not his *actual* mother, thank God, who before being ravaged by dementia was a viper and also, incidentally, a drunk). Suddenly it turns out his young plaything is a Jew, a member of his own tribe, and he has been trespassing on his unwritten rule, held fast to for twenty years, not to shit where he eats. Okay, that was a shock, but really, who's he kidding? Eli is a secular guy and the girl's name is *Mary* and her ass is something else and whatever, *what the fuck ever.* But now. It's like a bad dream. Now she has some terminal disease? Now her biological father turns out to be a channeler for the dead, a keeper of two households like some Hasidic Mormon! *And* a pathological liar to boot, claiming to Mary that her mother was dead — no wonder the poor woman went running for the hills, to escape Daniel. Of course, she could have taken the baby with her. But fine, she left. Now somebody will have to tell Mary the truth, and it will be all the more appalling in the wake of Daniel's palatable lie. Well, screw it, that somebody won't be him.

He tries to spoon Mary. She's always receptive to affection; she's all woman that way, loves to be held. Thankfully this extends, as is not the case with all women, to a healthy appetite for sex. Eli doesn't let himself question, in the light of everything he's learned, whether this sexual voraciousness was born of desperation, a frantic fight to cheat death, to not be alone in what short time she may have left. Well, okay, yes, he does. He does question it. He just doesn't want to know the answer. Fuck the answer. The answer isn't his fault. If she doesn't want to be alone, she shouldn't have hooked her sail to a man married two decades. What's he supposed to do, now that she's a Jew, now that she's ill? Leave his wife, for God's sake? He's always assumed that, sometime *soon,* they'll just part ways, clean, with their stockpile of dirty memories to take into their respective futures. But what kind of man leaves a lover who might drop dead at any moment — a woman barely more than a girl who should have her whole life ahead of her, a life in which to relish and then forget him? Should he just say, *Hey, it's been fun,* and ride into the sunset with his family and his middle-aged good health and his cultural agnostic Judaism and leave her to her fate? Didn't he think just this morning that he could imagine staying here with her, making a life with her? Oh, sure, he thought that—that was *before* he knew she was sick. That was before her ballbusting father came around to shine a big fat light on everything that, like all secrets and perversions, like anything worth having, looked better in the dark.

She's letting him hold her—that's good. Though *letting* would be the operative term; she's still not moving. Eli wants to shake her. He's flooded with the irrational fear that maybe, despite her feverish skin, she is, in fact, already dead. He scoops her tighter, curling his knees up into hers, his cock against her ass. Still, she doesn't speak, doesn't respond. The numbness he thought he felt is evaporating, and what's left behind is something like a simmering cocktail of confusion and rage. She's a liar, just like her father. Why did she let him come here? She must have known truths would come out. Maybe she's been trying to trap him all along.

He's hard. If they could only fuck. Sex would restore familiarity, safeness, something that would make them feel good. Then her father can tuck her under his arm come morning and shuttle her away and it'll all be fine. By the time she returns to work, her nice Kettering parents will no doubt have convinced her that he's no good for her, and Eli won't have to do the dumping after all. So: a good-bye fuck. One for the road. Her hot skin is making him sweat. She needs more than whatever's in that little orange bottle by the bed, anyone can see that. Her father must know it, too. She's not his anymore to let go of; soon enough, she'll just be *gone*.

He whispers into the nape of her neck, "I want you." He knows he should apologize for reprimanding her in front of her fathers back in the sitting room; he knows she's pissed, but for some reason her anger only makes him want her more, and he doesn't want to soften her, doesn't want her forgiveness now. His hands go to work, lowering the black leggings she's sleeping in, the same ones she wears to work under her miniskirts in Columbus. Her ass pops out at him like a secret present. He thinks of this ass cold and inert, lifeless in a box lowered into the dirt. He envisions himself fucking the life right out of her and it makes him want to shout at her, to call her names. How could she do this to him? How could she come to him wrapped in beauty and youth and careless, adventurous freedom and then make a monster out of him by turning into something else entirely, something he *still* has to leave? Her body in his embrace is stiff and furious. He growls at her, "Have you ever been fucked up the ass?"

He doesn't think she'll respond. Clearly she's not speaking to him. It comes as a shock, then, her voice like a jolt even though it's a whisper, her "No."

He finds he doesn't like the answer, though. Irrationally he feels as though, had he asked this question in Columbus, in her single-girl apartment, in the early morning when he's pretending to be out jogging, snuggled deep under her duvet whispering pervy come-ons to each other—he feels that there, in that setting, before the things he now knows, her answer would have been yes. It's crazy—she's either been fucked up the ass or not, it's not a gray question, and if the answer is no, it's no. But wait, that's not it. Had he asked in Columbus, when she was wearing her mistress disguise, it wasn't always the truth he got, and he knew that and liked it. There, her role was to be the antithesis of a wife. Her role was that of the younger, sexually liberated woman. The answer might have *been* no, but she'd have *said* yes in that other lover's skin. And it would have driven him wild, wondering who else had ever had her that way, how this young slip of a girl had done so much in so short a time, and whether he could teach her anything new, leave a mark on any untouched space, make some indelible impression inside her to leave behind. The knowing he *couldn't* would have made him sick, and the sickness was part of his desire.

He tries to make her play along. "Sure," he whispers at the back of her ear. "I'll bet you've been taking it up the ass for years. I'll bet ten men have been there before me."

She twitches violently, jolts around to face him. "I'm not lying!" And the lover's game between them, the game on which the sexuality of the world hinges, the game of approach and retreat and interrogation and erotic deceit, evaporates, so that the bed feels cold but for the patches of sheet touched by her feverish skin. "What's the *matter* with you?" she demands, pushing her feet off against his legs to distance her body from his. "Are you fucking blind? Can't you see I'm *sick*?"

"I—" Dear God, his lover is dying. His sweet, young lover, who rumples his hair, whose taut, skinny thighs are as shapeless and innocent as a child's. She may not even be alive by the time her Somali grant money comes through, those refugees from a world of horror outlasting her. He sits up, and his old, arrogant back twinges with the sharpness of his movement. His arms reach out to hold her, to rectify, but too late.

She's standing, pulling on an old sweater Eli distantly realizes belongs to him, right over her pajamas. Layered up this way, she looks like something to peel, right down to the skeleton. "I'm sleeping in another bedroom," she tells him, and her voice has changed, everything about her has changed. "God knows there are enough of them."

He should run after her.

The man playing his role in the movie would pursue her, flinging back doors until he found the girl and gathered her up in his arms. But the real Eli knows that the script for the scenes ahead is already written and offers no such happy ending. Why should he pursue her, force her to let him hold her? So he can get on the plane on New Year's Day and go home to Diane? So that he and Mary can go back to avoiding each other's eyes at staff meetings? Who is he kidding? He has already been removed from the world of romance, and without the possibility of being the romantic hero, what's the point? He feels like a woman, abruptly, wondering this, but without the possibility of love, exactly what is the point?

WITHIN AN HOUR in Mexico City, Mary has blown three hundred bucks. She's heard of CF patients who died right in the middle of flights because of the low oxygen, and though flying's never bothered her before, and she's needed oxygen only when she had her infection in Osaka, she's scared to board her next plane. The rickety flight from Querétaro to Mexico City was only an hour long, which somehow hadn't frightened her (irrational—as if she could hold her breath for an hour and emerge unscathed), but after spending that time hacking and breathless, pulling in air that never seemed to reach bottom, never seemed to hit its destination, and left her as short of breath after each inhalation as each exhalation, reality has set in. Panic gripping her insides like a magnet, twisting everything into knots, she heads straight to the AeroMexico counter and demands to speak to medical services, in hopes of scoring an Ecylinder that will last long enough for her to get home.

An hour later and I've missed my connecting flight, money down the drain while I'm stuck waiting in this sterile office watching airline personnel jabber on the phones in Spanish. Even in their hideous airline uniforms, these women all look hyperbolically sensual, in that beak-nosed, shiny-skinned, just-been-fucked way of heroines from an Almodóvar film or something. Me, I'm dry skinned and phlegmy, dizzy with airlessness—I am the opposite of sex. I am Cincinnati, I am Hospital. Idiotically, I didn't even bring the phone number of 18 Hidalgo with me when I tore out of there this morning, feverishly wheeling my suitcase over uneven cobblestones until I got to the taxi stand, a woman on the run, as fucking usual. Now I have no way of reaching my dad or Eli for help. I should have waited for Dad at least, should have let him change his return ticket to fly back with me, a human shield from other passengers gawking at my decrepit state. With his engineer proficiency, he'd have figured out how to work the Ecylinder. Now watch me do something to goof it up and start asphyxiating midflight like a fish on land, more entertaining than the lame in-flight movie. But no, I ran out of there too fast, trying to prove some kind of point, and now I'm fucked.

Except she's even more fucked than she realized. Because there will *be* no oxygen. She would need a doctor's note, they finally tell her, which she does not have. She would need to have called forty-eight hours in advance, which she did not do. In desperation, she spreads everything she has out on the counter for them as proof of illness: albuterol and Cipro and her Flutter device. But all they care about is her "fitness to fly" letter from Dr. Narayan, translated into Spanish by one of his nurses. *This* someone makes a copy of, no doubt planning to use it later to avoid an American lawsuit should she expire on the plane. She's coughing, flushed with fever, and feels everyone in the office studying the letter, debating whether they should let her board. Perhaps they wonder if she is contagious. (Typhoid Mary, Nix used to call her. *Oh, Nix, oh, Nix, can we really* both *die on a plane, could that really happen?*) Mary swallows her cough as best she can, pops two more Tylenol for her fever, clutches her bag with wild purpose, and sets about changing her ticket so that she can get on the next flight, which is not for four hours. Ticket in hand, she drags her bag to her gate, sucks in more albuterol, and reclines on the floor, feeling her jittery heart pounding into the carpet under her ribs, coughs mucus into napkins while Mexicans gape at her as though she has the plague, and finally passes out with her sweater over her face.

GEOFF IS THE low man on the totem pole, so he's working New Year's Day. Not that he's hungover or anything. He's been in Cincinnati for less than a month and has yet to form anything that passes for a friendship. The holiday season is a shitty time to relocate. Everyone is too busy with their own nuclear family to bother with newcomers. Geoff took the residency at the University of Cincinnati Medical Center mainly to be closer to his father, a diabetic, half-blind, fanatically independent man whose farm is two hours away. But in his month in Ohio, with his breakneck schedule, he has seen his father exactly once: on Christmas, when he did not have to work, since some Jewish residents put themselves on the roster. He'd have seen his father at Christmas anyway, even if he were still in Boston—even if he had moved to Chicago and let his stepfather, the hotshot cardiologist, pull some strings at a big deal cystic fibrosis center there. On Christmas, his father repeatedly called him "Harvard Boy," as always, and did not buy him a present. His father does not buy gifts; that was always Geoff's mother's terrain, though his parents have been divorced for more than twenty years. Geoff's mother and sister warned him that it was stupid to take the job in Cincinnati, a city he never liked, in order to be close to a man they glibly reassured him "doesn't want you around." These past few days, Geoff has taken perverse comfort in the fact that this may be true, since as it turns out he has only enough free time to collapse in his condo (which he has taken to calling "the barracks," since all he does there is sleep) and no time whatsoever to save a dying farm, dispense insulin, and prepare diabetic-friendly meals. The truth is, Cincinnati is beside the point; he could be anywhere. The sounds of rubber heels and snapping clipboards and oxygen machines have become his home.

The hospital is a frontier, his patients pioneers. Adult CF clinics were barely *necessary* a decade ago. These patients are the survivors. They are less heartbreaking than the kids, and—this is the part that makes Geoff tick—these clinics are where the most cutting-edge miracles happen. The crazy-ass, defying-all-expectation triumphs: Those tenacious CFers who keep running 5Ks into their forties. Heart-lung transplants handed the possibility of a middle age more healthy than their youth. Women who give birth and live to become soccer moms. They are an entirely new human population: adults with cystic fibrosis. They go where none have gone before.

Of course, those are the exceptions. Most of his cases, because of their very adulthood, are in the end stages of their disease. He doesn't get to live a lifetime with them but meets them only on their way out the door. It's a manic-depressive kind of existence, the kind that leads to feeling hungover even in the absence of a New Year's celebration. Geoff's daily life in this brave new world consists of oscillating between the sterility of the hospital and the loneliness of his prefurnished condo five minutes away. His med school debts are mammoth, his longtime girlfriend couldn't wrap her mind around *Ohio* and broke things off, and in one piddly month two patients at the clinic have already died.

Well. His work is good for nothing if not perspective. At least he can breathe.

He approaches the room of a patient who arrived last night with raging pneumonia contracted in Mexico, a nice little drama for the night shift. Now she's on a colistin-TOBI combo and oxygen. As always, he reads the chart before opening the door. He's still scanning as he approaches the bed, not wanting to miss anything crucial, lose the patient's trust by not realizing something he should have known. He doesn't remember to look at the name. Of all the things he might forget, a name seems *most* forgivable. He moves forward and—this is especially important in *B. cepacia* cases, but he's gotten into the habit with everyone—holds out his hand.

It is only then that he sees her.

The girl from Greece.

Her curls, her shoulders, her downcast eyes: all clicking into place in memory.

That yellow sea-foam hair, cascading over her shoulders on the dance floor.

Her knee still damp from the surf, pressed against his in the flatbed of the truck.

Mary—*his* Mary. Behind an oxygen mask, in front of him. Still alive. After all this time. At last.

"Holy shit." He says it softly, his would-be handshake frozen in the air. She had seemed unresponsive at his approach but now looks up, the familiar dark shock of her eyes against pale skin and hair. Her hand, IV dangling, moves to her mouth as she gasps aloud in recognition.

"Geoff. Oh my God. What are you doing here?"

And he says it as if it is the most natural thing in the world, exactly as he hoped so many times to say it: "Waiting to run into you."

She doesn't smile, doesn't laugh, doesn't even look at him suspiciously as though he may be crazy. Instead she begins to cry. This surprises him, but also does not surprise him exactly. He is accustomed to tears by now. It sounds as if she had quite a scare yesterday. She's probably exhausted and afraid. Pneumonia can be painful, too. Her FEV values look all right, but maybe nobody's bothered to tell her that. Overnight staff tends to be shitty.

When she opens her mouth, however, what she sobs is, "Geoff! Oh, Geoff. Nix is dead."

He drops the chart on the floor with an indecorous clang. One of those stupid wheeled tables is perched over her bed, but he knocks it out of his way and climbs in with her, feeling the plastic mattress crackle under his solid weight. He takes her into his arms, a watery mermaid, as she was that night almost seven years ago, only this time attached to tubes that are keeping her alive. By the time he notices he is crying, too, he can already smell the ocean in her hair.

Home.

Where Are We Going, Where Have We Been?

(GREECE: ZORG)

The Down Under is the fourth bar they have entered in the past thirty minutes. Geoff, his buddy Irv, and the two girls, Mary and Nix, duck and twist through a mass of Aussie tourists to the most remote corner of the bar, knees bent, staying low. Geoff is kicking himself for letting TJ and Bill cut out after they got the girls out of the disco, all walking in a boisterous gaggle reminiscing about fake people from "home" and talking at once, just moving toward the door like one body with twelve legs. Geoff, surging with anger and bravery, had even called over to the creepy assholes who were making trouble for the girls, "Hey, you guys wanna come?" but the kidnapping losers stood there, stiff spined and incredulous, not even deigning to answer the question, watching the girls leave surrounded by male bodies.

Man, fuck those guys!

Geoff wishes now he'd told TJ, Bill, and Irv that they should jump them, kick the shit out of them when they had the chance. Four against two, and that one Greek dude wasn't that big—probably the girls would have even joined in and thrown a few punches. But no. He'd been cocky, and when it was clear that he and Irv were the ones the girls were talking to at the first bar they ducked into, TJ and Bill went on to greener pastures, hoping to hook up with girls of their own, and so Geoff and Irv and Mary and Nix sat drinking for a while, the girls telling their wild story, Mary doing most of the talking because Nix seemed like the quiet one, seemed more upset by their ordeal, didn't seem into Irv even though Irv was trying hard to be funny and attentive. Nix didn't smile much, but she was cute, and who could blame her for being upset? Those guys were some pieces of work. Geoff and his buddies should have jumped them in the bar and taught them a lesson. Geoff hasn't been in a fight since he was eight years old, but still. He works out. He was on crew. Fuck those guys. He held Nix's eyes for a moment in the first bar, even though Mary was the one he was into. He just wanted to show her he felt bad for what they'd been through. He put his hand on her arm, but she flinched and he dropped his hand, embarrassed. He shouldn't have let TJ and Bill leave. What was he thinking?

Because now, here they are, running scared like little bitches. They'd only been in the first bar maybe half an hour when Zorg and Titus (they even *sounded* villainous, like mustachioed bad guys in a Disney cartoon!) showed up with two buddies of their own, looming in the doorway of the bar, scoping it out, looking for Geoff, Irv, and the girls. These bars are so crowded that it's easy enough to hide if you see your stalker first, so they'd all crouched low, waited until Zorg and Titus came inside, then scuttled along the sides of the bar like rats until they could saunter right out the door, leaving their would-be assailants searching. They did this twice more, even sneaking out a side exit once. But now, here they are in the Down Under, and fucking A, those guys and their goons are probably going to show up here, too, any minute. Poor Nix is getting visibly freaked out, worn down like a runner in a marathon who can't go the distance. And let's face it, Irv's a little guy: Geoff can't take these four on his own. Mary's been saying they should go up to some fellow tourists and ask for help, tell someone what's happening, but Geoff's not sure.

Because he's starting to think in the back of his mind, what *is* happening, exactly? They're being followed, yeah—though they can't really prove it. *Everyone* goes to these bars: all of Mykonos is crowded into them. Why shouldn't Zorg and Titus be here, too? No one has touched or even threatened Mary and Nix. When Geoff and his friends left the disco, Zorg and Titus didn't try to prevent their taking the girls. And though Geoff likes these girls—they don't seem crazy, and it's clear Nix is genuinely shaken up—their story sounds a little sketchy, like maybe they imagined the threat. What it amounts to, that he can piece together, is that the Spanish asshole, Zorg, was driving fast to freak them out enough to get them to agree to go to the Greek asshole's villa (*villa*, for Christ's sake!). But there, at the villa, then what? The girls had been served drinks, and Mary had taken a nap, and then the alleged kidnappers had taken them out to a disco? It doesn't exactly sound like the height of danger. Everyone knows what Mediterraneans are like: those guys were probably just trying to get laid and thought manipulation was courtship. But now. Yeah, now what Zorg and Titus and their miniposse are after isn't to get *laid* but rather to kick Geoff and Irv's American asses for intruding on their territory. The girls could probably walk away and it would be Geoff and Irv those four would follow. He's even suggested this to Mary and Nix, but they insisted they aren't going anywhere; they're too scared.

Mary goes to the bouncer, an Aussie with a mullet. Geoff hears her describing Zorg and Titus and their friends, asking the bouncer if he'll detain them when they show up, find some reason not to let them leave the bar. She's slipping him an American twenty-dollar bill like some con woman in a movie, if con women wore bikini tops at 10 p.m. And then, just like that, they're off, running hand in hand, the four of them, down the labyrinthine streets of Mykonos, dashing to Taxi Square and jumping into the first cab they see. "Take us to Plati Yialos," Mary says authoritatively, and Geoff feels even more turned on than he did when she let her hair down in the disco. They zoom off into the night, staring out the back window of the taxi, but no, they are not being followed. They are safe. No one—not even anyone crazy—would think to look for them out of town! Geoff settles back against the torn seat, relaxing into his drunken excitement. Mary's half-bare leg is pressed against his. Her skin feels cold and he offers her his sweatshirt, which hangs on her like a dress, covering the short skirt, so that she's even sexier, as though she's naked underneath, like they've just made love and are lying around. He feels a flash of pity for Irv, who clearly isn't going to get anywhere with shy, jittery Nix. In all truth, Nix may be a little prettier than Mary—more delicate in her features—but Geoff finds (he has never thought this before) that he likes his women tough, a little take-charge and adventurous, not fragile or nervous. This girl Mary, she's probably not really a slut, as he first imagined. It turns out it's not really her choice that she's wearing a bikini top at night in public. He's a little disappointed because this means it's not a sure thing she'll sleep with him later, but he's kind of glad—senselessly maybe, since he'll never see her again after tonight—and kind of relieved, too.

Plati Yialos is deserted. Geoff didn't know what it would be like; it's only their second day on Mykonos and they haven't really done anything yet except drink and hit Paradise Beach to see naked girls. Even at night, the beauty of the place is evident. Nobody's on the beach now, of course, and all the blue-and-white-striped lounge chairs are empty, lined up in hushed rows, waves lapping at the curved beach, distant hills darkening the sky like a jagged horizon. The taxi driver leaves without a question and they walk clumsily in the sand, plunk down on their choice of chairs, laughing and excited but without obvious direction now that they are no longer being pursued. Well, except Nix isn't doing any laughing. Here on the picturesquely romantic chairs, with the thrill of the chase over, Geoff's got to admit there's something shell-shocked about her that makes it a little weird to imagine some parallel make-out session—her continued silence, now that the danger is done, feels ominous. He shoots Irv a look to signal, *No, let's not make a move*, but Irv isn't looking his way. "I love your rings," he's busy saying to Nix, still in pickup mode. Geoff watches him take her limp hand in his. "This one—tell me the story of this ring."

But abruptly Nix stands and starts walking toward the surf. Mary, who has been holding Geoff's hand with more volition, drops it, too, her neck craning after Nix. She gets up and goes after her, her footsteps making small thuds in the sand. It looks playful at first, sexy, two girls running along the moonlit beach, but suddenly Nix's pace picks up and she seems to be trying to *escape* Mary for real. Geoff watches, stunned, as Nix begins to pull off her clothes, hurling them onto the sand behind her.

Irv elbows Geoff and says, "I know I should be psyched, I mean, look at those tits . . . but man, I don't know, that chick's a little freaky."

And Geoff. Suddenly Geoff *gets* it, a code locking into place, cracking everything wide open. The way once you understand something, there are no other possible computations. He barks too loudly, "Shut up." Stands, body unsteady in the thick sand.

Mary is running after Nix, but Nix is gone, a flash of legs and ass receding until nothing's left but a billow of hair floating on the waves, and the small headlights of pale eyes in the dark. Geoff sprints off after Mary; he runs until he catches her on the water's edge, where she's calling out with futility, "Nix! Nix!" He catches her up in his arms, and he means to tell her right then—he even begins, "Listen, at the villa . . . ," but what he thought of saying morphs without his consent into a weak stammer of, "Uh, so, you said you took a nap?" No matter, Mary's so busy yelling she doesn't seem to hear him, and to his surprise he can't make any more words come. Because for Christ's sake, what's he supposed to *say*? And who the hell is he to say it?

He watches, tongue-tied, as Mary walks away from his embrace, toward the surf. She pulls the sweatshirt over her head, starts pushing her skirt off her hips fast and jerky as though it's covered with bugs, muttering to herself, "Crazy, reckless, show-off, can hardly fucking swim," like she's talking to Geoff and not talking to him at once. He follows her but doesn't touch her, doesn't *catch* her, and before he can figure out if he is supposed to prevent her from going into the water, she has already plunged in, wearing her suit at least, and is swimming with surprising strength out toward her perilously bobbing friend. Irv is still in the far distance on a lounge chair, staring at the luminously bright stars or at the swimming girls, Geoff can't tell. Yeah, what kind of heroes are they now? Those girls could fucking drown out there. Geoff spent summers on his grandparents' farm near Yellow Springs, Ohio, nowhere near an ocean or lake; he does not know how to swim more than the width of a pool. If he went into this wild night sea, he would die, as simple as that. So he watches—he watches Mary reach her friend, the two of them out there in the dark, presumably telling women's secrets, elusive to him.

Perhaps it would not be fair to say that this is the moment he falls in love. If anything, he feels excluded and slightly angry, mostly at himself for his paralysis. If anything, he feels regret—again—that he did not jump Zorg and Titus when he had the numbers on his side, that he didn't kick them in the nuts until they spit blood, though he knows somewhere behind these fantasies that such an action is beyond him in its violence and impulsivity, and that's what makes him angriest of all. He watches Mary, and if anything, he feels that this mermaid in the water is something he didn't know existed until tonight, some strange hybrid of several common flowers that, when combined, yields a sweeter, more intoxicating scent. He watches her and Nix, bobbing in their sea of womanhood, and he feels it might make sense to take off his own clothes and walk into the sea, just on the chance that he might be able to hear their secrets, to touch Mary's wet arm before the waves engulfed him.

Instead he only stands on the shore, waiting for what he knows will be her eventual return.

Three Honeymoons

(CANARY ISLANDS: GEOFF)

What would happen if one woman told the truth about her life?
The world would split open.
—MURIEL RUKEYSER, "Käthe Kollwitz"

On New Year's Eve, 1994, she didn't think she'd make it to '95, but here it is almost spring, and she is not only still kicking but feeling inconceivably fresh off another overseas plane ride and holding a fruity welcome drink in the main house of the most luxurious resort she's ever seen. Its architecture resembles that of a turn-of-the-century village, as envisioned by a partnership of *Travel and Leisure* and Gaudí. Instead of one big hotel, approximately twenty "villas" dot the elaborately landscaped gardens like mini fairy-tale castles, all squat turrets and shiny tiles and pastel shutters. Instead of outhouses or vermin carrying bubonic plague, the place is so clean that Mary would feel perfectly comfortable licking the floors.

"This looks like someplace Snow White would hang out if she had a price on her head," she whispers, and she and Geoff laugh into their drinks, intoxicated by their shared delight at the absolute lack of authenticity. They will be on Tenerife for a week, and their covert plan is to never leave the premises of the resort. In their first few days, they stroll the gardens, eat gourmet meals or quick snacks at their choice of restaurants, read novels and drink on the private beach, and then go back to their villa to make love until they are exhausted enough to sleep, only to wake and do it all again.

Geoff calls this a "no stress" vacation. No backpacks, no flooding bathrooms, no hitchhiking. "I don't want to see you while I'm at work," he tells Mary, meaning *at the hospital*. Over their first shared paella he informs her, "I'm going to fatten you up."

Imagine a man saying he *wants* his woman fat! Envisioning a fuller swell in her breasts, her thighs brushing one another when she walks, Mary orders a third margarita — plus crème brûlée.

"No more slumming in the third world for you," Geoff says later, as they float aimlessly in their personal Jacuzzi, sprinkled with fuchsia flower petals, the aroma deepened by steam, so that the air is thick and perfumed like an opium den. "I'm going to make you take it easy if it kills you."

Then he grimaces.

PLACES TO MAKE love at the resort abound. The hammock on the hill, late at night when no one is around. Their Jacuzzi, Mary lying on her back outside the tub, droplets chilling on her body, while Geoff, standing inside the water like a statue of a Greek god, thrusts his hips, her legs slung over his shoulders. The crevices of the garden, on all fours behind bushes, peacocks gazing on. Mary and Geoff sneak around like children, looking for new places to copulate. A deserted chaise longue at sunset, while the rest of the guests are at the dinner seating. "This is what I wanted to do to you on that chair in Plati Yialos," Geoff says, diving between her legs. For a moment the ghost of Plati Yialos — of Nix's nude body hurling itself into the surf — hovers, but then Geoff's tongue sets to work, sun looming above the water before dropping under, a giant yolk falling into a bowl, and Mary's back arches and her thighs grip Geoff's head and muffled voices in the distance only spur them on.

IF HAPPY FAMILIES are all alike, the only thing more homogeneous still is a happy couple. See Mary and Geoff lying poolside with the other young men and women, all paired off like animals marching onto Noah's ark. Pretty, tanned twentysomethings chatting around the bar, swapping meet-cute stories (Mary and Geoff's always wins) in their various German, English, American accents. If Mary coughs now and then, even pulls out an inhaler, nobody seems to notice. If she disappears into the villa for a stretch of time to do her PT, surely everyone only assumes she and Geoff are in there swinging from the proverbial coital rafters.

Or maybe that is too simple. Mary's lungs are still suffering the aftershocks of her Mexican infection; her daily life continues to revolve around time-consuming physiotherapies; now that she lives with a pulmonary specialist, she is less able than ever to forget about her illness. Geoff even does bizarre things like invite his supervisor, her longtime physician Dr. Narayan, over to their house for dinner, and insists on calling him by his first name, Laxmi, though Mary blushes every time, and lives in perpetual fear that the elderly man who has handled her lungs since she was seventeen will now accidentally encounter a pair of her thong underpants or, say, her vibrator while visiting.

She knows that her current bliss cannot be explained away as her feeling "exactly like everybody else" suddenly, but precisely the reverse. To be in such normal love, while simultaneously cognizant of her own difference, makes it seem that the bond she and Geoff share must be deeper, more profound or extraordinary, than bonds shared by the other, regular couples at the resort. Yes, for the first time since high school, Mary has been granted entry to the Normalcy Club, but this time undercover. She and Geoff are complicit in their pretense, so that the *average* itself has become exotic: every ordinary moment carries an electrical thrill.

Is this finally "happiness"? she wonders. Is this what she always craved? And if so, how long will it last?

ON THE FIFTH day, guilt-tripped by the other couples who rave about the casinos and discos in the touristy *Playa de las Américas* section of the island, Mary and Geoff venture outside the walls of their resort and head for the beachy boardwalk. But despite a dearth of American tourists in the Canary Islands (mainly because most

Americans have never heard of them), it turns out that Germans and
Brits are just as adept as any ugly American at co-opting a place until
it becomes a Fort Lauderdale–like strip mall, complete with fish-
and-chips joints, bratwursts, and endless pints of beer, with neon
signs and fat senior citizens in sensible shoes. Bombarded by gaudi-
ness, Mary and Geoff scurry past the casino, the dance clubs with
wildly pulsating 1980s tunes shaking the sidewalk, the bars in the big,
glitzy chain hotels, bypassing the crowds. They amble along the rocks
that line the beachfront, until they once again reach seclusion. Mary
takes off her clothes and Geoff looks around nervously but then removes his, too, and they do it up against some rocks that poke and
scrape their skin but provide good foot leverage for Mary, since usually she is too short for them to have sex successfully standing up.

Mission accomplished, they hurry back to the idyllic world of their
resort.

THIS, THEN, IS love. That elusive bird that managed to fly
forever out of Mary's reach even in the great cities of Europe and the
African bush. That state of being or beast or concept, impossible to
pin down, that had started to seem to her a great, mythic hoax — or
if not that, then some salve for the simpleminded, not worth its hype.
But how underrated, *joy*. How incompatible with everything she
thought she knew of life. In real life your boyfriend ditches you the
moment you get sick; in real life planes explode in the sky; in real life
your long-lost father is a polygamist shaman. Now, only two months
in, Mary is a zealous convert to love and its attendant happiness: an
optimism junkie.

She never wants to go back.

ON THEIR LAST night at the fairy-tale resort, they dine in
its five-star restaurant. There is only one seating per each evening's
three-hour affair, and you have to dress for dinner. Mary and Geoff
wait in the cigar lounge for the seating, sipping cognacs. Geoff has
put on what Mary's father would call a sports coat, and he looks so
handsome her brain hurts. At twenty-eight, he is less muscular than

the boy she met years ago in Greece (he says he was on crew back then), but his new spindliness becomes him, has taken the macho edge she distrusted in Mykonos off his appearance. He looks kinder now, more vulnerable in his beauty. Sometimes Mary thinks Geoff looks like an actor cast to play the role of himself in a film; his face is too pretty to make sense in the context of a Cincinnati hospital and seems more Hollywood's idea of what a "good-catch doctor" would look like. His dark hair falls softly in a curve over his eye, making him look like a boy in a 1980s band, sans the eyeliner and with his square jaw for a dose of masculinity. Mary is pretty sure every woman he encounters would like to fuck him, though Geoff says this is ridiculous; he has slept with fewer than ten women, her included. Still, she sits in her strappy black dress next to him, euphoric. *This is my boyfriend. This is my life.*

At dinner, they order the catch of the day, filleted tableside. They drink a sauvignon blanc from South Africa, which Mary is relieved is dry. She doesn't know much about wine but recalls having had a sauvignon blanc with Geoff before and its being distastefully sweet. Geoff explained that this has to do with where the grapes come from and in what region the wine is made, but sauvignon blancs seem to come from all over the place, and she cannot keep it straight. He claims it's his favorite white wine, although Mary finds this perplexing, since it never tastes the same. However, she likes that Geoff knows about wine. It seems a grown-up thing to know about. It makes him seem the antithesis of Joshua or of Mary's parents. It seems an obscene, glorious luxury to be genuinely invested in the idiosyncratic taste of a grape and to have protracted discussions on this topic without the slightest tinge of irony.

"Look." Geoff points toward the entrance of the restaurant. "There's Olivier."

Mary turns her head. Olivier is what they call the Frenchman who wears a skimpy black Speedo at the pool, his penis coiled like an enormous snake inside. They do not know his actual name, the penis being too terrifying to permit small talk, but Mary, Geoff, and all the other couples have been laughing about him for days. What is he doing here

fingers into the delicate bowl of it and fishing out the ring, thrusting it forward at Mary. "I want you to listen to me," he says, sliding the wet diamond onto her finger. "Your FEV values are amazing for your age, you have a milder gene mutation—I think you're going to live for a long, long time, Mary. And as far as a baby goes, I'd never want you to do anything you weren't comfortable with, but studies are showing that women with good pulmonary function don't usually decline from pregnancy—some show that women who have children actually live longer. Plus, when the pancreas isn't affected, as in your case, a transplant could someday offer an entirely new lease on life, where you're not sick anymore at *all.*" He gets out of his chair and comes over to her side of the table. For a moment Mary thinks he will get down on one knee, but he is too dignified for that, too full of midwestern reserve, and merely crouches next to her chair. "Look, I'm not kidding myself—I know there are no guarantees. But if I were ever to lose you, the only thing that could make it even slightly bearable would be if I were raising our child and still had a part of you in my life."

If they were in a movie, this is the part where Mary would begin to cry—where she would fling her arms around him and shout, *Yes!* to the cheers of the other restaurant patrons. But she is too numb with relief to even speak. She cannot cry. She cannot even *feel*, precisely, except for an enormous wave of letting go, of surrender. She looks down at her ringed finger and nods, unable to meet Geoff's eyes. He hugs her tightly, and she wraps her arms around him and hangs on, thinking of the first day he brought her back from the hospital to his condo, and the way she wondered at her lack of nervousness or even, precisely, lust, when they fell together onto his bed. She felt, in contrast, as though they had already been making love for years and had returned to each other after an involuntary absence. For the first time, nakedness seemed neither a costume nor an escape route. Above Geoff's bed was a framed Nagel print, and abruptly Mary cackled and said, *I didn't realize we were back in 1986,* so Geoff, naked with his hard-on bobbing up and down, had stood on the bed, taken the picture from the wall, and put it inside his closet. "I guess since my decorating skills are so awful, you're just going to have to move in and save me from myself," he said, and although he had not even been inside her yet, the deal was done. She had already resigned from her job in Columbus and was unlikely to find a new teaching job before the fall, but the very next day Mary took the art she'd acquired in France, Japan, Kenya, and Mexico and, clutching the emptied travel tubes to her chest, spent five hundred dollars having it all framed.

"Hey," Geoff says, standing quickly, discreetly, before the other restaurant patrons start to stare, "maybe we should come here again on our honeymoon."

"I can't believe it," Mary whispers. "I was just thinking that."

THEN IT IS 1996.

Geoff first sees the carnival on his morning run, when he impulsively hops in a cab and gets out in Santa Cruz, Tenerife's proper city, instead of just running along Playa de las Américas. *Spanish carnies,* he thinks, surprised by how eerily identical the carnival is to one you might find in a school parking lot in rural Ohio. An old-fashioned menagerie of cheaply constructed, unsafe metal rides. He jogs right past it—he did not particularly like carnivals, even as a boy—increasing his stride, relishing the sun. It was snowing when they left Cincinnati.

Mary is still asleep. At home, she leads a borderline nocturnal schedule. She's in her second semester of pursuing her master's in education, and many of her classmates teach full-time by day, so most grad classes begin after 3 p.m. Geoff, Laxmi, and Mary's parents all agreed that, although Mary has her certification to teach high school English, having her own classroom in addition to her course load would be "too much." Last summer, when Mary was offered a teaching job that they all urged her to decline, she put up quite a fight. Even after turning down the opportunity, she was usually up at the crack of dawn, running off to swim at the YMCA or study at the library. On the days she had no class, she tutored ESL kids in an after-school program. Since Christmas, though, Mary's been sleeping in past noon, struggling to make it to class on time as the sun goes down.

She's awake on Geoff's return, and he feels instantly guilty. It's the

first morning of their honeymoon, and he shouldn't have just disappeared without her. She doesn't seem taciturn, but still, he omits mention of having run anywhere other than down the touristy Playa de las
Américas boardwalk, since he knows Mary hates it there. Somehow,
though, they end up wandering, by mutual unspoken consent, beyond
the boundaries of their resort and "back" to the boardwalk (Geoff is
grateful to have, in fact, not seen it twice in one day). Clearly Mary is
as restless as he, though they have only just arrived. Within the walls
of the resort, it feels strangely as though they are on a *Twilight Zone*
train car from which they can never disembark, and with relief Geoff
beholds the fat German and English retirees waddling around Playa
de las Américas: proof of the world outside.

Although he jogged through breakfast and Mary presumably slept
in and missed it, they sit together at a café table on the boardwalk and
order beers. "Beer only tastes good when I'm hungry," Mary says, proclaiming the carbonation "too filling." Normally Geoff would find this
adorable, but today he doesn't comment. They sit drinking their beers
on empty stomachs at eleven in the morning, surrounded by tourists,
most of them unattractive.

Mary looks pretty. Warm weather becomes her. Already her face is
flushing with sun and drink, and she wears a skimpy batik sundress
that shows off her swimmer arms, her flip-flops kicked off under the
table. In the humidity her hair winds itself into golden corkscrews.
After one beer, she begins making fun of the passing tourists, invent-
ing dialogue for them and having them talk to one another about inane
things like where to find a proper sausage roll. Her British accent is
spot on. The mania of her spiel makes Geoff anxious, but he also likes
that she's trying so hard to perform for him and laughs appreciatively.
He wants to be allies again.

Some hippies walk by—a ragtag bunch, six or seven men, two
women among them. They seem a natural choice for some of Mary's
funny dialogue, so Geoff waits expectantly.

"I smell their hash on the breeze," Mary says, and her voice is so
nostalgic, so unmocking, that for a moment Geoff thinks she is about
to break into an improvised poem (earnest in a tongue-in-cheek way)

on the joys of hashish, still for his amusement. But no, no such riff is forthcoming, only Mary staring longingly at the receding backs of the hippies.

Indignation rises in Geoff's esophagus like a bad meal returning to haunt him. Obviously Mary never smoked pot, even when she was younger, not with her lungs. The hippies are about their age, late twenties. Their women are unattractive, which surprises Geoff not at all—why would a beautiful woman settle for such a life? He finds them all ridiculous. To clarify: he doesn't begrudge them their lifestyle or wish them ill. He is as liberal as the next guy, after all; he voted for Clinton even though both his parents, who can agree on nothing else, are staunch Republicans. Geoff prides himself on being nonjudgmental. But come on! Walking around in ratty, mismatched clothing, smoking drugs in public, and sleeping on the beach when you are pushing thirty seems absurd to him. Would seem absurd to anyone.

Except that, apparently, to Mary it doesn't. The expression on her face is caught between nostalgia and longing, which Geoff interprets as an affront. If you like hippies, it doesn't take a rocket scientist to figure out that you shouldn't marry a doctor. Plus, if Mary took to smoking hash and sleeping on the beach, she would probably be dead in a matter of months. Perhaps this is *why* she is sitting here with him? His beer tastes warm and sour now.

Mary has stopped looking at the hippies. She turns to him and says, "That's all we do, isn't it? Look at things and try new drinks."

Geoff jumps a little in his chair. It seems bizarre and apocalyptic, her saying this.

But Mary laughs. "You know," she says. "'Hills Like White Elephants.'" And slowly Geoff feels his body relax. He has never read the story, but has heard of it, of course. It's unclear now why he reacted so badly. Even in light of the hippies, the quote obviously isn't true of him and Mary at all. "Remember?" Mary says, as though the possibility that Geoff may not have read the story is inconceivable. "How the girl says everything tastes like licorice? We should order a pastis—have you ever tried one? I used to drink them in France. And in London, there was this derelict old geezer who used to come into the Latchmere every morning at eleven and stay until closing. Everyone called him Pernod because that was all he ever ordered. Except me. I called him Norm."

Geoff does not, thank God, ask Mary if the guy's name was Norm. *This* reference he understands.

Mary signals the waiter. But Geoff doesn't want a fancy French aperitif now. He wants to go back to the room and retreat behind the *Herald Tribune* and forget about Mary for a while, even though it is the first day of their honeymoon and he has no choice but to take her with him. He pulls out some money, claiming exhaustion, to which Mary says, "If you didn't wake up so damned early to run around," but fondly, unaware of his mood shift, and they head back to the resort.

It isn't until dinnertime, however, that Geoff remembers about Santa Cruz and the carnival. Back at the resort, Mary sucked his dick without his having to ask her to, and so he liked her again. *Liked* her again? But of course he likes her all the time, loves her too much—that is the problem. Of course he wouldn't mind about the stupid hippies (to whom she didn't even speak) otherwise. He came in her mouth, and she dashed off into the bathroom to spit it into the sink, but he forgave her because that is just what girls are like after you get serious with them, even if they swallowed in the beginning. Geoff is no Casanova, but he is old enough to understand such a simple thing and not be offended by it anymore. Once, the girlfriend who later dumped him for moving to Ohio asked how he would like it if she shot a wad of menstrual blood into his mouth and told him to swallow it, and he had to admit he wouldn't like it much, though he isn't convinced the two things are exactly comparable when you come down to it. Nonetheless, his dick sucked and drained, he forgave Mary the hippies and fell asleep without the *Herald Tribune*, and later when he woke and found her poolside in her boy-shorts bikini, reading *Justine* by Lawrence Durrell, his dick got hard again and he remembered the carnival and offered it to her, like a fancily wrapped candy, a reward.

So here they are. They have ridden the Tilt-A-Whirl and the Scrambler, and everything feels happy, exciting, and light. Mary leans against him as they walk, her hand in the back pocket of his shorts. As in

Greece, she stands out here with her blond hair. She has on the batik dress and flip-flops again, while all the Spanish women wear leather heels. Mary, a world traveler, must understand the footwear customs of Spanish women, but she never wears heels, even though she is short. She dresses, Geoff thinks, like a girl in junior high, though her breasts, clearly braless behind the dress's gauzy fabric, are nothing a father of a junior high girl would be thrilled to see his daughter parading around at a foreign carnival. Against his body, she feels lithe and fragile, as though he could rip the dress off with one hand and leave her standing, abandon her to the crowd, with her gaping, pale titties and tiny underpants and the flip-flops still on her feet. Not that this is something he would ever do, or even the kind of thing he fantasizes about—though it strikes him as something Mary might whisper to him suggestively while he is fucking her, during one of her stretches of sexual intensity, when her drive borders on the desperate or depraved, and after long hours on call Geoff can barely keep up with her: a predicament both alarming and thrilling. Although she has not been in one of those periods since the fall, Geoff thinks that maybe later, when they make love in the hot tub, he will tell her about this fantasy that is not *his* fantasy quite, and he imagines her wetness gliding over his dick and how, even if she doesn't say so, he will know she is turned on. He has forgotten the hippies now.

There is alcohol for sale at the carnival, so they get drunk. In Cincinnati, Geoff is not a big drinker, Mary even less so, given all the meds she takes, but here, why not? Here for one week, why not be the people from her Hemingway story? The twirling Octopus, in combination with liquor, makes them ill. And yet there is a thrill in the air. They dance in the open lot to Madonna booming "Holiday," just as in Greece nearly eight years ago: in any country in the world, "Holiday" is playing. They take this carnival for all it is worth, and Mary's hand caresses Geoff's ass inside his back pocket, and everything feels right and fresh and good, even though they have both been to makeshift carnivals and danced to eighties songs and touched each other's asses a hundred times before, and that saved them from nothing.

When they leave, it is as though they are simply being led onward, to something else. They still haven't eaten dinner, and Geoff napped through lunch, just munching some Pringles out of the honor bar, so not only is he famished but his intoxication level is teetering on the brink of dangerous. They planned to eat dinner at "their" restaurant — the one where he proposed — but they've remained in Santa Cruz too long and missed the seating. And Geoff finds, really, that all he wants to do is meander until he and Mary find another place — the kind without set seatings, a place concierges do not recommend and that is not in any guidebook — and wander inside. He will know the right place when he sees it. They will drink red wine and eat seafood or paella, and years from now they will still talk about the restaurant, though they may not remember its name.

"Look," Mary says, jerking his hand. "What's going on?"

Up front, a parade seems to be blocking the street, though this seems an odd hour for it. The audience, rather than standing on the sidelines watching, follows the procession. Geoff tightens his grip on Mary's hand as they rush forward to see.

Ah, okay, yes. This is part of Carnaval — the *real* Carnaval — because tonight is the day before Ash Wednesday. Geoff isn't Catholic, isn't really anything, although he and Mary share a common later-in-life addition of Jews to their family, since Geoff's WASP mother is now married to one. If there is some hidden Catholic meaning to the fact that the procession is composed of men dressed in drag, then Geoff isn't savvy to what it is. Or wait — not just in *drag* but as *widows* in mourning, all in black but for red flowers on their hats, or a red shirt beneath a jacket or cloak of black. They shriek in falsetto, dabbing their eyes with handkerchiefs in a mock sorrow Geoff doesn't understand. Is it a parody of the Inquisition, perhaps? He looks at Mary for some Catholic insight, but though her eyes are shiny and aroused, she shrugs at him and shouts above the din, "I have no idea!" as though she's read his mind. Suddenly Geoff catches sight of a giant macramé fish being carried atop a float — he cannot work a fish into the Inquisition — and Mary begins to hop up and down, her airy dress flapping around her legs.

"Come on!" she shouts. "Let's follow them!"

They race along on the sidelines, trying to catch up, but the crowd is thick and they can't quite penetrate into its center. From where they are, Geoff can see that both men and women dressed as nuns and priests are part of the procession. Several of the nuns pretend to faint dead away as they move through the narrow streets, and this splinters the crowd a bit so that Geoff and Mary can finally get in closer. Just as they do, priests anoint the onlookers with buckets of holy water, which splatters onto Geoff's face. Beer.

Then come the ghouls. Masked and ominous, followed by clowns with white, ringleted wigs. Three girls dressed as prostitutes dash up to an older tourist couple nearby and fan their ruffled skirts, babbling in Spanish; the older couple laughs, but Geoff notes that the man backs up in a series of small, quick steps, knocking into the people behind him.

Abruptly the procession shrieks together, screaming in voices that sound indicative of real pain, and a chill runs down Geoff's back as it has on occasion in the hospital, when a patient's agony or fear becomes unbearable and restraints must be used. He knows this is *theater*, merely an improvised performance, but something in the collective hysteria frightens him. The people carrying the fish wear executioner's masks and black robes, and every so often they spin around and chase the crowd, the onlookers shooting off to opposite sides of the narrow streets. Mary is right there with them, caught up in the excitement, letting go of Geoff's hand, so that he has to bolt forward to keep up or lose her in the crowd. He thinks he hears the beating of drums, though over the voices and shrieks it's hard to be sure. Members of the procession are so disguised that several times, when Geoff sees friends meeting up with each other, both parties seem astounded at the recognition. A man dressed as a widow bats his false eyelashes at Geoff, and suddenly there is Mary again, whipping a brightly colored Mexican shawl out from her straw bag and wrapping it around Geoff's head, nudging him, but by the time he catches on and tries to bat his eyelashes back, the "widow" is gone. The procession moves on, but Geoff remains still.

"Come on!" Mary cries again. It may be only the second or third
time she's said it, but it feels to him like the hundredth. "Hurry up, we
won't be able to see what happens next."

He wants to give her this. He wants to hand it to her the way he did
the familiar parking-lot carnival—the way he handed her this *luna
de miel* as a substitute honeymoon when, at the last minute, they had
to cancel their original wedding plans on New Year's Day at Daniel's
majestic courtyard in Querétaro, sending notes to guests that Mary
had an "infection" and couldn't travel. Only Mary's parents knew the
truth about the miscarriage—knew that Mary had been pregnant at
all after seven months of trying, or knew that, in mid-December, they
had seen the baby's heartbeat on an ultrasound, Mary's pregnancy being treated as "high risk" because of her CF and so early ultrasounds
being standard. They went in, then, for their next appointment on the
day before Christmas Eve, holding hands and referring—like naïfs
begging fate to smite them—to their baby as their "Christmas present," but the heartbeat was gone.

In the dark room, after the ultrasound machine was turned off
and Mary was instructed to get dressed and proceed to her doctor's
office, Geoff burst into tears, crying loudly in a fashion he couldn't
remember doing since childhood, since before his parents' divorce.
He went to embrace Mary, the way he had the day they were reunited
and she told him about Nix, but instead she gave him a withering
look and rose to put on her clothes. The fertility specialist explained
to them that miscarriages at this stage were common—that in all
probability the fetus suffered from a chromosomal abnormality that
prohibited development, that most likely this had nothing to do with
Mary's CF and they would go on to have another healthy pregnancy
just like "normal" couples. Geoff watched Mary stare straight ahead
with eyes blank as a fish's. The doctor suggested they schedule a
D & C immediately to spare Mary the pain of waiting for her body
to expel it, but Mary said she would wait and let her body do the job
on its own. She waited for three weeks, but nothing happened except
she developed back pain so severe that by the end she could barely
walk, until she had to call her doctor back in defeat and ask for the

procedure. "My body can't even miscarry properly," she said bitterly, and after the surgery, which her doctor said they had put off longer than was ideal, she bled for two weeks, wearing thick Kotex to her classes and only finally, near their wedding day, being able to brave a white dress. She'd chosen a Mexican-style peasant dress, off the shoulder, for their grand Querétaro affair, but Geoff stood helplessly by as she tossed it in the trash, its fabric overflowing the crowded, plastic bin. Without her mother's help, she went out and returned with a stunning red gown embroidered with gold Chinese patterns, its bustier top and curve-clinging skirt a sophisticated antithesis to the innocence of the Mexican dress. She had her hair blown out on the snowy day of their ceremony, and it shimmered long and slick; at the dinner reception afterward all Geoff's relatives and colleagues raved, but to Geoff the bridal Mary seemed a glossed and polished shell of her usual self: cold, regal, and frightening.

Tonight is the first time Geoff has seen Mary exhibit excitement since the miscarriage. Even at their consolation prize of a wedding held on Valentine's Day in Ohio because Mary didn't feel up to dealing with Daniel anymore, Geoff felt her going through their vows on autopilot: a numbed-out zombie bride. He knows that he should offer her this night as the *true* beginning of their marriage—that he should follow wherever she leads now—but his senses are overwhelmed; he's drunk and tired and can't stop seeing himself at a great distance, shirking from the executioners and ghouls, cowering beneath the giant fish that looks as if it could topple and crush a dozen men. The procession has moved on and still he remains static. Confusion spreads across Mary's firelit eyes.

"I feel like we might be an intrusion." The words come out false—there are other tourists, many of them, in the crowd. He offers instead, "I know it's a performance, but there seems something private about it, too, something sacred, like they're putting it on for us but they hate our presence at the same time. Don't you feel it?"

She stares. Clearly she does not. And he's not sure that's precisely *it* anyway, what he means. He knows only that he wanted a small, quiet restaurant after the frenetic Tilt-A-Whirl and Octopus, after the nausea of the rickety Ferris wheel and dancing with her braless, rhythmic body, no trace left of a pregnancy that had never shown anyway. He wanted intimacy, privacy, a renewal of romance after loss, but instead he got strangers in drag shouting in his face, and bodies pushing up against his, and a roar so deafening he cannot, still, make out whether there was music playing or the racket was all human-generated. The crestfallen look on Mary's face makes him all at once remember the hippies, and he wonders irrationally whether they are in this crowd, whether now they have disappeared down some winding, narrow street to hump one another like dogs against the old buildings' crumbling walls—whether this is what Mary wanted from *him*, too. They are standing outside a tiny restaurant, Geoff notices, and he could almost cry: it is exactly what he had in mind. Its pink awning reads LA FORTUNA, and the small outdoor café is full, but inside there are several empty tables. He takes Mary by the hand and almost pleads, "Let's stay here. You must be starving—let's just eat."

Inside La Fortuna, all the other patrons are women. The women occupy three separate tables on far ends of the matchbox restaurant and do not appear to be together, yet each (there are seven in total) is dressed in a different-colored pastel dress: pink, blue, green, yellow, orange, lavender, and another pink that is more like dusty rose. The dresses are not all of the same cut, but they are, to a one, solid colored and old-fashioned in effect, so the women appear like scoops of bright ice cream in a surreally Technicolor 1960s sitcom. Something about their presence in the restaurant is both comic and creepy. In the cramped room, Geoff can tell that they all have English accents. Is this some kind of *club*? But no, the women at the various tables do not even glance at one another or interact in any way.

Geoff looks at Mary and says, "This has been a very strange night."

"It was unbelievable!" she gushes. "I wish we knew where they were taking the fish! I wonder if it was to the water—if they were going to let it drift out to sea."

Geoff feels beaten down. He feels as though he has been punched. The word *relentless* pops into his mind. This is what she is: relentless. And yet she has done nothing. She is sitting here, at the table across from him, not complaining, not berating him. She is compliant, but the fervor still sparks in her eyes. Back at Carnaval, she looked like Joan of Arc. Like a zealot: someone who saw visions. Slowly, right in front of him, she is transforming back into his wife, just a woman who has suffered one too many losses and is trying to outrun pain with stoicism, secrecy, and parades—and who the hell can blame her? What does he want from her anyway? On the night he fell in love with her, she was a zealot, an apparition from the sea. When he saw her again, she was aflame with fever—*genuine* fever—fresh from the brink of death and bringing him news of a plane that had exploded in the sky, and he loved her again, wildly, like a sailor loves a siren. Now, though, he just wants a normal dinner companion, not a visionary. But how can he expect her to turn her fervor on and off like a light switch when it suits him? She is racing for a finish line, and sometimes the romance of it blinds him, and other times he simply cannot keep pace.

"I wonder how late they stay out in the streets," Mary says, and it takes him a moment to realize she is still speaking of Carnaval, of the procession. "Maybe we'll see them again on our walk home."

All he wants is a wife who will cry over their lost baby, who will let him hold her and comfort her, but she will not give him this, instead darting her restless eyes around the restaurant. "Jeez," she says breezily, "have you noticed all the crazy-looking chicks in this place?"

He puts his head down on his arms. He has lost it. Is Mary to blame for noticing—just as he had—the pastel-colored women at the neighboring tables? Is she responsible for the fact that the people of Santa Cruz run around enacting some strange death ritual about a fish?

"Geoff?" Mary says, and he hears a hint of her intensity returning—but this time tinged with fear. He knows he should look up; he knows his behavior is inappropriate. "Geoff, what's wrong?

"Nothing," he says into his arms, but then he raises his head to face her. She *is* just a girl, just his wife. What was he so afraid of? He can't tell. Her eyes are her eyes, nothing more. Inside her chest, her lungs are working, doing their job for now. Under that sundress, her ovaries are producing eggs. *Look on the bright side,* her OB had said. *At least you know you can get pregnant.*

"I think I've been drinking too much today," Geoff says. "Do you mind if tonight we skip the wine?"

Nix,

I knew I should leave it alone, but I asked our waiter in Spanish what the deal was with the fish. Entierro de la Sardina, he says it's called. Basically they bury the fish at the water the night before Ash Wednesday. He didn't speak any English and my Spanish is rusty, so I wasn't able to sort out exactly why. Why a burial, why a sardine? Is it their symbol for Jesus? Somehow my lack of comprehension made it all feel even more like magic. When I found out I'd missed the burial, I felt like throwing things, but Geoff doesn't deserve that, so I just smiled.

And what the hell would you know about it anyway?

I guess since I keep defying my life expectancy, this was bound to happen eventually. I have finally gotten old enough to understand how young you were when you died. If you, the you of my memory, were alive today, I would not be telling my secrets to a twenty-year-old college student. If the ticking time bomb in my lungs counts for anything, then I am already past middle age, already an old woman. But even if you don't grant me that jump in maturity, still I have passed those places we shared. I am a married woman. For all of six weeks, I was a mother of a baby girl named Nicole Rebecca. I shouldn't have named her after you, I know. I keep making that same fucking mistake. But what can I say? She is my Nicole now.

When you left me at the Athens Airport, like when you left me alive in this world, you were the "traveler" among us simply because you were going to an American college in English-speaking London. Now I have lived all over the world. What possible reason can I have for still writing to a girl I met in kindergarten, to my "best friend always" from high school? I outgrew you long ago.

Your death was tragic, but if life has taught me anything, it's that tragedy is cheap. You were a force of nature, Nix, I'll give you that.

Unlike me, where my own body seems to attack me at every turn, it took an enemy of the whole free world to fell you. But what of it?

I remember all the times you said you would never be your mother, some dumb twit knocked up young and spending her life changing diapers and getting fat. I remember you wanted to be Anaïs Nin. I remember that you hated children — that when we passed a baby on the street and I would coo, you'd roll your eyes, plug your nose, and laugh that throaty laugh I found so intoxicating.

You were just a dumb kid yourself. I'm sorry. I've got to go.

M

RAIN AGAIN.

On the last day of their honeymoon, and for the third day running, drizzle piddles down onto the villa's low roof, small, staccato explosions of sound that Mary alternately tunes out, then thinks will drive her mad. Geoff lounges on the king-size bed in striped boxer shorts, his olive skin against the shocking white of the duvet like a J.Crew underwear ad. Though she has never thought this before, he seems too clean to be exactly *sexy*, his perfection utterly incompatible with the turmoil she feels. On TV, CNN is covering the third anniversary of the 1993 World Trade Center bombing that killed six people and wounded more than a thousand. They're showing footage from that day, and already Mary knows that it will loop around continuously, so that if the weather does not let up, this is what she will be stuck with on her last day on the island. She imagines Mom home in Ohio, watching similar coverage, perhaps calling Nix's mother, Sandy, and asking her to dinner after work so that Sandy will not sit home and obsess over the television, over the bodies of those dead from terrorism. Mary's mother is considerate that way, knowing something about dead daughters even though her daughter is still alive.

Mary gets up to shower, though breakfast in bed does not require such hygiene and she will need to shower again in only a few hours, since once Geoff tires of CNN, they will surely be engaging in sex. Mary came prepared for frequent honeymoon copulation (though in truth, before the rain, they'd made love only once), her luggage crammed with Monistat 7 and some stronger prescription cream, since even in bed her body has become mutinous lately. Although the frequency of sex that first year with Joshua sometimes reached epic proportions, it is only now, since she has been trying to conceive, that she has become plagued by the infamous yeast infections to which women with cystic fibrosis are prone. The brochures will tell you that this is because women with CF have thicker mucus. Mary will tell you it is because Geoff has a gargantuan dick, which does not sound like something she would ever have filed under the category of "problem," but when your vagina is itching and discharging like a motherfucker because you and your faulty mucus have been rubbed raw by a purple-red flagpole that pulses with its own heartbeat, your vantage point tends to change. Thus far, she has had a yeast-free honeymoon. Compulsively she showers, as though this will keep her that way.

There is little point to sex today anyway. She isn't likely to conceive again until her menstrual cycle returns to normal. Thus far, although she effectively hemorrhaged between the legs for fourteen days straight following her D & C, losing so much blood she had to take iron pills and got dizzy standing up, she has yet to have a real period. When they first arrived at the resort, they had not made love since losing the heartbeat, and Geoff seemed afraid to touch her. The bleeding is over, though; there is no reason not to resume her normal life. Under the steaming water, indistinguishable from the patter of rain on the little pastel roofs and dripping from the million insipid palm trees, Mary tries not to feel as though she will claw her own face off if the downpour doesn't end.

She reenters the bedroom naked. She should go to Geoff. Even among healthy women, one in four first pregnancies ends in miscarriage. Mary knows she is expected to understand that having CF or being adopted or having a dead friend does not "exempt" her from the ordinary trials and heartbreaks of life, like some karmic system in which her dues are already paid. And Geoff does not *blame* her for what happened. Half the women at this resort have probably struggled with infertility or lost pregnancies. Still, standing naked while her new husband fails to turn in her direction, his eyes glued to the repetitive loop of CNN, she feels like an imitation bride, and Geoff some one-man Make-A-Wish Foundation who was assigned to make her time-limited dreams come true, and as though they have both failed, proved their marriage a sham before it even began.

She goes to the closet to dress but instead pulls out her Vest. She hasn't used it much on vacation, relying more on her Flutter device. She didn't want to bring the Vest at all—it weighs as much as a toddler!—but finally allowed Geoff to pack it in *his* suitcase to avoid a fight. Now she puts it on like a suit of armor that cancels out the invitation of her nudity. Geoff cannot touch her while she's wearing it. It would be like trying to make love to a vibrating carburetor. She switches it on, and finally, at the sound of it, Geoff looks away from the TV.

"Awesome!" he says, giving her a thumbs-up from the bed.

Sometimes doctors can be a little bit crazy.

Geoff bought her the Vest for her birthday in late August. It cost something like fifteen thousand dollars. He is already in debt from med school and could not afford such a lavish gift, especially one Mary did not want. Yet he claimed that wearing this would increase her lung functioning. He put her on a regimen in which she wore it every evening while they watched reruns of *Thirtysomething* together. On that show, which Mary had never watched during its original run, yuppies have parties and gossip and go to therapy. Bad things happen, too. The main female character has a miscarriage, in fact. And another character, Nancy—played by an un-Hollywood-looking actress named Patricia Wettig—gets ovarian cancer. Nancy is married with two children. She gets better, but her friend Gary, who was never sick, dies. This, of course, is how life goes. Nix did not live to get married, but Mary has. Maybe Mary will yet have a child or two, and she and Geoff will spread out on a big bed with them, reading elaborately illustrated children's books and sleeping in a huddle. After turning twenty-eight, she wore the Vest religiously at home, so as to assure Geoff he hadn't wasted his money. Six weeks went by in that fashion. Then, at her next visit to the CF center, her lung functioning was up from its usual 80 to 85 percent to 102 percent. Her lungs were functioning better than the average person's without CF! Something wild pulsed in her chest. She felt dizzy, infected with a new bacteria called hope. That night, when she went to put on her Vest to watch *Thirtysomething,* she began to cry. Television shows are all about healthy people; a sick person watches them like a tourist or an alien ambassador. Yet Mary felt the invisible wall between herself and the ordinary world crumbling. She was just a woman watching TV with her husband, watching a show about young couples just like them. Geoff had *given* her that—had believed in a vision of her until it came true.

They conceived on her next ovulation.

She switches off the Vest. CNN is still rehashing the developments in the World Trade Center bombing, discussing the trial of the two masterminds. Mary hasn't followed the details of this case, but she remembers four men being put in prison in the early days of her court-ship with Geoff, and it provoking her to tell Geoff, rather stridently, that she wanted to go to Lockerbie to see where everything had hap-pened to Pan Am Flight 103, to Nix. At first he seemed shocked that, for all her travel, she had not already been there. Then he said simply, "I don't think it's a great idea," and Mary was surprised to find that *she* didn't really think it was either and that she was grateful he had said it—grateful he had named this truth so that it would seem less her own cowardice and more as though she were following his recommen-dation to appease him. She didn't write Nix much after that either. Her grieving felt processed at last, her life ready to move forward.

How soon, how unacceptable, to be *stuck* again. Her lungs are still thriving. Her husband is still kind and gorgeous and devoted. Here they are, in a luxurious paradise. *Enough. Enough.*

"I don't think you kept that on long enough, Mar," Geoff says, turning his head in response to the Vest's silence. "Were you timing yourself?" He clicks "off" on the remote control, and her heart abruptly soars.

"Come on," she says. Beneath the Vest, her pubic triangle looks out of place, disconnected from the whole, sexy in a macabre way. "It's our last day—screw the rain, let's go for a walk."

Geoff, though, doesn't stand. According to the patter on their roof, the pelting has slowed to a trickle, but he doesn't even go to the window to investigate. He simply pats the space next to him on the enormous bed, his palm hitting the duvet several times, as if he were calling a dog.

"You don't need to go wandering in the rain getting sick. No trips to the ER to practice your Spanish, okay? Let's just stay here where it's warm and dry. Do you want me to read to you?"

At home, like watching *Thirtysomething* reruns, this is one of their rituals. Already he has read her *The Age of Innocence, Tender Is the Night,* and *The Sun Also Rises,* classics that they both somehow managed never to tackle on their own. At home, this strikes Mary as incredibly romantic. When she mentions it to her mother, Mom all but swoons.

Now she thinks that she may bolt for the door, fling it open, and race outside, still undressed, before he can stop her. If the rain does not touch her face soon, her skin may just harden like plaster and crack in two. The Vest, however, weighs her down. Mary waits and waits, but nothing happens; her face does not crumble or disintegrate, and even now the tears will not come. So finally she merely stands and holds her arms out wide, an actor pantomiming a hug, and waits for Geoff to come undo the contraption and release her.

SOMEHOW IT IS 1997.

Mary and Geoff take the overnight ferry from Tenerife to La Gomera. Because, bizarrely, the last ferry on which Mary set foot was the one that shuttled her and Nix away from Mykonos, she cannot help thinking of that interminable ride. They were *supposed* to be moving onward to the party island of Ios, but at the last second Nix insisted on going back to Athens instead, then would not even consent to find a civilized, urban hotel in which to think things over but bounded straight for the airport to get herself to London and Mary back to the cloister of Ohio. By that point Mary was furious, confused, and weeping, saying irrational things such as that Nix couldn't force her onto a plane and that she would just stay and travel the Greek Isles alone. How little Nix even pretended to believe her threats only added to Mary's frustration.

These memories do not appeal, so Mary spreads a beach mat on
the floor of the La Gomera ferry and reclines on it, hoping the rocking
motion will soon cure her of consciousness. Geoff gazes down at her
from his small seat, which he dwarfs. The smile on his face is half-
aroused, half-paternal. "My Mary," he playfully chides. "You'll still be
lying on floors when you're forty, I bet."

Mary lets her eyes stay closed. "Who's going to be forty?" she says.

DEPENDING ON THE part of the world, on the hospital doing the study, anywhere between 3 and 15 percent of all cystic fibrosis
patients colonize *Burkholderia cepacia,* the most antibiotic resistant of
all the bacteria to which their damaged lungs are susceptible. Though
Geoff swore she was imagining it, Mary *saw* the accusation in her
parents' eyes—even in Laxmi's—as though she had only herself to
blame. Rather than washing her hands after touching any foreign object like a good CF patient, Mary was freshly back from a winter-break
trip to Mexico, where she'd gobbled food from street vendors on New
Year's Eve and frolicked glibly with primitive toilet germs at small
Querétaro cafés. She had all but sent an engraved invitation to the
cepacia syndrome that might now invade and ravage her lungs at any
moment, so that death could blindside her within a matter of weeks,
even *days.*

Even if cepacia syndrome never strikes, the increase in morbidity
associated with the bacterium is clear: everybody knows *B. cepacia*
heralds the beginning of the end. In the larger CF community, Mary
has become an overnight leper. She has to schedule her visits to the
CF center at the end of the day so that the non–*B. cepacia* patients
will not be endangered by her presence. If she had any friends with
CF, she would be told to substitute phone calls for visits. As it is, from
now on when she is hospitalized she will be quarantined from others
with cystic fibrosis, since even those also positive for *B. cepacia* might
have a different strain of the bacterium than she. She will never see
any of her old hospital acquaintances again.

As a white girl from Ohio, Mary has found herself for the first time
part of a minority it is far safer to discriminate against than to include.

What does it matter, she sometimes thinks the reasoning goes, *when the lot of them will be dead almost before they can complain?*

Of course *B. cepacia* is of no threat to the general, healthy population, and Geoff is nothing if not healthy, so Mary is not a leper to *him*. He can go on licking the inside of her mouth, her armpits, her clitoris, her toes, with impunity. When she coughs until her face turns purple, Geoff doesn't need her to cover her mouth. He fetches napkins and Dixie cups, leaves the room only because she is afraid the coughing will bring on an episode of incontinence that will be terminally unsexy, not because her bacteria can actually be terminal *to* him.

"I shouldn't have let you go to Mexico," he said, only hours after the diagnosis. Unlike her parents and Laxmi, Geoff's blame is reserved for himself. "I shouldn't have let you have surgery," he continued. "The biggest risk of infection is in the actual *hospital*." He was referring to a fibroid cyst she'd had removed just before the Mexico trip, because their fertility specialist thought it the culprit in her failing to conceive since the miscarriage. She had only just finished healing from that minor surgery when she and Geoff rushed off to visit Daniel. In his castle, they made love in a different bed every night, making bets about under which canopy their baby might be conceived.

When they came home, Mary's lung functioning and sputum tests had seemed a mere formality. Her FEV values had been out of the park for over a year. Geoff and Laxmi joked that they should write case studies about her: the model CF patient, nearly thirty and healthier than the general population.

Then they got the news.

THEY DISEMBARK ON La Gomera by early morning sunlight. Their plan is to rent a car and drive to the other side of the island, where the guidebook says there is a black sand beach and a little town. The ride over the mountains will take them through a protected laurel tree forest as well as banana plantations. They will dine on La Gomera and return by sunset, to take the ferry back to their resort. "It'll be like stepping inside a Gauguin painting," Geoff promises. "Look how much more quaint this place is than Tenerife, Mar—we should have been coming here all along!"

It is late February, a couple of weeks past their one-year anniversary. On Valentine's Day, Geoff brought home diamond earrings, and Mary's hands trembled as she held the box. She envisioned the square-cut studs in her ears while Geoff stood over her casket, even though she planned to be cremated. She wondered if diamonds could be burned down to ash, or if afterward somebody would merely pluck them out from her remains and give them a wash. "Please," she said in a whisper. "I don't want jewelry. Just take me someplace beautiful, someplace I can remember." Geoff was resistant at first: she needed to *avoid* risks like that now, foreign germs that might attack her immune system. But neither of them had ever been sick in the Canary Islands, and they often talked about how sad it was that all the rain on their honeymoon had prevented them from island hopping, and so, although the little blue earring box remained exactly where Mary had left it, Geoff came home a week later with airline tickets and told her to pack her bags.

At the car rental, Geoff slings an arm around her shoulders. "Let's rent a scooter instead," he says, guiding her to look at them, all lined up, cute and brightly colored and quintessentially European. "It'll be cheaper, and more fun."

Mary shrugs. Okay, a scooter. It's the kind of thing she would normally like—he is probably making the suggestion for her sake. And yet something nips at her heels, a residual haunting from the ferry, a ghost from the waves who may not mean her well, who harbors some malevolent will.

"Cool," she says, and she tries to mean it.

IT TAKES ONLY a minute for Geoff to infer that his plan may not have been a stellar one. He has never driven a scooter before, and it's more difficult than he imagined. Twice, trying to get the thing started, he loses control and sputters right onto the sidewalk and into the wall of a building outside the rental place. Mary yelps, "Maybe we'd better switch to a car," but Geoff brushes her off with, "Don't worry, I'll get the hang of it." Meekly Mary gets on the back. Her helmet is gigantic above her slender neck, lending her an E.T. resemblance. Rigid with determination, Geoff takes off.

This could be our last vacation. Today could be the last time she ever does something this adventurous. This is what the narrative loop in his mind sounds like now.

The roads aren't that bad, considering. Geoff has driven Independence Pass (albeit in a car) to get to Aspen, where his stepfather the hotshot cardiologist has a time-share. *That* is a road to give you nightmares: unpaved, no guardrail, narrow enough for only a single car, the occasional shell of a ruined vehicle below on the rocks. You snake along the whole way, white knuckled, listening to the stones splattering under your tires, never sure if the earth below is where it seems or if suddenly your car will just pitch. You'd better hope you die fast, too, because nobody would find you.

This, despite La Gomera's being the second smallest of the Canary Islands, is a proper highway. Two lanes, smooth pavement, with a civilized guardrail more than solid enough to hold back this piddly scooter should Geoff happen to lose his grip somehow. He's still smarting with embarrassment over Mary's suggestion that they throw in the towel and take a car. He speeds up a little, hoping to demonstrate his increased confidence—he's got this puppy under control now—but Mary's grip on his waist tightens like a vice and she hollers in his ear, "Slow down! Slow down!"

He was going maybe fifty miles per hour, tops: nothing on this highway populated by Europeans. Great. She doesn't trust him. This is a plot twist he hadn't anticipated. The instant he saw the scooters in the shop, he pictured them taking the curves slightly faster than caution might suggest. His wife is a risk junkie, and a scooter seemed a risk he could live with. Mary is no more likely to die on a La Gomera highway than anyone. A scooter isn't going to give her an infection or worsen her FEV values; she's safer on this road than she is using a public restroom. He's tired of hovering over her like an overprotective mother lion. He wanted today to be perfect, exciting. The air is sweet and fragrant with laurel trees. Geoff has never smelled a laurel tree before and is surprised by its intoxicating fragrance. Banana plantations decorate the landscape below.

But what difference does it make? What difference, when the love of his life has colonized the most dreaded bacterium known to CF patients, and he's running into freaking walls and can't get a damn thing right?

MARY'S HEAD THROBS under her heavy black helmet. In the highway's other lane, heading back to the port, tour buses whiz by at an astronomical speed. One skid, and Geoff could send the scooter careering under the wheels of one of those monsters. Violent air whips her scantily clad body, but inside the helmet she feels she might suffocate, trapped, peering at the world through the narrow prism of a camera lens.

She is trapped in Greece, circa 1988.

Nix's terror had been palpable from the backseat, but Mary cannot remember feeling terribly afraid as Zorg hugged the cliff-side turns. She did not think of what it would feel like to be eaten alive by the teeth of the rocks, her head and bones smashed before she hit the sea. No, she was pissed off, with no intention of giving Zorg the satisfaction of begging him to slow down. He had chosen the wrong girl, she remembers thinking, to challenge to a game of chicken. Though he didn't know it, his own stakes were much higher than hers: he had more years to lose than she did. If he wanted to sacrifice himself to the Aegean Sea to teach her a lesson, let him. He would be saving her parents years of pain and hospital bills. He would be saving her from drowning in her own mucus. *Go on*, she thought. *Do it. I dare you.*

She relented only because of Nix. She didn't want her best friend's death on her head. It had been at her insistence that Nix agreed to ride with her in this psycho's car, so she swallowed her pride and let Zorg touch her knee, apologized to him to save Nix's life. Ha-ha, very funny, since it turned out that Nix's life was even cheaper than her own. *Drive faster,* she should have told Zorg. *Get it the fuck over with.*

I dare you.

But she doesn't mean it; maybe she never did. Even now, she wants too badly to live, when one miscalculation by Geoff could put her out of her misery just as surely as Zorg's antics could have nine years ago. They are racing downhill, on the downward slope from the mountain's peak, and soon they will reach their destination. The black sand beach; the oxygen tanks and hospital beds and air hunger that await Mary at the bottom. Those "fifteen seconds" Mary read about in one of the Pan Am Flight 103 reports: that narrow window in which its passengers would have known something was wrong before they exploded into the airless air. Mary *knows* what those seconds were like for Nix because Nix had experienced them already in Zorg's car: an anticipation of death, in that case briefly deferred. When Geoff stops the scooter, she practically throws herself off its vibrating back, wobbles on shaky legs, and collapses under the weight of her helmet, clattering to the ground and blinking up at the too-bright sky.

GOD, THIS ISLAND is a postcard. Geoff feels drunk with beauty, his body heavy and languid. Mary finally settled down on the scooter, and once he could relax and take in the scenery, there were no more episodes of driverly incompetence: he just needed to get a feel for the thing. This little beach is—there's no other word for it—*sexy*. The black sand; the palm trees and tiny *tiendas* across the street; the water a violent blue. It's the antithesis of the white-washed beaches of Playa de las Américas on Tenerife; of the fat Brit tourists wearing socks with their sandals and wide straw hats above their burned, Porky Pig faces. Geoff doesn't see a single tourist on this beach. There's hardly anyone at all except for a few families with running, splashing brown kids. He wishes he'd brought a bottle of wine, but then even that wish evaporates—they can get one across the street somewhere, he's sure. A perfect day after all. He can't smell the laurel tree forest anymore, but already he's looking forward to its drug-like infusion on the ride home. He'll have only a little of the wine, give most of it to Mary, since he has to drive.

They find a patch of beach. Some women on the beach have kept their bathing suit tops on, but Geoff loves how Mary never lets this stop her: if it is legally permissible, she will go topless. Chaise longues litter the rocky black sand, and Mary gets right on one and stretches out, not tentative, not looking around to see if it might belong to someone else or if she has to pay a fee. Her sense of entitlement about such things baffles and bewitches him. She suffers, he has told her, from the disease of not giving a shit. She laughed at that. *Yep,* she said. *It's a secondary disease brought on as a side effect of my primary disease.*

In Geoff's experience, though, that's not quite it. To be fair, he knows far more people with CF than Mary ever has, and yeah, they tend to be different from other pulmonary patients in that they grew up with their condition—they've never known a life without it. Some even seem attached to it, have a sense of pride in the identification and community. This isn't true of Mary, though, since she was diagnosed so late (something he doesn't let himself think about much—all those wasted years when she could have been treated). In fact, *many* of the things that usually plague his patients have never bothered her because of her pancreatic sufficiency. She doesn't have to take enzymes to digest her food, much less face the prospect of feeding tubes. He isn't sure why, though her stellar lung functioning must help, but her fingers, littered with thick, silver rings, show no sign of clubbing.

The truth, Geoff thinks, is that Mary's entitled hedonism seems less a commonality among the *sick* than among smart, pretty, sexy girls—girls who have it all and know it. Sure, he's seen the phenomenon of sick people believing themselves "special" because of their illness, and maybe that is part of it. But here, as she lies with her breasts upturned to the sun, head thrown back and curls spiraling out on the chaise behind her, ultradark sunglasses shielding her eyes, and hipbones rising up slightly from her flat pelvis, one knee bent, it is hard to believe she is anything other than healthy and invincible.

He struggles to imprint this idea in his memory. When he treats her as though she is frail—ministers to her like a doctor or a father—she hates it, chafes against it. He needs to hold on to this, the colder, glittering truth of her, and not let himself fall under the sway of spending every moment enacting a private *Camille*, turning her into a heroine whose sole purpose is to die.

"I'll go to one of the little restaurants," he says, this resolved. "I can get us a picnic lunch and a bottle of wine."

Mary bolts upright, her sunglasses falling askew, and in an instant the image of her carefree brazenness is gone. "Wine?" Panic floods her voice. "You can't drink wine—you have to drive that contraption all the way back to the other side of the island!"

"Don't worry," Geoff says smoothly. "I'll only have one glass. You can get drunk, and I'll take advantage of you on the ferry. We'll find a quiet corner." He chuckles.

"I don't feel like drinking. I'm not hungry either—just sit down. We're not staying here long, right?"

He feels, not for the first time, as if Mary is testing him, though he isn't sure to what end. "But we don't have to take the ferry back for hours," he reminds her, taking a deep breath to keep calm. "It doesn't leave until sunset. What's the hurry? We'll get back to the port in time for dinner and eat at one of those local restaurants on the waterfront. They're more your style than the ones on Tenerife anyway, right?"

Mary just looks worried. Her hands knit together, twisting her rings.

"Come on," Geoff says, and he can't keep the edge out of his voice this time. "You're not still upset about the scooter, are you? You have to admit, I did pretty well in the end, didn't I? Are you going to hold one mistake against me for the rest of our lives?"

"Two," Mary says, as if on autopilot. "You slammed into that building *twice*."

"Jesus!" Two of the pretty Spanish children stare at Geoff in shock, though he has used the English pronunciation. He lowers his voice. "We haven't eaten since dinner last night, Mary—I'm starved and I'm getting us some lunch. If you don't want wine, fine, don't have any, but I'm going to have *one glass*. What's with you today?"

"I don't like winding roads," she says quietly, and though he can't see her eyes through the dark lenses of her sunglasses, he watches tears spill out from under the frames, down her cheeks. "They remind me of Mykonos."

Her words stun him like a punch. He stares, dumbfounded. All this time, he thought she didn't *know*. She has never mentioned it to him, anything about what those guys did to Nix, and Geoff has never brought it up. Not that it's been on his mind all that much. Nix, after all, is dead, no longer living with the ramifications of whatever may have happened at that villa, and he and Mary . . . well, they've had plenty on their own plates, haven't they? Still, in some small way the secret he's held about Nix and that night has weighed on him like a boulder forever in his shirt pocket, creating a barrier between him and Mary. Is it possible that, all this time, she has been carrying it, too.

"You never told me you still think about Mykonos," he begins. "Did you and Nix talk about it much—what happened with Zorg and Titus? After you left Greece, I mean?"

Mary snorts, her hands swiping away under her glasses frames. "Oh, she blamed me," she says hotly. "She thought it was all my fault because I was too weak and too sick. She couldn't wait to run off to London and be with her normal friends, her sophisticated East Coast friends, and leave me by the side of the road, because I was a liability—I wasn't any fun."

Geoff doesn't know what shes means; this doesn't make any sense in his scenario. He tries to fit the puzzle pieces of her words into the picture in his mind, but they just won't click—they seem of an entirely other context. "Wait," he begins, and he moves to Mary's chaise, nudging her legs over with his ass so that he can speak in a lower tone of voice and not startle the children again. "She thought it was your fault because you took a nap, you mean?"

"Nap?" Mary says. "What nap?"

A shiver runs up Geoff's back. *What nap?* She told him that night, when they were moving from bar to bar—she *told* him that she'd taken a nap, which implied that Nix was left alone with Zorg and Titus. In all the years since, while she has never mentioned that incident again, she *has* spoken of Nix, many times. The portrayal she gives is . . . well, of a girl much the way Geoff was perceiving Mary herself only a few moments ago. A brazen, vibrant, slightly lawless girl sure in the power of her own youthful beauty—a seeker who wanted to devour the world. But the Nix Geoff met that night in Mykonos bore no resemblance to that portrait. Mary seems to have been talking about *herself,* whereas the Nix Geoff met barely spoke, jumped at shadows, ran into the surf, not out of any impetus for adventure, but as though trying to outrun a demon—maybe even trying to end her life—so that when Mary told him, all those years later, that Nix had died, his first thought was *suicide,* and thank Christ he didn't say as much, because immediately afterward Mary told him the truth about Lockerbie. He feels suddenly unmoored, dizzy, wishing he had saved this conversation for after he had some food in his stomach, maybe some of the wine for fortitude. Because if Mary never took a nap, is it possible . . . did those assholes hurt his future wife, too, and Geoff let them simply get away with it? He can't decide, in the blinding sun, watching Mary wipe her hidden eyes, whether this hypothesis would explain a lot about Mary or whether it is merely redundant in the face of everything else she has borne. His hands curl into fists.

"Listen," he says, his voice low and angry, though the anger isn't at her, not anymore. "You told me you took a nap. You said you fell asleep at the villa, and Nix was left alone with Zorg and Titus. Did you or did you not tell me that?"

She takes off her glasses and looks at him with transparent confusion. "Yeah," she says, "right. She wasn't alone with them, exactly—I mean, she was *already* with Titus before I went to the guest room. I think she probably fucked him, though we never talked about it. Why are you asking me about that—what, do you think I slept with that psycho Zorg and never told you or something?" She looks away, out toward the children playing, and Geoff sees her focus shifting instantly, the way it always does when she looks at children, the way it always will, now that pregnancy is a risk well outside the boundary of what is possible for her anymore, in their new *B. cepacia* world. He wants to snatch her focus back, but he watches it dissipate, away from Nix, away from him, off in the direction of those small footsteps in the sand. When she looks back at him, she is smiling, but oddly, like a ghost herself.

"I probably *should* have," she says, and it takes him a moment to realize she means that she should have fucked sociopathic Zorg. Geoff has no concept of why she would say such a thing; his entire body flinches at the thought. "Then maybe she'd have known I was capable of helping. Then maybe she wouldn't have sent me away like a useless child. *I'm* the one who snagged you and Irv, aren't I, and got us out of that bar? She never even gave me credit for that. I worshipped her, and she acted like I was nothing."

Then her head turns again, watching a brother and sister chase each other along the shore, some innocent parody of the way she chased Nix on the sand that night at Plati Yialos. This time, Geoff holds his tongue.

THE SUN HIDES behind a cloud. Mary feels an encroaching chill in the air and shivers as she picks up her bag, slips the straps over her shoulders for the ride back to the port. The black volcanic sand looks more ominous than beautiful, biting into her bare feet as she crosses it, so that she has to stop and put on her flip-flops. Geoff waits on the scooter, his square jaw set in a kind of irritation that reminds Mary of the way her mother sometimes looked in the supermarket when Mary was a child and pestered her to buy junk food: as though he knows Mary is going to be difficult and is steeling himself to rise above it. Shamed, she shuffles over to the scooter and gets on.

Geoff revs up. All at once, the scooter shoots forward and knocks into a palm tree, clunking over some island resident's bicycle. Geoff mutters, "Shit, shit!" and kills the motor, gets off, and rights the bike. *Mr. Nice Guy.* Mary would have left the bike lying there. They have bigger problems.

He starts the scooter again, driving shakily upward toward the treacherous cliffs.

Mary's heart pounds in her ears; the sound is deafening, oppressive. It has ceased to be lost on her that what is happening is irrational. Geoff is driving slowly. Teenage kids—illiterate or revved up on hormones—drive these scooters worldwide, whereas her husband is a thirtysomething, Harvard-educated pulmonary specialist, for fuck's sake. Still, her head spins. She hears the echo of complicit male laughter—Titus leaning over and whispering something to Zorg, the deadened slits that were Zorg's eyes suddenly sparking to life as the two begin to laugh. She can hear their chuckling as though their exhaled breath is right there on her shoulder—that shared joke that never fit into any of her scenarios of that day. Not with the revelation of her terminal illness, which Mary has always assumed prompted Zorg to turn gentle, to send her off to bed like a sick child. Later, that moment in the disco when Zorg's hand lingered too long on Nix's knee, yet Titus didn't even flinch. Finally Geoff's voice, all those years ago, at the water's edge of Plati Yialos: *You said you took a nap.*

Mary's hand shoots up, irrespective of her will, desperately pushing the helmet off her head. Coughing, she gasps for breath. The helmet soars behind her, crashes onto the highway, rolling.

Geoff screams, "What the fuck!"

Mary is hacking hard now, clutching his waist. There are tears. Shit. Maybe if he just keeps driving, he will not see them. But no. Of course he will stop the scooter—he is stopping the scooter. Of course he has to get the fucking stupid-ass helmet, just as he had to right that bicycle. Yeah, Mr. Nice Guy—he was never a match for Zorg and Titus, never a match for what happened that day. Mary lets go of his waist, almost loses her balance, clutches the back of the scooter until it comes to a halt, then pushes Geoff's body away from hers futilely. She has started to shake.

Geoff runs after the helmet. It takes him a while—it has rolled pretty far. A bus whizzes by, almost knocking Mary over with its gust. She stands close to the guardrail, sobbing.

"Okay," Geoff says. "Okay, I get it. You don't like the scooter. I will drive very slowly, I promise—I'm sorry, Mar, I'm not trying to scare you. Come on, let's just get back to the other side of the island and return this thing, and then we'll be done with it."

"You think they raped her," Mary accuses, not looking at him.

Geoff steps closer to her, though he holds the helmet like a shield between them. "Yeah. I do."

"You don't understand." She shakes her head. "It's my fault. They were already *planning* it—that's why they sent me to bed. And I just went. I slept for something like two hours, maybe three. I just abandoned her to them."

Geoff sets the helmet very carefully on the scooter's seat, like something breakable and precious. He goes to Mary, his large hands on the sides of her arms, but his touch feels wrong and she jerks away.

"Listen," he says. "Be realistic. What could you have done? You were two girls in an isolated house with men who were older and stronger than you were. You didn't speak the language—you didn't even know where you were. Do you really think you could have stopped those sons of bitches from doing whatever they had a mind to do?"

"I didn't even try! I could have stayed with her, and maybe they would have reconsidered—maybe . . ."

"Do you really believe that? Isn't it more likely that they would just have raped you, too?"

She starts to walk, mindlessly, uphill. Geoff stays rooted on the highway's curb, not following, waiting for her, but she can't bring her body to turn around and reapproach him. Her hands are still trembling, her tears still falling, but something about all this feels wrong, as if she is acting something out, reciting lines that don't belong to her. How is it *possible* that Geoff would know all this time what happened to Nix and she would not? Nothing makes sense. He wasn't there. How could she have slept through the kind of gang-rape scenario he obviously imagines? He didn't even *hear* Titus and Zorg laugh. Mary's legs move numbly, her knees buckling, so that she has to hold on to the guardrail. They were all a little shit-faced—okay, really, really fucking sloshed, from the wine at the restaurant, the barrage of cocktails at the villa. The moment her head hit the blindingly white pillow, Mary was out cold. But was she really so drunk, so deep in slumber, that she wouldn't have heard her best friend scream?

Nix never screamed. On this, Mary would bet her life. But how does this fit into the rest of the scattered truths of that day? How does this reconcile with what Geoff thinks he understands?

He pulls up alongside her, on the scooter, helmet hanging from its handlebars. "Mary," he begs, "please get on."

Nature is in collusion with all manner of trouble. Just as she feared back at the beach when the chilly air teased her arms, a drizzle of rain begins to fall from the sky.

"We have no choice," Geoff begs. "Look at the sky—it's going to storm."

Nix's face on the villa's balcony, set with some kind of blind resolve. *I will get us out of this,* she promised. *Don't do anything,* she warned. Nix, the reckless one, always too brave for her own damn good. But how far could any girl be willing to go? Afterward, Nix was a shell of herself, nothing resembling victorious. What was the line between rape and a premeditated scheme? What was the possibility that *anyone* could so calmly orchestrate and carry out her own annihilation?

And what sense would such a sacrifice make, if both of them were only going to die anyway? What difference all the feelings Mary has had for Geoff, when after everything, love is just nowhere near enough?

"I don't care!" Mary screams at the idling scooter. "Go ahead, leave me here—it doesn't matter!"

Like everything else, Geoff's stare contradicts itself. There is anger, unmistakably, but also confusion, also fear, and she understands in a brief flash of clarity that he, too, has reached the end of some kind of rope. That he is summoning all the calm and generosity he can muster from a place very far away, a place he cannot feel. "Who do you think you're talking to?" he mutters, low. "I'm not going to leave you. If you make me push this scooter all the way down this damn mountain in the middle of a rainstorm and it takes all night, then that's what I'm going to do. But I will not be happy about it, Mary. You can't ask me to be happy about it anymore."

"You think you understand so much," she accuses. "You didn't see Nix in that car, when Zorg was speeding on the cliffs. We really believed we were going to die. She was . . . so afraid."

"But babe," Geoff says, killing the motor, "Nix *didn't* die in that car. Whatever happened at that villa isn't what killed her. She died on an airplane, but you're not afraid to fly. Your best friend died because some militant extremists bombed a plane—because the world is a fucked-up, terrible place, with terrorists and rapists, okay? But you can't help her anymore, Mary. This all happened almost ten years ago. What's done is done."

"Maybe she should have died on that car ride," Mary says icily. "We both should have."

"I'm not going to listen to this."

At the airport in Athens, when Nix pulled away first, Mary thought, *I will never see her again.* All these intervening years, that moment of fear has seemed prophetic, when really it was too late: Nix was already gone.

Cars blur past. Rain pours down.

"Oh, sure!" Mary shouts at Geoff through a rising mist. "Don't listen to anything you don't want to hear! You've been living in a dream world anyway! Like we were going to have babies and ride into the sunset. Like that was *ever* going to happen! You should never have married me."

"Why?" He leaps off the scooter to approach her, then turns abruptly and kicks it so it falls, hard and clean, to the ground. "Jesus, this is ridiculous! You're right here in front of me, aren't you? Nix is the one who's dead—you're not her. She was, like, a *person,* okay? She wasn't just some symbol for your own doomed life. Her death wasn't *about* you! Stop hiding behind her already!"

Mary wraps her arms around herself to keep out the rain. Her hair is damp in her eyes. She glares at Geoff, but she can't even see him for the drops of water, the wet strands. "I wish sometimes," she says, "that you had kissed her that night instead of me. Then every time I tasted you, I'd taste her, too. You think I didn't know something had happened? It was . . ." She sinks to the ground, legs finally surrendering. "It was fucking obvious, even to *you,* and you were nothing but a stranger. From the minute I woke up at the villa and Titus went to get Nix out of that room, she was a ghost already. There was nothing left of the person I'd known. I must've always suspected—but that's not fucking true either. It *never* occurred to me. Still, it was always there. I'd have done anything to bring her back—if I could have given you to her, if I thought that would have made her feel better, I would have."

He pulls her to her feet with a roughness she has never felt in his touch, and she thinks, for one crazy moment, that he will strike her, and finds she is wild with anticipation—that she is eager for the blow. But instead he clutches her to him hard. He holds her, whispering, "Stop it, stop it, don't say anything more."

Her legs, though, will not hold. She and Geoff sink to their knees together in the downpour, red dirt staining their bare skin like paint. Geoff rummages inside his pack, still holding fast to Mary's arm with one hand so that she cannot escape. He roots around until he finds a can of Coca-Cola Light, extracts it, and flips off the top. He tosses the can to the side—Mary is surprised, even amid everything, by his blatant act of littering. Grasping the tab of the can in his fingers tightly, he holds it out to her and slips the oblong opening uncomfortably onto her ring finger.

Can I say "My Dearest Nix"?

You do not fit into the narrative of my life anymore. I am a grown woman with B. cepacia and a husband I love but who wants to keep me in a beautiful cage, and I long for a child even more than I did the night I fled Kenya or the morning Geoff first walked into my hospital room like the answer to all my deepest questions, but there will be no baby now, and that has become an immovable, irrevocable fact. So here I am, trapped inside my own skin, waiting for my body to finish its unromantic assault on itself. But what, suddenly, is this? Everything I have believed about you turns out to be wrong.

He says, "I'm not going to let you do this. If you want to get away from me, you're going to have to get on that scooter and ride it back to town and leave *me* here on the road. Because I'd marry you all over again, and I don't care if you think that makes me an idiot. I accept you for who you are, whether or not you can accept yourself. I don't care if we can't have a baby. I don't care if you die — I, Christ, that's not what I . . ." But he stops. He clings to her hand, pressing its aluminum soda tab into the delicate flesh between her fingers. Under the rain, his eyes are leaking, too. "I know you're going to die," he says, his voice steady. "And I have no regrets."

"You will," she promises. Tourist buses roll past, racing toward the final ferry of the night, unmindful of the storm. "Nix died on me, and look at me now. I'm a mess. I'll go, and I'll ruin everything."

"I don't care," he insists again. "I want to be ruined."

Here is what I have left of you that you never meant to give me. The feel of your foot through the back of my seat in Zorg's car, your will to live overriding my temptation to just lie down and be done with it. A terror of winding roads. The rushing of the ground, coming for me, too. Yet also, the will not to just survive but to live, *rushing hard in my ears like the inexplicable roar of the sea inside a fragile, finite seashell.*

Here is what I have tried to give back to you, best friend, blood sister, fellow adventurer. A vow to keep moving, keep going, as you always told me you were going to.

Soon Mary and Geoff will have to get back on the scooter. At the speed Geoff will drive, they will never make it back in time for the boat. They will spend the night in town, will walk the dark, narrow streets looking for a place nothing like their Tenerife resort. At last they will find a little room, and later that night while her husband sleeps, Mary will finish her letter.

All this time I've viewed your life as some wild freedom jaunt, cut short by random tragedy. But you faced your own isolating hell, a secret that cut you off from me. Everything, from your failure to scream to the fact that you ushered me back to the States without explanation, points at some effort to protect, to keep this ugliness from me. Even your strange letters from London, so curiously devoid of your spark, your soul, make a dark kind of sense now. What can I say? As usual, you succeeded in your aims. All these years, and still I've looked at you the way you wanted me to, with awe and envy and even (lately) disdain. But your life was not a child's, though you died too soon. All this time, you faced a woman's sorrows, no differently than I.

In those months between August and December 1988, you somehow refused to give up or lose sight of beauty. You could easily have run home to the haven of your childhood bedroom, but instead you forged on, beyond Kettering or Skidmore, to London alone. Where does a courage like that come from? How can it be that even now, when I am almost thirty, you are teaching me still, inspiring me? Maybe I conjured you on that ferry, on the winding roads, as a reminder that I cannot just lie down and die either. Whether I have four months or four years, I have to find the strength to make my time count.

Someday it will be here, to the Canary Islands, that Geoff will return alone to scatter Mary's ashes. First, though, long before death, before sleep, before lovemaking and a whispered renewal of vows, Mary and Geoff will simply need to eat. And so they will wander in the rain to find an open door, plunking wet into folding chairs at a small table, the storm still raging outside. Afterward, they will always call it "our little place" because they never learned its name. The food will be nothing special, but they will eat as though famished. They will fill themselves with the sound of water pouring from the sky, the taste of the chicken's crispy skin, the tiles on the floor slippery beneath their shoes, the beating of their hearts in their ears. They will try to remember every last detail as though their lives depend on it.

I hear you, Nix, I hear you always. Urging me on.

Where Are We Going, Where Have We Been?

(GREECE: ZORG)

The first ferry to Ios leaves Mykonos at 6 a.m. This has been their goal. Nix walks with Mary and the two Harvard men through the empty streets until they reach the open port. Mary and the men keep turning to see if they are being followed, but Nix does not turn. Her attention is focused on the small adjustments to her movements she must make — on the way she would normally walk and use her limbs in the absence of pain. Before sleep, she had not yet realized the pain. This, she thinks numbly, is what somebody referring to injured victims of a roadside accident would call shock: *She's still in shock. The shock is wearing off.* She wants to wave her hand to an imaginary waitress and say, *I'll have another order of shock, please.* It is hard not to laugh and never stop; it is hard not to scream and never stop; it is hard to walk. She urinated into the sea last night at Plati Yialos so as not to have to touch herself, but now she has to go again badly.

Sandpapery Greek toilet paper is wadded up inside her underpants to catch the blood. She brought tampons, of course, in her rucksack, but she is aware from some distant place that if she uses them the way she would have to now, she will never be able to use them again. This is what her day has come to: preserving the sanctity of tampons. Mary kisses the good-looking Harvard one good-bye, and the other one waits for Nix's kiss, but Nix pretends that she is alone, that he does not exist.

On the Plati Yialos beach chair, she would have let Irv fuck her right in front of Mary and Geoff if those yowling cats had not materialized. This seems a sick joke now, not entirely possible. Her body is barely a thing that can walk. Yet it had seemed briefly possible that Irv's innocuous dick could be a scouring pad, erasing traces of what was there before. It had seemed briefly logical that one should immediately get back on the horse or one would be doomed.

It had seemed briefly conceivable that she was not already doomed.

There is another ferry, headed for Athens. "We're getting on that one," Nix says. "Forget Ios, we're going back to the airport and getting the fuck out of this country."

Mary begins to protest. Mary says things. Mary talks, gesturing with her hands.

"Look," Nix says, to make Mary stop. "You should never have come. You were a fucking wreck yesterday on that balcony. You're lucky you didn't drop dead from all that albuterol you were shoving down your throat. I should have known better—this is no place for you."

The two Harvard men hang back. They are headed to Athens tomorrow themselves, then to Boston or someplace, though Nix reminds herself that is also entirely possible that they are only real in this context, and after she and Mary leave Mykonos, they will evaporate. At one point Mary says, "This is crazy, you're acting like a total bitch. Fine, you want to go back to Athens, then go, I'll stay with Geoff and Irv and their friends!" and just for an instant Nix feels a spark of life inside her, a fight-or-flight adrenaline injection at the prospect of Mary's remaining on this island with Zorg and Titus, but no, the Geoff one comes over and says, "Look, you two, don't fight. After a night in Athens, things may seem different. You need to stick together."

Nix watches Mary fold her arms across her chest like a betrayed child. She watches Mary storm onto the ferry without giving the Harvard man her address in Kettering, her body rigid with confusion and fury. Once Mary is safely on the ferry to Athens, Nix, too, boards.

NOTE HOW OUT of place they are among the other passengers: locals commuting for business, or families—tourist and Greek—with young children. Other backpackers of their ilk are all still in rented rooms rendered dark by drawn curtains, sleeping off the island merriments of the night before. Wordlessly the girls find a bench in the sun, in their exhaustion mistaking the air for chilly, though already the sun beats down relentless. If they were thinking straight, they would find seats inside, away from the glare, but instead they sit on a white painted bench out in the open, jean jackets clutched around their shoulders, hair piled up in disheveled knots atop their heads, rucksacks on the bench between them so as to have something on which to lean or a barrier to deter each other from sitting too close. The ferry sets off into rocky waves, and still the two are silent.

THE WAVES MAKE Mary's stomach ill. She attempts to hide her nausea from Nix, who is treating her like some combination of a sick baby and a mental patient, thereby rendering any admission of nausea impossible. She reclines farther on her rucksack, the sun beginning to seem oppressive already. Dramamine helps on these ferries, fellow travelers on the way to Mykonos advised them, but she and Nix did not think to take such precautions. Such precautions had seemed for other people then.

The old woman across from Mary prods her with a twisted finger. It is not an unfriendly gesture, yet Mary jerks in alarm. The woman is smiling. She clutches her own stomach in a pantomime of seasickness, then points at Mary, and Mary feels exposed, irritated. The woman sports a babushka on her head, as though this is an amateur high school production of a Greek ferry instead of the *actual* thing, where people ought to know better than to look like such clichés. The babushka woman bears a box of candy and extends it to Mary, still smiling (in the high school production, she would be missing teeth, but in real life her teeth all seem accounted for). She shakes the box of candy a little bit, the way one might a bag of cat treats, and Mary understands instantly that while the woman pities her sour stomach, she nonetheless assumes Mary to be stupid, her intelligence on par with that of a domestic animal at whom shiny or tasty things must be shaken for the animal to understand the connection of such things to itself. For some reason this knowledge makes her want to bury her head in the woman's lap. Instead she surveys the box, stuffed with plump, powdered-sugar-covered candies, and her stomach roils. She has not truly eaten since midday yesterday, when she and Nix feasted on wine and freshly killed fish with Zorg and Titus at the hillside restaurant overlooking their own windswept beach mats below on the sand. She is ravenous and snatches up one of the candies, smiling gratefully at the old woman and nodding vigorously, happy to feign simplemindedness if it will help her score candy and sympathy. She pops the sugared square into her mouth whole and bites down.

It is like chewing a rose-scented, gelatinous bath cube, more disgusting than anything she has ever tasted. Mary's stomach rushes into her throat; her hand covers her mouth. This distress must be glaringly visible, because Nix, hidden behind dark sunglasses, not even facing Mary's direction, says under her breath, "You can't spit it out. She's watching. You have to eat it now."

Slowly Mary chews. The woman's smile tentatively returns; she keeps nodding. Although the cube tastes poisonous, Mary understands that it is *meant* to taste this way—that nothing is wrong other than her own lapse in knowledge, her own assumption that the candy would taste like candy she understands, instead of like the candy of this world in which she's found herself, where none of the usual rules apply. She should have known better, and out of the corner of her eye she sees Nix's shaded gaze on her and realizes this is punishment for something. Though she is still not precisely clear on her crime, she accepts the ruling—Nix's ruling. She swallows the sticky cube in partially chewed lumps, as quickly as she can, but already her stomach is rebelling. The moment that enough of the candy is down her throat so she can speak, she stands, mutters, "Efharisto," to the babushka woman, and dashes from the ferry's front deck toward the rear, where a cluster of passengers stand at a rail watching the hilly white buildings of Mykonos fade until they resemble geometric children's blocks in the distance. Mary leans into the back rail, hoisting her body as far over as it will go without diving into the sea, and pukes all the alcohol and mucus and terror of the past twenty-four hours into the water, a bit scattering at her feet. She wipes her mouth ruthlessly on the sleeve of the Harvard sweatshirt, only at that moment realizing she forgot to return the garment to Geoff, who is already disappearing into the ether of her past. Just six hours ago, she was kissing him at Plati Yialos, his hands beneath the sweatshirt warm on her back, but now he is gone, clearly never to be seen again. She is not a seasoned traveler, yet some of travel's laws are apparent even to her.

The world seems terrifyingly huge. A small speck on the giant blue earth, Mary hugs the rail of the back deck of a rickety ferry to Athens, the other anonymous passengers who once stood nearby having retreated from her.

Something pokes at the skin of her abdomen. Still hunched over the railing, Mary searches with her fingers and plucks several strands of straw out of the fleecy underside of Geoff's sweatshirt: relics of the ride they hitched from Plati Yialos back to Mykonos in the open flatbed of a truck that had reeked of wet sheep's wool. Because Mary does not know what is to come, she flicks the straw away thoughtlessly. After all, who would save a handful of dirty straw as any kind of memento?

Nix STARES UP into the sun, provoking her eyes to water. If her eyes will only water, like a signal, then maybe the tears will come. If tears come, then maybe she will do what she is supposed to and reach out to Mary, tell her everything, spill her guts like some silly child who's skinned her knee as a result of her own recklessness, and accept comfort. The sun bores into Nix's sleepless eyes until she sees spots, but still she feels nothing like crying. Nothing like doing anything except falling under the blanket of waves back at Plati Yialos and never coming out. Why, why did Mary come after her? And Nix, some shadow of a good midwestern girl clinging to her skin, had not wanted to make a scene and cause the men to dive into the water, too, so she swam back to shore, her limbs on automatic pilot. *Pilot*, ha-ha:

All the words that will be loaded now. All the things she will have to fear, now that fear knows where to find her.

She has to be nice to Mary. She cannot punch Mary in the face. She cannot shout at her, not only here on this ferry but anywhere. It is not normal; it is not acceptable. Mary has done nothing wrong. It is Nix's own fault, all of it, her own.

She will put Mary on a plane, back to Ohio, back to her doting parents, back to safety. Mary will never know what really happened at the villa. Some blind, guiding impetus that keeps echoing in Nix's head: *She will never know, she will never know.* People "get over" things. That is how life is. Awful events occur, and somehow time flattens them out, stops the flow of blood, stills the jumping of your skin. Nix did not disappear under the waves, and so this is what will happen, clearly. She will get over it. Everyone knows Mary has no *time* to get over anything. Mary needs to get the fuck home before Nix's mouth begins to leak, before it becomes impossible for the dam of her body to hold back the torrent of truth.

Still she stares at the sun, willing it to swoop down and incinerate her whole, like a moth that dared to get too close to its flame. Can it be just yesterday, on the winding cliffside roads, that she feared for her own life so intensely—that her life *mattered* to her so? But a moth has the gift of wings with which to achieve its own merciful destruction, whereas Nix, wingless, nothing but the weight of her rucksack on her back, is grounded here, all gritted teeth and *calm the fuck down get a grip it is not her fault act normal,* awaiting Mary's return.

ALSO CLINGING TO the ferry's railing, Mary notices a kid— pale haired, mildly sunburned—puking, too. This little girl, who cannot be older than nine, is too small to propel her body far enough over the rails, and so she mainly throws up straight onto the deck, on her own pink shoes, crying. Mary darts her eyes around in alarm: Where are the girl's parents? What kind of world *is* this, where little girls are left to vomit on themselves unattended, holding on tight so as not to be knocked over by the waves? Mary thinks to reach out to the girl—to ask whether she needs help—but all at once she is sobbing, too, huge, phlegmy sobs, her back shaking, the mixture of her body's spasms and the bumpy ferry ride causing her to knock her forehead a couple of times into the rail. What the fuck is the matter with her? What, does she think Zorg and Titus and their posse are going to follow them all the way back to Athens or something? Maybe Nix is right about what a weak basket case she is. Still, she cries violently into her arms for a little while. When she finally composes herself, pulls her head from her sweaty arms, the little girl is gone.

I really know how to clear a deck, she would quip to Nix, if Nix were the same Nix of yesterday, if those old rules still applied.

First she lost her mother, to that look of grief and horror Mom wore on her face for at least a year following her diagnosis. Simultaneously she lost Bobby Kenner, to whom she was apparently never a real person, only the *idea* of a girlfriend, and once she failed to resemble his idea, he was gone. But no, no—even *that* isn't right. Long before her diagnosis, before those losses, there were others. Her original parents, who perhaps suspected the dark genetic secret in her lungs and who may have thrown her away for that reason. Nix is the only one who never flinched, who never viewed her as less. Now her illness has somehow driven Nix away, too, although she does not understand precisely how. What is happening makes no sense.

The bar offers some illusion of clarity. It is not yet 7 a.m., but they are selling beer, as though the ferry itself might serve as an after-party for those tourists, like Mary, who have yet to sleep. Numbly she walks to the concession stand and orders two beers, paying with her last drachma. She opens hers quickly and takes a huge gulp so that her breath will be hoppy rather than sour, should Nix get close enough that their scents might comingle in the old, familiar way. She takes no pains to clean her sandaled feet, which she will blame on the little girl if it comes to that, but walks straight back to where Nix is lying on the brilliantly sunny bench, staring up into the sky. Although Mary is sometimes envious of Nix's straight, smooth hair, right now it looks dank and insubstantial, as though it has failed in fulfilling some animal, evolutionary purpose and left Nix naked and defenseless. Mary cannot see Nix's eyes behind sunglasses but understands she is not asleep. She sits as close to Nix's head as their rucksacks will allow, and holds the can of beer above Nix's face, as if to shield her from the sun.

Nix sits, gingerly, like an arthritic old woman. She takes the can. She begins to chug, as though it were a bottle of water. Mary holds her own beer, and though it does not take a great deal of worldliness to conclude that beer and hunger and vomit and waves do not make good company, she does the same.

They drink. The cans are almost empty. Back home, neither girl cares for beer. The past two years at Skidmore, Nix actually took to carrying a flask (usually vodka, she said, but she liked to mix it up) to parties where only beer would be served—she wrote about this to Mary in her letters. Nix claimed not to care if she seemed pretentious; she had not fled Kettering to be stuck still drinking beer out of plastic cups. She wrote this as though Mary understood, since the maddening nature of Kettering with its myriad shortcomings had always been a favorite topic of theirs. Since Nix left for college, however, Mary rarely attends parties anymore.

It is possible Nix may have enough drachmas to buy two more cans. The beer has pleasantly gone to Mary's head, and she would like to continue this pursuit of oblivion.

"Do you have money?" she asks.

"I'll check," Nix says, but she does not move to do so.

Across from them, the candy woman is speaking Greek, her box of repulsive treats stored away now. In the bright sun, Nix's skin looks translucent; Mary sees thin blue veins along her sharp jaw. Nix's nose is pink. Although nothing in her limp hair, her thin skin, her shiny, sunburned face, her arthritic movements, should add up to beauty, Nix looks luminous, like a wounded, exotic bird. Often enough, Mary has resented the common knowledge (among their peers, even among their mothers) that although the girls look surprisingly alike, given that they are not related, Nix is the "pretty one" of the pair. At times Mary has stared into a mirror, thinking, *She's just a bigger flirt, that's why people think she's so hot,* but suddenly she can see, in the ruins of their day, the raw, elemental beauty that clings to Nix, not like a costume carefully applied, not like some dumb accident of nature, but like a soul. She bites her lip.

"Why are you mad at me?" she asks quietly, as though the Greek people around them would understand or care. "What did I do?"

Still, Nix doesn't look at her. Mary is stuck tracing the map of veins along her jaw.

"There are just two things that are important in life," Nix says, staring out at Athens approaching on the horizon. "You have to be honest with yourself, and you have to be really mellow about harsh things."

Mary gapes at her. In the old world order, she would have demanded, *But what about being honest with* me, *your best friend?* Somehow, though, they have both moved irrevocably outside that old world, and not together. So instead she, too, only looks away, toward the last city where she will ever see her best friend alive.

Red Light

(AMSTERDAM: LEO)

In the mind of a woman for whom no place is home the thought
of an end to all flight is unbearable.
—MILAN KUNDERA, *The Unbearable Lightness of Being*

Only minutes after meeting Leo at Schiphol Airport, Mary sees that
the bohemian lifestyle she abandoned long ago is alive and well, with
her half brother smack in the middle of it. Leo, who is a younger,
even more handsome version of Daniel, is dressed in a pair of leather
pants, Chuck Taylors, and a ratty wool sweater under a clearly expensive blazer Mary would bet her ass is Armani or Prada, rolled up
at the cuffs so the frayed wool of the sweater pokes out. He is, for
God's sake, ridiculously beautiful! His hair is shoulder length and
crazy sexy, and his fingers are long, slender, and graceful. Mary isn't
sure what she expected exactly, but it wasn't *this*. Yes, their shared
father is a wolfishly handsome, sexually charismatic man, but somehow she always imagined her older brother—the product of Daniel's
dysfunctional child rearing—as mildly overweight and nebbishy, like
a character played in a movie by Albert Brooks.

The first thing he says to her is, "I was going to hold up a little sign
that said BECCA BECKER and see if you got it—God, how relieved are
you to have escaped *that* name? Not like Mary *Grace* is any better.

You were fucked either way." Like a singer ruined by smoke and whiskey, he has a laugh that is deeper than his voice. And that fast, Mary
is smitten, crushing on the big brother she never had.

She and Leo could have met easily, dozens of times, during the
years she was in Cincinnati and he in Brooklyn. At the time, though,
the thought appealed to her not at all. She was still adjusting to *Daniel*.
Then just over a year ago, Leo moved to Amsterdam in tandem with
Mary and Geoff's relocation from moderately dull Cincinnati to positively mind-numbing Lebanon, New Hampshire, where Geoff has
joined the pulmonary medicine staff at the Dartmouth-Hitchcock
Medical Center. Wasting away in a town so small that their street was
literally called Rural Route 1, Mary began to feel the pull of Leo's life
in Amsterdam like a Siren's call. What kind of fool fails to visit her
long-lost brother if it means a free stay in Europe?

"I may not have given you two much else, but your hunger to see the
world, that you get from me," Daniel boasted on the phone. "I know
you and Leo will enjoy each other. You have a lot in common."

It seemed a crazy thing to say in reference to one's actual *brother*.

Mary is tipsy from her long flight: her usual combination of wine,
extra hits of albuterol, and the thinner oxygen of air travel. She hasn't
eaten since before boarding in Boston, and her stomach is crawling
with the scraping emptiness of meds and lack of food. Leo lives in the
artsy Jordaan neighborhood, on Keizersgracht, directly across from the
canal and around the corner from a hole-in-the-wall that cranked out
the red-curry tofu on which Mary and Joshua subsisted in the winter
of 1991. That joint—at least where Mary thinks it used to be—seems
gone, the neighborhood gentrified to postcard prettiness. On Leo's
street, everyone's shutters are open, so that you can see into their apart-
ments, which tend to be dimly lit in a soft, gold glow and brimming
with flowers and books. Leo explains this phenomenon as *gezellig*,
which is not translatable into English but means something like cozy
or quaint.

"*Gezellig* is the national pastime," he quips like a jaded native. "Even
the sex shows here are *gezellig*. The people onstage wear Batman capes

and smirk and wave and give these cutesy little shrugs if someone goes soft—it's like a naked cartoon. It's the least sexy thing I've ever seen. Thank God everyone here is tall and gorgeous, or it'd be like living in Munchkinland."

A young blond woman rides by on a battered bicycle, flowers and bread poking from a basket on her handlebars. "See what I mean?" Leo says. "Don't get me wrong, I'm into it—I'm such a poser, I love it really. Everything here is relentlessly pretty and comfortable. But it's oppressive all the same. It's a form of fascism."

Mary blinks. Their father makes frequent, casual references to fascism, too.

Leo's ground-floor apartment opens onto an overgrown garden, and they sit in rusting (*gezellig*) wrought-iron chairs and drink a pitcher of Pimm's, which Leo has made with carbonated lemonade instead of ginger ale, and into which he has sliced apples and oranges like a sangria. Mary eats the apples and oranges from her glass and finds to her astonishment that this works wonders on her hunger. She feels better already, her buzz beginning anew.

Leo is thirty-eight. In the gray daylight, lines crinkle around his eyes. He smokes, offering her a cigarette even though she is certain Daniel will have told him she has CF, but instead of being offended, she relishes the offer like a token of camaraderie above safety. She knows it may be carelessness on Leo's part, or a lack of awareness of what cystic fibrosis even *is,* but still she receives the offer as though he is trusting her to make her own choices, and in that moment she realizes it has been a long time since she has been so trusted—since she has not been treated with kid gloves and supervision. At home she is fairly certain that Geoff has taken to counting her birth control pills to make sure she isn't skipping any; she nearly grabs the cigarette, but she fears she would make a fool of herself by going into a coughing jag. She is entirely drunk already, and it feels magnificent. Leo's untended garden, enclosed by a crumbling stone wall, seems to hum with magic.

She leans forward. "I can't smoke anything with my lungs, but when I lived in London right after college, we made cakes with hash oil so I could finally experience being stoned."

Leo blows his smoke away from her, the way Nix always used to do. "For a long time I wouldn't touch drugs," he says. "I was so afraid I'd turn out like Daniel. He was such a pathetic sack of shit when I was a kid. I'd come home and find him with his face in a plate of food, or OD'd. I was calling nine one one when I was eight, giving them our address, like, every other month. All through high school, I wouldn't touch weed or speed or coke. I was popping Ritalin like candy, mind you!" He laughs, and his Adam's apple bobs in his thin neck just like their father's. "Your mother, Rebecca, was the one who kept telling Daniel I was hyperactive, but he didn't drag me to a doctor until after she was long gone. Then he pretty much diagnosed me to the clinic doctor, and the guy just wrote out the prescription and sent us away. My whole childhood is a fog of Ritalin. I thought it was like magic and it'd keep me safe. Daniel stopped shooting up by the time I started high school, and then he got all psycho vegan and kept trying to take my pills away from me, saying the chemicals would kill me. I went after him once with a knife when he'd hidden them and I couldn't find them anywhere, and he kept saying, *I'm saving you, I'm saving you,* and I stabbed him in the shoulder and then called nine one one again. He told them it was an accident, but after that we just kinda stayed out of each other's way."

Mary does not know what to do with this story. She wants to ask whether Leo still avoids drugs — it seems by the start of his story that he was intending to tell her about how he changed his mind about that — and whether he still takes Ritalin, though she thinks maybe it isn't used on adults. Instead she manages, "When did you move out?"

Leo shrugs. "Dear old Dad took off my senior year of high school — he was living out in Eugene for a while. We had a dirt-cheap apartment in Brooklyn, and I had a job waiting tables, so I just paid the rent until I graduated, then got a scholarship to RISD and declared myself independent. After art school, Daniel and I didn't really talk until I wound up in the hospital half-dead . . . they had to track him down as next of kin. He told you *all* about that, I'm sure."

Mary stays quiet, digesting. It has been a long time since someone has told her so much about himself so quickly; that it is her brother makes it all the stranger, all the more loaded. No, Daniel never mentioned Leo's being sick. She does not talk to her biological father often, but considering that she herself has a life-shortening disease, the fact that Daniel's other child was near death might have organically come up. Clearly he does not have CF, so what can he mean? AIDS? She's ashamed of the thought—just because he is gay? Then she realizes, with further self-recrimination, that the thought of Leo's being ill excites her: it would make them seem like real siblings. Mary puts her arms around her own shoulders. The decrepit stone wall casts a long, chilly shadow. She thinks of Leo's sofabed, her body alone in it later tonight.

"You're shivering," Leo says, standing up. "Did you bring a jacket? I can loan you something. You have great hair." He shoots his arm forward and touches her curls contemplatively. "Perfect for the humid weather in Amsterdam. I fucking hate the cold, but Daniel passed us good hair for rain. The curl's so thick and tight it doesn't even frizz. You don't have to brush it, right? You just leave it, and it always looks good." His hand moves down and touches her nose now, as if he might be if inspecting a sculpture by a fellow artist. "You have our Jewy nose, too. Daniel says you didn't even know you were a member of the tribe until you got his letter. Shit, how could you have missed it with this thing?" He laughs, and his Adam's apple bobs again. Mary's face burns pink.

"So let's go out," he says, jumping to his feet. "Hey"—and it feels almost as though he is interrupting *himself,* he has changed tracks so fast—"I've just been talking about myself on and on. Christ, I hate it when men do that, I hate that about being a man, we're all totally self-important. I'm sorry. I want to hear all about you, too." If Mary is not mistaken, his eyes are full of tears. "I'm just too excited. You're married and all that, and you have your nice square parents in Ohio—Daniel told me all about them. But I don't have anybody, you know? He didn't get *me* any new parents. I never had anybody but him. Until you."

Oh . . . *oh*! Things snap into place so fast Mary blurts out without thinking, "Shit—you mean the *psychiatric* hospital! God, what a relief!"

Leo waves his cigarette. "Oh, sure," he says casually. "I'm an artist. We're all bipolar, right? Hey, my friend's having an opening tonight. We've been sleeping together, but I think he's in love with this other prick who's not even a real fag—want to come and meet him and give me your opinion? You're normal, right? I can trust you."

"I'm not so sure how normal I am," Mary says—and while bipolar may not be quite as good as AIDS, she thinks she can love Leo a little for this, too.

So how can it be that just this morning she was kissing Geoff good-bye at Logan Airport, and now she is here feeling like Alice in Wonderland, the dramatic gallery—high ceiling, huge windows, splashes of vibrant, almost menacing color—enhancing her feeling of surrealism as she trots about arm in arm with a virtual stranger she feels she has known all her life, ridiculously inebriated, dressed in a slinky black dress she does not remember having packed, and surrounded by huge canvases and tall, gorgeous men?

Well, there *are* women at the gallery, too. But Leo's world is a male one, and he introduces Mary to a stream of handsome Dutch art fags, each more fashionable and sexy than the last. Mary's body hums with pleasant, safe arousal. The crowd is mainly Dutch, but they all speak fluent English. Leo's lover is missing. Though it is a group show, all the other artists seem to be there—Mary has met them all. To each, Leo has said, "This is my long-lost sister, Mary. I've just met her today for the first time." Some of the men have squealed when Leo said this, and all have kissed her three times on alternating cheeks, the way Leo greeted Mary when he saw her at the airport, and it took her by surprise, so that when she went to pull away after the first cheek peck, Leo had to almost yank her back to finish the cycle. Now Mary knows to remain in place and peck back, though she keeps getting the starting cheek wrong. The lover's absence from his own show seems to confirm Leo's statement that he is "trouble." Mary finds herself anxious, hoping the man will not appear and wreak some kind of havoc. Leo, she believes (perhaps irrationally—he survived their father, after all), is fragile. Though she is younger by seven years, she feels it her duty to protect him.

"Look over there!" Leo says abruptly. Then, grabbing her arm, he stage-whispers, "No, sweetie, don't really look—he'll see you. There, the guy in the pompous little boho scarf. That's my nemesis!"

Mary glances out of the corner of her eye. She can see the man only from behind, but the scarf is visible because the man has a nearly shaved head. He looks, even from the back, quite Germanic. The stubble of his head is sharp yellow, and he is tall and lanky in an awkward, straight-spined way that differs from Leo's languid grace. If you put a little hat on him, Mary thinks, he would look like a server in a Disney World version of a German restaurant. Though she has not seen his face, she finds it extremely difficult to believe that this gawky, yellow-stubbled man could possibly compete with Leo in any arena. Leo has her tightly around the upper arm and is breathing a fast stream of talk into her ear. "This guy is un-fucking-believable. He's a complete whore, he'll sleep with anyone, even *women*, if it'll get his art anywhere. Pascal"—this is Leo's lover—"claims he's bi-sexual, but what the hell does that mean, bi-fucking-sexual, have you ever known anyone who was truly bisexual?"

Mary has to admit that she has not.

"He's just trying to position himself as the bad boy of the Dutch art world," Leo continues. "He's more serious about his reputation than he is about his art itself. He has all these affairs with gallery owners and collectors, and now that Pascal is up and coming, well, he deigns to fuck him. Before that, he would never have looked at him."

Mary is curious why beautiful Leo would be involved with Pascal if this balding faux German would not even have looked at him, but she does not get a chance to ask. The nemesis turns around, and

Mary inhales sharply, coughs, and drips wine on her mercifully black dress.

It is Sandor.

"Pascal is young," Leo is explaining, "and naive—"

"Jesus Christ," Mary says in an outdoor voice. "I used to live with that guy."

"What?"

But across the room, Mary has caught Sandor's eye. "Sandor," she mouths without sound, and though they are separated by half a room, he sees her, and his eyes go narrow and then, in seconds, wide with surprise. "Oh God," he says. She can hear him from where he stands. "Wow! It's you!" He is striding across the room on his long, skinny legs, and she remembers at once, in his movements, in his face, the secret of his strange charisma.

In a flash, Sandor has her by the arms—one of which was still in Leo's grasp, so Sandor wrested it away as though Leo were not even present—and embraces her American-style, long and hard and without the cheek-bobbing kisses.

"This is my brother," Mary says numbly, gesturing ineffectually in Sandor's arms.

"Your brother! Unbelievable!" Sandor exclaims. "I never thought I would see you again, Nicole!"

Leo actually snatches her arm back, so that her body whirls around. "Who the hell is Nicole?" he demands.

To her surprise, Mary sees not indignation but terror on Leo's face. Then she remembers: When Daniel first contacted her, Eli was so suspicious . . . Now, at Sandor's calling her Nicole, Mary sees in Leo's eyes the fear that he's been *had*—that Mary is not really his sister but some weirdo masquerading as family to scam him for a shadowy but ominous end. Panic welling in her throat, Mary takes Leo's hands. "No," she says, "no. I was lying to *him*—to all the people I knew then—about my name."

"Why would you do that?" Leo asks, still unsure, but before Mary can answer, Sandor slaps Leo on the back. It is a very heterosexual gesture and both Mary and Leo jump a bit in alarm. "Brilliant!" Sandor proclaims. "A double life! Your sister, Leo, she is like the spy with a secret identity. Very glamorous." He laughs aloud.

"We barely knew each other," Mary tells Leo guiltily.

Sandor looks perplexed, as does Leo.

"I thought you lived together," Leo says.

"Well, yes," Mary admits.

"Ah, Leo, my boy," says Sandor, patting Leo's arm less violently now. "Nicole, you see your big brother thinks I was fucking you. He is thinking we lived together in the biblical sense. Your brother does not like me, so this makes him sad. No, Leo, it was not like that! She was fucking some other boy, not me. That one, a very dear boy, very sweet, with him she ran off and joined the circus! It was spectacular." He beams.

"We all lived in the same house," Mary adds, unable to improve on this strange explanation.

"Yes," Sandor concurs. "This very strange house in London, full of very strange people. We all knew each other quite well there, I think. Except we lied all the time, everyone there. We knew nothing about each other. But it was very intimate."

Leo looks horrified. Mary, though, feels tears well up in her eyes.

"Yes," she whispers. "That was it exactly."

"Leo!" Sandor cries out again, and Mary fears her spindly, delicate brother will actually deck him. "Pascal is not here, as you see. Fuck him, yes, let's fuck him and go out for a drink."

Leo sighs petulantly. "I'd rather not," he admits.

"Look," Sandor says. "Come on. Don't be that way. You don't really love that little boy toy, do you? Don't waste your time! I want to catch up with your sister." Sandor gestures widely around the gallery, and abruptly Mary recalls sitting with him and Joshua on the floor of the small, underground kitchen, waiting for the first batch of hash brownies to bake and arguing over whether the Holocaust could have happened in Britain. Joshua, seeing England as a bastion of liberalism compared to his homeland, maintained it could not have, whereas Sandor insisted that all of the European continent suffered from both rabid anti-Semitism and potentially militant nationalism.

In that conversation, Sandor flung his arms around like a mad puppeteer, and Mary—oblivious to her own Jewish blood—grew bored and weary of their stoned, hypothetical debate. She remembers longing not for sleep but for Sandor to finally shut up and make himself scarce so that Joshua could fuck her. In those days, her body ran on the fuel of Joshua's semen; for a time it had truly seemed that, so long as she got laid, neither sleeplessness nor hash fumes nor lack of funds nor illness nor even the clawing grief she carried inside her chest for Nix could touch her.

Abruptly the air inside this cavernous gallery feels thin.

"Fine," Leo consents. "Let's go dance our fucking asses off, then."

"Brilliant!" Sandor hooks one arm through hers and the other through Leo's (he is, Mary realizes, at least as intent on annoying her brother as on "catching up" with an old flatmate). "Let's take her to April, yes, Leo? Who knows, maybe we'll even see our boy Pascal there posing for some other poof. Ah, Nicole, don't you just love Amsterdam?" His arms, locked with hers and Leo's, twitch like small, trapped animals with the apparent desire to gesture again. "Everyone passes through here eventually—even all the Arthog House companions!"

Mary's heart thuds up through her esophagus. "What?" Her voice comes out so weak she clears her throat, tries again. "What do you mean? Has Joshua come back here? Oh my God, Sandor—have you seen him?"

"Oh." Sandor laughs, "No, no, I'm sorry, I don't mean him, the nice musketeer. But you'll never guess who I saw playing the saxophone at this fabulous shitty little bar in the middle of a Sunday afternoon—what, only one, two months ago? That bastard Yankee!"

"Yank?" Now her voice is strong, almost violent. "You saw Yank—playing a sax?—here?"

"Well," Sandor drawls, "I think it was him. I certainly didn't go up and say hello. This guy"—he turns to Leo with a roll of his eyes—"was a piece of shit."

"No," Mary interjects. "He wasn't!" Leo looks at her, and he seems now to be trying to follow the story—to be filling in the missing episodes in his mind so that he can watch the new season unfold. The look on his face as he actually exchanges a conspiratorial glance with Sandor indicates that he assumes they are talking about the man who was Mary's Arthog House lover. Agitation washes over her, and she pushes at Sandor's arm. "He just didn't like you because he thought you were stealing his tapes."

"He thought I was a fag," Sandor intones flatly. "Oops, he was right—I am!" At this, Leo actually laughs. "I should have snuck into his bed sometime," Sandor continues, "and stuck my dick up his ass just so he could stop wondering. Did you ever see that film—Nicole, Leo, you're Americans, you must know it—*Deliver Us,* something like that? *Squeal like a pig*—that one. Can't you just see Yankee squealing!" Now Sandor and Leo are both cackling, and at last Sandor shrugs. "Except, well, he was big—skinny, but very tall—and mean, like, you know, Leo, like the cowboys. He was like a real cowboy, ridiculous but mean. He was like, *Punk, make my day*—like that badass Clint Eastwood, not the fat little squeal like a pig actor. Plus, probably he would have given me a social disease. He was a junkie, wasn't he?" He looks to Mary for verification.

"Take me to that bar," she says. "Let's go there now, for our drink." She knows she sounds deranged. "Maybe we can find him—it'll be a real Arthog House reunion."

"Oh, that place is too far," Sandor says, shrugging. "We can't go there now. Who knows if they're even open?"

Desperation wells in Mary's chest. It seems preposterous that a place with live music on a Sunday afternoon would not be open during typical bar hours. But already Leo's eyes are glazing. He no longer cares about the Clint Eastwood junkie and whether he was Mary's lover. Mary notices that Sandor's arm is still linked through Leo's even though she herself has disengaged. Her emotions feel runny and nonsensical, her needs impossible to articulate. She tries to remember the last time she ate.

"Let's go to April," Leo says. "You're here without your husband, so we might as well take you somewhere your husband would never, ever go." He and Sandor both chuckle. Mary surmises that April must be a gay bar, glamorous and decadent. Half an hour ago, nothing would

have pleased her more than to continue this illusion of walking on the
illicit side, surrounded by steamy men. Now, though. Sandor is steering them toward the door. Outside, the breeze is chillier than it should
be, and Mary longs for New Hampshire, where the seasons know what
they are supposed to be, and you are not cold and wet all the fucking
time, and for reasons she cannot pin down, even to herself, Sandor has
already come to seem a consolation prize.

It seems like every letter I begin to you lately starts, "I'm sorry it's
been so long since I've written." As though I believe you can even hear
me — as though I believe you would care if you could. Probably it's safe
to say that, if the dead could think, you'd have other things on your
mind. Nix, I would never have described my old feelings about you as
"clean" or "easy," but looking back, they seem that way. I remember my
survivor guilt, that sense that I was the one who should have died so
that you could continue your healthy, indomitable life. Now, instead,
there have been nights of tossing and turning, imagining what two
men might find to do with one girl for nearly three hours in an isolated
villa . . . and finding that my female body can imagine it all too well,
as though I carry an unwitting genetic knowledge of what it is to be
violated. Instead, there is awe and confusion about your silence, both
as it was happening and later: Would you ever have told me? Did you
simply run off to London and "forget" it — is anybody on earth really
that strong? Instead, there are nights I pore over the four letters you
sent me during your semester abroad, looking for traces of trauma, but
I find only the implacable distance that had sprung up between us in
Mykonos. Now, I find myself feeling guilty not only for living, but for
failing to save you, for remaining un-raped, for my pretty life in New
Hampshire with the same man who once carried your body across the
sand, away from those screaming cats. I find myself more inspired than
ever by your bravery, yet more than ever, too, ashamed of my fear.

For Kenneth, there has been no consolation, no prize.
Across town, in the doorway of a fourth-floor walk-up, he stands with
his lover's wrist grasped too tightly in his fist as she berates him.

"Sukkel!" Agnes shouts, trying to jerk her arm back. "Watje!"

"Fine," Kenneth says. "I'm a pussy—I'm a whatever the fuck you just said. Come back inside." He knows he's holding her too tight and loosens his grip to take her sleeve instead, but like most of her clothes, Agnes's sleeve is purposely frayed, and the strips slide through his fingers loosely, a few breaking off as she yanks back—he can hear the cheap fabric ripping. She stands a foot away from him in the hallway, hip jutting out like a chicken bone, a taunting look on her face.

Then, all at once her mouth grows serious. She shrugs, looks at him pleadingly. "Baby," she begs. "Kom met mij."

"Fuck off," Kenneth says, turning his back to the doorway. "Uitgewoonde heroinehoer."

"It know one to take one!" Agnes retorts, and Kenneth gives up, heads through the kitchen into the rest of the apartment, where he can no longer see her. *It know one to take one.* Yeah, that about sums up their whole fucking relationship, doesn't it? Nothing more to say.

From the window, he watches her emerge onto the street: a bony figure clad in black, skin so pale she's almost indistinguishable from the washed-out white gray of the buildings across the street. Later, when she gets home, she'll be high, but it's impossible to say whether that'll make things better or worse. He can hardly tell the difference anymore; her brain is going, so that she always seems twitchy and dangerous and a little stupid in a way he used to find sexy but now finds increasingly frustrating.

Ruined beauty, that's his specialty. He is forty-five years old and exhausted by ruin.

He's been clean for seven months.

Pussy, she called him. *Wimp.* He's not a man to her, clean. His needles were the phalluses she craved. His cock's in way better shape clean, but that doesn't even factor. She'd rather run off with her girlfriends to some club and shoot up in the toilet, zoning out like the zombies in *Night of the Living Dead.* Then, once she's run back to the toilet to puke, she'll come out looking horny and fine, dancing wild, and making all the men who see her crazy with desire, because

Agnes has something raw and lit in her when she's just the perfect degree of high — has it even now that her looks are going to seed. Used to be that coke was her thing at clubs, but now she's all about the H; she can't get enough.

She has him to thank for that.

He should have run out on her before he kicked it himself. Then she wouldn't be his responsibility; you can't blame one junkie for walking out on another. Now he's stuck. He came out of the blissful cocoon of his own addiction to find her living in his apartment, spending his money, smoking his cigarettes, crashing in his bed, and refusing to put out. Fuck it. Agnes doesn't need him. She got herself all the way from some backwater Czech town to A'dam on her own, survived picking up tricks illegally on the street before getting taken in by a bordello; then all on her own she left that life behind and got a real job waiting tables, even dancing at RoXY's dyke-themed night, "Pussy Lounge," for extra cash, a gig any hot girl would covet. She was something then, beating out all those trendy wannabes. Lately, though, RoXY won't have her with her protruding ribs and bruises. Kenneth's not sure even a bordello would take her, or whether she'd end up back on the street should he walk. He'll give this to Amsterdam: when you put the governmental stamp of approval on whoredom, you get a better class of dames. In some cities, a desperate bitch like Agnes might be the best you could get, but here you can have your cock sucked by a gorgeous, multilingual, twenty-one-year-old Dutch college girl and sip champagne while you're at it, all aboveboard. Agnes's non-English-speaking junkie ass need not apply.

And now he's all she has. He shouldn't have let her leave, should have kept her here with him even if it meant he had to knock her down. He should have, but he wanted a break from her. He permits himself to fantasize: Maybe she'll meet some kid at the club, run off with him. Maybe she'll become Someone Else's Problem and he'll be free.

He's not tending bar tonight, so what to do with himself until Agnes gets back (because fuck it, he knows she'll come home). This is what he misses most about H: when the needle was his mistress, he never had to wonder how to kill time. Now, days and nights stretch out before him in want of some kind of productive activity. He's been in Holland now for more than five years, since the *last* time he kicked H and found himself with a Dutch wife as a means of killing all this extra, no-drug-taking time — thank Christ she never had kids, at least. He knows better than to believe he'll never touch a needle again. Once a junkie, always a junkie. But he's on hiatus, at least, and this time — though he's afraid to dwell on this too much — he just doesn't crave it like he used to, no matter how long he went clean before.

This time, he seemed to just wake up one day, Agnes naked next to him with a busted lip he didn't remember (did she fall — were they in some kind of accident? — or did he do it himself?), and he felt done. The H seemed like a burden, the way going to work for his father had been a burden in the years after Will died and he was promoted into Will's position. He felt like getting high was what he was *supposed* to be doing, but he just wanted, more than anything else, to play hooky: to not heat up the spoon, not tie off his arm. He wanted more sleep. He stayed in bed all day, and even after he started feeling sick, sweating and shaking, and knew the H was there in the apartment, he couldn't work up a taste for it. The sickness felt good somehow. He started drinking to help with the withdrawal, as Agnes sat on the corner of the bed, her long legs drawn to her chest like a sylph's, lecturing him on how bad the booze was for him. He threw the bottle of Famous Grouse at her and ordered her to take his stash and get it out of the house, give it the fuck away, for all he cared.

He should have told her to leave with it.

The night stretches out before him. He's avoiding friends who use, which has him tending bar at a touristy Irish pub. *Another Saturday night and I ain't got nobody. I got no money 'cause I just got laid.* He remembers Will singing that, parodying the new Cat Stevens version, probably two, three months before Will put a bullet in his brain. Kenneth switches on the TV. On CNN they're still yammering about Clinton's being cited for contempt of court — they'll never finish persecuting that poor bastard even now that he's been acquitted. That damn blue dress with his jism on it will probably hang in a museum someday with a white laundry pen circling the spot where he shot his wad. Jesus. Kenneth rolls another cigarette, sprinkles a little hash in it even though he's been telling himself he won't, lights up, and listens to the English of the newscasters until the words blend together and sound foreign to him, until nothing makes any sense.

WHEN THEY FINALLY do make it to Café de Engelbewaarder, on Sunday afternoon, Mary, Leo, and Sandor find it in full swing on their arrival. Immediately Mary is frightened for her lungs. The place is a cloud of smoke; she can even smell hash, the odor drifting in from the back of the bar. Yank is nowhere to be seen, certainly not on the stage playing the sax. However, the place is so packed that he *could* be here, somewhere in the back maybe or in the throng by the bar. She, Leo, and Sandor enter the smoky haven, Mary tucking her face a bit into her brother's arm as if to breathe air filtered through his skin. She will be able to stay here only so long before she starts hacking, so she'd better make it good while it lasts.

It's the kind of bar she hasn't experienced since she was last in Europe, with Joshua. Packed with a predominantly male crowd, full of aging hippies dressed in faded tones of black and gray, everybody smoking, drinking Duvel and small glasses of whiskey. Most of the men have long hair; the women wear fringy scarves wrapped around their necks. These kinds of people annoy Geoff. He thinks they're putting on a show with their shabbiness—trying to indict others as bourgeois pigs if they deign to take a shower and comb their hair. Mary doesn't agree, but that doesn't mean she fits in. Her engagement ring alone set Geoff back 10K, plus she's carrying a Kate Spade tote. She looks like a freaking yuppie or, worse, a doctor's wife: exactly what she is.

But the music! Well, Geoff would approve of the music. Cacophonous and wild, a jam session of roving musicians is in full swing at the front of the room. She, Leo, and Sandor stand where they can watch the rotating musicians; maybe Yank will materialize out of the crowd. Maybe any moment, the front door will burst open, letting in shards of light that make everyone wince, and there he will be.

Sandor goes to order drinks. Mary asks for bourbon as though for luck. She and Geoff always drink wine. However, she feels for the second time in her life as though she is going by an alias—as though she has slipped into someone else's skin. In the course of twenty-four hours she has transformed from a bored New England schoolteacher to a kind of madcap Euro detective accompanied by two faithful sidekicks, roaming Amsterdam looking for the Man Formerly Known as Yank. On the day of her bleed, he *told* her his real name; she remembers the moment but not the actual words, which she never used or heard again. She imagines Sandor asking the bartender in Dutch if he knows of a man called Yank and the bartender laughing in his face.

Which is exactly what happens two hours later, after the musicians have gone home or are clustered in the back and Mary is starting to cough but doesn't want to leave. The bartender (a) snickers and (b) indicates that he doesn't know anyone by that moniker, not in any language.

Mary does not wish to take no for an answer, so they take seats at the bar and Sandor continues to speak to the bartender in Dutch, describing the time when he saw the mystery man in question playing the saxophone. This doesn't ring a bell with the bartender, who adds that, as they've just witnessed, De Engelbewaarder sometimes gets more than twenty musicians jamming together on Sunday afternoons, and clearly he cannot know them all, but that the girl they saw is the usual saxophonist and not—the bartender winks—easy to forget. Mary would like to leave right then, go take gulps of fresh air outside, but Leo and Sandor have ordered more drinks, so she has to sit and sip her third bourbon and pretend not to be impatient. Sandor and Leo converse with the bartender in rapid Dutch, after a while forgetting to translate what is being said. Leo's mastery of the language is impressive. Mary pushes her glass away, but instead of leaving, Leo enthusiastically begins drinking it himself.

All at once, the bartender slams his hand on the bar so loudly they all jump, and Leo gives a squeal of alarm. The bartender, though, is smiling. He says something else in Dutch, and Mary catches only the word "jam." Then, not waiting to be translated, the bartender mimes wildly for Mary the actions of tending bar.

"He says," Sandor explains, "that he just realized we are talking about the old bartender. He's not a musician. Just sometimes he would play for fun, on Sundays, with the others in the jam session, when the girl was busy." Sandor says "jam session" as though it is in ironic quotes.

"The thing is," Sandor continues, pantomiming a discouraged look as if to forewarn Mary that the news is not good—Mary thinks, suddenly, that he will tell her the "old bartender" is dead—"he says this man now works at an Irish pub. And I know for a fact that Irish pubs here in Amsterdam, they always hire people from Ireland, with the Irish accent. Maybe they hire some Brit and think the Dutch people don't know the difference. But they *don't* hire the tall cowboy with the Yankee accent, that much I promise you. So I'm thinking this is not our man."

"He doesn't have a Yankee accent," Mary explains. "He has a southern accent. In America, a Yank is a northerner. The nickname never even made any sense."

Sandor looks at Leo and shrugs as if to say, *They all look alike.* She is not sure who "they" would constitute. She is also not sure why her body has clenched up, tight and alert and suddenly ready for action, at this new clue.

"ALL I CAN say," Leo announces the next day as they peruse a phone book looking for names of Irish pubs, "is that either this asshole better owe you money, or you had better desperately want to fuck him, because otherwise why are we working so hard to find him?"

Mary blushes. It is abundantly clear that committing adultery would not exactly shock either Sandor or Leo; still, she feels exposed and foolish.

"We never slept together," she explains to her brother. "We were just friends. But he did me a favor once . . ." She pauses.

What did Yank *do*, really? Wouldn't anyone—barring the part about leaving her in the flat alone so he could run out and score—

have done the same for a sick girl far from home? Yet the connection forged between them that night felt important, intense. Still, what possible bond could offer a rationale for a married woman's tracking down an aging, homophobic junkie? Wanting to "fuck" him surely does not quite cover it. What would Geoff say if he could see her jotting pub names and addresses in her Nix notebook, directly beneath the messily scrawled sentence, *What does it mean to heal?* This is crazy. Memory stirs, and Mary wonders for a moment what the elusive Hasnain, Nix's boyfriend, is doing now—if he is still in London after all these years, and if *he* is the one she should be trying to find. But no: she was chasing someone else's memories back then—the memories of the dead. Her search for Yank may be futile, it may be immoral even, but it is her own.

Inexplicable things are happening around her. Friday, when she arrived, Leo was in love with a younger man named Pascal and hated Sandor for trying to steal the boy's affections. But if Mary is not mistaken, Leo and Sandor slept together last night, after they returned from an elaborate *rijsttafel* at a hole-in-the-wall Indonesian joint, and Leo and Sandor sat up gossiping about their mutual art friends until Mary gave in to her exhaustion and trudged to Leo's bedroom to do a PT. Her Vest is at home, so she had to use her Flutter device, and halfway through she lost all energy and tossed the thing across the room into her open suitcase, passing out in Leo's bed, believing she would wake with him beside her. They have been sleeping side by side since her arrival, like children on a sleepover, making up for lost sibling time, and the intimacy of it has been delicious and touching, her favorite part of the trip. Yet when she rose this morning, Leo had unfurled the sofa bed and he and Sandor were still asleep. She couldn't swear to what was hidden by the bedding, but both men were naked from the waist up, and Sandor had a tattooed arm slung over Leo's darker, frailer torso. She scurried back to Leo's bed in titillated alarm, rising only when she smelled coffee, to find Sandor sitting on the (now folded) couch in his outfit from last night, Leo impeccably dressed in fresh jeans and a button-down blue linen shirt, feet bare and hair still wild.

All day now, she has been watching her brother and Sandor, looking for clues. If anything, Sandor seems more intent than ever on annoying Leo, suggesting they should call Pascal and see if he's in the mood for Irish whiskey, since their plans clearly include a pub crawl. He even continues to call Mary "Nicole," though Leo has asked him three times to cut it out. Sandor's tormenting of her brother has a crackling sexual energy to it, intimate enough to make Mary feel like an intruder.

There are about half a dozen Irish pubs in Amsterdam. Leo is not familiar with any of them. Mary has already gathered that her brother has an almost unfathomably poor sense of direction and faulty visual memory, which seem to her odd traits in a visual artist. Sandor, however, knows of several and says that Mulligan's is the only "tolerable" one of the lot, so, hoping for the best, they head there first. They have been drinking all day again at Leo's, and Leo and Sandor have been smoking cigarettes and hash. Mary's lungs feel as though they've been scraped along a gravelly parking lot and hung up in the sun to burn. She did her (only third of the trip) PT in Leo's bedroom while he and Sandor continued their banter and smokefest in the living room, but it helped even less than last night's.

The wet air outside enters her throat like a cold knife with each inhale, then turns heavy and warm the moment Sandor throws back the door of Mulligan's. A man and a woman are, inconceivably, playing spoons for a boisterous, approving crowd. Sandor and Leo immediately start elbowing each another and affecting brogues. Mary's eyes, though, dart straight for the bar.

It cannot be this easy. It cannot be, but it is. The world is small. When Geoff's parents, now divorced far longer than they were ever married, were in Venice on their honeymoon, they ran into four separate people they knew from home. These encounters were so strange to them that Venice became forever infused with a kind of magic in their memories, as though everything that happened there was larger than life; they even returned to Venice for a "second honeymoon" when trying to revive their marriage, although this time they saw no acquaintances and succeeded only in realizing that they, too, had become strangers.

As for Mary, her "Venice" was the Cincinnati hospital room, five years ago, into which Geoff walked, sealing their romance with a sense of fate. Now, however, small-world coincidences seem to be occurring in such rapid succession that she's unsure what meaning to take away. Just Friday night at the Jordaan gallery, there was Sandor, whom she had never expected to see again, and now the same thing is happening again, albeit this time at her orchestration. Was this *all* predestined, the way it felt with Geoff, or is life mere chaos, bodies thrown together, flung apart, then colliding again at random? To say that the world no longer feels real, feels *smaller than life* in the largest possible way, would not be an overstatement.

She walks toward the bar. She was afraid she would not recognize Yank, but now that she sees him, she realizes how impossible this would have been. Sometimes—in airports, mostly—she has wondered whether travelers from her past have walked right by her and she has failed to notice, ravaged as they have all been by time. Yank, though, had an old quality to him even when she knew him at thirty-five or thirty-six. He had a ridden-hard-and-put-away-wet vibe that made him seem a haggard, dangerous old man, though in retrospect she realizes he was still quite young. He was strikingly attractive then, in the spooky, half-dead way of an outlaw on the lam. She still has photographs of him, too, of course. In most, he is reading or looking elsewhere—like many photographers, he did not like having his picture taken. But in one, he looks straight at the camera, and in it Mary was able to capture the ghostly, haunted quality of his dark blue eyes. From the distance, as she approaches him tonight, his eyes seem the same these nine years later. His hair has gone from mostly brown to entirely gray, but there was enough gray in it back then that they all ribbed him about it. His body is still rangy-skinny, but as she comes closer, Mary can see that he moves with a stiffness she doesn't recognize, as though he is aggravating some injury with his motions behind the bar. When she's close enough to speak to him, two women cut in front of her and begin ordering drinks in Dutch, and Yank wordlessly goes to pour. Mary notices Leo and Sandor behind her now, Sandor starting in with, "Squeal like a pig!"

and Leo breaking into peals of inebriated laughter. The women ordering drinks move aside.

Mary is right in front of Yank now. He catches her eye and waits for
her order. She scans his face, smiles tightly, waits for the recognition
Sandor exhibited, the sound of her own former alias, "Nicole!" from
his lips, for he called her that to the end despite knowing otherwise.
Instead, when she fails to speak, he asks her a question; the words
seem hazy, and only once the buzzing in her ears stops does she realize
he is speaking Dutch. "What can I get you, darlin'?" he says, on her silence. Mary can hear English spoken, mainly in Irish accents, around
Mulligan's, and he has apparently inferred that she, too, is Irish.

He does not recognize her at all.

Sandor steps forward and stands face-to-face with Yank, equally
tall. Yank looks at him just as impassively, as cluelessly, still waiting for
their orders. For a moment, Mary fears he will give up and turn away.

"It's really you," Sandor says in English.

"Oh," Yank says back, "yeah, it's me. Hey, buddy. I thought I'd seen
you around here and there. You're like the portrait of Dorian goddamn
Gray—you ain't aged a bit."

Sandor doesn't smile, but he seems mildly disarmed. He glances
at Mary, whose body is burning with an angry heat. How can this
be happening, right in front of Sandor—in front of her own brother?
She has led them on what seemed like an impossible mission, only to
catch their prey more easily than she could have imagined, and now he
remembers Sandor—Sandor, whom he couldn't stand—and not her.

"Look, buddy," Sandor says, his voice dripping with vitriol. "Don't
you remember Nicole?"

Her first impulse is to run—to duck and crawl along the floor of the
bar until she is out of the range of his gaze. Instead she stands rooted
while Yank's eyes move abruptly in her direction, scanning her up and
down. The motion is lazy and indifferent, and it occurs to her that he
may not only fail to recognize her but fail to remember the existence
of a Nicole at all—that she may have made not even a ripple of impact on him. While she has stared after hippie travelers even when on

romantic getaways with Geoff, hungering for what Yank represented to her—a lost tribe of drifters living outside conventional law, even the law of her own body—their brief time together at Arthog House meant *nothing* to him. And why should it, really? The truth of their shared past clicks into place in the instant it takes his eyes to take her in: He was not her lover. He was close to Joshua, but even Joshua was something of a little brother figure, not an equal exactly, perhaps not even a "friend." This is a man who was wanted for murder! What impact could she honestly have expected to make on a man like that?

"I figured," he says after a moment, his eyes still revealing nothing, "you'd be long dead by now."

Instantly something in her body is released. Not happiness exactly, not vindication, but some distant cousin of these. Something messier that she is suddenly unsure why she ever wanted to touch—something she fears.

"Right back at you," she says.

He smiles. In the smile, something old is transmitted between them. Or does she only imagine this? No matter: her realization of a moment before—the truth that their lives have been entirely disparate—is gone before she can even remember it.

The bar is loud, exploding with the incongruous sounds of spoon playing and laughter, with nothing that matches the silent thudding in Mary's body. The man in front of her does not ask any of the questions she anticipated. He does not ask whether she and Sandor have somehow kept in touch all this time. He does not ask what she is doing in Amsterdam. He does not ask if they knew he'd be here or have run into him by accident. He does not ask, even, if she is married, if she is a *mother*. He keeps looking at her. Sandor says to Yank's silent smile, "Ah, I remember it well—all the stimulating conversation of Arthog House." His voice is ironic, yet the joke falls flat. If the conversation at Arthog House perhaps mirrored conversations of nomads all over the world, riddled with tales of stoned misadventures and pseudophilosophical clichés . . . well, maybe it did, but it was stimulating to them at the time, and they all know this.

"Sit down," Yank says to Mary, ignoring Sandor. He pulls out a bottle of Southern Comfort. Mary has not tasted Southern Comfort in nine years. He pours one for Sandor and passes it to him, then one for Leo, who says, "This stuff is crap—this stuff is like cough syrup," then one for himself, and finally one for Mary, which he passes to her slowly. "To life," he says, and Sandor says, "To old times," and Mary says simply, "Proost," strangely determined to avoid nostalgia. They are in Amsterdam; it is 1999. They are not dead, not ghosts, not living in the past. There is now; there is even a future, maybe, both she and Yank having already defied overwhelming odds. Here they are, and what they will do about it is up to their bodies and the liquor and the night. She intones her Dutch toast, and they all three, without waiting for Leo, slam back their Southern Comforts in unison, while Leo takes a dainty sip of his and passes it over to Sandor, saying, "Jesus Christ, I can't possibly drink this, help me, please."

It could easily end here. The warmth of the shot in their bellies, then a hug, a chaste kiss, kiss, kiss, on alternating cheeks (like all good nomads, "When in Rome" would be their credo), a *good to see you again.* Then off, back into the cold knife air and her brother's apartment, back on the plane in two days, back to the normal life she has painstakingly forged, back to Geoff. If there were ever a moment to stand up and leave, this would be it.

Instead she leans over a little, close enough to smell the boozy, wet-rag aroma of the area behind the bar, no doubt permeating Yank's already less-than-clean clothes. "So," she says, "you're pretty old by now—did you ever get married?" She does not ask about kids. She doesn't want to be asked in turn.

"Yep, I was married again," he says. "Dutch girl, that's why I'm here. Not for long, though. I live with someone now."

Mary persists: "How long have you lived with your girlfriend?"

At this, he looks confused. "I'm not sure," he says. "Maybe six, eight months. She's not my girlfriend exactly. Neither one of us can speak Dutch better than a six-year-old, and she can't speak English either, so the communication's pretty limited." He looks at her so straight-on that Mary suddenly becomes aware that Leo and even Sandor have started to look elsewhere. "She's real fine, but she's had some serious shit go down in her life," he says low, "so she doesn't like to fuck. We help each other out in other ways."

For reasons clearly inappropriate, Mary feels enormous relief.

"So you and this *fine* woman can't talk and you can't have sex. What do you do, just do drugs together?"

Yank eyes her with a kind of overt disappointment. "Ten years is a long time, sweetheart," he says, but Mary isn't sure whether by this he means he no longer uses, or whether the lapse in time since they last saw each other disqualifies her from asking such personal questions. "And I didn't say we can't have sex," he clarifies. "I said she doesn't care for it. I implied it was an *infrequent activity*. Now, in my old age, I actually kinda dig it if the woman wants to be there. Funny thing, I don't remember caring about that much in my youth. Middle age takes all the fun out of everything—don't worry, you ain't gonna be missing much."

A cold shiver runs down Mary's back, right in the middle of the hot, crowded bar. In the fourteen years since her diagnosis, every single person she has ever spoken with, even Laxmi Narayan, has acted as though it is somehow possible that she will live to ripe old age. In all that time, no one has ever spoken of her imminent death unless she badgered him (usually Geoff) into it, and then the topic has been broached in a state of high drama and afterward never spoken of again. This drifter is certainly not up to date on the latest cystic fibrosis treatments; for all she knows, he does not even remember the name of her disease. Yet he speaks as though Death is simply a friend of his whose approaching shadow he recognizes on her face. No one has *ever* casually remarked on the ticking time bomb in her lungs as though it were merely a given, not worth getting worked up about—perhaps even a relief.

Kenneth, she remembers abruptly. Yank's given name. It does not suit him.

And she wants to kiss him, this namer of her death.

It would be fair to say she has never wanted to kiss anyone so badly.

THE CLOCK NEXT to the sofa says 3:49. Leo gingerly lifts Sandor's arm and slides out from under it; the motion is familiar, one he has been engaging in for two decades now—he has it down to an art. Most men fall asleep so easily, such a careless surrender, but to Leo, sleep has always been an elusive beast, threatening and seductive at once, a monster he has alternately hunted and been hunted by in return. Under the thin sheet, Leo is naked, which makes sleep come none the easier. Like his father, he is usually cold, and when alone he sleeps in sweat pants and a fleece sweatshirt, sometimes two pairs of socks. Long ago, though, he began staying naked for his lovers. They enjoy it, and there is so much Leo feels unable to give, unable to summon within himself, that he tries not to skimp on the easy things.

Barefoot and still nude, he pads down the hall to his bedroom. He feels the need to check on Mary. It is less that he fears she has died in the night (though as with an infant, he fears this may be possible: that he may open his bedroom door to find her simply not breathing anymore) and more that she may have been gripped by insanity and escaped, scaled the garden wall, and run the streets to find that man, Kenneth, who means something to her, and who Leo can tell is dangerous. The entire night, waiting for Mulligan's to close, Leo worried that Mary would not come home with him and Sandor, that she would stay with Kenneth and become lost to him—lost to her husband and her decent life, all *because* of him, because of having come to stay with him and having accidentally been infected by all the things that ail him, that ail their father. The things she escaped. Now, though, in the dark of the night, he understands that these things have ailed her, too, even without their proximity. She is already infected. He and Daniel run through her veins, and this makes him love her insanely and fear for her and want to protect her even though he is not up to the task.

He sits on the edge of his bed. She is asleep. Her mouth is open and she snores, unladylike, probably from her disease. She is less pretty in her sleep, but even more childlike, tinier under the blankets than she looks in regular life, her face scrubbed of makeup, without defense. He stares at her, trying to remember whether she looks like

Rebecca. She is blond like Rebecca, that much he remembers — the opposite of him, of Daniel. But the rest of her seems like Daniel to him: her thinness and her nose, that unruly hair and slightly feral beauty. She is not as beautiful as *he* is, and he wonders if she minds. Leo's looks have served him very well, but perhaps Mary has not needed them, not the way he has, given she had normal parents and didn't have to fight for every scrap of luck. Perhaps what beauty she has is enough.

Her eyes are open. She surveys him, sitting naked on the bed, but doesn't jump, doesn't say, *What the hell are you doing?*, does not seem alarmed. She receives him as Leo imagines a mother would receive her little boy, woken by a nightmare and standing at the bedside. She pulls back the covers, murmurs, "Are you all right?"

Leo gets in. He doesn't touch her with his body — he doesn't want to be creepy, even though he would like to snuggle up to her — but takes her hand in the dark and holds it. He is so happy holding her hand that it takes a moment to notice that she is crying.

"No," he says, half pleading. "Don't cry. I'm sorry."

She scoots closer to him, wiping her eyes with his knuckles. "Why are *you* sorry?" she says, and she sounds slightly snotty and slightly not — he isn't sure. "What did you do?"

"You shouldn't have come to visit me," he explains. "Things go wrong around me. I'm bad luck."

"Leo," she says, "don't take this the wrong way, but not everything is about you. You've been totally nice to me. I'm wild about you, I wish I never had to leave you." She laughs a little, though she is still crying. "Sweetie, do you have a doctor here?"

"Yeah." He laughs a little, too. "Don't worry, I take my meds. I take them better than *you* do what you're supposed to, I bet. It's just not enough. Nothing's enough for me, Mary."

"Is that always true?" she asks. "Or are you having a hard time right now — is something new going on? Because you seem a little different even from a few days ago. You seem . . . younger maybe? Scared."

"It's just the sex," he explains. "I'm great at all the other stuff, the

parties and the restaurants and the putting flowers in a vase and picking the right outfit so it looks like I didn't think about my outfit. God,
I love that shit—I'm the Daisy fucking Buchanan of Amsterdam." He
sighs. "My therapists tell me I'm not good with real intimacy. *Not* that
getting fucked is real intimacy."

With her free hand, she strokes his hair. His lovers have done
this—they love his hair, they always love his hair—but no woman has
ever stroked his hair before. It feels foreign and frightening and good.

"So what was my mother like?" she asks. "You lived with her. Are
we anything alike?"

"I was just thinking about that," he says. He speaks quietly so that
his head won't move too much—so that she won't stop the stroking.
Then all of a sudden he is mad at himself. He is the older brother.
He sits up, the duvet falling back. "Don't worry about her," he says.
"Rebecca. She wasn't that great. She used to tie me to a radiator so she
could go downstairs and get cloves of garlic stuck up her ass by the
quack doctor who was our landlord."

"Jesus Christ!" Mary squeaks. She sits up, too. "Are you fucking
serious?"

Leo shrugs. "Well, it was the sixties, everyone was weird. After she
ran off and Daniel gave you away, the landlord's girlfriend used to baby-
sit me. She was awesome! Her name was Denise and she was Indian—
as in Native American, not from India—and had that fabulous hair.
You would have loved her. I wished she could be our mom." He pauses,
then reaches out and touches Mary's eyes to see if they are still crying,
though they feel the degree of wet where he can't be sure if it's old or
new tears. "She wouldn't like how I'm relating this," he admits. "She
respected your mom. She thought she was right to save her own ass.
I don't want you to like Rebecca, though. Even if you were better off
without us, I don't like what she did to you."

"What about what she did to you?" Mary asks.

Leo thinks about this. "I gave her reasons," he concludes. "But you
didn't do anything wrong. You were just a baby."

"Leo," Mary says, and the way she says his name kills him; he wants
her to stop and he wants her never to stop. "*You* were just a baby too."

He doesn't like to hear this. It makes him uncomfortable. "She was hot, though," he concedes. "Your mother. What's your other mother like? Is she pretty?"

Mary smiles in the dark. "No. I mean, she's not ugly, but she's not hot either. Pretty wasn't a big deal in our house. You and Daniel—everyone around you guys is really beautiful and flamboyant and fucked up." She laughs out loud. "At my house it was just the opposite. Nobody had any special talent, and everyone was kind of plain and ordinary. But they were all . . . solid people. Stable people. They did the best they could for me."

"You make it sound like what they did didn't work," Leo says.

"I don't know." She leans back again, and now, finally, he can reach her hair easily, without suspending his own arm awkwardly in the air, so he strokes her head the way he should have before, the way a big brother is supposed to. His lovers stroke his hair, but he does not stroke theirs. He is not a stroker of hair. Not until now.

"My mother and I were really close," she tells him quietly. "Then I got diagnosed, and it just . . . she was terrified. Something snapped in her—she could hardly look at me without crying. There'd be this panic in her eyes, and I was totally humiliated, like she was looking through my skin and could see all *my* fears. I felt naked and pathetic, but I needed her—she had to help me with my physiotherapies and medications, I was totally fucking clueless at first. And the more I needed her, the more I resented her. I was too afraid to go away to college, and I hated her for that, too, like it was her fault, like she'd infected me with her fears. Once I finally left home, God, it was like"—she laughs again—"it was like *breathing* again. We get along fine now—I mean, I know intellectually that she had every right to grieve for the fact that her daughter was terminally ill or whatever. But it just never ends. At every stage—like now, she keeps doing research, trying to get me to have a heart-lung transplant when the time comes . . . There's this hospital in Toronto that does transplants on people with my kind of lung bacteria. After a transplant they put you on immunosuppressant drugs so you don't reject your new organ, and that makes you susceptible to infections so they put you on antibiotics to fight those, but the antibiotics typically don't work on us, so we die anyway. My mother just can't accept it. I feel responsible for her grief, and I just want to run."

Leo doesn't know what to say. He knows nothing about mothers. He keeps stroking his sister's hair, and she sighs like the purr of a cat, and he feels happy again, the way he did when she held his hand, so happy his skin could burst. She is his sister. His sister! She is his.

"What," she begins, rolling onto her back, "is going on between you and Sandor? I thought you couldn't stand each other. Are you guys a couple now? What about Pascal?"

"It's complicated," Leo says. "I have no idea what's going on."

Mary laughs. "Oh yes," she says. "Yes, you do."

All at once, Leo notices that his dick is stiffening a little at the mention of Sandor—at the memory of Sandor still on his sofa bed. He wishes he had put on his sweatpants instead of being a goof and not thinking things through. He bunches the duvet a little around his crotch to hide it, says, "Sandor is completely in his body. I'm not in my body at all. Sometimes I forget I even have a body. I get so caught up in my head, I can't feel sensations, like I'm painting and later I'll realize I threw my back out and can barely walk, but I didn't notice at the time because I was somewhere else. I have a hard time with sex—I mean . . ." He pauses, embarrassed. "I don't mean a hard time like a *soft* time, that's not what I—"

"I know what you mean," she says. "A hard time just being there, in the moment. I have that sometimes, too."

"You do?"

"Well, I don't know if it's the same thing," she says. "It's just like, sometimes I want to have sex so badly, I feel so hungry for it, and then when I get it—I mean, I come or whatever, and if you're a woman that's supposed to be feat enough—but it's never as pivotal as I think it's going to be. When it's over, I still feel separate, like my body is cased in glass and no one can reach me."

Leo closes his eyes. "No," he says. "It's not the same thing. I mean, I feel separate, too, I feel what you're talking about, but it's more than that. It's like my body is there, but I'm not in it. It's like my body has nothing to do with me, like it's some kind of trinket I bought at a store and can give people as a gift, but I'm not inside the box, I'm over in the corner watching them open it." He thinks of earlier, of Sandor. "Sometimes," he says, "if it's painful enough, then I can feel it, I can snap into my body and be there. But that's a tightrope walk—I mean, pain can get me *there*, but if I'm not careful, if I don't choose carefully, it's like snapping awake to find myself in the middle of a horror flick. With Sandor . . . I don't know. I guess he seems like he can keep me grounded but not kill me in the process. Does that make sense?"

"Leo," Mary says, "no. No, it doesn't. Or maybe it does, but I don't like what I'm hearing. Are you saying Sandor is hurting you—that you want him to hurt you?"

He doesn't answer. In truth, Sandor hasn't really hurt him, not yet. All they've done is fuck, which was risky enough, Mary in the next room and all. Plus, in Leo's experience, most sadists are fetishists, not hedonists; Sandor's sexuality isn't narrow enough to fit that bill. Suddenly he doesn't know how to explain himself. He is anxious that his straight, married sister will think he's some "beat me, beat me" weirdo who wants to wear a dog leash and get shit on, yet agitated that she doesn't understand the fundamental truth of how hard it is to stay in the present fucking moment, how easy it is to drift away, and how it takes a strong hand, a commanding hand, to pull you back and hold you in place. He isn't sure Sandor can manage it, but Sandor's smart, he's manipulative, he's ruthless, he's a natural top—so much so he'll even do it with a *woman,* for God's sake!—and that's all a reasonable start. And yet with Sandor . . . so far, he doesn't feel afraid. He thinks Sandor could actually be a friend.

"What I meant," he tries again, "is just that Sandor is this cool combination of Dutch and Spanish, you know, from his parents. He's got that Spanish aggression and sensuality, but mixed with the Dutch irreverence, the Dutch way of being so casual in your physicality. And that funny Dutch mannerism—like he's *gezellig,* even when he's trying to be all assertive."

"Oh God." Mary giggles now. "Don't tell him that, he'll die."

"I know." Leo joins her laughter. "He's trying to be all hot and commanding, and it's like he's this adorable little doily on top of an antique wooden table. He's like an adorable doily with a big dick!" Even as he says it, he is imagining the painting he will make: a doily with a dick in its center. He will call the painting *Amsterdam,* and two years from now, shortly after Mary's death and when New Yorkers are dragging around their PTSD like invisible albatrosses in the wake of 9/11, the painting will be commissioned for an exhibition called *The New Surrealists* at MoMA, though such a confluence of events—such awesomeness and terribleness—seems wholly inconceivable now.

All at once, Sandor stands at the bedroom door. He, unlike Leo, had the presence of mind to put on his pants. He takes one look at the bed and quips, "So, I am sorry to interrupt this lovely scene of brother-and-sister incest, but Leo, I think maybe this girl needs to go to sleep, and I *know* I need to go to sleep, so shut up, yes?"

Leo looks from Sandor to Mary. He doesn't want to leave Mary, exactly, but he thinks Sandor has done the right thing in coming to claim him—coming to rein him in and make him behave normally—and he appreciates it, so he stands. At his nudity, Sandor shakes his head with exaggerated dismay, clucking his tongue and saying, "Leo, Leo, do you want to scar your sister for life? She is American and they are very afraid of naked people, you know that—what are you doing?" and Mary starts laughing all over again, and Sandor puts his arm loosely around Leo's shoulders and ferries him back to the sofa bed, lying him down, putting the blanket over him. Before climbing in beside him, Sandor takes off his own pants.

MOVING IN A single-file line at the Anne Frank House, she finds it impossible not to think of being herded like cattle—of people during World War II crammed into train cars shoulder to shoulder, hardly able to breathe, the shorter ones like Anne (like Mary herself) unable to even see over the heads of the others. The aisles in Anne's annex are narrow, and Mary can look only to her side at whatever object, photograph, or letter is on display. She stares at a child's phonograph, which Anne and Margot must have played records on before their lives became enshrouded in silence. It is painted yellow, bright and flagrantly innocent, and Mary's eyes fill with tears.

The world is a terrible place. She does not need the Anne Frank House to tell her this. Young girls have been paying the price for the violence of men for as long as the world has existed. German soldiers, Spanish pilots, Libyan terrorists: all the same. Some men are driven by hatred, as though little girls they have never met are their enemies. She thinks of Anne's final hours at Bergen-Belsen, dying of typhus. Who is *she*—a thirtysomething American woman—to fear death? Hers will be sanitary, civilized, full of morphine and machines and relatives gathered at the bedside. Not like Anne's. Not like Nix's. She knows nothing of suffering. She cannot breathe.

Out on the street, on Prinsengracht, she gulps air, cries a little more. If she had lived in Holland during the war, she would have been a Jew, would have met a fate similar to Anne's. *Would have been a Jew.* Well, of course she *is* a Jew, according to the rules delineated by the Nazis at least. Judaism is in the blood, not in the practice. Many of those who died in the camps were secular, products of mixed marriages, even practicing Christians. She is a Jew. Just like her brother, Leo, the bipolar atheist homosexual, who could have been sent to Bergen-Belsen several times over, if such a thing were possible, for his "crimes." Just like Daniel, the new age American shaman. Just like her biological mother, Rebecca, the hot blond who tied Leo to a radiator and had cloves of garlic stuck up her ass by a quack. Jesus Christ.

(*Or not, as the case may be.*)

Mary walks along Prinsengracht, heading to Sandor's apartment, quite a walk away, near Vondelpark, or Needle Park, as Leo says it's called after hours. Leo is finishing a grant application on a deadline, compiling slides and filling out forms, so she is without him for the first time and already missing him in preparation for her imminent departure. She doesn't want to leave Amsterdam. This is causing her significant guilt. She is supposed to miss her husband.

She does miss her husband. She does.

Just not enough to want to go home yet.

Their life in rural New Hampshire is peaceful. They rent a wooden house that opens in the back onto a wooded area. Sometimes they see bears in the yard. They do their shopping at a funky, organic grocery store called the Co-op, and Mary and Geoff have gotten into the vibe, started baking their own bread and making yogurt from scratch, cooking while listening to Geoff's jazz albums on a vintage turntable and sipping Bordeaux. Mary teaches at Hanover High School, in the same town as Dartmouth College, and her students are the well-bred, Aryan-looking offspring of professors and Dartmouth alumni. The girls mostly have eating disorders. Geoff works far longer hours, so after work she comes home to an empty house and grades papers or watches TV while wearing her Vest. On the weekends they hike Mount Cardigan or Mount Tom; they have picnics and sometimes rent a canoe. Every once in a while, Mary goes to dinner with the other teachers at Hanover High. She cannot complain about her colleagues, who are nice people and, just as her mother used to do with her teacher friends, tell funny stories about their students. Sometimes (less frequently) they get together with Geoff's colleagues, but many of his fellow doctors are Chinese or Indian and have their own communities, and those who aren't tend to make Mary feel self-conscious. Word has gotten out that Geoff's wife is a former patient of his, and Mary feels like a specimen, as if they are all waiting to see how this experiment turns out: the doctor and the sick girl. They are waiting to see if Geoff's heroism will pay off, or if, like a Peace Corps volunteer who goes too native and starts letting flies collect on his open wounds, he will be saved by somebody who swoops in and helicopters him out when the going gets too rough.

She feels sicker since landing in Amsterdam than she has felt in years. Than she has, in fact, felt since the Mexico City Airport in 1994. It's her proximity to cigarettes, her constant diet of alcohol, her lack of sleep. In only a week, these things can build up, smack her in the face. If she were here much longer, she would end up hospitalized. As it is, Geoff will make sure she goes in for a "tune-up" the moment she gets home. It will be her first hospitalization in New Hampshire, and she isn't looking forward to it. She would feel like the new kid at school, except that she'll be quarantined anyway. Geoff will hover and make sure her pulmonary numbers swing up again.

Unless, of course, they don't.

Vondelpark is huge. She would like to wander around in it, get herself lost. According to her guidebook, there are free concerts in the park, and playgrounds. She would like to go to one of the playgrounds and watch the children. Or maybe she wouldn't. Maybe that falls under the category of Not a Good Idea Anymore. She remembers a story her mother told her once, about how when Mom miscarried for the sixth and final time, her father ran up and down their old block, shouting at the sky and cursing God, until a neighbor brought him home. Mary tries to imagine herself here in Vondelpark, losing control and wailing, running amok and raging at the sky, but she cannot picture it. Maybe she does not deserve a baby if her grief is less than her sense of decorum.

The baby she lost would have been a Jew, too. In Hitler's Europe, her child would have been dragged from Geoff's Gentile arms and loaded with Mary into the train cars. Mary thinks of *Sophie's Choice*. She barely remembers the plot other than that scene. She sinks down on a bench, crying again. Sophie should have refused to give up either child. Then they would all have been shot on the spot, and that would have been preferable to the guilt, to the separation from her son, who died alone in the camp like Anne Frank, like Nix died alone in the sky. *Go ahead,* Mary almost told Zorg in the car that day in Greece. *I dare you.* No, she will not die alone, despite not having a baby. She has her parents; she has Geoff. There is no need to stay in Amsterdam and abuse her lungs and pretend to be twenty-one again with her damaged brother and Sandor. There is no need to rage at the sky, at a God in whom she's not sure she even believes.

She has the address of Kenneth's apartment in her pocket. She doesn't know how to get there. It's not central, not in a touristed area, not on her guidebook map.

By the time she arrives at Sandor's, her mascara is no doubt smeared. He ushers her in, does the Dutch cheek-kissing thing; she gets the impression that he would stoically observe ritual and peck her on alternating cheeks even if she were on a ventilator, and it makes her laugh, which makes her cough. His apartment is all clean lines and modern Germanic furniture—the total opposite of Leo's cozy, bohemian lair. To her immense relief, instead of pulling out a bottle of liquor he puts on a kettle for tea. She sits in an offensively bright red chair, pressing her knees together.

She knew Sandor first, but he is Leo's now. No matter what we tell ourselves in an effort to be sophisticated and free, there are bonds in this world created nowhere else but in bed.

"Now this is how I remember you," Sandor says, sitting across from her, not too close. "This is the Nicole I knew, not so much with these grown-up clothes and the grown-up smile."

"You remember me crying?" she says, and she laughs shrilly.

"No." He doesn't smile. "No, but always looking like you might. Like you had lost something and were looking room to room, hoping to find it."

"That's a good observation," she says. "Yeah, I'd lost something. I certainly had." He goes to pour the tea, and she thinks, *But life is loss. So what? It isn't an excuse for anything.*

When he sits down across from her, she says, "Do you ever want to have kids, Sandor?"

His face registers visible surprise, much more so than at finding her teary eyed and trembling on his doorstep. After a moment he says, "I don't think I want that, no. My mother was a good mother, you know, not like what Leo says about his childhood, nothing like that. And children are very happy, very beautiful things, sure. But until you just said this, I think I never considered about it before in my life!" He opens his arms wide, a teacup held precariously in one hand. "So that means probably it isn't for me, don't you think?"

He leads her toward a closed door. For a moment it occurs to her that he may be taking her into a bedroom to seduce her. She imagines herself lying back, letting her brother's lover do whatever he wants to her body even though she's not attracted to him and never was. Is this what she's come to, then? That she would betray her husband and her brother all in one fell swoop, for a man she doesn't even desire, whom she's fairly certain doesn't desire her? *No, she resolves. If he touches me, I'll refuse him, even though my body is aching right now for some kind of comfort, some kind of release.* She is so caught up in her resolution that when she finds herself surrounded by Sandor's canvases, she feels dizzy, drunk somehow, despite the tea.

The canvases are huge, with life-size human figures on them, each — Mary realizes with a sharp intake of breath — supposed to be dead from some kind of violence. The paint on the canvas is so thick that the knife wounds, the bullet holes, the decapitations, are deep enough to stick your fingers into. Quite a few of the figures wear soldier's uniforms, of various nations. Others are civilians, mostly male, but there are girls' bodies, too — some naked, with bright, open wounds of red paint gashed into their sides, across their breasts. She has never seen anything like it. They are like the paintings of a serial killer. She stands gaping, momentarily afraid.

"I have different series," Sandor explains animatedly. "For different wars, regimes in different countries. I just finished the Mirabal sisters — you want to see them? For years I have wanted to make them but I was too in love with them to do it. Finally, you know, I think about them for so long that we become like an old married couple and I get a little sick of them, and then I see their flaws, and then finally I can paint them, once the infatuation is gone. Now, now that they are out there, out of my head, I love them again. They're beautiful, don't you think?"

The three dead Mirabal sisters don't have gunshot or knife wounds like so many of the others, but they are bleeding in places from their beatings, and their necks are bruised. Mary puts her hand up to her mouth. Sandor has painted the girls' skin so that she can see the network of veins underneath. Their hair is splayed out messily, some individual strands matted to their faces with blood.

"Jesus Christ," Mary says. "Sandor, these are incredible. You're unbelievably talented. God, they're horrible to look at! Does anyone actually *buy* them and hang them in their house?"

Sandor looks around him. "That has been a serious problem," he admits. "They're good for shows, but not so much for the cozy little Dutch house."

"I didn't realize you were so obsessed with war and carnage," she says cautiously. All at once, though, she remembers again the argument with Joshua in the Arthog House kitchen: Sandor's insistence that World War II could have happened anywhere, even in civilized England. He must have been fascinated by war, a student of it, even then. An idea suddenly strikes her. "You don't have any paintings of the victims of the Lockerbie disaster, do you?" she asks, but he is shaking his head no before the question is even out. She isn't sure why she asked. Was she planning to give him a photograph of Nix and ask him to paint her, broken and mangled, still strapped to her airplane seat, dead in a Scottish field? Jesus, talk about high treason. Better she should just take Sandor into the other room and fuck him than *that*. Her eyes fill with fresh tears. What is wrong with her?

"You can't call me Nicole anymore," she blurts out. And realizes with a bolt of relief that she has *time* — not for everything, but for this. Someday she will tell him why, but it does not have to be today. "I'm not asking for Leo's sake," she says simply. "I'm asking for mine."

He doesn't answer. "I love your brother," he begins instead, quietly. He is next to her now, arms at his sides still. "I have loved him for a long time, I think, from the time I first knew him. Then all of a sudden *you* are here . . ." Before she can blink, both her hands are clutched in his, as if they are a couple making wedding vows. "I'll look after him for you if he lets me. I'm better than that pretty little *aarsridder* Pascal, so I think Leo lets me stick around, but who knows, maybe you can put in a good word. You don't have to worry about him, Mary."

She sniffs. "That's good." Even though Leo is the last thing on her mind, and she is certain Sandor knows it, she manages to look up, to face the canvases around them full of human wreckage, and say to the man who painted them, surprised to find how much she means it, "I feel better knowing Leo's in your hands."

THE CASE IS CLOSED: *your life remains a mystery. The blank shell of you running into the water at Plati Yialos, your cold rejection at the Athens Airport, your impersonal travelogues from London, culminating in that giddy final letter that defies all my dark imaginings. I can never know the truth of what happened inside that room. I will never know if you were impacted the way I would have been. I will never know if Hasnain was proof of your "recovery," or even if he existed at all. I can never ask if you faced Zorg and Titus alone in an effort to save me, or look deeply enough into my own heart to predict whether I could have done the same for you. The only thing I know for sure is that you aimed, in some way, to spare me. Because I was sick, because you thought me damaged or tragic — maybe. But also because you loved me. Your protection was an act of love, and if you could see how far I've come you would beam your glowing smile, and then, at my continued hand-wringing, smack me upside the head.*

And so, Nix, what does it mean to heal? To heal while my body simultaneously attacks from within? To heal in the absence of answers, here at the end of an incoherent, schizophrenic trail? What does it mean to trust unconditionally? What would it mean to finally — finally — let go?

AGNES IS DEAD. Kinga doesn't speak English or Dutch, but it's not hard to figure out what she's saying. Kenneth stands in his doorway watching the girl — she can't be more than twenty-four — pantomime Agnes's death for him like he's going to guess the name of a flick in a game of charades. She's in the hall, junkie eyes bugging, acting out Agnes's snorting coke and shooting H in tandem, though he figures it didn't happen exactly like that, more like Kinga doesn't know how to convey the lapse of time, whatever it was. The fucking insufficient lapse of time. He's spoken to Agnes about it over and over again: that a real heroin overdose is rare, it's mixing drugs that can get you killed. Agnes didn't drink. They knew too many people who'd OD'd mixing H with booze or tranquilizers, so Agnes avoided the combo. She was a damn vegan, wouldn't touch eggs or milk. Coke, though—that was a different story. Coke went with everything. Even her addiction to heroin couldn't quell her craving for that old friend completely. Kinga's mouth pours out a facsimile of an ambulance siren, mimes a sheet pulled over Agnes's head.

"Zaterdag?" he asks, and she nods, points at her wrist as though it contains an invisible watch, says, "Zondag," to indicate it was Sunday morning, of course—past midnight. He doesn't know how to ask the rest: What took her so long to come and tell him? Did she tell anyone who Agnes was, or did she disappear into the crowd the minute the ambulance or police showed up? Was this at the club, or later, at some party, and where?

Is she certain Agnes is really dead?

Of course. That much he knows. If she weren't dead, she'd have gotten word to him. He's been telling himself all week that she ran off with some guy, but he's known it was bullshit. She never came back for any of her things. It took Agnes years to acquire anything of her own; she'd never leave it all behind, not for some new man. Christ, she didn't even *like* men.

He's talking himself down in his head. He wants to scream at Kinga, but it's not her fault, she's just some young junkie, someone Agnes wouldn't even have been out with if he were any kind of man. Agnes never carried ID with her, in case she got into any trouble: she wanted to be able to lie her way out of it. And even if the cops or the morgue or who-the-fuck-ever knew who she was, they wouldn't con- nect her to him. Agnes's address on all her paperwork was still in some backwater Czech town. She had no legal Dutch address; they didn't share the same last name; Kenneth doesn't even own a telephone; and *his* paperwork puts him at the address he shared years ago with his ex-wife, who doesn't even live in A'dam anymore. He and Agnes both existed off the grid, and if Kinga hadn't shown up now to tell him, he'd never have known shit.

He watched Agnes leave, knowing exactly what she was going out to do. She asked him to come, called him "baby" in English, and he called her a heroin whore. He sent her off with his blessings, to kill herself.

Kinga stands in the hallway pretending to cry—she's the worst actress he's ever laid eyes on, and he's seen some bad ones. "I not come to now for I more upset," Kinga tells him.

"Yeah, yeah," he says. "We're all fucking upset." He shuts the door in her face.

Now what? Should he go to a local police station with Agnes's passport, try to track down her body? It's been nearly a week; surely it wouldn't still be lying around? He has, he realizes, no idea. If this were Atlanta, he'd know what to do; if it were London, and he weren't hiding from the cops himself, he'd even have a clue. But he's a foreigner here, after all these years. The cops would speak better English than Kinga, but who knows the real story of Agnes's death, and if there's something fishy going on and he starts sniffing around, maybe they'll start sniffing *him*. He's got less to hide than usual, less to hide than in a long, long time, but *less* doesn't translate to *nothing*. The cops aren't his friends, not in any language. His hands are tied.

He sits on their bed. Reclines all the way back. The more his mind wanders, the worse this gets. Agnes had people in her hometown. Shouldn't somebody let her family know? But Agnes's old lady isn't married to her daddy. She's with some other man, and Kenneth doesn't even know his last name, probably never would've met any of them even if he and Agnes had been together ten more years. Where were they when Agnes was walking the street, getting her face bashed in by johns? Where were they when Agnes was picking up *him*, a man more than fifteen years her senior, and letting him tie off her arm? Yeah, he's sure they'd welcome him into their home like a hero, if he could even find it. Take one look at him and kill the messenger, more likely, and he'd sure as hell deserve it. No, Agnes will lie in an unmarked Dutch grave, and her people back home will be happier for it, sitting round their kitchen table bemoaning how she wrote them off, thought she was so high and mighty with her pretty face and big tits, went off to Holland, and never looked back. They'll take some joy in the story, in rehashing it over their Eastern European booze and inbred hardships, passing it around so that its implicit end is Agnes somewhere else living high on the hog, thumbing her nose at them. Not a bad fantasy, if you can hold on to it. He wishes someone could have given his mother that, with Will.

He should cry. He doesn't feel like crying. He should call some-body, tell somebody, but this is his life now, clean or what passes for it: there's nobody left to call. He should go out and pick up a girl, but if he got some stranger in front of him right now, some hole with a language barrier and no common past, God help him, he's not sure he could trust himself, he's not sure he could stand it, he's not sure he wouldn't just hurt her for the sport of it. It should have been *him*. Not because Agnes was any better than he is, or because she wouldn't have followed suit soon after even if he'd died first, but because then he wouldn't have to lie here anymore and tally up the body count. Will first, his mother not long after, and then he ran, so that Hillary and his baby son, they might as well be dead, too: dead to him, just like his father. And all at once he *is* crying, but it's not for Agnes. It's because it spooked him: thinking his son's as good as dead just because he's not around. The boy's better off without him. He's gotta be in college by now; he won't even remember Kenneth, won't remember having just learned to say "Daddy" when Kenneth ran. Still, knowing that his boy is out there somewhere, living a normal life, a life without him around to taint it, is the only thing that's kept him from putting a barrel to his head, from loading the dose to turn it lethal all these years. *Please, God*, he prays, *don't let my boy be dead.*

The number is on the back of a Mulligan's coaster, right on the floor next to his bed. Her cell and e-mail, exchanged as the bar was closing and she went off with her brother and Sandor into the night, leaving him to clean up. He'd thought she would stay. He believed all night that they were going to hook up; he hadn't questioned it; it seemed a given—and then suddenly she was gone. *Mary,* the coaster reads, but he can't think of her that way and noticed Sandor was calling her Nicole still. Kenneth wouldn't stoop. It'd make her feel too important, like something he'd held on to all these years, which isn't exactly true. He hadn't thought of her at all really. But then there she was across the bar, and something old reignited between them, with a life all its own. It isn't some lost innocence. He was already ruined when he knew her back then, already beyond repair. He can't put his finger on it. Something like recognition.

He doesn't have a phone anymore. He pitched his cell when he kicked H; he didn't want calls from anyone, didn't want to make any either. There's nobody he's wanted to talk to. He has no computer, no e-mail account. The fact that this American wife gave him a bloody e-mail address, of all things, just indicates the gulf between them, how ridiculous the whole thing is.

There is a phone in the Indonesian restaurant downstairs.

She answers in this normal voice, this "English is my native language and I am a normal person and nobody I know just OD'd" voice, and he does not, for the first time he can recall in his entire life, know what to say to a girl. When he doesn't answer, she says, "Babe, is that you?" and for one fucking insane elated moment he thinks she means *him,* but then he realizes she must mean her husband — her husband at home in America, waiting for her.

"It's me," he says. He doesn't know how to refer to himself. She never called him by his proper name, but he hasn't gone by Yank since his thirties. "My, uh . . ." Nothing in his life, nothing that he is, makes sense in words. "My girlfriend just died. I was wondering . . ." He is a crazy person; he will scare the living fuck out of her. "Do you think you could maybe come over?"

The girl, though, doesn't miss a beat. "Well, that depends," she says. "Do I have to bring a shovel?"

He starts laughing. Falls against the wall of the phone booth, cracking up, and can't stop — he is too relieved by her almost sociopathic irreverence. Yes, he remembers now. She looks normal, but she's *not* normal. She's wrecked, too, just not by him.

"Nah," he says. "I didn't kill her or anything. I mean, I sorta did, but not the way you're talking about."

"Okay," she says. "Then I guess I'll come."

He says, "Did you keep my address?"

She says, "I'm not sure," and he does not for a moment believe her now, and feels better, better than he has any right to ever feel, with all he's done. "Give it to me again just to be safe."

"Bullshit," he says. "You'll find it." And he hangs up.

MARY'S HEAD THROBS like a heart. Kenneth's sheets feel vaguely wet, as though the humidity in this city never allows anything to truly dry. Her body hums with the exhaustion of a wounded athlete. There is energy under the fatigue, a current that jolts her muscles and renders sleep an impossibility. The night is still black, but a weak, murky black that hints at daylight.

She guesses it must be around 5 a.m., though Kenneth does not seem to have a clock in his apartment. His bed is just a mattress on the floor. Nothing in the whole place looks anything like what she has come to think of as "home." His shower curtain is made up of laminated postcards from places he has been, pinned together with safety pins; the effect is stunning, like something they'd charge hundreds of dollars for in some chic boutique, yet the rest of the bathroom is unkempt, uncoordinated, even dirty. The walls of the apartment are covered, ceiling to table level, with photographs. All the photographs are black and white and are held on the walls with tape, unframed; she recognizes some from years ago, though none are of her. His kitchen is so small it could pass as a foyer. It appears to be used as storage for his photography equipment and musical instruments; a sax case sits propped up against the refrigerator as though it would never occur to him that he might need to access anything inside.

Signs of the dead Czech girlfriend are everywhere and nowhere in the apartment. Her clothing—small and black and often made of fabric that looks like netting—is littered on almost every conceivable surface. That shower curtain and the photographs and the saxophone, though, reveal nothing of the dead girlfriend. There is only one toothbrush on the bathroom sink, although Kenneth says the girlfriend took nothing with her before she died, so Mary is not sure what to make of that. Maybe they shared?

Next to her, Kenneth snores faintly and steadily. She remembers him, the still-young Yank, as a silent sleeper, quiet as the dead. Now, the middle-aged man who has just become her lover snores beside her into the night.

Mary is ravenous, but there is nothing in the refrigerator—she has already gotten up and moved the sax case to investigate. Literally nothing, save some film. He does not even own, as she would have expected, a bottle of alcohol. It seems preposterous. Why would anyone invite a woman to his apartment if he couldn't even offer her a glass of wine, a shot of whiskey, a fucking cracker? Was it that certain, that preordained, that they would have sex?

Of course. Of course it was. She wanted him from the moment Sandor told her he was in the city. Even now, in the soreness and familiarity following their copulation, Mary feels a damp embarrassment under her arms at the memory: He did not recognize her! She tracked him all over the city, and he did not even know her! He would never have contacted her again but for the death of his lover, or nonlover, or whatever she was. *Whoever* she was, Mary has fucked Kenneth on the dead girl's grave. For this, this grave fucking, she has betrayed Geoff. For *this*.

Treat me, she told him when he was tearing off her clothes, *like something that couldn't possibly break.*

She is not a neophyte. She has been the other woman; she has been a wife. And yet. Through it all, the men in her life have felt distinctly separate from her: *other*. It was true from the first. She and Joshua were entirely different continents, their liaison a tiny island between two worlds, kept tenuously afloat through omissions and lies. With Eli, too, attraction was a carefully orchestrated dance in which deception played no small role, until she became merely a looking glass in which he could see his own fantasies shining back at him.

Now, with Geoff these past five years . . .

Until tonight, she has had no secrets from Geoff. He knows her; he even knew Nix. Still, her mind's unlit, off-road paths, down which he cannot follow, seem to multiply by the day the closer she gets to the finish line. While he is the most intelligent and responsible man she has ever met—*mature beyond his years,* her mother says—there is a lightness to him as incompatible with her weight, with her darkness, as Joshua's South Africanness was with her Americanness years ago.

Next to her lies a man whose life has been lived mainly in darkness. On the surface, he and Mary have nothing in common. Jesus, that's an understatement. *Nix* was the one who liked the bad boys, but if Nix met this man, she would run. No, worse than that. She would turn her nose up and not even give him a second thought. The Man Formerly Known as Yank would be, in Nix's or any reasonable girl's estimation, a lowlife. The opposite of a good catch, naturally, but not even the kind of "walk on the wild side" that would appeal to most women like them. He is past his prime; he has no money. Unlike the bad boys of soap operas and prime time—glamorous mobsters or decadent play-boys—he exists in a poverty-ridden underbelly of society: a subculture Mary would not even know existed had she not stumbled onto Arthog House.

He has called out her death as if it were nothing. He has bitten her mouth, grabbed her by the back of her hair, and when the coughing took over, he pinned her to the mattress while her body shook, shoving himself inside her and fucking her right through the spasms until she was thrashing like a fish, pushing at him in fury and confusion, and then, when her lungs stilled and she had grabbed his discarded shirt and covered her mouth with it, spit into it, immediately Kenneth's mouth was on hers again, as though nothing had happened. Her face is scraped raw by his stubble. Oh God. Eli used to talk dirty to her, but it was never like this. *Get down on your belly,* he ordered, pulling out. *I'm going to fuck your ass until you howl like a dog.* His face was older, wilder than it'd been in the bar. For a moment she felt herself falling—Eli's body pressed into her back their last night at Daniel's house—and an old anger rose, stiffened her limbs. Kenneth kept look-ing at her straight-on; she felt her eyes widen like a startled bird's.

Then she remembered Sandor's *squeal like a pig,* and for another moment she believed she would laugh, would explain it to Kenneth, and he would chuckle, too, so that the moment, the danger, would be shattered: they would be back on safer ground.

With Eli, that is what would have happened.

And with Geoff? With Geoff, nothing that had transpired in the past forty-eight hours would be even remotely within his frame of reference.

Treat me like something that couldn't possibly break.

Kenneth jolts awake next to her, sitting upright like someone waking from a nightmare. His eyes are open, but he does not seem to see her. She is sitting up, too, too restless to lie down anymore. It takes a moment for his eyes to focus, to seem to take her in. The room is cold; Mary is shivering; even her breasts have goose bumps.

"I shouldn't have done this," she begins.

"Girl," Kenneth says deadpan, "If you thought you shouldn't've done it, you'd have put some clothes on for the conversation."

In the half darkness, she feels herself blush.

"Come on," Kenneth says, prodding her with his foot. "Stop looking at me like I want something from you. There's nothing I want. I'm done with all that. Relax."

"Done with all of what?" she asks.

He gestures at her. For a moment she doesn't know what he means, but then she sees he is sort of pointing at her ring. "That," he says. "Re-la-tion-ships. That ship, if you'll pardon the pun, has sailed. I don't mean because of Agnes. Way, way before her."

He stands up. Naked, his gray hair long and mangy, he looks like a hungry animal. "So your brother lives in town," he says, pulling on his jeans. "Say you come over and see him now and then." He reaches to the floor and finds the belt he extracted the night before, and Mary's legs feel hot. "I've run enough in my life. This is where I am now. You want to find me, I'll be here. Or if not *here,* here," —he gestures at the apartment— "then around."

Four hours ago he pushed into her so hard the sheets sprang loose from the mattress. Electricity seemed to ride through her skin and shoot from her fingers and toes; she felt cracked open, obliterated, no room for the anger anymore. Afterward, he'd put a hand out to her and said, *Look, I'm no expert on marriage, but you said you've been with your husband, what, five years? If he knows you, really gets you, there's no way he'd be as shocked by what just happened here as you think. So probably you can let yourself off the hook.* She knew he meant the words as comfort, but they chilled her. She couldn't begin to guess whether Geoff *did* know her—her core and what she was capable of. It seemed a fifty-fifty crapshoot.

Abruptly she pulls the humid sheet up around herself and stands. "You always used to call Sandor a faggot," she says. "Like it was an insult, like the problem was him and not you."

Kenneth, though, doesn't even look in her direction. He is heading for the kitchen. "You ain't gonna believe this, but I've got coffee. Want some?"

She gets up and follows him, annoyed.

"You thought he stole your jazz tapes, but it was *me*—I took them. I don't even remember why." Mary is not sure what she's waiting for. Anger? An apology? If anything, she feels buoyed by his flagrant lack of guilt. Where is she going with this?

He still doesn't look her way, but says low, "You stole the tapes." His exhalation comes out as a whistle. "Baby, you sure know how to make an old man's day."

Her eyes fill inexplicably. Some flood of trust welling up in her: unstoppable and potentially lethal. She does not know how to slow it, how to stick her finger in the leak. This man is like no one she has spoken to in a decade; he is like an alien. Yet she has never in her life slept with anyone who felt so much like kin.

Still, she repeats stubbornly, "You were always calling him a faggot." Then finally: "What in God's name am I doing here?"

Soon he will say, *You and your buddy Sandor keep talking about Arthog House like it was some utopia on earth, but it was just another place I lived and not real long. The only thing worth remembering about that place was you, that day, those pictures. Be a real bad girl for me and maybe I'll dig 'em up and show you next time.* Soon she will vow that there won't be a next time, and he will stride over and lay her out on the dirty kitchen floor, and she will think momentarily of the floor on which she lost her virginity; she will think of Leo and how in the span of one night she has come to understand everything he said to her about what it takes, sometimes, to hold a person in place. Then they will begin, and she will not think of Joshua or Eli or Leo, or even Geoff anymore.

But for now, Kenneth keeps digging in a kitchen cabinet. "Yep," he says, voice muffled. "I always knew that boy was a faggot. Can I call it or what?"

"You are," she tells him slowly, "the complete opposite of *gezellig*." She thinks of a line from *The Unbearable Lightness of Being* and smiles. "In the world of *gezellig*, you would be a monster."

Like a present, he turns around, holding up coffee in a dirty glass jar.

Where Are We Going,
Where Have We Been?

Here, then, is what Geoff will remember: The way sea foam clung to Mary's skin as she emerged from the surf, her arm around Nix, whose pubic hair was covered in foam, too, so that she seemed a pornographic mermaid, and the way his dick got hard at the sight, and the shame of that, and how he jumped up to gather her clothing and hand it to her before Irv could see her nakedness, too, and only afterward realized he should have turned away, should not have touched her clothing or looked at her at all, though neither girl reprimanded him or really seemed to notice; he had become invisible. How he believed they had reached a clear "crisis point" at which it made obvious sense to leave Plati Yialos, to find a way back to town somehow, but instead as soon as Nix had her clothes on she headed straight to the lounge chair where Irv was still gawking in the distance, her eyes so big she reminded Geoff of a junkie or a prisoner, even though he had never met either a junkie or a prisoner, and leaned over and kissed Irv with a force that seemed to knock Irv onto his back. Later Irv would claim her skin trembled—*really fucking vibrated*—under his hands as though she were an overcharged electric blanket, as though she could send off sparks and shock him, and how that really got him going. Geoff stood at the surf watching them make out and he felt like he should wave some kind of flag and call a time-out, but nobody else seemed to be in the same place in which he'd found himself; they were all still playing a different game, Mary coming over and putting her wet hand on his arm. How he kissed her mainly to avoid looking at Irv and Nix, and though only a moment before he'd believed himself in love with her, at the touch of her cool, small tongue he felt little of anything. Then she pushed her breasts up against him, and he slid his hands up the back of his own sweatshirt to feel her prominent spine and the gooseflesh of her nipples still damp from the sea, and his body's pendulum swung wildly again, so that he ground his groin up against her like an animal without conscience. How out of nowhere, like a sound track to his conflicted desire, these yowling cats materialized, running along the beach, and the sound of them was like someone being tortured, a pain so big it could drive the humanity from a person, though that made no sense because these *weren't* people; they were just skinny, half-hairless cats, probably howling not with agony but because they were in heat, their feral bodies close to an explosion that had nothing to do with morality, just like Geoff's. Still, at their approach Nix leaped up on her beach chair and screamed, short and loud, over and over again. Geoff heard the muffled, intermingled-with-the-waves sound of Irv trying to talk her down off the chair like it was a ledge, but she continued screaming with a pain so singular she drowned out the cats. And Mary saying, "She must think they have rabies. *You* don't think they do have rabies, do you? You don't think they're going to attack us or something?" Geoff heard himself say no, then strode over to the chaise longes, past Irv's pleading form, and picked Nix up and carried her in the opposite direction of the screeching cats. How he carried Nix's body across the sand and felt for himself the vibrations of which Irv would later boast, as though they had anything to do with Irv at all, and how later, at Irv's bragging, Geoff would secretly resolve never to hang out with him again once they were back on American soil, and with a couple of exceptions like friends' weddings and shit where they ran into each other accidentally, he kept to that resolve, though who knows why, Irv was a pretty good guy, and who knows where he is now? How three years later, when it came time to decide on a specialization in medical school, Geoff, to the shock of his mother and his stepfather the hotshot cardiologist, announced his intentions to focus on respiratory medicine, in particular cystic fibrosis, though he had always intended to be a heart surgeon, those glamorous cowboys of medicine. How he had no photos of Mary, but from the moment he dissected his first pair of lungs, he felt, under his hands, every individual knobby bone of her spine; he felt her hair pouring into his hands like his own private ocean; and he never, ever looked back.

HERE, THEN, IS what Mary will remember: That this was supposed to be the night she would lose her virginity. How a gorgeous Harvard grad fell straight into her lap, but even after they got back to their room in the middle of the night, and that poor guy Irv was lurking around confused and demoralized in the shadows because Nix had pulled the blanket up over her head in her twin bed, when Mary whispered to Geoff, "We could go somewhere, the two of us. We could find someplace quiet—" he cut her off, said, "I don't think you should leave your friend," and the shock of the rejection almost knocked her down. Her cheeks burned; she was thankful for the dim room, and although her overwhelming desire was for Geoff not to witness her embarrassment, some base impulse in her could not take no for an answer, could not *believe* that the way he'd tenderly held her hand in the flatbed of the truck or taken off his sweatshirt when she was cold meant nothing but politeness. Could not believe she would so misread the signs on which the adult world hinged. She tilted her head toward the door and quipped, "Well, thanks for saving our asses. Have a nice life," and the way Geoff's face fell surprised her yet again, as though he had expected something else entirely—as though it really *mattered* to him. How she found herself saying, "It's okay, I have cystic fibrosis anyway," as though to console him, as though it were a social disease he was fortunate not to have the opportunity to catch. She closed the door in his face, regretting the loss of him even before the lock clicked. But within only a minute, Geoff and Irv were back, rapping at the door, and when Mary answered, Geoff said, "They're right around

mother would say if she could see her hitchhiking on a deserted road past midnight with two strangers in Greece, and how eerily unafraid she actually felt—how nothing seemed dangerous anymore. The way Mary's hand kept reaching out to touch her, and how hard it was to care that shrugging it off was hurtful, but something in Mary's touch stung, and the two Harvard men felt safer. How the bland, yielding lips of the boy she'd kissed on the lounge chair had seemed almost inanimate, though not comforting, and that sexy British men did not hold the promise they had less than twenty-four hours ago, and suddenly Nix was not sure why she was going to London at all, but the thought that she had been doing so primarily to sleep with accented hotties incensed her, made her wonder who she was and what she was doing on this earth. That when the door to Titus's bedroom first reopened as she sat primly on his bed, wondering whether it was even necessary to sleep with him to seal the deal, or if a few kisses and gropes had proved sufficient for her plan's execution, she genuinely believed for a moment that the tall frame of Zorg in the doorway was a mistake—that Zorg had gone into the wrong door looking for the bathroom or something. Then she saw Titus coming in behind him, and all at once, she *knew.* How in the seconds it took them to approach the bed, speaking Greek to each other as they would throughout, she had to choose: to scream and fight and hurtle down a road of explicit struggle and escalating tempers that could end with her and Mary buried under the house, or to grit her teeth when they approached in tandem, one pulling her shirt over her head as the other tugged her shorts down. How she was not certain Zorg would murder them if she resisted, but she *was* sure it was not impossible, since men's killing was a fact of life, just like girls' sometimes opening their legs to a man who might be a killer, in order to get out alive. How she believed, in that brief instant before things really *began,* that if she could do this for Mary, it would make everything all right about Bobby Kenner, that they would be even—and then, in the brutal hours that followed, the way that neat little story she had told herself shattered and shattered and shattered again. Until part of her hated Mary, sick Mary who had to be protected at all costs, whom she was protecting still with her silence, as though admitting what she had done on Mary's behalf would endanger *Mary*, napping in the spare room, her stupid precious virginity intact. All that, Nix would remember, plus the cats, wailing like refugees from an underworld, straggly and sick and mad as demons, and how the sound played something inside her gut like the strings of a cello, humming, bringing up her own screams like her body was a helpless instrument.

AND THIS: THAT the world was full of airplanes, and I could get on one and go home, to safety and refuge and boredom—that no one was making me go through with anything. Yet knowing I would not, that something more powerful than the sound of the cats, or the feel of Zorg's knees grinding into the backs of my calves, drove me on, not only to London but beyond—that I would keep going, that already I was past the point of return to Ohio. That even then, I did not wish to change places with Mary, my best friend, whom I loved and wanted with an urgent totality never to see again. Mary, who was trapped.

The Moroccan Book of the Dead

(MOROCCO: KENNETH)

The body is a tidal flat. Wave after wave washes — or pounds — across.
You stay open to the world as long as you can. Then blood draws the line.
—MARK CUNNINGHAM, "Blood"

She calls from Gibraltar. It takes three tries before he answers his cell. She tells him, "I don't want to land in Tangier alone. Come down and take the ferry with me."

He says, "I can't just take off work like that."

"No," she says. "I mean quit work. I don't know when we're coming back."

"Well," he says. "Now you're talking."

She exhales hard. "Two rules. First, no drugs."

"Jesus," he says, "when're you gonna stop that? I've been clean three years."

"Let me clarify something to you. Not being a sniveling junkie isn't the same thing as being clean. I don't just mean no heroin, I mean *nothing,* don't bring anything with you, and if you get something here, you do it when I'm not with you, and don't bring it back around me. You might think acting out *Midnight Express* would be some big adventure, but a Moroccan prison would kill me. Do you understand?"

"Fine," he says amicably. "Shit's cheap there. Disposable drugs. Done."

"Two," she continues. "No sex. Wait, I don't mean no sex exactly. I mean no sex with me."

It is his turn to sigh. "Get real, girl. You're inviting me to give up my cushy life for the third world, and I've gotta be some poster boy for clean and sober living in the deal . . . all for the promise of, what, your legs glued together? Some incentive."

"I'm inviting you," she says, "for the company. Something I think we both could use. I'm inviting you." She stops. "It's been a long time since I traveled with a friend."

From: mrgrace@yahoo.com
Subject: Re: Re: Re: Safely in Spain
Date: August 16, 2001
To: geoffreyjs@hitchcock.org

Hey.

Gibraltar is full of English pubs, like the boardwalk in Tenerife. Obviously I don't care for it. The weather's good but I got a little burned from the antibiotics, so now I'm hiding from the sun and waiting, just reading a lot. Leo and Sandor will be here soon, and then we'll head to Tangier.

Geoff, I'm sorry. I wish you were here but I understand why you wouldn't come. It's just that I need this trip for closure on what has been a defining part of my life. The time has come to nest, take it easy, drag out my time for as long as I can . . . I know that, I swear I do. Since I'll miss the start of this school year, I'll see how my health is holding up come spring, and IF it's advisable (according to Dr. Fox, according to you), I'll put in applications for a new position then. I hope I can go back to work and keep that measure of normalcy in our lives, even if it's only for one more year.

Please, Geoff, please understand. I didn't want my last trip to be something I'd taken without intent, without knowledge of its significance. I couldn't face the prospect of going so quietly into the night. This does not mean I take your love lightly.

M

THEY ARRIVE BY dusk. The first thing to hit Mary is the smell. Under her feet, discarded trash has become a gray, sticky paste from the rain and the trodding of travelers' feet. The port teems with hustlers, vendors, Islamic women shouting at boisterous children in Arabic while the self-proclaimed "guides" accost those off the ferry in English, French, or Spanish. Kenneth pushes through, declining offers to help them find hotels, to drive them where they want to go. She is surprised to hear him bark in French at one of the hustlers, though since she doesn't speak the language herself she isn't sure whether perhaps he just threw out a curse word picked up from some French lover, or if he's spoken with authority. The air smells like a carcass. Impulsively Mary puts her pashmina up to her mouth to inhale the scent of her own body and perfume, as though this will save her lungs from the air, and almost immediately a man shouts at her in English, "The problem is not Tangier, the problem is you!" She drops the pashmina before Kenneth can notice the provocation for the man's verbal assault. To their right, another man sings the praises of America. Though they turn up the rue du Portugal, heading in the direction of the medina, he follows them, talking of his American friends and ignoring their insistence that they need no guide. When Kenneth at last successfully shakes the man off, he is replaced almost instantly by another, this one shouting, "You are as bad as the Israelis!" at their rebuttal of his services. The man taunts, "You don't want help, okay, maybe someone stabs you and you are better off dead." Still he follows. Kenneth turns onto a quieter street (Mary questions the wisdom of this, given their stalker) and, as soon as they appear to be alone, turns on the man and pushes him up against a wall. Mary's heart races, waiting for a group of the stalker's friends to materialize, but the man merely skulks off, shouting obscenities as he leaves.

They stand on a corner with their rucksacks, unsure of where they are.

Kenneth says, "You have a guidebook, right? Girls like you always bring guidebooks."

"Girls like me? You mean girls who leave their husbands to travel with lunatics who attack the locals? I didn't realize that was a type."

"Whatever, Cystic. I didn't attack that guy, I just got rid of him. Where's the book?"

She winds her pashmina around her neck high enough to breathe into it with her mouth and takes her Fodor's from her pack.

"Rue Magellan," Kenneth pronounces. "Here, this way. We'll go have a drink."

"Shouldn't we find a place to stay first?"

But she follows. His legs are so long that it's hard to keep up. A couple of streets in, he stops wordlessly and takes off his pack, takes hers (a small hospital contained within) off her shoulders, puts it on, and hands her his, which is immensely lighter. Probably, she thinks, he has two changes of clothes and that's it.

By the time they get there, Mary is exhausted. This is the sort of thing to which she cannot adjust: how tiring things are now, ordinary things that for thirty-two years she did without thought. This is how it begins. One day, you can stroll aimlessly around for hours without thought; you can take hikes with your husband and swim laps. Then abruptly you cannot even sing along with the radio without getting winded. The infection is gone, but your lungs are not the same. Suddenly you spend more time lecturing your students from your desk than pacing the room with the restless energy you have possessed all your life. Suddenly you cannot carry your own rucksack for more than a few blocks. Suddenly you do not dare travel alone, and when your capricious brother bails on you at the last moment, instead of changing your plans, you stick to your guns and call another man.

"Burroughs, Kerouac, Ginsberg, they all stayed here," Kenneth is saying. They have to step over thick trash on the slanted street to get to the slightly dilapidated white building bearing the sign HOTEL MUNIRIA. Mary's relief at the word *hotel* is palpable. "You teach lit," Kenneth says. "Well, this is it—this is where it happened for real."

"I don't teach the Beats," Mary says. She does not add that she has never understood their appeal exactly, that they always seemed to her some posturing dick club.

The hotel's bar, the Tanger Inn, is like a shrine. Photos of Beat writers litter the walls, and even some pages of their manuscripts are tacked alongside. It is heady, she has to admit: the life they led, touching it like this. Regardless of whether the art that emerged is her thing, these were men who lived life on their own terms. Of course, from what she understands, women were often the casualties. She and Kenneth sit under a photograph of Burroughs. "I always wanted to come here," he says, a rare excitement in his voice. "I worshipped these cats when I was young. Even built my own Dream Machine."

Mary is not sure what this means.

The bourbon burns going down, but its burn is good. She imagines it dissolving everything in its tracks like acid, eating the mucus inside her. "I hear these guys beat their wives."

Kenneth snorts. "They were all fags anyway," he says. "Too bad your buddy Sandor's not here—him and your brother could ask for the room where Kerouac and Ginsberg shacked up together. It could be like their honeymoon suite."

This is it, then: the chance to say what she has been waiting to tell him. "They'll be here in a week. They're meeting us in Casablanca."

He stares. She puts her head down on her arms. The bar is not crowded, but everyone inside is a foreigner: a traveler or expat. The bourbon is starting to scramble her brain and she would like to walk around the room and study the photos and pages more closely, emerge with a clearer picture of these howling men and what they stood for—the ways in which adventure is necessarily lawless, the ways in which freedom always demands a price and someone else is left footing the bill.

"What're you playing at?" Kenneth says, so quietly she can barely hear him through the filter of her arms. "I didn't come for a reunion with those boys." He takes the top of her arm so that she sits up to face him. "Don't give me any shit either about how I hate queers—I don't care who they fuck. But if I wanted to get together with Sandor, all I had to do was cross town. Where's your husband, girl? What am I doing here?"

Across the room, a bald man in a white linen suit sits alone at the bar. Something in his dapper attire strikes Mary as out of another time. At a nearby table, four kids in their twenties laugh over beers. They look like a poster for the United Colors of Benetton: One girl is Asian and drop-dead gorgeous; one of the men is Latino and equally beautiful. The remaining girl and boy are white, less splendid, but full of a young vitality. They cannot be more than five or six years younger than she is, but she feels as if they are another species.

"Eight months ago," Mary begins, "my lungs were working at ninety percent. That's probably better than your lungs. I was one of those weird case studies. My lungs have been colonized with two of the deadliest bacteria someone with CF can get, but for some reason it barely seemed to be impacting me. Other than tune-ups, I hadn't been in the hospital since 1994." She drains the rest of her bourbon, picks up his, and takes a sip. "Then in January, a month after my dad's heart attack, things just went to shit. Maybe it was the stress, but I got pneumonia for the first time in years. I'd pretty much just gone back to work when one day I'm sitting there in class, talking about *The Crucible*—you know, Arthur Miller?—and all of a sudden I have this pain in my chest like I'm going to die, and I can't breathe, every time I try it's like my chest is on fire, I can feel it burning all the way into my back. I was gasping for air, I thought *I* was having a heart attack, too, and would die right in front of my poor students." She laughs, and she can hear how her own laugh—with its hollowness, its bitterness—is different from that of the four young travelers at the next table. "I wasn't that lucky. I just had a collapsed lung."

Kenneth is still watching her. He hasn't done the things the teachers at Hanover High do when she talks to them about her health: make faces, gasp. He hasn't asked questions like Geoff's doctor friends. She's not sure if this is because nothing can faze him at this point or if it's because he doesn't really care, though if he doesn't give a shit, she isn't sure why he's here.

"Next thing you know, I'm back in the hospital with a tube in my chest. It was almost spring by the time I went back to work, but it wasn't the same. I was tired a lot, coughing more than usual. They put me on this antibiotic called minocycline—one of the *few* that works pretty well for the bacteria I've got. Anyway, I started feeling really crappy. I had stomach pain, and no matter what I did, trying to take the medicine with food or whatever, it got worse. So I go to the ER and they give me every fucking test under the sun. Finally they said I was having an attack of acute pancreatitis. You have to understand, you can only even *get* pancreatitis if you have a functioning pancreas, which most people with CF don't. It was just ridiculous, the one thing you don't expect. They think maybe the antibiotic was causing it, so they took me off it, jammed me full of IV fluids, I'm home in a few more days. By now, it's May. And over a four-month period, my pulmonary function has fallen from ninety to less than sixty percent. Geoff doesn't want me to finish the year out teaching, he wants me to rest, focus on getting my numbers back up, right? So I just leave—I take a leave of absence for May and June, and all I'm doing is sleeping, eating, wearing my Vest, doing my therapies. I'm spending maybe four hours a day on therapies and meds. That's my summer. But the numbers don't go up. In fact, they fall further, not much, but enough to put me on the brink of being classified with severe lung disease for the first time in my life—to have gone from literally numbers that were normal to *severe*, skipping right the fuck over mild and moderate. I always was an all-or-nothing kind of girl."

She stops. She is not sure what she's supposed to do now. She wishes she could cry to demonstrate to him the gravity of what she's saying, because she's not sure he gets it, but she doesn't feel like crying. She just feels like ordering another drink.

"It's over," she says at last. "I can't fake it anymore. I used oxygen to fly to Spain, which I've never done on a plane before in my life. At home, Geoff had me sleeping with oxygen just to give me a boost, because it made my sleep better. I don't *need* it—I don't need it *yet*—but I won't deny that it helped."

Kenneth says, "Where is he now?"

"It's complicated," Mary says.

"Did you leave him?"

She cackles a little. "Well, obviously as you can see I *left* him physically, yes." Abruptly the tears are in her eyes, but she doesn't want them anymore, blinks them away. "I came because I needed to, and he didn't think I should. He didn't have time off anyway—he took a ton of personal days when I was in the hospital all those times. Who knows if I'll ever go back to work, so we need Geoff's health insurance. He couldn't sabotage his career to come even if he wanted to. Which"—she chortles again—"he definitely did *not.*"

"No," Kenneth said, "I don't get it. I don't care about the health insurance shit. How could he let you come here alone? He sure as hell doesn't know you're with me."

"He thinks I'm with Leo and Sandor. Leo agreed to come, but then all of a sudden he got offered some fabulous show in Paris. It's a big deal—a one-man show at some really prestigious gallery. I mean, he's forty years old and he's waited his entire life for this. He got this grant—did I tell you about that when I saw you last year? Twenty thousand dollars. His paintings have been selling, his career is taking off. He couldn't say no, but he's only staying for the opening and then he's coming here."

The four tourist kids have gotten up to leave. On the walls, Kerouac and Ginsberg stand watch like bemused sentries.

"You could have waited," Kenneth says. "A week in Spain's no hardship. I've seen you, what, three times in two years for one night apiece? Why did you call me?"

"I shouldn't have called," she admits.

"Let's leave," he says, and for a moment she thinks he means leave Tangier, get back on the morning ferry, and give up, and the tears do spill over hot and fast before she can banish them. But then he says, "We should get us a room. We should fuck our brains out. What do either of us have to lose?"

"I told you," she says wearily. "I *told* you."

"I don't give a shit what you told me."

"We're getting two rooms," she says. "If it's too expensive for you, I'll pay."

"What the fuck, girl," he says. "I'm not taking your money. I can afford my own damn room. But you're the one who turns up at my bar or my place every time you come visit your brother. You're the one

who called *me* and said 'quit your job.' Don't tell me I don't know what
I'm good for in your eyes, and how it's not what you want."

"It's not," she says. "I don't know how to explain it. I don't care about
sex right now. Maybe I've moved beyond it."

"Oh, Christ," he says. "Your lung falls down and now you're beyond
sex. You're not Joan of Arc, baby. Get over yourself."

She starts laughing. "This—" she says, "this is why I invited you.
Not the fucking. This."

"Well," he says, "it ain't why I came."

"Leave, then. Go, and I'll wait here until it's time to meet Leo and
Sandor."

"Right. Like you didn't tell me that whole sad story so I couldn't
cut out. Like you didn't say all that shit to make sure I'd know it's not
safe to leave your fifty-percent-lung-capacity, cystic ass on your own."

"Do what you want," she says. "I thought you're such a Bad Man
anyway—isn't that your shtick? What do you care if I end up dead in
Tangier, Mr. Bad Man?"

He stands and throws some bills on the table, and she's shocked to
see that he changed guilders for dirhams before he came, in anticipation of the trip. She thought she'd have to charge their drinks; surely
Kenneth does not own a credit card. "Come on," he says. "You want
your own room so bad, then cut out the foreplay." He lifts her rucksack, but when she stands to grab his, he's already slung it over his
shoulder like a duffel, like it is nothing at all.

WALKING BACK TO the hotel on his third morning in Tangier,
Kenneth thinks maybe he'll just stay on here. In their room, Cystic is
still asleep. He's got to see her through meeting her brother, but then
he'll be free. He's been in Amsterdam longer than anywhere except
Georgia, longer even than his time in London, which seemed like
forever when it was happening. Time to move on.

Tangier could be the place. Since he's been here he's been taking photos like a motherfucker; he's feeling an old hunger he hasn't
known in years, eager for the next thing. This city is the kind of place
that could fuel him. Seedy, dirty, teeming with people and odors and

sounds — but something beautiful underneath the filthy facade, something old and eternal. Yesterday he and Cystic took a taxi ride up to the top of the hill the city's built on and looked down. The taxi driver said it's one of the only places in the world where you can view two continents at once, and Kenneth felt almost dizzy, a sense of the world's simultaneous vastness and accessibility overwhelming him. When he was young, he left home to see the world, and he *believed* in it, that goal — he thought himself on an honorable quest. But all that time in New Orleans, Taos, Los Angeles, London, the Caribbean, then back around Europe before he settled in A'dam — something was lost early on, before he even hit British soil and things got really bad. The journey itself had ceased to be the point of anything, and instead he was always on the make, looking for a buck, looking for somebody to take advantage of, looking to score. He was already a junkie when he left home, but a junkie could still have a soul, at least for a while. Finally, though, the drugs ate out anything left in him of the noble wanderer, turning him into a grifter, a dealer, a con man, an enforcer, whatever he needed to be.

But that's too easy. These past few years, even before Agnes's death, he's been clean (or clean enough), and it hasn't changed him much. All that time in Amsterdam, a city overrun with tourists sucking up its quaint beauty and amusement park of vice, he wasn't ever moved. Here his eyes are like a camera lens again, and there are two visions: the messy, cacophonous one he and Cystic are traipsing through in the flesh, and the one he can frame just so, cutting out anything extraneous and boiling things down to their surprisingly harmonious essence.

He wanted to walk up that hill, but she couldn't. They had to take the taxi up, and Cystic insisted on paying because it was her "fault" they couldn't walk like normal people. At the top there were four other travelers. Kenneth recognized them from the first night at the bar. They were just kids, but they'd taken a car, too, with a guide. He wanted to say, *See, most tourists don't walk it, there's nothing to feel guilty about,* but she wouldn't have liked that. She doesn't like him to be nice, and he's no good at it anyway, so he steers clear.

Under the worn-thin bedspread, she barely stirs. She sleeps like an infant, scary deep. Maybe he'll walk up the hill today. She can hang at the bar downstairs and read—she picked up a copy of *On the Road* from the hotel lobby, where someone else had left it—and he'll go on his own. Even though he did more sightseeing yesterday than in his entire life, he's having a hard time sitting still. He got some great shots at the Caves of Hercules. The silhouette of the caves looked like the bust of an old hag, mouth agape to cackle, dark and crazy water looming beyond. And they trolled the Kasbah, walking under all those Moorish archways, photographing a bright green Matisse door with Cystic standing in front of it, looking skinny and hollowed out. In the past she used to look healthy, almost objectionably so, like some cheerleader or TV sitcom wife. Now there's a sharpness to her that makes her look like a bird of prey. Under her gauzy shirts her elbows are bigger than the tops of her arms. Eating tires her out. She looks like a breeze could knock her down. Pared down, like everything else here. Like something elemental and pure. Like his hands could snap her bones.

At the medina, she bought gifts. A hookah, of all things, for a fellow teacher in that small New England town. A hanging drum with a hennaed hand decorating one side of the sheer skin—this she said she'd keep herself. Some bowls with that blue mosaic design for her just-widowed mother. She likes to barter. A couple of times he had to get involved when someone wanted to speak French, but for the most part the merchants are fluent in English just like the young Dutch. She's asked him twice how he knows French and he just said he used to live in Louisiana and left it at that, though he didn't know any real Creoles there and never heard French there except in the jazz bars.

He hasn't bought anything except more film. Well, and a hooker.

At night they've been sleeping in side-by-side twin beds like he and Will used to when they were boys. She goes to the toilet down the hall to change, as though he hasn't seen every inch of her from the inside out, each of the three times she's come to A'dam. The first night at the Hotel Muniria he lay awake, having consumed not nearly enough booze to put him out, wishing for some hash at least to help him unwind, thinking about crawling into her bed. He imagined just getting on top of her and pinning her down, letting her wake to his dick pushing its way in. He was about 50 percent sure this was what she expected. There was only one room left at the hotel, a double, and she consented to it saying they could find another place with two rooms in the morning, but then they went sightseeing and gift buying and mint tea drinking and no new hotel was procured. The second night she must've *wanted* him to push things, to just not take no for an answer. She was pulling that girl shit where it would all be his idea, his fault, like he'd forced her. They're both too damn old for that game, so when she came back to the room in her sweatpants and T-shirt ready for bed, he just stood and said, "I'm going out."

He expected her to grill him at the very least, but she said, "Good. You should."

He has hash now from the taxi driver. Soon she will get on the train to Casablanca and head to meet her brother and he will be done with her. Game-playing, cock-teasing bitch.

At the Caves of Hercules she said, "If I were here with Geoff I'd take off all my clothes and make him take my picture. He used to love it when I did things like that. Now I think it just makes him uncomfortable."

"It won't make me uncomfortable," he said, laughing. "Here's the camera."

But she stayed dressed.

He imagines the way her rib cage would protrude, the shading underneath it like the shadows the rock formations cast on the water. He can't decide if she would look more close to death naked, or less so. Her clothes, exactly the kind of gauzy, concealing cotton shit a good American girl would wear in an Arab country, give her the airy appearance of a ghost. He'd like to see the shock of her pubic hair, darker than what's on her head, against her wan skin. He'd like to hear her scream with an energy that shows she's still kicking. He'd like to smell *her* up close instead of the perfume she dots onto her wrists and throat, which could be the bouquets around a coffin. When he puts her on the bus, it's the last he'll see of her. There won't be any more trips overseas, she's said. She won't show up again at Mulligan's (where he might still be able to get his job back—or maybe he'll just stay on in Tangier). She will disappear into the void with Will and Hillary and his mother and his bastard father and his now-grown son, with Shane and Agnes and the legions of others just like them, some of whom he can almost taste like it was yesterday, and some whose faces he can't even conjure anymore.

He spoke to his whore in French. He wore a condom. Afterward they smoked hashish together and it was fine. The whore had a pockmarked face but he didn't mind. Her tits were big, and he liked to sample the local flavor. There were plenty of North African whores in Amsterdam, but he'd never gone to one. Will had come home from Nam with a taste for prostitutes—back in Atlanta, they became goddamn connoisseurs. It was good to screw the Tangier whore; it gave him a sense of nostalgia and new beginnings at once. Better than to fuck a pale skeleton of a woman, a woman who didn't want him. Not that the whore *wanted* him exactly, but she wanted his money and he was glad to pay and everybody was happy in a simple way that made the world go round. Nothing new in that game, nothing personal. Sometimes Will used to rough up the whores, but Kenneth never did. Later, of course, there were girls who'd paid their debts to him on their backs, junkie girls who had only one thing with which to barter. Yes, it's better for her to take her gauzy clothes, her clean hair and flowery perfume and wedding band, and get on the train.

He stands up, goes over to her bed, low to the ground and rickety like all beds in these kinds of places, like every bed he's slept in for twenty years. The fact that she is comfortable enough around him to lie there sleeping in the bright sunlight irks him. He didn't ask for this intimacy. He didn't ask for this comfort.

He prods her with his foot. She sits up with a sharp gasp like someone choking. She's sweaty from the stale heat, but her lips, without the gloss she usually wears, seem a little blue.

"What's going on?" she asks. "You're dressed. Have you already been out?"

"I just got home," he says. "About an hour ago."

He catches that he has said "home" and wants to amend it, but that would just draw more attention to the mistake. This isn't home. There is no home.

"Are you hungry?" she says

"No. Let's get out of the city." Suddenly he doesn't want her here anymore. He doesn't want to spend the rest of his time in Tangier, after she leaves, bumping into her ghost. "Let's go see something on the coast."

Her face lights up like a little girl's, suddenly beautiful. He can't look at it. He fusses in his bag.

"Awesome!" He remembers sometimes hearing her use that expression with Joshua when she first moved into Arthog House, and the way he'd cringe—how easily dismissal came then. He motions at the door with his chin.

"There's a beach town an hour away, Asilah. We'll check it out. Get dressed." It's only once she has left for the toilet that he can breathe normally again.

From: mrgrace@yahoo.com
Subject: You would love this place
Date: August 20, 2001
To: geoffreyjs@hitchcock.org

Hey babe.

I'm in Asilah at an Internet café. This town is so spectacular. Everything's awash in white, almost like Mykonos, with the blue ocean, the blue sky, blue tiles everywhere, as though the entire world is white and blue. There are funky murals on the walls and a summer jazz fest that apparently attracts people from all over Europe. You would love this place. It's nothing like Tangier, which I loved, too, but you would hate. Here, cute little kids run around at the beach with their huge, dark eyes and skinny legs—they look innocent but try to get you to give them coins to take their photographs, ha. In the town there are still places where you can go watch old men baking bread for the villagers in a giant brick oven. There are camels everywhere, walking on the beach, dozing at entrances of buildings. The Berber women don't like having their photographs taken (even for coins);

they think, we've been told, that the camera will steal their souls. But I can't resist zoom-lensing to try to catch them, they're so mysterious and beautiful. Geoff, I just want to eat this place whole. The air is so much cleaner than in Tangier—everything smells like flowers and the sea and the leather of the marketplace, the mint of the tea. I know it isn't true, but it feels impossible to be ill in a place like this. My energy is higher than in Tangier. There are things I love that are no good for me now, and it breaks my heart but I know I have to accept it. Everything that Tangier is falls into that category now.

You asked when I'm coming home. A fair question and I wish I could answer fairly but I don't know. A month, I think? We're making our way down the coast, Casablanca after this and then farther south to a hippie beach town called Essaouira, and finally inland to Marrakech and the High Atlas. Don't worry, I won't hike (as if I could). I'll stay at some little hammam or something and wait for Leo and Sandor to come back for me. We want to make a trip into the desert and camp (don't worry, I've got salt tablets, I'll stay hydrated), and after that we'll head back to Spain by way of Fez, where the medina is supposed to be like going back in time. ALL of Morocco feels that way so far to me. I wish it were still possible to say that we'll come back here together someday, but I know that isn't going to happen now, so I can only ask you one more time to be patient.

Me

KENNETH LOOKS CLEAN for the first time she has ever witnessed. On the endless stretch of sand, he wears a linen shirt in a color she has come to think of as Moroccan blue and a pair of lightweight trousers. He completely surprised her this morning by going into a store in Asilah—not a tourist shop but an ordinary clothing store where the few other customers were Arab men—and speaking to the shopkeeper in a French already less halting than it was on their arrival five days ago. He carried his small parcel back to their noisy little hotel on the beach, where he took a shower and changed into his new outfit, combing out his long hair. For a moment she thought he would produce a razor and shave his beard, but perhaps he doesn't own one, because the beard remains intact.

Mary did not know what to make of this transformation, but she took the opportunity of his cleanliness to suggest that they go and see the nearby resort their driver told them about, Le Mirage. She wanted to see it yesterday but was embarrassed to bring Kenneth along: a fact that shamed and annoyed her at once. It is not in her guidebook, but no taxi driver or guide has failed to offer to take them. And so, Kenneth sparkling clean and looking more like a shaggy Hollywood producer than his usual cross between an old Deadhead and a too-skinny biker, they arrived by taxi with all their luggage. The plan was to stay for lunch and then head back to Tangier in time to have a drink at the Tanger Inn.

Instead, Mary took one look at Le Mirage and announced that they would stay the night. The simplest suite was two hundred dollars. Before Kenneth could even weigh in, she plunked down her credit card.

A boy helped them carry their luggage out of the lobby into the open air, the panorama of sea stretched out below their hilltop. He led them to one of the individual villas, each with its own sitting room and private patio with lounge chairs. Mary immediately imagined herself and Geoff lying on the chairs in their bathing suits, Geoff's skin growing dark as an Arab's. She doubted Kenneth had owned swim trunks since boyhood. Years of drugs and nocturnal habits have left him looking like he might be allergic to the sun. When she imagined him lying on a lounge chair, she saw him still in the cowboy boots he wore in London and Amsterdam. She wasn't sure why she even wanted to stay at a place that so clearly didn't suit her traveling companion. No doubt Kenneth would think her materialistic, a typical American, always looking for luxury over authenticity. Well, fuck him. He could endure one night.

She tipped the boy before Kenneth could. She knew she was emasculating him and didn't care. Perhaps he didn't even *know* about tipping at hotels. Who could say what ordinary customs he might not be privy to?

Kenneth said noncommittally, "I'm gonna go down and see the beach."

She followed . . .

Now, splashes of purple and pink flowers burst everywhere. Mary catches a glimpse of giant sunflowers set back from the water, taller than she is, moving gently in the wind. Sand and rockless sea stretch as far as her eyes can discern. Though there have to be other guests at the hotel, the beach is completely deserted, as is the terrace of the small restaurant looming above. It reminds her of the place where she and Nix lunched with Zorg and Titus, the way it overlooks the beach below, the perfect isolation. She imagines herself here with Nix, the two of them in their shorts and flip-flops hounding the woman at the front desk to arrange an in-room massage, maybe nude sunbathing at the foot of the sunflowers. She envisions Nix's silver toe ring, crusted with sand.

But no. She is here with *Yank,* of all people!

Self-destructive, Geoff maintained on their way to Logan Airport. *I can't support this, I can't assist you in your suicidal mission.* And she put her head on her knees in the car and muttered, *Why do you have to be so dramatic? Why are you trying to take all the joy out of this for me?*

Kenneth has rolled up his trouser legs and taken off his sandals, water spilling over his ankles. In three years, he will be fifty. Fifty: for Mary an inconceivable age. One more serious infection and her lung function could plummet to 30 percent almost overnight, heralding the end stage of her disease, of her life. It is more a question of whether she will ever return to work; whether she will celebrate her thirty-fifth birthday in two years. No, fifty is not even a pipe dream. After all he's done to himself, all his years of self-abuse, Kenneth is walking in territory she will never chart.

She reaches his side and he looks down at her, face grave. He is going to reprimand her for bringing him here, for paying, for tipping that luggage boy. He is going to say he's calling a taxi, waiting for it outside the gates of the resort with his dusty rucksack alongside all the sleeping camels, heading back to Tangier, leaving her here.

"I've never been anyplace like this in my whole damn life. Thanks."

She almost jumps. "You *like* it here?"

He looks surprised. "You see something not to like?"

She stares at the water. There have been times she has felt almost symbiotic with this man — sometimes when they're talking, usually when he's fucking her. But now he seems an utter mystery.

"Mary," he says. He never, ever calls her that. "Honestly, girl. This has been fun, it's been . . ." He hesitates, smiles. "It's been goddamn awesome. But tomorrow, you're gonna get on that four o'clock train to meet your brother. That's what you told your man you were doing, and that's what you should do. I'll go with you to the station, but once Sandor and Leo come on the scene, you don't need me. This is as far as I go."

She doesn't say anything. It is only two o'clock; there will be hours of sun left before they go to dinner. It still seems, here, impossible that Tangier even exists, that tomorrow will ever come.

"If I sleep with you" — she lifts her chin to him — "will you change your mind?"

He takes one step closer, his hand moving slightly as though to touch her, and she doesn't know what kind of touch it will be. Sometimes he can be tender, almost sweet, and she can glimpse the southern boy he once was, a college student who wanted to study art but whose father insisted on something "practical" that would help him go into the family business — that boy who was obsessed with D. H. Lawrence and played the piano and married his high school sweetheart. Other times . . .

His hand, though, falls to his side. "No," he says. "It won't."

But he's lying.

THEY DINE ON the terrace, against a sunset backdrop un-like anything Kenneth has ever seen even in the Caribbean: a giant ball of molten lava, red as a blood orange trickling toward the horizon. He snaps some shots, though sunsets rarely come out right, and he and Cystic watch it fall, taking their drinks to the edge of the wall as if to get as close as possible.

On the way back to their villa, Cystic carries her sandals in her hand, walking barefoot. The effect is sexy as hell until she steps on a sharp rock and cries out, hopping around on her one good foot while blood drizzles onto the ground. The restaurant is higher up the hill than their room, so Kenneth scoops her up and carries her, though at first she protests. She is a woman, he has noticed, who requires a lot of maintenance but always chafes at its offer, as opposed to the kind of girls he grew up around: girls who expected bucketfuls of chivalry even though they could run the world. She's alarmingly light now, must be under a hundred pounds. He's used to skinny girls, to how they waste away from within; he's seen that plenty. Still, he holds her carefully, afraid that if he trips and falls, the weight of his own body will crush her.

In their fancy bathroom with the ornate tiled sink and big tub, she sits on the edge of the toilet washing her foot. The gash is impressive. They have no Band-Aids, but she says the concierge will procure one for them; it's always that way at hotels like this. Still, she doesn't call. She sits with a washcloth on her foot turning red fast. Kenneth feels stupid hovering over some little flesh wound; he starts to leave the bathroom, go put some music on the stereo (he's never been in a hotel with its own stereo system before), but she calls out, "Hey. Do you want to take a bath?"

He runs the water. This is something he hasn't done since Hillary, taking a bath with a woman. It has to be like riding a bike—it has to be like using a needle: you never forget how. They did this on their wedding night, and afterward whenever Hillary wanted to reach out to him, she'd run a bath. By the end, though, their tub was full of baby toys, crowded and usually with a ring of dried bubble bath around the edges, because Hillary didn't always scrub it out when she was done bathing the baby. By the end, Kenneth showered fast in the mornings and didn't get home until after the boy was already in bed, so he missed those times when his son splashed in the bubbles and Hillary carried him, dripping and pink, in a towel to the nursery. On the morning Kenneth left, he didn't shower at all. He didn't want to look at anything of the boy's, didn't want to step over any of his shit. He just got up and threw on his jeans and left.

There's bubble bath here in the fancy Le Mirage bathroom, but since he has never used it before and doesn't know the protocol, he leaves it be. She's perched on the closed toilet seat with her red wash-cloth, watching him test the water with his hand. "I like it hot," she says, and he responds, "That's gonna make the blood start up again," but cranks it hotter anyway. When the water reaches halfway up the tub, he doesn't look at her, just strips and gets in.

It is the first time in memory he's bathed twice in one day. There is something humiliating in this knowledge, though it would have seemed all right, just fine, until a few days ago. He has to stop think-ing like this, the way he's thinking about himself—it makes him want, not to kiss her, not to lick her tits and feel her ass, but to do something *else,* something to punish her for his feelings. Soon he will put her on the train to Casablanca and she will become Somebody Else's Problem. Tonight he doesn't want to go overboard if it's the last time he's ever going to fuck her—he doesn't want her to remember him only that way.

She removes her white sundress in one fluid motion. Under it she wears no bra, which is often the case. Her breasts are small and still girlish, the nipples translucent pink like the inside of a seashell. They are not the kind of breasts he usually prefers, but they look all right on her. She steps out of her lacy blue panties, and she looks differ-ent down there than he remembered: her ass less full, her hip bones pushing against the skin, the hair waxed or shaved down to a landing strip perhaps in anticipation of a holiday in a warm climate, though he hasn't seen a skimpy bikini yet. She lowers herself into the water and immediately her body becomes distorted as if viewed through a funhouse glass. He wishes he'd used the bubble bath so he couldn't see her at all.

He wants to kiss her; he wants to wrap his hands around her neck and squeeze; he wants to put her on her knees in front of him; he wants to run.

She says, "Will you wash my hair?"

It is a relief to laugh. "My first wife used to always want me to do that, too. What's with you girls and somebody washing your hair?"

"Robert Redford," she says. "Ralph Fiennes." But he doesn't know what that means.

He cups the water in his hands. Her hair is porous like a sponge;
it soaks up more water than makes sense. He turns her around in the
tub so that her back is to him and he can bend her backward a little
to keep the water from falling all over her face. He's no good at this,
probably. He should have bathed the boy at least once or twice when
he had the chance; then he would know what to do, how to control
the water's direction. He lathers her head, not using enough shampoo
at first (her hair soaks that up, too!), and rubs the bony shape of her
skull. Her head and neck seem bumpy and too small. It seems crazy
that she is actually *in* there, in a space so small.

He rinses her hair with a water glass from the sink. Her foot must
not be bleeding anymore; the water isn't pink. She leans against him,
and his cock presses hard against her spine. He isn't sure what it's
thinking exactly; he isn't sure he can go through with its plan. Yet he
obeys his body—puts a hand on her breast.

"No," she murmurs, almost a purr. "Don't. Just stay like this."

He pushes himself back away from her, water sloshing on the floor.
He thought he might feel *relieved* if she refused, but no. She turns to
face him, the knobs of her spine twisting as she contorts her torso. The
tub is too small for a man his size to share, and though the water fills
the space where her body was, he is still too damn close.

"This isn't a slumber party," he says coldly. "I'm not your dead
friend."

She contemplates him for a long time. He meant to make her mad,
but she doesn't look mad. If she were mad he could push her against
the cold tile of the tub and cover her mouth with his; he could let his
body do what it knew. He keeps still, the water quiet now.

"You're certainly not," she says. "She wouldn't like you, I don't
think." She is smiling, though oddly. "But I do."

"Yeah." He says it quietly. "I like you, too." Then he gets up to crash
on the couch before he can get himself into any more trouble.

LESS THAN THIRTY seconds after exiting CMN Airport in
Casablanca—a city more French than Arab, more cosmopolitan than

Old World, more generic than not, worthy only of a stopover in their minds—Leo grabs his sister by the arm, his spindly fingers tight like a vice.

"What the hell," he demands in a stage whisper, "is that freaking guy *doing* here?"

Mary tosses her head and ignores him.

LEO'S BODY FEELS so alert he is almost sick. Maybe it's the fumes. They're sitting above what seems to be an exhaust leak. Leo thanks God (the god of exotic scenery and surprisingly lucrative painting sales) that Mary is sleeping, because even if she's breathing this foul exhaust, at least she doesn't know it and can't feel anxious the way he does on her behalf. They are the only tourists on the bus, though it's crammed with people. Leo is no stranger to foreign bus rides, having visited his father in Mexico, but this is something else entirely. Outside his smudged window it's like a biblical scene is unfolding. Young girls give water to mules; men herd cattle on expanses of brown land; dryness and more dryness. Small communities are walled in by smooth sandstone, and another lone wall stands—crumbling and rocky in more the English fashion—amid an isolated field, its purpose now long lost. *If I saw a painting of that wall I would think it was sentimental crap,* Leo thinks. *So why do I feel so moved?*

Next to Leo, Sandor is reading a book about Moroccan history but not actually looking out the window at the country itself. That is Sandor to a tee. Sandor and all his damaged dead from the history books, but in real life he keeps it light, things seem to roll right off his back; he's oblivious to anything truly unsettling. It is a gift, Leo has come to believe. It keeps a person sane, and Sandor is very sane, almost alarmingly so.

That fucking bartender's sleeping, too. Leo cringes, imagining what nocturnal activities might have this asshole and his sister so tired out. He hasn't had any luck getting Mary alone to find out what the fuck's going on. When he talked to her a week before her flight to Barcelona, he told her to wait for him in Sitges, lie on the beach; he even gave her some phone numbers of friends she could look up if she wanted someone to take her to dinner or if, God forbid, she got sick. But the night he arrived in Paris, she e-mailed him, saying she was already in Tangier. Then when they landed in Casablanca, *this*.

The bus rolls up to a tiny, fly-ridden café, all male clientele of course. The bus must be a hundred degrees; Leo is experiencing a hot flash, veering dangerously close to claustrophobia. He has to get off this thing, out into the world.

"Let's go get some tea," he tells Sandor.

"Excellent idea," Sandor says, not looking up. "Wait, just let me fetch my *Lonely Planet's Guide to Sodom*. Then we should make out a little bit, too, at that café, Leo, so Mary and the Yankee have a most exciting story about their trip — how they watched us get killed."

Leo tries to kick Sandor's leg, but they're sitting too close together and he can't get a decent angle. "Come on," he says, waiting.

"You think I jest? Seriously, what are we *doing* in this country? Those crazy villagers out there, they may start pounding on the door and ask that we be given up for the crowd to rape. And we, we are not angels, nobody will sacrifice their daughters instead."

Leo stares at him, confused. Commie-junkie-shaman fathers, it should be stipulated, rarely make their sons read scripture.

"This coach ride," Sandor explains, "—I feel like we have not just traveled miles, we have traveled *time*. Those robed men squatting in the fields, you keep pointing to say, *Oh, look, aren't they quaint?* Those same men would stone us in the town square, just you remember that!"

Leo sighs. "So does this mean you're not gonna blow me on that Jimi Hendrix beach in Essaouira?" But before Sandor can answer, he leans across the aisle, grabs Mary's shoulder, and shakes her awake.

"Come on." He's whispering, too, but for fear of waking the godforsaken cowboy. Mary blinks rapidly, then follows gamely. He notices with some trepidation that she brings her entire day pack, and that at the café, mint tea in front of them in the suffocating heat, she pulls out her inhaler. "Look, they have an outlet," she says. "Do you think anyone would be freaked out if I did my DNase here? You know, the thing with the mask?"

Leo envisions his sister being mistaken for a biological terrorist wearing a face mask while releasing deadly poison onto the rest of them. "Hmm," he offers, not wanting to give Sandor the satisfaction of their collective murder. "Maybe they have a toilet?"

"It takes about twenty minutes."

"Oh."

Apparently deterred, Mary drinks her tea. She makes a few snorting sounds with her nose as though trying to clear it. She gets these nasal polyps; she used to have them removed, she says, but now she just deals with them because surgery poses a danger, a risk of infection. Even her fingers on the small glass look different than they did only a couple of years ago. They're wider at the ends near her fingernails and slightly curled under, as if she were a child playing dragon. It must be part of the disease, though he's not sure why and doesn't want to ask. Her physical attractiveness is like a constant high-wire act: a balancing between feminine charms and the harsh facts of the disease. Leo would tell her you can barely notice this finger deformity, but that isn't true, not anymore; she can't wear all those chunky silver rings she used to wear, and he thinks he might start to cry. They both stare out at the orange-brown world surrounding them.

Mary says, "If I lived here, I'd be dead."

"God, absolutely," Leo says. "Me, too."

It is true. The world from which they come is one of absurd luxury. A world in which you can be born with a disease that once killed children in infancy and instead live to be past the age of trustability according to the old hippie creed. A world in which you can be born with the mad urge to kill yourself and try several times, and it turns out that you can just take a pill and suddenly you are walking a perpetual high-wire act yourself. They are indulged. Even now they are here, soaking up this timeless land, but without any purpose to their trip other than to expand their own horizons, delight their own senses. This is decadence: the ability to live long past the point when nature tried to rule you out; the ability to turn the world into your playground rather than your burden or job.

"Honey," he says, "does Geoff know? Does he know that man is here?"

She almost drops her cup. "Of course not!" Then angrily: "Not that he'd care."

"Did you split up?"

She laughs mirthlessly. "I don't even know what that means anymore."

"Do you want me to call him?" Leo says. "Do you want me to get him to come and meet us?"

"Oh, Leo," she says. "You're so sweet. That's total nonsense, though."

The colorful Berber passengers, the men in their monochromatic Arab garb, are getting back on the bus. Leo settles the bill and he and Mary get back on board. Sandor is sitting with his nose still in his book, not even sweating. The bartender is still asleep. It is as if he and Mary have simply stopped time, stepped out, and had some magical interlude, and now everything is as it was. Leo is full of an intense sense that no one on earth except Mary is cognizant of where he is, and Mary does not count, when in any world except their absurdly rich and modern one, neither of them would even exist.

They sit across the aisle from each other as the bus starts up again. Mary takes out her little inhaler and Leo refuses to react, tells himself to behave normally. She sticks it in her mouth, then suddenly withdraws it with her nose wrinkled theatrically. "Holy shit," she says, "it smells like exhaust. Something must be wrong with the bus."

From: mrgrace@yahoo.com
Subject: checking in
Date: August 25, 2001
To: eggrace@yahoo.com

hi mom!

sorry i haven't written much, there aren't that many internet cafés around compared to europe. everything's fine. essaouira is gorgeous. it's this cool beach town where jimi hendrix and bob marley used to hang out, and is famous for its woodwork and spice market. all the colors are on fire in this country. there are these old, shriveled merchants in brown hooded robes who sit out on blankets, and they're surrounded by sprigs of every spice you can imagine, so it's like an explosion of color around these plain brown men. the medina is blue and white like so much here, charming and friendly compared to the aggression of tangier (don't worry—by "aggression" i don't mean we were mugged or anything, please don't panic, ha-ha). the air smells fresh and fishy, except by the port, where they grill out so much fish that it's like a perpetual smoke cloud—i've been avoiding it there even though the most famous restaurant in town is right there and leo and sandor say it's really awesome. today we went to buy a carpet for geoff . . .

THE CARPET MERCHANT had served them mint tea. Berber whiskey, he called it. Mary sat in the shade while he spread rug after rug on top of one another for her perusal, and Sandor and Leo pelted her with questions about her house's color scheme, pronouncing most of the carpets "too blue" until at last one with the right prominence of green in the weave emerged. "You should know better than to take artists shopping with you," Kenneth said, as though he wasn't an artist, too, as though he hadn't been taking pictures nonstop since his arrival in Morocco. Did he just not like the task of buying a gift for another man? Mary wondered—let herself wonder. But if he was jealous, he didn't show it, had come along gamely, just like the others. He sat next to her on the ground with his long legs crossed Indian-style, effortlessly for a man of his height and age, then moved farther away to smoke, flicking the ashes into the ornate ashtray and taking such a shine to it that abruptly, as she bargained with the merchant, Mary threw the ashtray in with the deal. Afterward, presented with the option of shipping her purchase home, Kenneth had balked, saying who knew if it would arrive, and if it didn't and she'd already have paid up, so the merchant proceeded to roll the rug in front of their eyes so tightly, so small, that when it was finished, though it would spread across Mary and Geoff's dining room, it had been reduced to the size of a baby in a blanket, so tiny that when Mary took it in her arms, its weight shocked her and she had to hand it over to Sandor to carry.

They had been at the shop for two hours. By the time they left, Mary felt spent, vaguely depressed that she had not shipped the rug after all. In her imagination she saw Geoff receiving it while she was still gone, spreading it out under the table where they usually ate, knowing she was thinking of him and forgiving her somehow for everything: all he knew and all he didn't. For the nights in Amsterdam screaming and writhing under Kenneth; for the fact that their knees had touched casually while she chose this gift. For the fact that she was weak and selfish when the ill were supposed to be strong and heroic. For the fact that she was squandering what time they had left to be together by running . . .

for *our* dining room i mean, it was for me too, mom. i really like it here. essaouira has almost a european vibe, in spite of the random camels and cows lying around the beach . . .

She had not planned to windsurf. Essaouira was the windsurfing capital of Africa, people said, but it wasn't until Mary hit the beach that she decided to try, dragged Sandor and Leo with her, though Leo kept claiming that he couldn't swim, that nobody who grew up in New York ever learned to swim and he was bound to be killed. Kenneth didn't own a swimsuit, hadn't touched the water since the day he'd rolled up his new trousers at the water's edge at Le Mirage, and Mary thought he would wander away without a word, the way he'd periodically been doing since their last night in Tangier and even more since Leo and Sandor's arrival. But instead he stayed and watched. Her lungs felt better than they had in weeks—maybe months—and she fantasized it was from the air rushing in them as her sailboard picked up speed. You could take lessons right on the beach. The salt seemed to have scoured her lungs the way it did her nasal passages, even though she hadn't coughed it all out afterward. She felt clean and replenished, her skin browning the way it always did when it came in contact with saltwater. She'd grown tired after an hour and had to stop, but even then the exhaustion felt good, pure, the way it had when she used to swim at meets in high school. Leo and Sandor were still going strong in the water, Leo's graceful, olive-skinned body blending in perfectly and Sandor's lanky paleness nearly glowing, but they were laughing and strong and young, still young—even Leo at forty seemed young, and why not? He could live another fifty years, and if that wasn't youth, then what the hell was? When she emerged from the surf, Kenneth looked so happy it took her aback. He smiled so infrequently, his smile usually inseparable from a laugh that was sardonic or irreverent, but now he was just plain smiling, looking like he had done something wonderful though he had done nothing but sit on the sand.

They walked along the beach. He said, "I might have to buy me a pair of shorts and try that shit, it looked crazy fun," and she felt inexpressibly glad and wasn't sure why. They walked a long stretch. Farther down the beach were rock formations that looked like a sunken castle sticking out of the water, but Mary hadn't consulted her guidebook since they'd arrived in Essaouira and she didn't know what it was. Nobody was around now. She and Kenneth walked over to some porous brown boulders and sat on them, though the sharp rock poked into her skin. She felt vibrant.

"I didn't expect to love it here so much."

Kenneth looked genuinely confused. "Why would you leave your husband and run off here when everyone told you not to if you didn't think you'd dig it?"

She shrugged. "Same old. I keep thinking I'm done with the exorcism, but I never am."

"You mean Nix? What, she wanted to come to Morocco and never got the chance?"

Mary looked up at the sun until her eyes felt raw. "Her boyfriend in London had a cousin in Morocco. They were thinking of coming here, I think to live. I don't even know how seriously they considered it—she might have only written that to impress me. Actually, I'm not even sure her *boyfriend* was real. She might have made him up, too."

"What the hell for?"

"It's complicated. To throw me off the scent of something else, maybe. She would have had her reasons."

They sat in silence.

"I watched that trial on TV, you know," Kenneth said at last. "I watched everything about it and thought about you watching in Vermont or wherever the hell you live. A lot of people in Amsterdam said it was all rigged, they said the US rigged the whole deal, but then other sides were saying how *more* people should've been convicted, how that Libyan didn't act alone. I thought about what you would think and how no matter who took the fall it wouldn't bring back your friend. They talk about deterrents, but there's no such thing as convincing someone bent on hate not to hate. In the whole wide history of the world, nobody ever talked anybody out of anything by stringing someone else up."

Mary watched minuscule fish swimming in and out of the holes in the rock. It seemed unfathomable that they looked exactly the same as the tiny fish in Ohio creeks. How could anything live both in Ohio and here and be so unchanged?

"I came to town right after the verdict," she said at last. She found his eyes and held them. "I showed up at your door and you fucked me and you never said anything."

"What'd you want me to say?" he asked, but she didn't know. She started to cry a little bit, but it wasn't because of Nix, or Lockerbie, or Kenneth's silence (she would have expected nothing else). It was only because her lungs felt so deceptively clean and she wished Geoff could have seen her on the sailboard, and the thought of his carpet bound so tightly and small and yet so heavy back in her room made her heart feel it could slam right out of her chest. And it did no good to talk about the fucking circus of the Lockerbie trial and all the justice never done in the world and all the families still haunted in a way even she could never fully touch—it did no good at all.

"Stand up. I want to photograph you."

"I don't feel like it."

He smiled, but a different smile from when she came out of the water. "Doesn't your brother talk to you about his work, Cystic? Nothing's any good unless it burns."

"Fine," she said. "Do me here then. I'm not getting up."

He took his lens cap off, started setting up the shot, took a test.

When he kept waiting, she finally reached up and pulled down her suit, still not standing, wriggled it off under her, and threw it to the side, so that the sharp rocks were even more pronounced against her ass. She looked away from the camera, said, "There's a picture of me Geoff took in the Canary Islands on a rock like this. We had it framed for a while in our bathroom until my poor father came to visit and freaked out."

He kept clicking. She leaned back against the rock. Her back hurt in a way she hadn't noticed when she was sailing across the water, and what had felt clean in her lungs just a moment before started feeling too scoured now: raw.

She said, "You're never going to show me these, are you?"

"Sure," he said, "I'll show you. I'll show you the next time you come to Amsterdam."

"I told you," she said. "I'm not coming again."

He lowered the camera, squinted at the sky. "The light's changed," he said. "It's no good anymore. We should get back."

i miss dad even more since i've been here. not because he'd ever set foot in morocco (can you imagine?!), but because i never even thanked him for following me all the way to mexico to interrogate daniel and confront eli. i don't like to think of you sleeping without him, worrying about me. i know he used to talk you down, just like geoff does for me. i'm coming to understand lost time in a different way since dad died. i've been a completely crappy daughter and now i live far away even when i'm home and maybe i can never rectify all the inconsideration, all the times i've held you at a distance, all the resentment for things that were never even for a moment your fault. mom, please don't worry. i know i said when i left that i didn't know when i'd be coming home, but i've decided on a month, no longer. i'll be home by late september. i don't like sleeping alone either. i wish i could say that coming here has been solely a mistake, but that would be a lie.

AND SO, WHEN he shows up at her door, she is still somehow surprised. Dinner has been had, the four of them together, a fountain gurgling as background music. Sandor and Leo have retired to their shared room (with two beds, given automatically without any request to that effect), and Mary is in her own room reading Paul

Bowles, as one is supposed to do in Morocco, and feeling horny and virtuous and filthy and ruined and hopeful, assuming Kenneth is out trolling for sex just like Port in the novel. He is not secretive about his activities and she is in no position to give even her blessing to his forays, much less anything else. It is possible that he loves her, but what of it? She lies on her woven bedspread, the glaring white of the walls blurring her vision, the tile of the floor chilly despite the heat outside. On the bed she is safe and warm and consumed with Port and Kit and their travails, until there is a knock on her door and she automatically assumes Leo, there for a postsex chat once Sandor has fallen dead asleep, Leo in some crazy silk smoking jacket with his hair a mess and looking hyperbolically beautiful, and maybe he will crawl into her bed and stay until morning, the two of them cocooned as though they come from the same womb.

But no, it is Kenneth fully dressed, the sand of the beach still clinging in spots to his jeans. He steps inside the room before she can invite him in or ask him to leave.

Not that she would ask him to leave.

She says, "Are you going out?"

For a moment he doesn't respond and she wonders if maybe he isn't going out but is instead leaving altogether, the way he said he would at Le Mirage. She tells herself that she shouldn't try to persuade him to stay, that she has to let him go this time, that not only is trying to hold on to him selfish and wrong (because she is willing to be selfish, willing to be wrong), but it also simply makes no sense. He is not a thing that can be held on to. It is like trying to grab smoke. It is the way he has described trying to recapture that first heroin high, which never returns again no matter how far you chase it. What there is between them does not translate into any coherent language. Even if Geoff did not exist—even if she had never married—she would not have a future with this man. Fine, then, let him go: to his brothel, to his plane back to Amsterdam, or to his train to a new life in Tangier that could never include her. Where is Leo? Why couldn't it be Leo at her door?

"I thought I'd—" Kenneth begins, then stops. "Can I sleep here tonight?"

She wants to ask, *Did you check out of your room because you're leaving?* She wants to ask, *Have you run out of money?* She wants to say, *I hope you didn't really quit your job at Mulligan's, because I'm not going to be here as long as I planned.* She wants to offer, *I'm sorry I misled you,* though she isn't sure if she would be referring to Mulligan's or to something else. He sits on her bed, removes his sandals, a sprinkling of sand scattering on her floor. She is not sure she wants him here, his sand and the smell of his smoke and his bourbon and his skin. It is possible she cannot bear his being here, possible she will strike him and push him toward the door. Except that if she did so, they would inevitably end up in bed. Her hands stay at her sides.

He is taking off his clothes. Her senses start returning; he doesn't have his rucksack, so he can't be leaving for good. No, he has left his room, the room he paid for, to come here. They have had sex a total of seven times on three different occasions, and each time they fucked, it began almost instantaneously, a frenzy of bodies pushing together, a feast of hungry mouths. Nothing like this, this quiet removal of clothing down to his underwear and slipping between sheets. He enters her bed like a husband of many years, soundless and without fanfare, yet he looks all wrong in the prettiness of her hotel bed. She turns out the light and realizes that in their times together, other than when they slept in separate beds in Tangier, the lights have never been off. They have never shared the ceremonies of sleep. She is already in her pajamas and doesn't undress further but gets into bed beside him, his body radiating heat like every man's body since Joshua's, so that her fresh white sheets are no longer cool.

He holds her in the darkness. The room has only a tiny window, too high up on the wall, as though they're in a basement, and the darkness around them is total. They have embraced in the past, of course, even on this trip, but he has never held her like this, gently, silently, with a tentativeness and need she is not sure how to decipher. He is holding her, she thinks, as though her entire body is bleeding.

"I've been thinking," he says through the excessive blackness of the room, "about going back to Atlanta and looking up my son."

"That's wonderful," she says. "You should absolutely do that."

"Nah. I shouldn't really. But I might anyway."

"Kenneth," she says, "I think that's seriously the best idea you've ever had."

"Okay," he says softly. "Okay."

She is aware that she thinks of touching his dick now, as a kind of reward for his good idea. She is aware that she is almost thirty-three years old and is still not sure what comes next, what she has to offer if not sex.

"I don't know what I'm doing here." In the darkness, the words feel like a time long ago, waiting with Nix in the somber, incense-filled church for their separate turns inside the confessional, where they would make up sins: *I lied to my mother; I cheated on a test at school.* Were they so without sin then, or were they just lazy? *Forgive me, Father, for I have sinned,* she thinks, her eyes closed. *It has been seventeen years since my last confession.* Now she would not have to make things up. "In Morocco, I mean. I'm like that Hemingway story where all I ever do is look at new things and try new drinks." She laughs. "I've never contributed anything anywhere I've gone. I taught English for about five minutes in Osaka. I should have *done* something, joined the Peace Corps, built a fucking house or gone to an ashram or volunteered at a refugee camp. I haven't made any impact. I drink mint tea and buy carpets. It's all been meaningless, and now it's all going to be over."

"Guess so," he says, and it feels like she's been slapped. She wanted him to argue, to tell her it was all worthwhile, to compare her life to his and judge it meritorious by contrast. Next to him, she has been Mother Teresa! The places where their bodies fit together are moist under her nightclothes and she knows his cock is hard though she cannot see or feel it. He chuckles and says, "I guess you could've gone over to Bosnia or Rwanda or something like that and caught some bug and died real noble on a stretcher for CNN and that would've looked prettier than being here with me."

She is aware that she is rubbing herself against him slightly, that her body cannot keep still now, is humming and tingling with a voltage she can't stop. In the past all their thrashing and shoving against walls and biting and screaming has been so much theater—genuine in the moment, but only noise. *This*—she could die of this. This desire could short-circuit her heart.

"Baby," he says. His hands have started traveling down her body, shocking the electric places. "I told myself I could make it through the night. I told myself I'd kiss you, that maybe you'd let me kiss you and I could be that guy who would be happy with a kiss—that it would be the first time I just *kissed* a woman since you in London. It sounded real good in my head. I don't want to leave, but I think I'd better."

"No." He tries to sit up, but she holds on to his biceps, hot like fever. "We don't have to sleep. We can just stay here like this and know we won't sleep and that we want something we can't have and it will be okay. We won't die of it. Don't go. Please."

"*I* want something I can't have," he says. "At least say what you mean."

"That's not true. I swear it's not."

"You can have it, then." He laughs, the sound slicing the room. "Christ, this is stupid, you can have it already."

"No," she whispers. "I can't." She is holding him now, cradling his head like a child's, wrapping her legs around him. It will happen, fine, it will happen and she doesn't care. She will go back to Geoff and lie about this just as she already has to lie about so much else. At least Kenneth will be happy then and she will only be torturing one man. She presses her body into his and feels his hard-on against her bladder, the tangle of his hair against her hands. They push against each other, but her clothes are still on and it's like pushing against a wall that sways but doesn't yield. She kisses his eyes, his hair, but when his mouth searches hers she keeps moving, eluding him, pulling him back down to the bed to lie flat, spooning his body, which feels in the dark like the skeleton of some large animal, like excavated bones. She thinks and thinks that he will turn around, that he will pin her down and pull off her pants and that she will let him, but he doesn't, and finally his breath begins to come more evenly, slow as though he may already be asleep.

"Cystic," he says finally, and she realizes that *she* was sleeping, that his voice startled her awake. "The things I've done. I know you think I'm just telling tales, but if you knew what I'm capable of, you wouldn't be here. I promise you that."

"I already know," she murmurs, forehead against his back.

"No," he says. "You have no fucking clue. You just think you do."

"Shh," she says. "Shhh, baby, shhh."

"I don't wanna *shhh*," he says, jerking a little, but he does, and soon his breath is calm again and he is sleeping in her grasp.

She is the one awake till morning.

NOBODY'S CELL PHONE worked in Essaouira, but the moment they get off the bus in Marrakech, Leo's starts beeping like a banshee. Mary waits in the shade with Kenneth and Sandor while Leo retrieves messages, pacing back and forth in front of them like a panther, narrating as he goes along. "Merel," he proclaims, grinning. She owns the gallery that represents him, and promised to apprise him of Paris sales. By the second message he's laughing aloud and saying, "Darlings, we will be finding ourselves some swank digs tonight." Mary high-fives Sandor, and they wait while Leo continues to play art diva, holding the phone to his ear and reporting, "Oooh, Merel again, she sounds pissed off that I haven't been at her beck and call—" But abruptly he stops dead in his tracks, a look of horror crossing his eyes. Mary's stomach jumps. "What's wrong?" she blurts out. "Is it Daniel?" Though her biological father is never sick, for some reason he has always seemed to her a marked man. Leo doesn't answer, merely passes Sandor the phone. "Her Dutch is too fast," he murmurs. Then: "The Reina Sofia? I shouldn't have smoked the last of that hash, it's giving me delusions of grandeur." He puts his hands up over his face and leans against a mildly slimy wall. He is shaking.

Mary puts her arm on his back to try to steady him. To her relief, Sandor, holding Leo's phone and listening to the messages, is making an eyes-bugged-out, half-smiling, half-disbelieving expression that would not be suitable to Daniel's untimely demise. He is nodding. He starts to cry, and Mary is taken aback and sharply embarrassed; Sandor is not usually prone to outbursts of emotion other than sarcasm. He hugs Leo, who still has his head in his hands. The phone has been flung onto a train station bench, and Sandor is embracing Leo right in front of all the Arabs and discombobulated tourists, whacking Leo upside the head a little and saying, "Cut it out, the lightning is not going to strike, you stupid boy, this is it, this is *it*, it's true!"

Leo says, "It can't be true. Stop looking at me. Oh God."

"It is only a *temporary* exhibition," Sandor says at last, withdrawing from Leo's arms. "It's not like you get to stay there, Leo. Calm down."

They sit on a bench, except for Kenneth, who nonetheless hovers close enough to hear what is going on.

"I have to go home," Leo says. "Or to Paris, or Madrid, I'm not sure." He starts laughing hysterically. "Sandor, holy shit. Did she even say where I'm supposed to *go*?"

"You don't need to leave today," Sandor explains calmly. "We will go back to Casablanca tomorrow and you can be in Madrid in an hour and a half if Merel wants you to kiss somebody's ass. We'll call her and work all of it out, no problem."

All at once it hits Mary: she should never have run off to Morocco! If she had only saved this trip, she could have gone to see her brother's work exhibited at one of the great art museums of the world! Or wait — maybe she can still go? They could all head back to Casablanca together. It's like Sandor said: only an hour and a half. She can call Geoff, and for something like *this*, surely he will fly out to join her? She imagines herself shopping in Madrid for something suitable to wear to Leo's museum debut . . . imagines her arm linked through Geoff's, flutes of champagne in their hands. Her mind lingers too long on the picture of her own hand holding the glass, and at once nausea roils in her stomach. For thirty-one years her fingers were normal — not just normal but lovely, thin, and tapered. Now she would be E.T. in a cocktail dress — now her fingers against a crystal flute would expose her new truth.

"Well done, man," Kenneth says. "You're going to be sharing digs with *Guernica*. Shit." But his eyes are already on the gate, ready to move on.

From: mrgrace@yahoo.com
Subject: Marrakech
Date: August 28, 2001
To: geoffreyjs@hitchcock.org

We got some unbelievable news today. Leo's going to have a painting in an exhibition at the Reina Sofia in Madrid! He insisted on staying here for my birthday, though, so he doesn't leave until the 31st. We want to do a small hike to celebrate (I promise: small!) before heading into the desert.

So for now we're here only for a night. Leo and Sandor have sprung for the most expensive hotel in town, La Mamounia, where apparently the Clintons and Winston Churchill have stayed. Out in the gardens there's an entire wall of purple flowers so dense that you can't see a speck of rock, and the bathrooms are so colorful and ornate that they look like enlarged versions of the intricate boxes sold in the medinas. It's kind of a freaky combo of art deco and Moorish, not very "authentic." But wow, it sure is a relief to be somewhere cosmopolitan enough that the concierge acted like storing my DNase in a fridge was no big deal, instead of acting like I was a drug smuggler, and to walk into the room to find a bottle of clean water I could use for my neti pot. I don't have to pull out the hand sanitizer in this place, it's cleaner than a hospital.

We even have a phone in our room! If you want to call, this would be the time. Geoff, I thought I'd celebrate every birthday with you for the rest of my life. I'm having an amazing time. But I never wanted it to come to this.

Love, me (still 32 for 2 more days . . .)

FUCK TANGIER. MARRAKECH is the place. Kenneth sits on the terrace of Café Argana overlooking the Jemaa el-Fna, waiting for Cystic and the other two. She's been in the business center at their palatial hotel, no doubt sending e-mails to her husband, and while the other two wanted to eat at the hotel restaurant, where you sit on pillows and watch a belly dancer (Christ!), at least Cystic backed him up and insisted on hitting Jemaa el-Fna. They agreed to meet at the conspicuous restaurant overhanging the square, and Kenneth left La Mamounia right away, the ostentatious bustle of the place making him cagey in a way Le Mirage, with its vast emptiness, hadn't. He thought an hour alone would clear his head, but his head is already *too* clear, clear to the point of stupidity—he's too sober to boot. Nothing he's thought in the past week feels even remotely sane.

He said that thing to Cystic about his son, about finding him. It hangs now, heavy as a rope.

What he should do, he knows, is wait till it's time for them to meet him, and while *they're* out, sneak back to La Mamounia, use his room key and retrieve his rucksack and disappear into the medina and never see any of them again. He knew it even before he headed down to Spain; he knew it in Tangier; he knew it at Le Mirage. Why, then, won't he leave?

The view is good at this tourist-trap restaurant, but still. He'd rather be down on the street where the action is. Down there is a bedlam that makes his skin buzz. Unlike in Tangier, where it was every man for himself, this place has a community vibe that intrigues him, draws him in. You could live in this square and want for nothing, never leave; it's like a walled city of old. Earlier today it felt like a movable circus, bursting with bare-chested acrobats with chestnut skin, casually defying gravity, while nearby, snakes slithered to the sound of music played by bored, fat men. Women wore shorts or burkas or anything in between, and through some of the veils you could see the shadow of a feminine jaw and it was sad and erotic at once. But just when you think you have the frenzy of Jemaa el-Fna figured out it shape-shifts after dark, so that the bright stalls of fat, fire-bright oranges and embroidered fez hats are gone. By night, the square has transformed into one cohesive, makeshift restaurant, full of the smells of human consumption. Beneath the giant cloud of barbecue smoke, the noise of the crowd rumbles with a sense of danger even more seductive than its daylight incarnation.

He thinks about blowing off Café Argana altogether, but Cystic can't eat street food. She has to be careful what she touches, what she lets inside. Some kind of bug that's nothing to him could wipe her out. Jemaa el-Fna is a virtual cesspool of germs, like those buses they've taken, like every square inch of Tangier, like all the toilets she's squatted over since they've been here, just holes in the ground, sometimes with nothing but a trickle of water running from some rock in the wall, or a dirty bucket next to your feet, which you're supposed to slosh on yourself with your left hand, as if using only one particular hand will make the slop inside clean. Her husband was right: she has no business here. A well of anger surges up his throat. Any real man would've smacked her face, taken the credit card away, told her to sit the hell down, that she wasn't going anywhere. Simple.

Except of course it's not that simple. Except that, of course, Cystic would never marry a man like that, and so her Good Man, her liberated Twenty-First Century Man, let her go traipsing around the third world with the likes of him.

Here they come now. The Flying Dutchfag, the Rising Artist, and the Fatally Ill Damsel. Walking across the square below him, they look like characters in a film: all shiny and clean, their cotton clothes billowing. They look *young*, even Leo, who's not that much younger than he is. They look too young to be anything he should touch, though he's touched a lot younger. He can hear their laughter all the way up here, and for a moment, panic rises in him: he was supposed to flee but he didn't. Abruptly he thinks of how easy it must be to score in this wild place, how it was a mistake to leave heroin behind, it left too many spaces inside him in its wake, and try though he has to leave those spaces in peace, they're still hungry and squirming and looking for something to fill them, and how stupid he is to think that it might be her. Under the table his legs twitch. He has his camera, and if he misses the H so much, it wouldn't be hard to find. He has his camera and his money, what's left of it, so who gives a shit about the rucksack? He wouldn't even need to go back to La Mamounia, to the room they're supposed to share because neither of them had the balls to require Leo to plunk down an extra four hundred bucks. Those boys must assume they're fucking anyway. Why else would he *be* here?

Run, you stupid fucker. Run.

They have reached the table. There is another man with them — barely more than a boy really, maybe his early twenties. Kenneth noticed the boy walking close to them in the square but thought nothing of it, since the square is teeming with people. Now he gawks as though maybe Cystic and the other two don't realize the boy is there — as though maybe he is stalking them without their awareness. Cystic, though, puts her hand on the boy's arm and says, "Kenneth, this is Tommy from La Mamounia. He has the next few days off at the hotel, so we snagged him to be our guide to the Atlas Mountains — he has friends there."

Leo and Sandor grin broadly. The boy is good-looking in that Arab way, and they must be enjoying the eye candy.

They all sit. It is a table for four, so an extra chair has to be procured.

"Tommy," Kenneth says slowly. "What kind of name is that for a Moroccan?"

"Oh," the kid says, "my real name is Khalid. Tommy is my name for La Mamounia." He speaks with less of an accent than Sandor. It's unnerving.

Kenneth snorts a little. "So Tommy is your alias?" Now the kid appears confused. "You know," he clarifies, "your alter ego, your code name, like that. The name you give fat Americans 'cause they're too stupid to pronounce Khalid."

"Khalid isn't hard to pronounce," the kid says agreeably, "but sometimes the guests at La Mamounia have a hard time remembering it, so Tommy is my nickname."

"Why *Tommy*, though?" Kenneth persists. He feels antagonistic, though he knows there is no reason. If the others wouldn't find out, he would kick the kid's ass just for fun. "It doesn't even start with the same letter as your real name."

Cystic shoots him a dirty look. Yes, there are moments when this is who she is: a polite girl from the heartland suburbs, the kind who — if she weren't damaged goods — would have grown up to be somebody's mother, saying shit like, *Is that how I taught you to speak to our guests?* Christ. This ordinary suburban girl is what all his internal chaos is about? This thirtysomething doctor's wife putting her hand on the Arab kid's arm maternally as if to deflect Kenneth's impropriety?

But what she says is, "Don't worry, we all have aliases around here, so you'll fit right in." And just like that, the mother has vanished and she is something else again.

"Okay then, Alias," Kenneth says, gesturing at his menu. "So have you eaten at this place? What's good?"

The kid shrugs, not deferentially but boldly now. "I've eaten here, yes, but nothing is good. There are other places — I'll take you if you like."

In one synchronized movement, they all stand.

ANOTHER UNRESOLVED MORNING. Under a merciless blue sky, the sun shining lustrous on their shoulders, the four of them plus the Arab kid head for the Kik Plateau. Alias's friend's village isn't accessible by car, so they've got to hoof it. Leo keeps asking Cystic if she remembered her salt pills, until she thrusts a skinny arm out at him and snaps, "Here, lick me if you don't believe it!" Kenneth can taste her from memory. Finally, he stops on the hot dirt road and strips his jeans off, hacking at the legs with his knife to make shorts. Everyone laughs; for a minute he's all right with being here; for a minute he can make it through this day. What passes for trees are tiny and pushed back so far from the road — amid fields of wheat and wildflowers — that they offer no shade. "The sweltering sky," he jokes. Ha fucking ha.

They arrive to find Alias's friend gone, no one but the boy's mother, Nawar, at home. They've come unannounced, but now that they're here, it's clear there probably isn't one phone in the whole village. They stand in the blinding sunlight, water bottles depleted and the midday temperature climbing past one hundred degrees. Silently, the small Berber woman moves from the doorway to usher them in, and so they step, sweaty and blinking in the sudden darkness, into another world.

Nawar guides them up a wooden ladder to the second floor of the house, the one designated for human residents rather than the sheep that dwell on the ground floor. Each story comprises one room, equally unfurnished but for the straw sleep mats. Almost instantly, their hostess retreats outside to prepare tea, leaving them alone, sitting on the wooden slats of the floor. Her kitchen isn't part of the house, and the one window faces in the wrong direction to allow them to see her outdoors, cooking.

Alias lounges easily on a straw mat smoking a cigarette and dropping the ashes into the cup Nawar supplied. Kenneth first launched into French when he greeted Nawar, thinking she would understand, but it turns out she speaks only Arabic. There's no school in this village, Alias explains, and even if there were, she would not have gone forty years ago, being a girl. Once she comes back inside bearing her teapot, Alias begins translating whatever is said—in English, in French—into Arabic for her, and then translating her Arabic back only once, into English. Kenneth has noticed that though the kid is what people call "fluent" in English, when he speaks French his words flow faster, with more quirk, more personality. Now when he makes conversation of his own, he's been lapsing automatically into French, directing his words at Kenneth as though the others are not there, and the cacophony of overlapping languages feels like a jam session back at the De Engelbewaarder: wild, messy, beautiful.

Since Alias is smoking, Leo and Sandor light up, too, and Cystic says she'll go outside. Kenneth stands and says, "I'll go with you," even though he too wants a smoke. His head brushes the ceiling. They descend the ladder to the first floor of the house and weave their way through the sheep until they reach the door. There are two doors actually: one leading toward the outdoor kitchen and the other to the front of the house, which faces the road, eclipsed by the village now. Kenneth maneuvers to the front door, where a handful of village children cluster and stare. Finally outdoors, he lights a cigarette, the still, hot air dispersing the smoke only marginally better than the trapped air inside the house.

Mary says, "I counted the sheep. There are nine."

Kenneth mutters, "Bet you anything there's more out in the fields just ain't come home for supper yet."

Low and furtive, they laugh.

"This is magnificent," Mary says.

"Sure," Kenneth agrees. "Long as you don't have to live here." But his body has lost its languid laziness, all its "I don't give a shit" bravado. He's tuned to attention, to a fine pitch, and it shows and he knows it. He has seen nothing like this in all his forty-seven years. He has seen a lot, but it has mostly been a lot of the same. This is something else entirely, wholly off the radar of his life. It is perhaps the first thing he has ever experienced that being stoned would in no way improve.

He will not realize until later that they spent four hours at the house and it never once occurred to him to take a picture.

Mary says quietly, as though the village children may overhear, "If you go back to Georgia, then maybe this isn't the last time we'll see each other. There isn't any law against being friends with someone you've slept with before. Georgia isn't that far from New Hampshire, so who knows?"

In an instant the world he has been drinking in seems to disappear. Her words and their mixture of condescension and promise obliterate everything else. Last night, they slept in the same bed together again. Nothing happened. Nothing but their bodies commingling in sleep and desire, her voice against his skin in the dark. Nothing.

"You can't get me to see my son by dangling yourself like a carrot." And he hates her for the way she just made the landscape narrow, for the way he held on to her last night, no longer even questioning her terms. The hating feels good, feels better. "Don't try to save me and I won't try to save you, and we'll keep getting along fine."

"I wasn't trying to—" She looks shocked. "That isn't what I meant! I just know we've both been . . . I've been sad about never seeing you again, and I can tell you're sad, too, no matter what you say. I was just trying to talk to you like a human being."

"There's your first mistake."

She takes the cigarette out of his hand. "You're not human, huh? Why didn't you smoke this upstairs, then? Why don't you blow smoke in my face like my sweet brother does? Who's trying to save who, Mr. Bad Man?"

He grabs her wrist, so quickly the cigarette flies out of her fingers and sails in an arc, landing still lit on the ground a few feet away. One of the little boys scurries to pick it up and the children run away with it. Now that they're alone, however—the thing Kenneth's wanted all day—he is at a total loss for what to say. He lets go of her wrist, but even that he does too roughly, almost throwing it away from him, so that it bounces off her body. She takes it between the fingers of her other hand, holds it against her chest like a wounded bird.

"Maybe I already know the things you think I don't," she says, voice thick, though he isn't sure if it's anger or pain or just her fucked-up lungs. "Why won't you let yourself believe that? Do you think it would shock me if you tell me you hooked Agnes on drugs? Jesus, I'm not an idiot. Do you think I'd be surprised if you said you hit her? What else did you do, Kenneth? Did you rape women? I hate rapists more than just about anything in the world, but even if you tell me you raped somebody, I'm not going to run into the mountains scream-ing. Maybe that means I'm stupid. But I know you *now*. If that's who you used to be, then you've changed."

If he feels anything, it is not reassurance, not even anger anymore, just a bottomless weariness, as though the heat, the stink of the sheep, the borderline dehydration and withdrawal from booze, have all finally caught up with him and laid their burden on his back. His sigh is heavy. "It's not black and white like you're talking, girl. You make evil sound like a cartoon decked out in a trench coat and lurk-ing around corners. You don't know the first thing about it."

"Oh, I don't know anything about evil? Is that so? You're the only one with a past, are you? You're the only one who knows what men are capable of?"

Too late he thinks of Lockerbie. He sees the pulse throb fast in her throat just before she turns and storms back into the house, and too late he wonders why she brought up *rape* among the spectrum of crimes he may have committed. But she is gone and he cannot ask her. He cannot ask if it is still rape if the woman never said no, never tried to get away. Is that the right word if someone owes you money, and you could have beaten or killed her for it, but instead you let her pay you back with the only thing she has? Is it the same if the men whose blood you've drawn have drawn other blood themselves, or do only crimes against the innocent count? Does it matter less if the body you dump in the Thames isn't someone you killed, only someone you called your best friend and wished dead in the same passive way you wished it for your own sorry ass?

And what he wants to know most is whether he is more afraid Cystic *would* run like hell if she knew his past—or whether he couldn't view her quite the same if she knew and still stayed.

ENTERING THE TINY house alone, Mary catches the end of Alias's announcement that Nawar is baking bread and it will be ready soon. Instantly her mouth begins to water. She's famished from the morning's long walk; Nawar's hot tea seems an abomination, but the water has cooled and its minty sweetness is surprisingly refreshing. Mary closes her eyes briefly, senses overwhelmed.

All the things she saw on the bus ride to Essaouira that seemed so picturesque from their moving vehicle seem to have expanded so that *they* are a part of the picture, so the picture is everywhere around them. And this—not the chaos of the medinas, not the fiery sunset over a beach, not the photos of Ginsberg or even Kenneth's body against hers—*this* is why she came. She feels lucky in such myriad ways it almost hurts.

Alias and Nawar are chatting in Arabic. After a spell, Alias explains that her son is working at a hotel in Erfoud and hasn't been home in three months. He writes down the name of the hotel on a book of La Mamounia matches and hands it to Mary, saying, "When you get there you ask for him as your guide and tell him I said hello!" Nawar's husband is at the market, getting supplies, Alias explains. He will be home tomorrow. The floor has only two sleep mats now, but Mary imagines the years when it must have contained three—maybe more. Where, in a home where every family member sleeps lined up on the floor of one small room, do married couples escape to have sex? Do they rely on sleeping children? Do they sneak downstairs and copulate amid the strongly aromatic sheep? Or do couples search out growing wheat in the fields and make love out in the open in order to escape the confines of family?

Nawar comes in with the bread. Dressed in the usual colorful

Berber weavings, her hair hidden under a bright orange scarf, her face round and flat, bones close to the surface, she seems old: not just old-fashioned but actually *aged*. She is probably Leo's age, younger than many of the women teachers Mary goes for after-work drinks with, who joke that forty is the new thirty and still wear their hair flowing and get alpha hydroxy peels in Boston. Here, in this world, forty is the new eighty. Nawar is already an old woman, skin leathered, back slightly bent, no doubt from carrying enormous piles of firewood as Mary saw women doing when she was on the exhaust-filled bus. Here, as in Kenya, death is cheap. No hospital for miles across rough terrain, and surely no one with any real medical training would live in such a village. *Here I would be an old woman already; here nobody would think twice at my death or even mourn me.* Though of course, as Leo said, here she would have died long ago, probably undiagnosed.

Yet the bread smells like heaven!

Kenneth reenters the house quietly, bowing his head to walk in the low-ceilinged room until he reaches the mats on the floor, where he sits next to Sandor and away from her. Nawar brings a bowl of fresh water in which they all wash; then with their right hands they tear off hunks of bread. There is honey for dipping, and Mary thinks that despite Kenneth's outburst she is fully content right here, listening to the French and Arabic she cannot understand, her eyes meeting Leo's as if to say, *See, see, isn't this better than Paris?* Downstairs, sheep occasionally bleat, the smell of them wafting up and competing with the aroma of the bread. Outside, children titter under the window.

She goes and looks down on them. One small boy has his penis out and is dangling it at them, sticking up his middle finger as he must have learned somehow, somewhere, even in the absence of TV. She feels keenly chastened. She had allowed herself to imagine that all the villagers were happy they were here, that they were welcome in the most biblical sense, where the traveling stranger passing through town is a treasured guest and hospitality an imperative. It occurs to Mary for the first time that she has no idea what her brother and Sandor are *paying* Alias to accompany them on such a long trip—that she has forgotten he is not here just for the fun of it. She looks at Alias with a new suspicion. He is sweet and charming, but he is not their friend. Maybe they cannot trust him.

As if on cue, Alias smiles and says, "I told Nawar it's your birthday tomorrow! She would like to henna your hands."

Without even thinking, Mary's hands dash behind her back.

The men are in a circle on the floor mats, munching their bread, the small Berber woman smiling expectantly at her. Mary is familiar enough with the custom of hennaing to know that she should receive the offer as an honor—that unlike at the beauty shops in Boston's ethnic neighborhoods, here henna isn't something you get just on a whim as decoration but is reserved for special occasions like weddings, for rituals like warding off the evil eye. God knows she could use a healthy dash of warding off evil. She thinks of Geoff and of how, if it were the two of them here alone with Nawar, she would hold out her hands in an instant, succumb to this honor, and hoard it in her memory to pull out later and savor. Geoff, for all her fury at him for not accompanying her, has never made her feel anything but wholly beautiful; it would never occur to her to be embarrassed in front of him about the shape of her fingers, or anything else. But now, after her spat with Kenneth outside, she feels vulnerable. And Alias. She can't help thinking of Hasnain and his phantom cousin in his presence. Hasnain was about Alias's age, and Nix said he was handsome and—asinine or not—Alias is the first young Muslim man she has ever known, handsome or otherwise (and he is handsome). She cannot imagine going to the center of this male circle and holding out her flawed hands and letting them watch while Nawar decorates them. What if Nawar has not noticed their misshapenness before now and recoils? Mary would die of shame.

She says, "Can I do my feet instead?"

Alias asks Nawar and then responds, "No, no, she says the feet won't dry in time for you to put your shoes on and make the walk back. Your sandals will ruin the feet. To do the feet, you have to have time to leave them bare. She says the hands."

"All right," Mary says. To refuse would be worse. She thinks for a moment of the ferry to Athens and the woman who offered her what she now knows was a rose-flavored Turkish delight, and how Nix commanded her to swallow the thing rather than spit it out. How she took it as a punishment, but how Nix was right. To refuse Nawar would be unthinkable.

Leo says, "Can I get my hands done, too?"

Sandor elbows him. "It's for girls. What, you want them to find you a husband here in the village while they're at it?"

"Why is it for girls?" Leo demands. "It's like a tattoo, and ink isn't gender specific." He turns to Alias. "Is that true? I thought in this culture a man can get whatever he wants, so if I want henna, why shouldn't I have it?"

Alias shrugs. "The men use henna for their hair and beard sometimes. But you have no gray yet, so there's no need."

Sandor snorts, "No gray? Look closer."

"I don't want it in my *hair*," Leo says. "I want to get it with my sister for her birthday. She shouldn't have to get it all alone. She's sick of being the only girl."

Mary has never realized, until Leo voiced it for her, exactly how true this is. She imagines herself and Nix side by side in this stuffy room, hands extended gleefully, comparing designs. So much she has missed. Nix was not the only girl in the world—not her only friend in grade school, in high school. There were others, girlfriends she laughed and shopped with and talked with on the phone, some even after her diagnosis. But after Lockerbie they all just reminded her of Nix in a way that hurt too badly, and then she began to travel in a world dominated by men, and recently her illness, work, and marriage have been more than enough to handle. Has she *purposely* avoided letting any new woman get too close, like a widow leading a celibate life after the death of her beloved? She grasps Leo's hand. "Will Nawar do it? Can you ask her?"

Alias shrugs and asks Nawar. To everyone's considerable surprise, Nawar laughs aloud, revealing several missing teeth. Her big grin lights up the room.

"She says this is a big experience for her," Alias says dutifully, doubtfully. "The American men are very different from our men, and she is happy to give you the masculine design." He frowns openly. "My sister does henna, too," he says. "In Marrakech. She wouldn't do your hands, though. She would not be allowed to touch you—if you came to my father's house, she would put on the burka so you can't see her face. You're not supposed to touch a strange man, one not part of the family, not Muslim. But the Berbers are different and they do things in their own way, so fine, she says it's okay with her." He folds his arms across his chest.

"Dude," Kenneth says, "You were drunk off your ass with us the other night, rambling about your girlfriend the French schoolteacher. I wouldn't get too high up on that holy horse if I was you."

"That's my life," Alias says stonily. "Not my sister's."

"Well, Nawar doesn't have to worry about touching *me*," Leo says, rubbing Sandor's leg happily. "She's as safe as a nun in a convent."

Alias does not translate this. Sandor looks as though he would like to kick Leo several times in the ribs. Kenneth, on the other hand, looks pleased, as though something interesting is happening, as though he approves of this turn of events. Mary and Leo scoot to the middle of the mats while Nawar mixes the henna. They sit knee to knee, suddenly giddy. Leo takes off his silver rings and hands them to Sandor. He takes Mary's hand again and brings it to his lips and kisses it.

"I'm so happy to be with you for your birthday," he whispers. "This is one of the best days of my entire life."

Tears smart in her eyes. She does not mind her fingers anymore. She breathes into Leo's ear, "Thanks for the save—now they're all looking at you, not me."

"Silly girl," Leo says. "Think of your fingers like a battle wound. They show what a courageous person you are. You have to get used to them because you're going to be looking at them for a long, long time." His eyes are teary, too. Their heads are draped together, whispering, while Nawar busies herself and Alias sulks and Kenneth and Sandor talk to each other about nothing so that Leo and Mary can have their moment. And this must be what sex is like in a place like this: the world gives you space because it has to. Because people will stake a small space for intimacy even when there is none.

SHE WAKES GASPING. Sometimes this is how it is. Air-hungry, nothing she sucks in able to reach bottom, breathing out when it feels like there is nothing to expel, desperate for the exhalation to end so that she can try again, pulling and pulling but empty. Her breath comes faster. This is what it was like in the hospital, when the nurses came in and gave her oxygen, and one, her favorite, Crystal, would smooth her hair and say, *It's all better now.* She staggers in the dark. Her portable compressor is recharging its batteries, plugged in with the adapter. Inside her pack is her albuterol, her TOBI just in case. Groping around, she shoves the inhaler into her mouth and gulps, waits for the relief, allows herself those moments of hope. She walked today for a total of something like six hours, not counting the midday rest at Nawar's home. There are people with CF who would give anything to walk even a few blocks without needing a two-hour nap to recover. She is lucky; she is strong.

But tonight the albuterol isn't helping. She used her Flutter before bed, but sometimes it's not good enough, and the DNase isn't for immediate relief, takes twenty minutes to even use. Maybe it *would* help, though, if she could get to it — it's in the freaking hotel refrigerator and there's no one at the desk at this hour to retrieve it for her. Dizzy, she switches on the lights.

If only Kenneth were here. After their fight earlier he got his own room, fabulously cheap — less than twenty bucks — clean, and pretty, with a small pool out back. In a few years there will be luxury *riads* all over this area and wealthy Europeans will be building summer homes, but right now that has only just started to happen; now you can still find bargains easily, you can pay for your own room and not break a sweat. Her lungs feel thick, the back of her throat coated with mucus. She makes herself cough but it's not productive, requires too much air. Panic washes over her like anesthesia until she cannot feel her hands and feet. Her chest hurts, and mucus this thick could be an infection. If she gets an infection here, she is doomed. She will have to go home right away, while she can still get on the plane without its being a major production. It is past midnight; she is now thirty-three. Her cough is getting desperate, loud. A knock on her door.

"I'm fine," she calls. She is not sure why.

"Are you choking?" The voice is Alias's, not what she expected. Why is it always the wrong man at her door? "Do you need help? I know the Heimlich maneuver."

She starts laughing. It hurts her chest, and when she sits up, spots burst in front of her eyes. What *is* the altitude here? What are her oxygen levels? If only she could get at her DNase and thin this shit out and cough it up. She opens the door, tries to speak, coughs violently in Alias's face.

He seems to realize at once that she hasn't just swallowed something the wrong way. "You are sick," he says, and she snaps, "Duh," then feels awful for it. She tries again, "I left my medication in the hotel refrigerator. Could you find it for me?"

"Of course. Do you want me to get your brother while I'm gone?"

"No, no, just hurry, please."

Back on the bed she pounds her chest, arranging the pillow under her back so that she's slightly upside down. She closes her eyes and imagines Mom's cupped hand: the patience, the perfection of the small blows, how invasive and infuriating it felt, so much that she never realized, too, how *safe,* how utterly without thought she was able to be, her mother responsible for her body's outcome. Alias returns with her ampoules, her name written on them with a Sharpie in Geoff's handwriting. Mary leaps from the bed, still coughing, and grabs her meds, shoos him away, and slams the door. She keeps coughing into the mask; it's hard to breathe in; she's getting everything wet. Out in the hall she hears shuffling, becomes aware that Alias must still be there. She leans her back against the bed, settles into the mist, counts backward. When she was in high school and wanted to calm her spasming lungs, she would sometimes say the Lord's Prayer in her mind over and over like a meditation. Recently, through all her tests and procedures, Geoff always insisted on staying in the room with her and would talk to calm her, or sometimes just sit at her feet and hold her toes. The space around her in her single room feels enormous now. What she would give to have a body in here with her: any body would do. Time passes; air moves in and out. She takes the mask from her face. Coughing is easy now, necessary, the mucus desperate to come up, streaks of blood in the sputum. She gets the toilet tissue she's been carrying—because it's rarely available except in hotels—and rips off hunks, spitting into it. She should go to the bathroom but it's down the hall and she doesn't want to see anyone.

Another knock at the door. Christ. She opens it and still it is him.

"I wanted to make sure you're okay."

Mary wipes her mouth gracelessly. "I'm fine," she snaps. "Look, no offense, you're a great guide—today was awesome—but I don't think you even like us very much, and we're not paying you by the hour. I want to be alone."

Alias blinks at her in the dim hallway. He is still dressed in his street clothes and she wonders why he hasn't been to bed yet, what he has been doing. "Why do you think I don't like you? I like you."

"Right," Mary says. "You wouldn't let your sister touch a gay male Jew, but you like us just fine."

Alias laughs. This surprises her. She has not seen him laugh before.

"You don't look Jewish," he says.

"And I suppose that's supposed to be a compliment."

He shrugs. "The Jew and the Arab, they look the same. It is not a compliment."

She coughs sharply, covers her mouth. "So you came to my room in the middle of the night to tell me I'm *ugly*?"

"I came to see if you are okay." Alias gives an exaggerated shrug. "If you choke, at La Mamounia they don't like that and I'll get fired. I'm just a guide, after all."

A smile spreads across her face. She feels it, big, and her breath is able to support it. She says, "You're funny. I don't get you, though. You seem like a normal guy—the way you dress, hanging out with us at a restaurant drinking and talking the night we met. But then you say these things. Like we're just infidels and you don't think we're the same as you are."

"The Koran is the one truth," he says somberly. "But I'm an infidel, too, just like you."

"See!" Mary realizes that she has flung open her door—that she has for all intents and purposes invited the boy inside. "How can you say that the Koran is the truth but then casually disregard it and not do what it says? If that were really what you believed, wouldn't you be spreading out a little prayer mat right now and not even talking to a Jewish woman? Wouldn't you be wearing a beard and not dating a French girl? Are the pleasures of this life really so amazing that you'd sacrifice your eternity in paradise for a Flag Spéciale beer? Come on! It's like you're just saying what you're supposed to say but you know it's all a load of crap."

He is nodding. His eyes have gone flirtatious somehow and it is the opposite of what she needs, she who already has more men in her life than she can handle. "The pleasures of this life are so amazing," he says. "Yes."

"I don't think so," she scoffs. "I've tasted Flag Spéciale."

He steps inside the room. "Where is your boyfriend? You don't share the room together? You are still a virgin, until you get married?"

She laughs. She wants to ask if it's proper for him to ask this question of a woman, but she can't stop laughing.

"Oh!" Alias's eyes widen. "He isn't your boyfriend then? He is homosexual, too?"

"No!" Mary says. "No, he's not gay. He is"—she pauses—"just a friend."

Alias is sitting on the bed now. Where was he when she started to cough? How is it that he is the only one who heard her? Maybe this is a dream.

"Your *friend* has the wrong idea about my girlfriend," he admits, and he looks a little bit embarrassed, uncertain. "I must have made a mistake with my words on our first night. She isn't French, she *teaches* French. She is Moroccan, Muslim, like me."

"But she's educated," Mary says. "I bet she doesn't wear a veil."

"Correct. Well, sometimes she wears one, if she visits her family and goes out someplace with them. But not in Marrakech, no, she doesn't. None of our friends do. This is not the Middle East. You Americans don't know the difference. Morocco is almost like part of Europe."

"It's Africa. In Nigeria, women get stoned for adultery, don't they?"

"I don't know about that," he says casually, but then abruptly the recognition hits his face. "Oh. So you are married?"

"Yes," she says. "How old are you?"

"Twenty-five. Time to marry, too, have some babies. You have children?"

"No." She gestures at the plethora of medical equipment littering her primitive room. "Because," she says, "I can't. I'm sick."

He stands. A kind of panic washes over her that she has frightened him. She's not sure she *likes* him even. The gulf between them feels enormous: a chasm of age, of nation, of culture. How did Nix ever bridge it? How could she, who had traveled not nearly as much as Mary has now, have fallen in love with an Indian Muslim in London? What did they have to talk about? She wonders again—with her usual pang of treason—if Hasnain truly existed, or if he was a salve Nix spoon-fed Mary to make her believe everything was just fine, to distract her from the truth of the rape, the way parents distract children with tales of Santa Claus. Maybe Nix casually met a boy named Hasnain somewhere, at a restaurant or a launderette, and got it in her head to spin an exotic fairy tale Mary would never think to question. But *why?* Why, when she could have claimed to love a fellow American student, when she could have claimed anything— why that? No, he must have been real. Mary isn't dizzy anymore, but still she feels her sense of visual perception is off, foggy. She can feel Nix on the other side of a veil. Mary is thirty-three; she has lived a full decade longer than her life expectancy at the time of diagnosis. And she may never turn thirty-four. She both believes and does not believe this. The possibility lurks on the other side of the veil, Nix egging her on, telling her that ordinary codes of ethics do not apply to her: that she could kiss this boy and it would not be a betrayal either of Geoff or of Kenneth. That she cannot be held responsible because she will soon be gone.

She thought that he was bolting—that her admission scared him off—but instead Alias is in front of her. The door to her room is still open, and he reaches out and closes it with the confidence of a man, not a boy. He has the most arched eyebrows she has ever seen, hooded like a cobra's despite his boyish face—mysterious, seductive. He says, "I think you are very pretty, yes. Not for a Jewish woman. For any woman."

He kisses her softly. Her mouth still feels foul from the mists of her medication, from coughing everything out, but he doesn't seem to notice or care. She lets him kiss her the way she would not let Kenneth kiss her just last night, and she tries to think of Hasnain, to feel a oneness with Nix, but instead she thinks of Alias's girlfriend, brash and veilless and probably the age Mary was when she lived at Arthog House. Instead, at the feel of Alias's arms encircling her, she thinks of Geoff's more substantial, more mature embrace—the way he held her at Logan Airport with a tight agitation, his anger at her departure surrendering to fear. There is in her the antithesis of arousal, and she pulls away from the boy and looks into his dark eyes, beautiful and perfect in the way of her brother. Yes, he was right about Arab and Jew: he and Leo could be related. In the biblical milieu of Nawar's village, Leo might even be the father of this young man. She pulls away to his murmurs of, "I'm sorry, please excuse me!" and she is not looking at Hasnain, who would be a middle-aged man now, but just at a hopeful, confused, intelligent, sheltered Moroccan boy who speaks at least three languages and believes in the Koran and who wants to touch an older, married, sick Jewish American because she is an experience, because she is as exotic as it gets. She doesn't hate him for his behavior because she has been there: collecting people, collecting experiences. Someday Khalid will be a man, but not yet. His manhood will be his own journey, his girlfriend's journey, and she will not be a part of it, will not be a story he can take out of the drawer of his mind and examine, even though some part of her wishes she could be.

Tomorrow she will go as far as the pass, take in the view, celebrate her birthday with three of the men she loves. And then she will go back down. It will be the perfect symbol of her completion. Then she will catch a ride back to Marrakech with Leo—let Sandor and Alias and Kenneth go on into the desert without her. She will fly back to Europe and call Geoff and ask him to come and meet her for Leo's show, but if he cannot—if he *will* not—she will go back home. It is over. She has no business here. She opens the door, and Alias, confused and perhaps relieved, steps out into the hall.

In the dim light of her room, she sits down at the small blue table. There is no computer access here, so she opens her Nix notebook. She has not written in it since her first visit with Leo, with whom she soon began engaging in such a passionate and high-maintenance exchange of letters, e-mails, and phone calls that her old notebook—to a correspondent who never answered—went untouched, forgotten. This, she supposes, is what they call closure. Still, she could not bring herself to travel without it, and even now she does not rip out a page, merely continues where she left off. She does not intend to mail this letter, so in a way it *belongs* with those old missives to Nix, as though she is writing to Geoff's future ghost—to whatever essence of him will remain, from whatever essence of herself. She begins:

> *You are the man of my life. You have tolerated more than any lover should ever be asked to bear and I can only hope that we can move on from here and instead of worrying about healing my body instead heal what distance has been between us because of me. I am placing myself in your hands because that is what love demands of everyone in the end: surrender. For too long I've confused the narrowing of the world that comes with commitment with the narrowing that comes with physical decline, and only now that I am truly facing the latter can I tell the difference. Maybe I would forge on further out into this feast of the senses that is the world if it were only my choice. But I want more to return to you, to stake our own piece of the earth and live fully on it for however long I have.*

She does not mention Kenneth. She will never mention Kenneth. There is never only one Truth.
There is only one truth at a time.

THE HOTEL IN Imlil is terrible, and everyone is angry. At one another, at the surroundings, at Mary for being too sick to hike and spoiling their last day together, at Leo for having to leave. The pillowcases at this dive are nonremovable, sewn on so that they cannot be washed. The toilets — a row of stalls in the hall — are overflowing with brown fecal water and don't flush. In the shower room, giant insects congregate on the tile walls, yet Mary and the others are all so filthy they *had* to shower, and Leo is furious at Sandor not only for all the henna cracks but because Sandor would not come into the shower with him and made him face those insects alone. The altitude is giving Leo a headache and kicking Mary's ass, but when they retired to Leo's room together to nap (safety in numbers), they were both afraid to turn out the lights, and when they finally tried, pulling the flimsy curtains, Mary kept bolting up and saying she felt bugs crawling on her, and this has Leo in a state of hypervigilant hysteria.

This is crazy. Even now Merel is boxing up *Still Life, with Men* to move it to Madrid, and meanwhile Leo is sleeping in a vat of African shit and bugs on a probably lice-infested pillow and all of it is rapidly increasing his count of gray hairs. Tomorrow he has to leave. He will not be able to make the hike with the others, and this is not the way he wanted to end his trip: his last trip with Mary, or so she claims. She told him this morning that she was leaving with him, but once they postponed the hike she changed her plans. She *needs* to make the trek, she says: it's like a symbol. Tomorrow Leo will get a ride back to the city without her and she'll remain with Kenneth and Alias.

"You have to stay and watch her," Leo begged Sandor the moment Mary was out of earshot. "We can't leave her here alone with them. Just stay a couple more days, go back to La Mamounia after the hike, and chill out by the pool. Then get her on a fucking plane and bring her back with you. Don't let her go running into the desert or have an orgy or whatever plan she has in her head. Come meet me and we'll call her lame-ass husband and get him out for the preview party, okay? We'll be shopping for party clothes in seventy-two hours."

Sandor has been difficult this entire trip. He folded his long arms in a way that made his chest look too narrow for the job. "I want you to admit this is madness," he said, too loudly. "I want you to admit that we should never have gone along with her big Morocco plan. What is she *doing* here, Leo? Your sister has a terrible disease, and she is going to climb the fucking mountain? This is crazy, and you talk about party clothes! How can you leave me here to cope with her alone?"

"It's only one more day," Leo insisted. "She's doing fine—she's holding up great! Everybody treats her like an invalid and that's exactly what she hates, don't you see? Just stay with her, Sandor, please. We'll meet up in Spain."

And so Leo will be flying home alone.

Sandor feels excluded, Leo suspects, by what's going on in Paris, in Madrid. His big show of worrying about Mary is to avoid admitting other, more personal resentments. Leo understands; he would be jealous if *he* were the one left out in the cold. He's seen this happen with other artist couples in their circle: one partner becoming envious, bitter. Sometimes, the relationship does not survive . . .

The thought of Sandor's leaving him is too awful. Leo dwells, instead, on the bugs.

The hotel is called Étoile; there's a little subheading on the sign in front that says STAR OF THE ATLAS like a Vegas strip show. There is a small terrace café in front, which is the most sanitary place to hang out if you don't dwell on what the kitchen must be like inside, where they're making your food. Sandor took off for a hike alone, and Mary has taken one of Leo's Xanaxes and is finally crashing. At the terrace café, Kenneth sits reading. Leo doesn't remember seeing Kenneth with a book earlier; he must have gotten it from one of those exchanges these traveler joints have in the lobby. James Michener's *The Drifters*—Leo starts cackling. He isn't Kenneth's biggest fan, but he has to admit that the guy, despite his penchant for incorrect grammar (obviously a pose he has held so long he's forgotten it's bogus) seems well read. Sometimes he reminds Leo of his father: the whole literate ex-junkie thing. This is, of course, part of why Leo dislikes him. And part of why Mary is screwing around with him: girls and their Oedipus complexes. Geoff and Kenneth, like a competition between Mary's straight-and-narrow adoptive father and her deranged biological deadbeat one. Sure, he gets it. That doesn't mean it isn't dumb.

"Ever read this?" Kenneth asks. "It's actually pretty good. Not *good*

good, but for what it is. The bible of my tribe. Or what used to be my tribe once upon a time."

Leo sits down, motions to get someone's attention. "I don't read stories," he says. "I mean, I read history, biographies, art magazines, that kind of thing. Not fiction."

"Whatever," says Kenneth.

He seems a little drunk. Leo's not sure how much Moroccan beer a man like Kenneth would have to drink to achieve that state, but it seems true nonetheless. Maybe when nobody was looking he procured more hash?

"Where's my sister?" he says, even though he knows.

Kenneth gestures toward the wider world with his beer can. "Hell if I know," he says. "Ask the Arab kid."

At first Leo doesn't get what he means. He thinks briefly of a one-eyed kid from back in Nawar's village but then realizes Kenneth means Alias. "Huh?" he says. His voice rises to a squeal. "Holy shit! You don't mean she's run off with him?"

Kenneth raises an eyebrow. "Well, they didn't *run* nowhere. But she kissed him last night."

"What!" Leo stomps his feet a little. "How the hell did that happen? Shit! I thought that kid was gay! Closeted, of course, but gay."

Kenneth snickers under his breath. "Man, you people think everyone is gay."

"Don't 'you people' me," Leo says.

"Why shouldn't I? You think I don't see how you look at me, like I'm some trailer-park redneck? What's good for the goose, Kemo Sabe."

"Hmmph," Leo says. "I take it I'm the goose in this equation. Fine, the gander buys the beer."

Kenneth doesn't protest, only mutters, "Take it from me, that kid ain't gay."

"Well," Leo says with a deep sigh. "Quite a loss for our team. He's stupid but pretty."

"He ain't stupid either," Kenneth says. "He's just young."

"What'd she kiss him for?" Leo gratefully accepts his own squat can of shitty beer. "And why would she tell you about it?"

"Why shouldn't she tell me?" On the terrace Leo notices several insanely large beetles lounging in the sun, fatter and even more repulsive than the leggy insects of the shower. "You and Sandor got it all wrong about us. We're just old friends."

"Old friends my ass," Leo says.

Kenneth signals for another beer. "You ever read a *biography* of Lawrence Durrell? 'Cause he wrote that once you view somebody as a confessor or a savior, they're outside the bounds of love to you."

Leo gawks, stupified. "What the hell would that have to do with *you*?"

"Good question, buddy. Good question."

Leo gulps his beer. He should have gone on the hike with Sandor even though Sandor's been skittish like some closeted kid himself, constantly fearing being "discovered" and stoned in the town square. As though they are truly an anomaly here any more than anywhere else. As though they are truly an anomaly anywhere.

"So are you saying Mary can't love Geoff? Are you saying—you don't want her to *leave* him or something, do you? I thought you were just here for the"—*sex*, he thinks, but he doesn't say it—"pigeon pastilla. For the bugs and the delightful aroma of sheep."

Kenneth doesn't answer. Leo waits for a moment, thinking he is considering his reply, but after a while he concludes that Kenneth has simply decided to pretend he hasn't spoken, that he isn't *there*, so he stands and leaves the table and heads inside the hotel, up to Mary's room. He knocks on her door but nobody answers. He knocks again and sees her wandering from the shower room fully dressed even though she already showered earlier that day.

"Hey," she says. "I just peed in the shower. The drain is way more sanitary than the toilets."

"Oh, I know," Leo says. "I did that this morning."

He goes into her room. They sit on the bed and she does another hit of her inhaler. Leo wonders if there's a limit to how much she's supposed to use, and he's guessing she's reached it.

"I just talked to your . . . um, lover? Paramour? Cowboy for hire? About how you're apparently some Mrs. Robinson putting the moves on our young Alias. I thought maybe I'd find him with you in here."

"I didn't put the moves on him," Mary says. "He put the moves on me. Sort of — I'm not sure his heart was in it. We kissed a little — very little." She stops. "Kenneth told you that? Why?"

"The question, sweetheart, is why you told *him*."

"I just wanted to be honest," she says.

At this, Leo is dumbfounded.

"Look," Mary says. "I'm leaving soon, I'll never see him again. I didn't want to leave with secrets between us."

"Oh, shit," Leo says. "That Durrell thing was applicable, then."

"What Durrell thing?"

"Never you mind." Leo puts his legs up on the bed. "Look, honey, what are you doing? Alias is a little boy. You have a husband — and a lover. What's going on?"

"I told you," Mary says. "Nothing happened."

"But what's going *on*?"

She's quiet then. She leans forward and wraps her arms around her bony knees. "I was just trying to live every day like it might be my last," she says finally. "Let's face it, I'm not a UN ambassador or a prima ballerina or a doctor who saves lives. I'm nothing special. You — you paint and that's your passion, right? Well, the rest of us, if we want to experience a high like that, we take drugs or have sex. I'm too sick for drugs, so that's it: I fuck."

"Funny," Leo muses. "If this were my last day on earth, I'd be careful. I wouldn't go pissing people off. I wouldn't make out with some inconsequential child even if he does have eyes to die for. I wouldn't betray Sandor or tell my lover truths that were only sure to hurt him, even if the guy was kind of an asshole. I'd only be that reckless and selfish if I had a long, long time to make amends and repair the damage. I think you've got things backward."

"Yep." She flicks a bug off the window with her hennaed fingers, and together they lean off the bed's edge and watch the bloated thing floundering on its back. "Step on it," Mary commands. "You have shoes on, you're the boy!"

And Leo does. He jumps off the bed and lands on the bug with a crunch, picks up his foot and stares at the mess.

"This is," he says, "the absolute most disgusting place on earth. It is a crime against nature to spend your birthday here. When you get to Paris or Madrid or whenever I see you next, I'm going to take you out for an amazing dinner and we'll get completely shit-faced drunk and wear inappropriately fancy clothes and celebrate properly."

"I don't know," Mary says. "We'll probably have to do that in boring New England. I doubt Geoff will really come to Madrid, so I'm probably going home."

"Oh," Leo says, "you'll be back."

"I really don't think I will, sweetie. You have to come visit me now."

Her face right then looks just like it does in the painting that will hang in the Spanish museum, haunted and hollow: the painting he wants her to see, and also never wants her to see. Her dismembered head surrounded by all their heads: their father, Daniel; her other father, the just-dead Paul; himself; Geoff; even Kenneth the way he looked that night at Mulligan's two years ago, hair straggly and eyes hard. The view is from above, heads arranged in a cavernous bowl like so many pieces of fruit piled atop one another, sideways and upside down with Mary's in the middle, alight with a glow, like the old paintings of saints. *Still Life, with Men,* he called it. He did not dare paint Sandor then—he wasn't yet sure he'd be around long enough and didn't want to be humiliated if their friends saw the piece at Merel's gallery. For Mary's lovers whose faces he couldn't approximate, he painted heads in profile or from the back, to create the appearance of clutter. "You said *still*," Merel pronounced at the time, "but this looks like a parade." Leo hadn't meant the word that way, though. He didn't mean not moving. He meant *for now*. Mary's hair falls in yellow strands over some of the faces, electric the way he remembers it in his garden the first day they met. The fruit bowl is lined in satin, with handles like a casket.

"I'll come visit, don't worry about that. But I know you—you can't keep a good woman down *or* off the European continent. Believe me, you'll be back."

Relief washes over him when she lets it stand.

• • •

OF COURSE, THERE will be blood.

First though, a long night at the fleabag hotel in Imlil, no one get-ting much sleep. Alias, crashing with a friend nearby, comes back the next morning early, too early, to collect them for the hike. He avoids Mary's eyes. Groggy farewells are bid to Leo in the hall outside the overflowing toilets, Leo in boxer shorts, his curls standing on end as though his fingers have been stuck in an electrical socket (Mary tries to memorize him), his elegant hands, decorated in henna symbols, waving at her and Sandor and even Kenneth as they make their way downstairs in hiking boots. By the time they return, he will be gone. The party makes instant coffee with boiled water, which Alias has procured from the hotel's closed café, and drinks it black in water bottles that feel wobbly and warm from the coffee's heat. Mary's hair is unwashed and tied under a bandanna. She and Sandor walk arm in arm, both melancholy about Leo's departure, while Alias and Kenneth walk slightly ahead, speaking French, occasionally laughing.

To head south would take them the way of true trekkers: Mount Toubkal. Instead they veer west out of the village of Imlil, heading for a less-challenging pass. Still, her going is slow. They pass through the village of Tamatert, chased by the usual adorable village children, and she catches her breath photographing two boys and a tiny girl with puffy hair and a dirty pink apron, sucking on oranges; she catches her breath, then loses it again with longing. The town behind them, they walk uphill for a small while, back down, maybe two miles in that fashion, and already she feels she has run a marathon. It's only at about 2,400 meters that the *real* uphill begins.

Soon they are switchbacking. Back and forth, back and forth, the path isolated and narrow, no other tourists on their part of the moun-tain. Sometimes they have to scramble, the terrain littered with crumbly dirt-rocks and spectacularly fat black beetles—maybe it is a blessing Leo is not here. Here there are no trees, not even those squat things like the ones near the Kik Plateau. The breeze is still cool—Mary shivers under her long sleeves—though the morning is warming up.

On the switchbacks, she sees the ground below her rushing at her in the opposite direction, the way the ground seems to spin when you have just gotten off a carnival ride. When she stops walking, the ground on which she's standing stops, too, but the ground below continues its rotation. This must be a lack of oxygen, even though they're only around 2,800 meters. Or more by now? How high is that in feet? You're supposed to multiply by three, she thinks, but her head can't do the computation; nothing feels clear. She does not mention the rushing ground to anyone but stops now and then to cough, and Sandor keeps saying, "We don't have to go all the way. Anytime you want, we can stop." She doesn't have the breath to waste on protest, but she sees Kenneth put a hand on Sandor's arm and say, "Man, she knows what she can do and what she can't. Lay off."

Mary realizes she did not actually believe it would happen, but they finally reach the pass. Wait—if she did not think they would get here, then why is she on this mountain? What did she believe would happen *instead*? This, too, feels foggy. Down below is her destination: the cliff bottoms of Mykonos; the black sand beach of La Gomera; the oxygen machines and quarantined hospital room and gulping for air while her parents and Geoff look on with agonized pain in their eyes. From the pass, she, Kenneth, Sandor, and Alias look down into a valley, the town below them like crumbs at the bottom of a bowl. Surrounding them, mountain peaks form the bowl's jagged teeth. They sit on the ground and look. In truth this view is less thrilling than the medinas, than Nawar's house; a mountain is not specifically Moroccan or even *African* but could be anywhere. It has taken them a stupidly long time to get to this view, and now the day is hot. Alone, the three men could have made it in half the time. They have been walking at a pace so slow that surely it felt confining to their long, healthy legs. Mary rests her head on Kenneth's day pack, gulping water. She's still chilly, though she's consumed the majority of the water they brought and cannot possibly be dehydrated. She coughs, and Sandor and Alias gape as she keeps trying again and again, hacking herself raw. "It won't *do* anything," she tries to explain. She's clogged, so that her lungs won't let in the air. She lies back down, gulping on her inhaler, then abruptly bolts upright again to cough violently into her hands.

Then. The blood.

Bright, unexpected mouthfuls in her hennaed hands, obscuring the intricate design. No sooner do the three men all jump to standing than there is another upheaval, the coughs convulsive, not voluntary now, and each lurching up more red liquid, thick like lava with blood's unmistakable smell. She is screaming but not screaming, the scream stuck in her lungs and drowned, and when the men rush to her, there is a small pause amid her drowning—a pause in which both Sandor and Alias are obviously afraid to touch her, so that suddenly Kenneth has her face in his hands, trying to lift her chin as though maybe there is an injury, an actual *injury* somehow undetected. As though he lacks the memory that this is exactly where they began. Mary's body spasms again, blood flying onto him as though she is the girl from *The Exorcist,* as though her head will spin. He is covered down his front with the color and smell of her.

He barks at the others, "Jesus Christ, we have to get her down!"

This has all happened in maybe forty-five seconds. In less than a minute, everything can change.

There is nothing wrong with her legs, but she cannot walk. She is a drowning animal, frantic and gasping, and Sandor rushes forward and grabs one of her arms, too, his hands slippery with sweat. Even this, though, doesn't work. The switchbacks aren't wide enough for them to walk this way: three people linked horizontally, her body convulsing like a fish. They are shouting back and forth to one another, but saying nothing that can help: *What the fuck? What the fuck?* Kenneth lifts her like a parcel and Alias shouts that he will run ahead, run back to the village to procure a car so that they can get her to a hospital— there isn't one *here,* Mary knows, nothing for miles, and if any is closer than Marrakech, it is nowhere you'd want to be. It is maybe three hours to the city, more, given how long it will take to even get her into town.

She will die here on the mountain—it is inevitable—and yes, *this* is what she expected, then; *this* is why she is here. *Oh God, oh Mom, oh Geoff.*

Alias hesitates, perhaps uncertain whether there is any point in rushing for help, or whether it will only brand him a coward not to have stayed with the others while she dies. Sandor pushes Alias so hard he nearly falls backward, shouts, "Hurry! Run!"

In Imlil, her cough suppressant is tucked away with her other medical paraphernalia. Along with the written CF protocol from Laxmi, because Dr. Fox, her specialist in New Hampshire, disapproved so strongly of this trip that Mary was afraid to ask her for the necessary paperwork and had Laxmi fax it instead. His instructions came with a handwritten note proclaiming *I am not happy about this,* which could have been for her or for Geoff, Mary didn't know. The note says to administer Cyklokapron by IV to clot her blood should she have a massive hemoptysis.

Whether there would even be fucking Cyklokapron in Morocco, Mary knew, was anyone's guess. *Your suicidal mission,* Geoff had said. She could not pretend to believe that Africa had ever been equipped to catch her fall.

Against Kenneth's body, her limbs thrash as she sputters blood. "Don't kill us," he says to her, and somewhere under the gush and panic she hears: She has to stop squirming so he won't slip, so they won't *both* plummet to their deaths. She has to be still so he does not become her casualty, too. Blood rushes. She can't control her limbs.

Then all at once it is over. Over. Her lungs' convulsions cease and she collapses in Kenneth's arms, spent, blood already drying sticky on her skin and clothes. All at once she is blinking dizzily and breathing again, lungs no longer full of molten liquid choking her. She starts trying to wipe blood from Kenneth's face, but her hands feel blind, fuzzy. He catches them in his and stills them.

Sandor murmurs, "Thank God, thank God," his voice transfixed.

They stare at one another, all three dazed. She is not dead.

Now what are they supposed to do?

KENNETH PASSES HIS pack to Sandor, puts Cystic on his back in its place. He thinks she'll protest but instead she clings to him and they start down the mountain. It will be hours before they reach even the minuscule little village of Tamatert, much less Imlil, where Alias could possibly snag a car. "Better walk behind me, buddy," he tells Sandor, and Sandor falls in line, the plan unspoken between them: if Kenneth falls, Sandor will catch the girl from his back. The dirt-rocks under their feet scatter and crumble; the switchbacks are steep. This will never work. It will never work. Kenneth can see Alias occasionally beneath them, zigzagging, moving fast. His youth, his strength and speed—suddenly it all seems obscene.

After a while he's got to stop, switch Cystic onto Sandor's back. She's not coughing anymore but seems to be doing little else either. It is understood that her walking is impossible, but Kenneth can't feel his body. Though the blood seems to have shed the last of what passed for substance in her weight, it was a matter, simply, of her starting to slip, of his legs buckling. There is no pain, no soreness, no exhaustion. Just the inability to go on with the load.

Thirty-five-year-old Sandor shoulders his passenger as though she is nothing, picks up the pace like the girl's nothing more than a day pack. Now it is Kenneth's turn to walk behind, though Sandor doesn't seem to need him.

Down, down, an hour this way, maybe longer. At one point she says she can walk and they let her try, but she is slower on her own than Sandor is carrying her, so they resume their positions. She is weepy, and Sandor glances back at Kenneth, his pace slowing, apparently unsure whether they should stop to comfort her. Kenneth barks, "Stop crying, you're gonna get everything flowing again!" and she gulps and buries her face in Sandor's neck, and Sandor says nothing, walks on.

Alias isn't in Tamatert, but at the edge of the village people are gathered, waiting for them—the kid must have actually tipped them off. In a town this small, most people speak no French, but Kenneth's able to communicate with a couple of the men. Their "guide" has gone ahead to Imlil, he is told, for a car. The women have bowls of water and rags to wash the blood, which Alias must have warned them about. Women approach Cystic as though blood is not a dangerous thing, begin bathing her still fully dressed. They think, it is clear, that she has been in some kind of hiking accident. They look for the wound.

It is then that Kenneth notices them. The four travelers he and Cystic first saw in the Tanger Inn: the dark, exotic couple and the white hippies. They are walking up the road, cameras round their necks, day packs on their backs, oblivious to the blinding heat, to their poor choice of hour in making this trip. They chat in their loud tourist voices, one of the girls proclaiming how cute the village children are just as Cystic did earlier this morning. "I'd just love to take a few of them home with me!" exclaims the pigtailed traveler, and Kenneth sees she has a Canadian maple leaf on her pack. They approach and there is Cystic, rust-colored water running from her listless body. The four travelers stop in their tracks. "My God!" shouts the pigtailed girl—a woman really, small lines already around her eyes. "What happened to her? Were you attacked?"

"Attacked?" Kenneth says blankly. "You got a car, by any chance?"

They all stare at him. One of the men nods: Yes, a car. Down below, in Imlil.

Sandor says, "We need to get her to a hospital."

Cystic murmurs from a few feet away, "Alias will be here before they could get down there and back with a car."

"We don't know what that guy's gonna do," Kenneth says coolly. "Could be he wants nothing to do with this and we'll never see him again."

Cystic shakes her head, eyes closed. He knows she wants to protest and it makes him dig his heels in. "Sandor, go with them and get the car and I'll stay here with her."

Sandor stands, ready to go.

"Wait a second," the Asian girl says. She is startlingly pretty, angelic looking, her skin poreless. "We need our car." Her voice is rising, panicked. "You can't just go take it. We have to *return* that car—we'll be held responsible for it. What if you just run off with it? Do you think we have the money to pay for a whole car? We'd be arrested!"

"We're not car thieves!" Sandor protests. "Come with us if you like—we're trying to get a sick woman to the hospital!"

"We can't all fit in one car together," the Asian girl protests sensibly. "There's no hospital around here anyway—I mean, I'm sorry your friend got hurt, but I don't see what we can do to help. We can't take you all the way back to Marra*kech*."

Kenneth feels his hands balling into fists at the girl's whine. The villagers are still standing around openly staring, and though they don't speak English, conflict is palpable in any language. Kenneth's eyes dart toward Cystic, and the rage in him feels like venom. He could kill this girl, this beautiful girl and her pigtailed friend and the two assholes with them. He could kill them with his bare hands for not caring, not trusting, even though *he* doesn't trust Alias, who knows Cystic better than these kids do, who has kissed her. Even though he's not the least bit convinced Alias hasn't just left them here hanging. The four travelers look at one another uncertainly, but not one speaks up to contradict, to offer up the car, and Kenneth thought only Americans were this full of righteous entitlement, this kind of callousness, but no: it is the whole world, the whole modern world, and the only way to escape it is to live in some godforsaken remote village where you share your house with sheep. Though he is not fool enough to think that in the Old World it would be any different—that fresh-baked bread and a roof to shield you from the hottest few hours of the sun and the way Nawar bent lovingly over Cystic's damaged hands means nobility—as if he doesn't know that those villagers would sell their daughters to the first bastard who came round with a buck, and that these women with their bowls of water and rags probably expect to be paid. The world is shit and he is part of it. He should never have let himself lose sight of that. But he would like to wrap his hands around this beautiful Canadian's throat until she, too, coughs blood, because the woman who *made* him lose sight of the world's ugliness is nothing to them, just an animal left on the side of the road to die: just a story they will tell back in North America over beers. He moves closer to the dark man, the beautiful girl's man, intending to punch him, to tell him his girlfriend is a heartless piece of trash, but no release will come.

"We'll go down to Imlil," the white boy interjects, stepping between them. "We can't give you our car but we'll go down and find you another one at a hotel."

"We're waiting for someone," Cystic says. Her voice is louder than it has been since the coughing began. "He's on his way back. We were just stopping to rest." She stands, and Sandor rushes to her side. She takes a few steps forward, pupils dilated like a junkie's and some flame inside her glowing, so that her face looks not pale but *white*. Sandor puts an arm around her and ushers her down the road, and at last Kenneth snaps back to himself and rushes with them, too, puts his arm around her body from the other side, so that he and Sandor are almost embracing, and like this they are about to walk on when Alias comes rushing down the road calling to them, car in the distance and, as they can see as they get closer, insanely, all her belongings loaded inside.

"What the fuck?" Kenneth shouts at him. "You spent your time pulling shit out of her room? She could have been bleeding to death up here!"

Alias blinks, out of breath, clearly terrified. "But her medicines," he falters. "Maybe she needs them?"

And it is the heat and the water Cystic drank so fast that there was none left for the rest of them and the fact that he is too clean, just too damn clean for this day to be happening, that makes Kenneth sway on his feet, head knocking against the frame of the car, so that Sandor almost has to help him in, too, as from the edge of the road the four travelers in the distance, the matter settled in their minds, move on.

SANDOR GRIPS THE passenger's door handle, white knuckled. Alias is speeding like they're in a Hollywood chase scene, though he's probably never had a formal driving class. In the backseat, Kenneth holds Mary in his lap. She's slugging cough syrup, the prescription kind, and Kenneth takes it from her hand, saying, "Baby, you weigh about fifty pounds, you're on the petite protocol," but Mary's head just lolls against his shoulder. Every moment on the road without the appearance of more blood feels a miracle. Sandor keeps an eye on his watch.

She is almost unconscious when it starts again, as somehow

Sandor knew it would. Her body jerks despite her closed, drugged eyes, blood spurting out with a life of its own, immense and terrible. Sandor puts his head between his knees, muttering "Sterkte" under his breath like a prayer. In his peripheral vision, he sees Kenneth pull out his knife and start slashing open the carpet they bought in Essaouira—a lifetime ago—wrapping the stiff thing around Mary's body so that her blood convulses right over it. Kenneth has his arms around the carpet; he's murmuring to her—*what,* Sandor can't hear. It almost hurts to look at them; he feels an intruder on a private scene, intimate and vulgar at once.

Then it is over again, just as suddenly as it started. That nightmare slips back inside some fissure in the universe and she's breathing again, the gurgling sound of her air filling the shell-shocked car.

"Sandor," she says, and he turns full on to hear, Alias still driving like mad and shouting, "We're almost there, we're almost there!" though they are nowhere near. Sandor thinks of what Leo would do and climbs over the seat, large gaps of vacant space on either side of the bundle that is Mary and Kenneth. He puts his arms around Mary's carpeted shoulders, too, so that he and Kenneth are holding each other by proxy.

"When Geoff asks what happened," she rasps, "say I passed out right away. Tell him I had no idea what was going on."

Sandor sobs. Christ, why didn't he force Leo to take her back to Europe—why didn't he stand his ground? This is un-fucking-believable. This cannot be happening. He holds her shaking shoulders inside the blanket and weeps. She pushes at him with her hands.

"Tell him I loved the trip. Tell him I missed him but I understood. Why he couldn't. I . . ." She fades for a moment, as though she is asleep, and Sandor makes an involuntary noise and shakes her to see if she's dead. "Tell him I understood why I wasn't mad," she says, and he knows what she means but the incoherence is terrifying. He looks at Kenneth, who turns his face to the window as though trying not to witness. But when Sandor says, "Stop this talking, you are going to be fine, they'll fix you up and you can tell him yourself anything you like,"

Kenneth looks back at the huddle inside the carpet, her blood on his face, and says clearly, "He hears. He'll remember what you said."

She is unconscious when they reach the hospital. There follows a frenzy of activity, only the basics of which Sandor understands. Blood clotters, an IV antibiotic. Mary wakes, incoherent, belligerent, tries to get out of bed over the protests of nurses. She seems to recognize no one. She's lugging her IV line behind her when the blood starts again, though by now, Sandor no longer feels faint at the sight of it. He can touch her without recoiling, the way Kenneth did from the first. Perhaps it is not so much old hat as that he assumes its *temporary* nature. She will bleed to death, and when she is dead, then the blood will stop.

She is drowning. Spitting blood into cups faster than the nurses can hand them her way. She leans against a sink filled with red. Her skin is the color of the graying porcelain. When they try to get a nasal cannula on her, the blood spurts toward it like a geyser; Sandor lies down on the floor, hyperventilating a little. Then they are *both* lying there, her head in the crook of his numb arm, the flow of her having stopped again as inexplicably as the last two times. Other than her raspy breath she could be a corpse, she's so cold.

The doctor, Boutell, is French, but Kenneth doesn't know French medical terms, so he switches to English, and the words Sandor hears could stop his heart: *bronchoscopy, emergency surgery, cauterization.* Kenneth has dug through her bag for the letters from her physician at home. When she is too groggy to sign consent forms, Sandor blurts out, "I am her brother, I will sign." All blonds look alike. They pass him the forms.

She sleeps. She's on oxygen, on morphine, IVs sticking out. When she wakes, she groans, "Don't tell Geoff until it's all over." She begs, "Don't let him see me this way." Other times she seems to have no idea they are in the room.

Leo knows nothing; Geoff knows nothing; Mary's widowed mother at home remains uncalled. Sandor stands at the hallway phone box. The hospital corridor is full of cats. He does not want to have this conversation—he does not, but if he fails to call, there is a chance Leo will never forgive him. He rests his forehead against the cool wall tiles, cats rubbing up against his legs as if they're in one of Leo's psychedelic paintings.

This hospital is mainly normal. Wealthy Moroccans, tourists, expats. Sure, there are these scrawny feral things roaming around as though they have the run of an abandoned building, but otherwise things seem all right here. Mary is in a private room even. Kenneth says her copious bleeding must have scared the hell out of them—they must not have wanted her anywhere near the other patients—but maybe it's merely a sign of civilization? She did not die on the mountain, after all. Tomorrow she will have surgery. Maybe it is as simple as that. Crisis averted.

Sandor feels drunk, dizzy. He can't remember exactly when he last ate. These cats remind him of the film *Betty Blue,* when at the end the male lead has euthanized his girlfriend and sits at home in their kitchen conversing to the cat as though she is the dead lover. The *unreal* seems, here, as though it could be real, and Mary seems as though she could be a dream. How has she possibly come back into his life after all those years? How has she come and with her arrival given him a window to Leo and changed everything? It has all been one elaborate hallucination. The real girl who played Nicole in the film of Arthog House (whose name really *is* Nicole, of course) is somewhere else entirely, and he will never see her again. Leo Becker is not his lover, just a man he desperately wants to fuck, whose work, the first time he saw it, struck him as the love child of Salvador Dalí and Francis Bacon, full of hyperprecision and dream and beautiful perversion. Leo is no one whose body he has tasted, no one who claims to love him, and this sick girl is not his Nicole and did not facilitate it. Sandor has done more crying today than in the past fifteen years. He has cried himself dry.

He does not pick up the phone. Instead he goes with Alias and Kenneth to get something to eat. Hunger and fear make them stagger. They are complicit. Out on the streets, people stare at Kenneth, cluck and hiss at him about his bloodstains.

"I will go to my place and fetch fresh clothes," Alias says, leaving

them at a café. Everything Sandor and Kenneth own is still in Imlil;
they will never see those things again. Even after Alias has proved a
genie on this trip, pulling vehicles and functional medical facilities
and race-car driving out of his firm little ass, Sandor wonders if they
will ever see *him* again either. Kenneth voices the same, but half an
hour later Alias is back with fresh-smelling powder-blue shirts, one
for each of them, and trousers for Kenneth that fit in the waist but
are too short. Cats prowl the café, too; they seem inescapable. Sandor
tosses them scraps of bread, though Alias tells him not to and the
cats don't appear interested.

Back at the hospital, visiting hours are over. They are told Mary
is "resting comfortably." In the morning she will be cauterized. This
sounds official.

"It'll stop the bleeding and we'll load her on a plane and go home,"
Sandor tells Kenneth, who has fallen silent as a stone. Sandor isn't
sure what "home" entails. Leo will be there somehow, and Geoff, too,
and definitely not Kenneth or the emaciated cats.

Kenneth paces the hospital corridor. Sandor wants to leave, wants
it perhaps more desperately than he has ever wanted anything in
his life, but can't admit it in the face of the damn Yankee's vigil.
He steps outside for a smoke and sobs a bit more, then curses himself until self-anger replaces the tears. On his return, Kenneth is
sleeping standing up against a wall. Sandor prods him with a foot
until he jerks alert. On the street, walking to Alias's apartment,
Kenneth starts tossing out titles for their predicament. "The Unbearable Lightness of Breathing," he says. "Death and the Maiden,"
Sandor counters. They riff. "Got My Invitation to a Beheading," concludes Kenneth, which doesn't quite make sense to Sandor. Still,
they laugh, punch drunk, and have to stop walking. Then the rest of
the way they can't look at each other.

The sky is black. It seems impossible that at Jemaa el-Fna tourists
are scarfing down food, musicians playing. That in the little rooms
above courtyards, couples are fighting, having sex. Alias lives in one
bare room with a small kitchenette. His girlfriend does not live there;
Sandor had automatically assumed she did. They crash on Alias's

floor in borrowed clothing, the sleep of the just or the dead. No one even mentions a phone.

Yes, if only things can improve *before* he calls Leo, then he will avoid the fallout. They will be locked in secrecy forever—the old Arthog House trio—and Leo and Geoff need never know how close things came.

By morning she is already in surgery. There was more bleeding during the night, her oxygen levels dipping so low she required a ventilator. These words conjure apocalyptic images in Sandor's mind, but when Mary comes out of the operating theater, the doctor pronounces her bleeding "fini." They found the source: both lungs at once. In recovery the ventilator is scaled down, so by the time Sandor and Kenneth are permitted to see her, she wears only an ordinary oxygen mask.

"Luke," she rasps through her ravaged throat, "I am your father." Then she giggles on anesthesia as they wheel her back to her room.

Crisis averted.

Kenneth rings Alias at La Mamounia to tell him the news. Mary still won't give them Geoff's number in New England, but Sandor tries Leo's cell, Merel's cell, even the Paris gallery. It is still early and every call goes straight to voice mail. He leaves no message other than *It's urgent, call.* If they hadn't given her medical paperwork to Boutell, they could track down her American physician and get word to her family, but those papers are gone, the French doctor seems to be missing, the nurses know nothing of the forms. Sandor rings Leo every half hour, to no avail. He isn't sure where Leo is staying, and last year Leo dropped his cell phone into a urinal by accident and just left it there. Mary goes by her maiden name; Sandor doesn't know Geoff's; Leo is the keeper of such things. Leo, her brother, who cannot be trusted with anything. They wait, more bored now that she isn't bleeding. Sandor and Kenneth bullshit about the London jazz club Vortex for a while, how excellent it was. Mary asks them to find her a *Herald Tribune*.

Crisis averted.

Except that suddenly she is spiking a fever. Except that when Boutell finally reappears, face more worried than it was yesterday, he says he looked up cystic fibrosis on the Internet because they have never had a CF patient here. Except the nurses clear her room and stick a central line into her chest, and when Kenneth reenters he says, "She doesn't like that, she doesn't want that there," and Sandor says, "I'm sure the doctors know what they're doing," though clearly this may not be true at all, and Mary says nothing now; she seems detached from her body. Her skin is no longer supernaturally white but flushed from fever. "I shouldn't have left her last night. I knew I shouldn't've left," Kenneth says over and over again until Sandor looks at him hard and says, "*I* left her, too. Just shut up."

IV-administered antibiotics can take as much as twenty-four hours to work. Just over twenty-four hours ago they were drinking coffee from toxic plastic bottles; Mary was crooning at Moroccan children; Leo had not yet boarded his plane. What if Sandor reaches Leo and Leo falls apart? There is something unspeakably fragile in him—what if this news is the thing that does him in? And how could Leo be *expected* to bear this when Sandor can hardly take it himself and he is the stable one, the sane one, the one who is not connected by blood to this woman they both love? Leo's phone goes to voice mail again and Sandor hurls his cell across the room so that its insides fall out. In the toilet his stomach retches but nothing comes up. Twenty-four hours.

Kenneth is waiting in the hall when he returns. "I'm telling that doc to call her husband," he says. "This circus has gone on long enough." But as he leaves to find the doctor, word comes that Geoff *is* on the line: he must have been alerted by Mary's home physician. A nurse comes to collect Sandor, the husband's alleged brother-in-law, saying, "Son mari pour vous."

Sandor has met Geoff only once, at Mary's father's funeral. He remembers him as exceptionally handsome in an entirely different vein than Leo. Tall, sturdy, masculine, well groomed. He and Mary looked vaguely wrong together, but Leo made more of it than it was.

"Leo." Geoff's voice is all business yet strangely intimate—the sound of his wife's brother's name in his mouth. "Is it as bad as that Dr. Boutell says? Why won't they give her the phone?"

Sandor clears his throat. "No," he says, "it's just me. Sandor. Leo had to go back to Paris, and then this happened. I told them she was my sister, I hope you don't—"

"I'm getting on the next plane. You do not let anything happen before I get there, Sandor. No one touches her—no more surgeries, do you understand? I'll be there in less than twenty-four hours. *Nothing* happens, promise me."

"You don't get it," Sandor begins, using the expression Leo often feeds him. "She was bleeding, there was no choice—"

"Listen very carefully," Geoff says with grave authority, so that even before he continues, Sandor is struck by the full impact of what he and Kenneth have wrought in hiding the truth: that they have been errant, disorganized children playing a man's game. "There is not a single cystic fibrosis center in Morocco. There are something like four on the entire African continent. Mary had no business even setting foot in that country—she has colonized bacteria that can attack her system and kill her just from forgetting to wash her hands in her own house. I begged her not to go, I refused to have any part of it, and maybe that could have been the end of it, but no, you and her irresponsible, oblivious brother were all for it and ran down to meet her with fucking bells on and took her hiking at nine goddamn thousand feet. Now my *wife* has been bleeding and cut open and intubated in the middle of Bumblefuck. Do you realize more people get pneumonia in the hospital than anywhere else, and that's in fucking *America*? If she's septic, nothing will help her—nothing. Do you understand what I'm saying to you?"

"I'm sorry," Sandor chokes out. "I'm sorry—"

"You tell her I'm coming. You tell her I love her and I'll fix—" Geoff's voice breaks. "You tell her I'm going to get her the hell out of there."

He hangs up the phone.

TIME'S MOVING TOO fast. Too fast when Cystic's alert and can talk, and while at first the hours in between dragged, now those are speeding toward Kenneth, too, hurtling him along. It's like snaking up the incline of a roller coaster real slow and you think the wait will kill you, but once the descent starts there's no time for anything anymore, not even the dread. It's all over before you know it. Three days, that's it. Three days they've been here and nothing's the way it was, as if that time before was a shadow life, a book he read long ago. There's never been anything but this. The hours he spent in agonized anticipation of the end of their trip, of the day she went back to her husband and he never saw her again, seem like an elaborate scam now, a children's story they were feeding themselves. It could never have played out any other way than this.

She's living in the in-between place, waiting to be ferried across. The doctors don't say it like that; Dr. Boutell doesn't say much — he's way over his head. Every time they see him, he has a phone in his hand, calling somebody to consult, even bringing Cystic his own cell a few minutes ago so that she could talk to her mother at Logan Airport, where her mom's hooking up with the husband, the two of them flying over together.

Turns out getting a flight to Casablanca isn't such a simple matter. Even JFK doesn't offer the flight every day, so it's turned into a scramble, Sandor says, as they compare flying to Europe first and then hopping some Iberia or Air Maroc flight down with waiting for the next day's flight out of Logan direct. In the end it must've been a wash: the husband's flying out tonight, will be in Casablanca by morning and in Marrakech later that day. Leo, too, is coming back, landing in Casablanca separately, but ultimately waiting for the same flight to Marrakech so that they will all descend together, a stampede of righteous family members demanding answers from Boutell, and hoping for a miracle Kenneth knows in his bones won't come.

When they arrive he will already be gone. A given. He will not be around to see the end, not be permitted any space at the bedside for final good-byes. Once that flight from Casablanca lands, even Alias will have more rights than he. No matter, her bedside isn't *territory;* no pissing contest can make this go any different. Her husband is coming and Kenneth is glad. The man is a doctor and at least this three-ring circus will end. The husband will arrive and see the truth of it and that will be that. They'll medevac her out of this joint, bring her somewhere high tech and gleaming. Then settle down to watch her die.

Who knows how long they'll have to wait, though? A body, even a body that's been through what hers has, can take a long time shutting down. He thinks of Cystic and how her eyes will twitch. How the morphine will stop the way she sometimes just starts gasping, the panic of her air hunger, the outrage of Boutell's saying that they *can't* turn the oxygen up any higher or she'll stop breathing on her own—this makes no sense to him, this makes no goddamn sense—that if it goes any higher she could end up on a ventilator, and the way she fought it the first time they might have to induce a coma just to get it in her, and then you're talking life support. Right now she's still breathing on her own, just with bursts of terror and biting at air that won't go down. As if this is a favor to her; as if torture is a treatment plan.

The husband will come in and speak medicalese and stop this; he'll make them increase the morphine and then either she won't know anything anymore or the things she knows, the things she sees behind her eyes, will be inaccessible, so at least everyone else will feel better with her doped up like that, they'll sit round the bed and say, *At least she isn't suffering,* like they have any fucking idea what goes on behind a person's eyes when the sweet, vicious knife of the drug claims your days.

He waits in the hall. She talks to her mother, and her voice has a hysterical edge but comes slow and groggy like a hiss. She says the usual things; he can hear this from the hall. The *I'm sorry*s, the *I love you*s. He and Sandor have slunk out into the hall so she can have her privacy, but maybe there's nothing private left anymore; things are too far gone for private. He wants this *over,* wants her free of it; he doesn't want to be sent away to imagine the end rather than bear witness with his own eyes. He doesn't want to abandon her to their civilized grief and pretty lies.

He has no right to her. He isn't trying to believe he has a right.

She keeps saying she doesn't want her husband here, but Kenneth knows this is just her own pretty lie—her fear talking. As long as the husband isn't here, she can keep some core of bravado up, some face she needs to keep in place to get through this, but the minute she sees him, the minute he walks in the room, Kenneth knows she'll fall. He's got no illusions about this. She's got no kids; if she had wanted to walk out on her marriage, she would've done it. She loves the man: simple as that. She loves him enough to have fought every impulse she had, to have beaten herself up every time she couldn't win. She loves him enough that even though she was going to have to lie anyway about Kenneth being on the goddamn continent with her—about the fact that he existed at *all*—she still wouldn't fuck him the moment it became something more than a game, more than a same-time-next-year thrill. And that kind of love is dangerous. She'll see the man and she'll fall apart, she will become abject regret and naked fear and then the morphine will come and Kenneth will be on a plane by then, so who knows, who knows?

She's so quiet.

There's so little left in her now that it takes a while to notice what's going on. Takes a while to notice that she's not talking anymore, that her bedclothes are covered in red. Maybe she was *trying* to scream but no sound, no air came. He and Sandor cry out and all at once there is a frenzy of activity: they rush the room, these dark nurses in their starched white uniforms, they shout to one another in French and when Kenneth and Sandor get too close they're shooed away. Christ, how much is one body supposed to take? Where is all this blood even coming from? He kicks the wall, but it is centuries-old stone, and there is no crash, only pain.

The last thing he sees before they pull the curtain is her mouth clutched against her own blood like a kiss, as a nurse strides and snatches Boutell's phone from her hand, snapping it shut.

SHE'S TOO SICK to operate on now. Her fever's still raging after twenty-four hours, the antibiotics ineffectual, like so much water flowing into her veins. They cannot cauterize and so it's just back to more blood clotters through her central line. Even the cough suppressant would depress her breathing too much now to risk it. The scenario in Kenneth's mind revises itself: No medevac. This is her final destination. Now there is nothing to do but wait it out.

"Do you ever think about Joshua?" she says. She is sitting elevated to help her breathe, her face so white there is no contrast between her skin and her pillows except for the blood still dried on her lips. She stares beyond him at the curtains, pale and stark like nothing else in this country, nothing like the blues of Asilah and Essaouira, as if those colors no longer exist.

"No," he says.

He's never before realized how boldly he's felt entitled to air.

"Will you think about me?"

"Not if I can help it, darlin'."

Her small laugh is a wheeze; it takes her time to recover. Soon, an hour, maybe less, she will start the alternation of chills and burning again, the cycle she's riding between pushing off her bedclothes and begging for more blankets, between lying limp and sweating on her bed and shaking so much that they thought at one point she was having a seizure. "Now's the time to start lying to me," she instructs, putting her hennaed hand on his, always the teacher.

He regards the winding lines, faded from black to brown and leading nowhere except back into one another like a labyrinth. How fitting it turned out to be that Nawar decorated her hands and those of her brother for her own funeral.

"That was me lying," he tells her, but this time he earns no laugh. Her eyes are already closed.

Behind the curtains, she says she sees people moving: a rippling in the fabric; the darting of a face into the morphine shadows. "I know they aren't there," she assures him and Sandor gently, "but I hear them talking behind the walls."

Is there a God, and does it matter, when he will not save them now?

And then all at once it's so clear. So clear he can't believe he didn't see it before. It is not because he ceased to be a *game* that the girl refused to let him inside; that's too easy, when what's been between them was never a game, when playing was never what they were doing. But he sees, as she lies here slowly dying, that despite all the noise she made about how long this trip would last, about buying souvenirs for home, there was only ever one way this could have played out. She came here to *die,* plain and simple — kept pushing beyond her endurance, overmedicating like her brother said, mingling with germs, inhaling smoke and exhaust, ascending altitudes and tempting fate until something was bound to crack. Whether she knows it or not, whether she can admit it to herself or not, she couldn't stand the thought of fading away in New England on her country lane, life's walls shrinking in on her bit by bit until she became somebody else, until she needed an oxygen tank just to take a shower like she said would happen someday. So she came out here for one last hoorah, one big bang, and look, as usual, the girl got what she wanted. It's so simple he can't believe he didn't figure it out in Tangier, call her on it to her face. Maybe if the words had been spoken aloud, she'd have seen it for all its absurdity and stopped, just stopped. Now, instead, the absurdity has taken on a life of its own.

It's so easy. She wouldn't fuck him this time because she wanted her husband to be her last.

ALIAS HAS PREPARED tea in his small kitchenette in anticipation of Kenneth's arrival. They sit and Kenneth makes his stomach accept the liquid, wills it not to rebel. Alias is shirtless and virile, wearing only his trousers, and for a brief and fractured moment Kenneth thinks about either pulling out his knife and stabbing the boy through the heart or fucking him. He puts his head into his hands as Alias talks about the gig he had at La Mamounia that day, the family of tourists he had to cart around. "I had to put on my guide face," he says, "but I don't feel like smiling."

Kenneth gulps his tea without waiting for it to cool, lets the scorching pain ground him.

"I came to ask you something," he says, cutting off the kid's complaints, his testimony of compassionate involvement. "You know a place I can score some heroin?"

Alias's face freezes. In the dim room, the black of his eyes blends in with the night outside. After a moment he puts on a smile, holds up his hands. "This is not a part of my job at La Mamounia," he explains calmly. "Sometimes, yes, people want to smoke some hashish and I hook them up, sure. But not this."

"You've lived here your whole life," Kenneth says quietly. "You see things. I'm not asking you to come with me, man. I could wander the streets looking for it and we both know I'd find it eventually—that's the nature of the city, every city in the world's the same like that. But I wanna get back to the hospital tonight. I need this done fast."

Alias stands. He begins to clear away the teapot, though he himself has not finished. He does not, it is clear, want Kenneth touching his glasses anymore, touching the place where he lives, and Kenneth feels relief: Maybe Alias will not show up at the hospital tomorrow. Maybe this will be the end of him. Kenneth steels himself for a night of wandering and thinks of the Tangier whore—how much he would like to see her marred face right now, how stupid he was to spend an entire night with her when he could have been with Cystic. He moves to leave and Alias puts out a hand to stop him, though the hand does not actually make contact.

"Sure," Alias says, his voice the same agreeable calm as before. "I don't do this myself but . . ." He shrugs. "It's like you say. I know this city, everything about it, good and bad." He begins to nod and in his face Kenneth sees barely concealed disdain and better-concealed sadness. "So of course, yes. I know a place like that."

LEO'S PLANE HAS been delayed. Sandor talked to him just a few hours ago while he was still at CMN. Leo had hooked up with Geoff and the mother and they were all waiting for their flight into Marrakech, so Sandor went to RAK in a rental car at the designated time to collect them, but the flight had not landed. In a panic he rang Geoff's phone but got no answer. He has been assured they are en route in the air. It is a short flight; they will be here soon. He waits.

Leo, of course, left his cell phone in Paris at the apartment of a friend before leaving for Madrid the day before yesterday, and there it lies still, uncharged. Sandor heard from him only when Leo took it upon himself to ring Sandor's own cell from his Madrid hotel, voice bright (though Sandor noted his trying to make it less so, perhaps fearing Sandor's envy over the exhibition—oh, how far away that all seems now), saying, "I'm just calling to check in!" And so Sandor had to tell him the truth. It surprised him: how close he almost came to lying, even though there was no way he could get away with it, even though he knew what withholding information from Geoff had cost. It was just that he couldn't bear to reach the moment, the one in which Leo's voice lost all its happy timbre and collapsed on itself—the moment of listening to Leo's sobs on the phone.

He had never heard Leo weep before. For a man whose eyes fill with tears every time they watch a film (even a sentimental American television commercial can do him in!), what Leo passes off as "crying" generally has little staying power, as though he loses the will for it barely out of the gate. Early in their time together Sandor mocked Leo for this, saying his tears were all about appearances, just like the fresh flowers Leo insists on buying every other day, and the way he won't set foot in the Albert Heijn and frequents only the small, picturesque corner markets for groceries. The way that, in the beginning, Leo knew how to take off his clothes and moan at just the right moments, but his eyes were far away, so that Sandor wondered whether he had really only made love to a shell and Leo was somewhere else entirely. But now, the sound of Leo's choked sobs is like being kicked in the stomach—he would do anything to stop it, say anything. When Leo spoke to him on Geoff's phone from Casablanca, he was crying still. Geoff's voice when he regained the phone was impatient, and Sandor knew he must think that *he* is entitled to all the grief and that Leo is just some upstart who arrived too late in the game to have any genuine claims on Mary.

But who owns grief? Leo longed his entire life for a family, and these past two years, in his sister, he has found it. Geoff was not there to see the way Leo prepared for her infrequent arrivals in Amsterdam—the way he grew sleepless leading up to the day. It was not Geoff who saw the exorbitant international phone bills from

Leo's calls to New Hampshire, or walked in on Leo writing her an eleven-page letter when he'd spoken to her only the day before. No: Mary adores Leo, Sandor knows that, but she *has* a family. What she has meant to Leo cannot be contained within two years, and Sandor finds his body restless, unable to keep still, waiting for Leo's arrival so he can go to him and hold him tight. He does not care who is looking, does not care what Geoff or the mother or every fucking rule-abiding Muslim in the entirety of this country thinks. He cares only for taking the edge off Leo's ache, of cupping his face in his hands and promising, *I'm here, I will always be here, you cannot scare me away, go on, try.* For the first time since arriving in Marrakech he does not feel like vomiting. He feels a sense of sadness and dread and the hole that begins to open up inside, making space for loss, but he is not frightened anymore. He feels steady, strong.

This, then, is love.

Though Sandor will not voice it for many months, it is at this moment that the first kernel of his desire to have a child with Leo is born. He has never thought of a child as something for parents to share, to bond over; *his* parents lived in different countries, after all. But there in the airport, waiting for the sky to return Leo to him, he thinks of what it means to stake something and declare it your own, to never run again. To turn yourself over to the eternal in the face of life's transience: giving and taking, growth and decline, again and again. Mary was adopted. It will be in homage to her, the woman who brought them together, linking their fates in a single, preposterous sweep. He thinks briefly of women, both lesbian and hetero, who might be approached and asked to borrow a womb, but no, this is a private matter between him and Leo. Somewhere there will be a baby born, a baby with a past in its cells already and yet also wholly theirs, his and Leo's alone. He decides it there and then: they will not ask some woman they know, for the only woman with whom they would gladly have formed such a happy little baby-sharing commune is *Mary.* Now that thread will be broken; it will be just the two of them. And love is not free. No, his love for Leo has proved both exclusive and costly. It has cost his carefree youth; it has cost him every ounce of envy and agitation he has to spare; it has cost him a world of sexual variety; it has cost him the leap from hating his father and all the fathers of the world to desperately longing to become one.

All he wants is to pay and pay and pay some more.

A DYING WOMAN lies in a hospital. The tubes and wires snaking from her body notwithstanding, she takes up very little of the bed, and the man in the room with her stands up from his chair, gathers the IVs and monitors in his hand, and moves them aside, lies down next to her. The woman puts her head on his shoulder, but her oxygen mask digs into her flesh; she tries to adjust the mask but fails, takes it off. The man does not question her, though all common sense would indicate that he should. They lie there, waiting for the call. Sandor will alert them the moment her family's flight lands, and then the man will have to leave and not come back. Airports and hospitals are places where beginnings and endings are cheap. As Sandor kills time at RAK, contemplating fatherhood, Mary and Kenneth prepare to say good-bye.

Mary watched Sandor leaving. He, too, would not be seeing Kenneth again. These two men, once casual enemies at Arthog House, stood in the doorway of her room as accidental allies. The room in which they have put her is in the corner of the building, where she is shielded from the other patients (or rather they are shielded from her). Sunlight does not fall on her end of the hall, and the view of the corridor from her bed is shrouded in gray. From there she observed their embrace. She watched their tall bodies holding each other, the light from her room's window not reaching them quite but illuminating the room, so that their forms appeared half-lit. It would have made a beautiful photograph: their matched height and thinness, the way they embraced like broken warriors, the last ones standing in a stadium. There was no space between their bodies, so that they could have been brothers, lovers. She watched from the distance, and then Sandor was gone, though she hadn't seen him walk away. Then it was only Kenneth coming back to her bedside chair and wiping his eyes. Then it was only the two of them and his hard bones next to her in the bed, both no comfort and a comfort she needs more than air.

"I'm scared," she whispers. "I've never been so scared."

His arms cannot get all the way around her because of the tubes. He puts one over her, his own body trembling the way hers has been shaking with fever, so that they knock into each other slightly, the respective tremors of their bodies ill timed.

There has been more blood, and when it came, a blackness claimed her and then there was nothing else, just the memory of air and the flooding, blind terror. She wants to *want* the blood to just keep on, to finish this, but she is not strong enough; she cannot want it. And so she still fights.

Between her legs is the catheter tube. Coming from her chest are the IVs, antibiotics past the hope of kicking in, now just for show. The oxygen mask hides her face; she is not human anymore. She is an animal that has crawled under the stairs to die, but they won't even let her go in peace.

"I'm going to tell you something," he whispers to her. "Are you with me, can you understand what I'm saying to you right now?"

She nods.

"Last night," he says, "I went out and bought enough H to kill myself." Her head jerks up, and with his hand he continues to stroke her hair, says, "Shhh, no, I'm still here." She tries to say something and he cuts her off. "I was gonna do it once they came, once I had to go, but the plan's changed." He lets the words sink in, feels her struggling to try to face him, to see his eyes. "You want it," he says, "it's yours."

"My God." But what flicks on like a switch behind her glassy eyes is hope.

He continues, forges on before she fades, before he loses his nerve. "This shit's so simple it's ridiculous. I go cook in the bathroom. Then I take the heart monitor off you and put it on myself. I shoot you up. When it's over I put the monitor back on your finger. By the time they get the flatline and get all the way over here from their station, I'm gone. You've got a 'do not resuscitate' order." He permits himself a small laugh. "You're scaring the shit outta them, so I'm guessing they'll be all too happy to oblige. But it won't matter either way. I bought enough for *me*. You've never used—all the morphine in your system and how small you are, even a quarter of that and it'll be too late."

Her teeth clack in excitement, in fever, in fear. "What if they catch you?"

"Baby, they don't even know my last name. They think fucking Sandor is an American Jew named Leo Becker. I go straight to the airport, fly wherever the hell you can get from Marrakech—Paris, I bet. From there I go home."

"Atlanta," she says. "You're really going?"

He nods. Kisses her forehead. She gasps a little and holds the mask on her face, huffing the air, and right away her eyelids get heavy. He pulls the mask back a little. "Wait," he says. "Please." He has no idea when he last used that word: *please.* "I promise. If I weren't going home to see my boy, I'd have kept this for myself and you'd have been on your own. Don't fade on me, baby, please. You've gotta tell me what you want me to do."

Tears are rolling down her face. "You just want to be the last person to see me."

"True," he says. "True."

A nurse could walk in at any moment. His heart is pounding hard and he feels hers, too, through her thin gown, fast against his chest, fluttery and unconvincing next to his, easy to distinguish even though they're beating right into each other. He has to sit up, has to get this show on the road. Probably right now the staff is gearing up for the onslaught of the Americans, the pulmonary specialist husband— they're all busy, quaking in their boots and waiting for some damn international incident. Like she's not even here.

She is nodding, biting her lip. "It won't hurt?"

This is the first thing he's been sure of. "No. It'll be good. And then it won't be anything."

She starts shaking her head. "But—okay, say you get out. Wait . . . you fly home, okay. But they'll find out." Her voice is urgent, a child about to get in trouble. "They'll see it in my system. They'll come after you."

He's thought of this. Of course. Even if Boutell is happy to chalk it up to her disease, the husband will want an autopsy: he'll be trying to prove what the hospital itself did wrong. They'll find the heroin easily, not exactly a needle in a haystack. He believes with everything in him that Sandor and Leo will be on *his* side. He knows this may be crazy but believes it nonetheless, can't fathom that they'd voluntarily give him up. But maybe they'll have to: the doctor and nurses have seen him with them, they can't just pretend he was a phantom. Sure, fine then: the law will come after him. He feels himself fighting annoyance. What the hell difference does that make?

"I don't care about that," he says. "This is stupid. This whole thing—it's . . ." And then it's on him, a dry sob he can't control, though he promised himself that he wouldn't break down, no matter what her answer was. "I've gotten out of shit before," he says, struggling to keep his voice even. "Don't you understand they're just going to let—I can't stand it. You, trapped like a rat, coughing blood and fading away, choking on the world. For Christ's sake, why shouldn't your last moment be a rush, be like the best fucking climax you ever had? Not like *this*."

She presses herself to him the way she did that night in Essaouira, urgent, but without desire now. He thinks of what she said to him in Tangier: *beyond sex.* She made it sound good, almost noble. There's nothing noble about it. Sex is life. She was wrong about that.

Somehow, though, she is smiling. Intermittently holding the oxygen up to her burning face because the need for air is beyond her control just like these sobs are beyond his. She's squirming in his arms, too hot for his touch, fever rising again. She regards him, and in that moment he is able to compose himself, to take this last of what she can offer and hold it, click it in his mind like a photograph. She says defiantly, "I'm *not* sorry. Nobody should go to Morocco without somebody who'd help them bury a body. Even if the body's their own."

"Good girl." He makes himself sit, feels the air invading the space where her skin has been. "We're running out of time, though. We gotta roll."

She is still smiling. "I can't," she says. "Kenneth. Thank you . . . so much. You know I can't."

In his eyes, Mary watches emotions flash. Relief is not one. Nor surprise.

"It's not about me anymore," she whispers, touching his face, her hand against the roughness of hair. And it would be so easy, so perfect, to stretch their secret liaison all the way to this, to turn even death itself into a collusive game they are in together. She could hand her arm over to him without fear, trust him to give her—as he has done before—exactly what she needs. "It's not about you, baby. They're coming. I've never seen anything through. I owe them this."

"You don't owe anybody anything," he says, but she lets her hand drop, closes her eyes at last. Behind the lids she can still see him. Him and the others in the room, those who have died here maybe, those who lurk in corners and behind curtains, just waiting for Kenneth to make his exit so they can have free rein. They do not fear her: she is too close to being one of them. They are not real; of course they are not real. But she does not fear them either. They can accompany her farther than the real ones can go.

So many things she meant to do but didn't. Learn to meditate; become truly fluent in Spanish; read those kinds of books her brother reads. Allow her mother to feel needed. Love her husband as exclusively as he has loved her.

She has been lucky, almost unspeakably lucky. There are women who spend their entire lives in one town. Women who never finish high school, much less graduate school, who never have a friend like Nix to lose, much less other, healing bonds like those she's found. Leo and Sandor: their tenderness, laughter, open arms. Kenneth: an unflinching eye beyond words or conditions. And Geoff—Geoff, who held her in memory and jumped worlds to find her, and who will now hold her in memory again. There are women whose lives are spent waiting by the phone, but although she was neither the most beautiful nor the most worthy, every man she has slept with loved her at least a little, even Eli, dear Eli, practicing for old age by now. There are women who have never had an orgasm, who have never seen a lover get down on his knees in the rain, who have never been photographed or painted, who have never tasted paella or watched the sun burst into color over Mount Kenya. Women who have been invisible and quiet for eighty or ninety years and called that a life. There are women, too, who have had all she has had plus babies, grandchildren, vibrant health, dazzling careers; who go gray gracefully and die fast in their sleep. There are, aren't there? They are out there somewhere; thank God she does not know them. She has *lived,* and in the world she's traversed, she has seen and been loved more than most. More than her mother, more than poor dead Agnes. Even more than Nix.

She does not think these thoughts. She has conjured them all before, dozens of times over years of dress rehearsal for thinking them when the time comes. But now she finds them slippery as mercury, utterly elusive.

"I wanted a baby," she manages to say, eyes still shut. "You could have forty years left, longer than I've had. It's not too late, Kenneth. Go and find him. Promise me."

"I already promised," he says. "I'm going. I'm going."

But he stays, waiting for Sandor's phone call. Beyond that even, watching her sleep, willing her to wake and speak to him just one more time, until it is truly too late and he hears voices approaching, cuts out and sees them only briefly: Leo and Sandor's mouths gaping with an almost comic surprise. For a moment he catches the husband's eye—*her* husband, Mary's husband—not enemy or competitor but just another man to whom an invisible torch has been passed. He is the keeper of all things now. Geoff sees the long-haired white dude staring, radically out of place in these surroundings, and a sense of déjà vu ripples up his back, then is quickly obliterated by the business at hand.

By then Kenneth is gone, has rounded a corner and left her to them, making his way swiftly down the opposite hall.

Epilogue

(GANDER: HASNAIN)

There was a crime. But there were also the lovers.
—IAN McEWAN, *Atonement*

Hasnain is not claustrophobic. When he was a small boy, he used to hide in a trunk in his parents' bedroom on occasion to spy on them and report back to Ali their goings-on. Usually banalities about the restaurant, or sometimes a mild row about the children: about Ali's poor marks and how Baba had ruined Hasnain's future by insisting that he take up piano. Nothing he and Ali didn't already know. Still, Hasnain studied their tones and inflections to do impressions of them later for his twin. They did not own a television, so on days they weren't forced to help out at the restaurant, there was little else to do. Their father did not approve of television, whether because it would rot their minds or because it would dilute them, turn them into slouching, smoking, cursing, drugging English punks, Hasnain and Ali could not be sure. His disapproval turned his children into spies, ferreting out any small kernel of interest. Ali could not hide in the trunk—it was small and felt airless, so he panicked—but Hasnain remembers liking it in there.

A woman in the aisle seat behind him is crying. She says, "I have to get out of here, I can't breathe. Can't they let us off already? Why can't we just find a hotel or rent a car? Why are they holding us prisoner? *We* didn't do anything." Her husband tries to calm her, though she is already whispering. Nobody wants to set off any alarms in case there are terrorists on board the plane. Upon the husband's shushing her, though, the wife increases her volume. "Do I look like I've got a bomb strapped to my leg, for Christ's sake; I'm a fucking housewife from Decatur!" Hasnain does not know where Decatur is. The husband shushes her again, admonishing, "Yeah, you sound like June fucking Cleaver with that mouth. Keep your voice down. Don't you know it's illegal to even say the word 'bomb' on an airplane? You can be arrested for that!"

This much Hasnain already knew.

THERE ARE FIFTY-THREE grounded planes. They clutter the tarmac as though for an aircraft show, as though at any moment the locals of the town, Gander, in Newfoundland, Canada, will materialize and mill between the planes to admire and touch them with curious hands. In truth, no one save security is permitted to approach the planes, any more than the passengers are permitted to disembark. They sit packed into cramped seats, breathing recycled breath and air-conditioning. In an effort to ward off staleness, the air is excessively cold, and many of the passengers have blankets wrapped around their shoulders or slung over their legs. Hasnain finds his eyes darting toward concealed legs, trying to ascertain what is hidden under the blankets, searching for an invisible bomb.

TWO MEN ON the plane wear openly Islamic dress, sport long beards. The other passengers mainly avoid them, though Hasnain notices a few overcompensating, being overly solicitous of the men, who do not return their friendliness. Or perhaps it is not overcompensation so much as *keeping your enemies closer*. Perhaps these passengers have appointed themselves ambassadors of sorts, and they are merely keeping an eye out.

He does not know why he brought the letters with him on this trip. It would make sense if he flew only rarely—if every time he anticipated being airborne he thought of her and took her letters along in homage. This is not the case. He flies frequently, both for work and to visit family in London. Yet he has not read the letters in years — five years, six? He has never taken them with him on a flight since the one he hopped to New York in 1989, on which he took everything he could carry, everything he owned.

The things I have been writing to you have been borrowed scraps of other lives, the usual semester-abroad adventures I hear my flatmates gossiping about in our kitchen every morning over PG Tips and cigarettes. I've regurgitated their stories for you, hoping to accomplish something by it, a tamer form of the same "something" I was trying to accomplish that day in Mykonos. It's just like my mother says, I never learn. In reality, I lie in my twin bed every day after the others have gone to class. They've stopped even asking me to take the Tube in with them because everyone knows by now that I'm the weird girl, the basket case, the one who has come all the way to London to fail out of school and hide under my covers all day. I lie here and tell myself not to picture it all, but I still do and it's always so real, like it's happening over and over again, whether I'm in my bed or in a classroom, it doesn't matter. The only time it stops is when the piano player next door practices every morning from 9:30 to 10:30. Mozart, Chopin, Ravel. I don't know the names of the concertos, but I remember them from my father's collection, from everything he took with him when he left. The walls must be thin because I can feel the pounding of the keys under my body in my flimsy bed, and the music takes me out of Titus's villa, out of their hands, and not back to being a little girl with my father exactly, but somewhere safe, somewhere else . . .

HERE IS WHAT they have been told. First, that they were making an unexpected landing in the Canadian town of Gander, to check out a possibly malfunctioning part that might need to be replaced. Quickly the crew went about the business of shutting down the plane. Hasnain was not concerned, but upon landing it was immediately clear that something was wrong. The pilot came over the PA system and joked, "I bet you're wondering if all these other aircraft have the same malfunctioning part we do," and there was a nervous titter of laughter, but most faces had gone serious. The human body carries inside it an archetype of knowledge that things can change in only an instant: that what has been an ordinary day can quickly become war. The pilot announced that there had been some terrorist activity in New York and that US airspace had been shut down—all transatlantic flights, including theirs, would be grounded until they received further word. Hasnain felt his skin grow clammy, slippery, his vision tunneling and turning dark.

It sounded abstract: *terrorist activity in New York*. It could mean anything. Had Manhattan become a war zone? Were there riots, people fighting in the streets and slinging grenades? Though they were not sitting together as a group, and other than traveling companions, none of them seemed to know one another, it immediately became clear who onboard hailed from New York: a camaraderie already beginning to form. Still Hasnain sat quietly in his seat, staring at his carry-on stuffed beneath the chair in front of him. He had brought the letters for no reason, or so it had seemed.

Now he knew why.

HE IS NOT claustrophobic. He is not, but the walls of the plane seem to be contracting, moving closer like the walls in that room at Disney World when he and Leslie took the kids. He imagines Leslie now, calling his mobile, but none of the phones on the plane are working. Canada has a different cell system and any call that gets through at all goes to a Canadian operator who keeps saying all lines to the US are blocked or jammed. They cannot reach the outside world. Back in New York, nobody knows they are here.

They have been on the tarmac for twelve hours and are down to only Pepsi, small bars of chocolate, and crisps.

LESLIE AND THE boys. They seem at this moment an abstract concept, too. For the overthrowing of New York, Hasnain conjures Leslie—the phantom Leslie of his imagination—donning guerrilla fatigues and bursting from the house to join the revolution like the good progressive she is: going to join the uprising. Except there is no

rising *up*. The Twin Towers have been brought down by Islamic terrorists; a plane has flown into the Pentagon. Onboard, passengers circulate rumors about the Sears Tower, so that for a while it is common
knowledge among them that Chicago is under attack also. Only later,
when they have access to television, will they learn that this never
happened, and they will be unsure why it seemed to them a fact.

He imagines his sons hiding in the coat closet, as they are fond
of doing: always spying just like he and Ali did. In his mind, Leslie
has left them in the house to fend for themselves while she runs the
streets in her fatigues, though in reality she would never do this, not
for any cause. *What is the cause?* He isn't thinking straight. In reality,
she is a stay-at-home mom, a pacifist, a lapsed Lutheran, and only
an armchair radical.

OF COURSE THE ones to fear are Islamic extremists. In
England, in his youth, often they were Irish, but now, in the landscape of today, the terrorists will be Arabs—Muslims, like him. And
Leslie will be stunned, her hand going to her mouth in alarm as she
realizes in one fell swoop that she cannot be on their side—that
their side is not what she imagined. That their side is monstrous.

ALREADY HIS FELLOW passengers are losing their fight,
their grumbles dying down. They will spend the night on the
plane—there is no getting around it—and so mothers tuck children into laps, and men stretch their legs out into the aisles. How
quickly human beings become like cattle; how quickly the drive to
resist settles down and what is enforced becomes what is inevitable.
One woman on the plane weeps while a cluster of seatmates around
her—friends now—console her. The woman's husband, Hasnain
has overheard, works in the Twin Towers. Even the pilot has at-
tempted to use his own phone to call the woman's home, but he has
not been able to get through. Time passes, and within a few hours
even this woman's tears die down as she settles into resignation, into
fitful sleep. She will have told herself, he knows, that her husband
could not have been in the building at the time, that today is the day

he goes to the health club in the morning and doesn't get to the office on time, that he seemed slightly ill when she left on her trip and right now he is probably feverish in bed. Hasnain remembers the stories he told himself in the hours after Lockerbie was announced—the way he got in the car and raced to Heathrow, convinced that he would find her there, lost and wandering among travelers, unable to leave him, unable to get her feet off British soil. As though death were simply an impossibility; as though the human brain is devoid of all deep history, of all memory. As though it can never learn.

EVERYTHING I HAVE *written you until now is a lie*, her first letter urgently begins. *This is the letter I meant to write but couldn't.* It is dated just days before he and Nicole met—the first of five letters she left behind with him, along with her black sweater from Neal Street Store, along with her tapes of Miracle Legion and Sam Brown and Chopin, along with a tattered copy of John Updike's *Trust Me* and Thich Nhat Hanh's *The Miracle of Mindfulness*. She kept a yoga journal, but she took it with her on the plane along with her address book. All of that became fire and ash and blood somewhere above Lockerbie, so that only these five letters—folded and shoved into the back of a biography of members of the Bloomsbury Group and directed to a friend from home sometimes addressed as Typhoid Mary—remain.

ARMED GUARDS LINE the path from the planes to the yellow buses as passengers, ordered to leave all luggage behind, are hustled off. Their pilot, whose voice has become like that which Musa heard booming from the fire—an unquestioned truth—stands by at the plane's exit, reminding them to remain calm and obey Canadian authorities, stressing, "Everything will be all right." An elderly man holding the arm of his wife freezes in his tracks, so that for a moment Hasnain suspects he may be having a heart attack. When he looks at the man's face, though, he is crying. He turns to the pilot and says, "I know you didn't mean it this way, young man, but that's exactly what they told us when we got off the trains at Auschwitz."

HASNAIN IS NOT the only Muslim here. He sees quite a few corralled into the buses, some clearly not speaking English and blinking in confusion, unsure what is happening to them. To the side of the tarmac, three women in full burkas, nothing but their hennaed hands visible in the morning glare, have been taken under the wing of some kind and folksy Canadian and are not being led to the buses. Hasnain knows they are probably headed for a private home, just as many of the elderly are being separated for their own safety, along with a couple of pregnant women. Yet he reminds himself mentally to check for these women when the planes are boarded again — *if* the planes are boarded again — just in case.

The Canadian authorities check his passport with interest at first, and then, when they see his name and British citizenship, the alarm lights that had flashed are quickly extinguished. In Kashmir, now the site of one of the world's most dangerous nuclear stalemates and once the home of his father's family, Muslim and Hindu surnames are mixed up, free floating, unlike in most parts of the world. For the first twenty-four years of his life, the fact of his Muslimness was a given, common knowledge, part of where he fit in among London's complicated brew; the name Hasnain announced it, yes, but did not need to. *All* the Indians he knew then were Muslims — that was the world his parents kept to, though they had every kind of patron at the restaurant.

As soon as he landed in New York in 1989, he began the process of changing his name from Hasnain to John. He meant it ironically, John being a name he saw then as quintessentially, almost comically American — a name itself devoid of any deep history and memory, just like his new country. *John Wayne.* It was common anyway in Indian culture to have anglicized nicknames, though Hasnain had never had one. And so his passport bore a name unlikely to belong to any terrorist, the fact of his Muslim heritage disguised by a mere omission, slipping into the cracks between language.

If he never mentioned it, it did not exist.

THE MORNING THE American girl arrived at his door he had decided not to play the piano. He was twenty-four years old and enough was enough. He had just started the final year of his master's degree in engineering, and as soon as he graduated he would marry his longtime girlfriend. Some of his English friends liked to ask if it was an arranged marriage, but of course that was not the case. True, they had known each other since childhood, and their parents were friends, but it had been their choice to date. Neither had even *been* to India. London was both their home and a place where they would forever be aliens, but in this experience, too, they were not alone, for London contains a sea of isolated exiles. After marriage they would be exiles together, but their children, second-generation Brits, would not.

The day the American girl showed up at his door, he had chosen not to play. For many years his dream had been to become a concert pianist, and even after relinquishing that possibility (without really pursuing it), he'd thought of music as the thing that sustained him. But that was foolishness now. No, his music was merely a *hobby*, and one did not adhere to hobbies with ritual and obsession; one did not need to play at the same exact time every day, the moment his parents left the flat for the restaurant, the moment he was alone, or with only Ali, since being with one's twin is no different from being alone. Ali didn't care for the lessons their father had imposed—he had no ear for music and less interest. His mother said Hasnain played well, but she, too, had little use for hours spent sitting at a piano, playing, as she called it, "the dead masters of colonialism."

It was late September 1988. The weather had already gone cold. These were the dark months when the music mattered to him most, and it was his being drawn to it that stilled his hands that morning, made him sit down with a textbook to study instead. A small decision: the piano could wait. A small choice, like what to have for tea, like which umbrella to bring. Small and without consequence, Hasnain sat, an alienated exile in a sea of alienated exiles: an ordinary man absorbed in an engineering textbook.

The pounding on the door was hard, staccato. The way someone would bang if the building were on fire, to warn you to get out.

He thought briefly of not answering. Only a religious fanatic aiming to convert you was likely to be pounding on the door on a rainy September morning. Besides, not answering the door would confirm the picture of himself in his mind as a man absorbed in his studies, not thinking about the piano. Yet he found himself standing, leaving that fantasy at the kitchen table with his book. He found himself walking down the stairs to open the door.

IN THE CHURCH basement, old Canadian ladies and high school students ladle soup into bowls, pass out sandwiches. The entire town has mobilized. Gander has only ten thousand residents, and there are rumored to be more than six thousand air passengers now grounded here, scattered among schools and churches and meeting halls and lodges. Sleeping bags and cots have been gathered. At the front of the room a television plays, continuously showing footage of the Twin Towers falling down. Some people are crying and others are standing round chatting and munching on snacks as though this is an after-church social. Phone calls are still being made, but if anyone here has lost a loved one, the Canadians must have chauffeured the bereaved off quickly to a private home. Instead, the energy in the air makes it feel like some combination of a funeral, a group therapy session for those with secondary post-traumatic stress syndrome, and a cruise. Hasnain, a.k.a. John, sits on a metal folding chair with a ham sandwich on his lap. In this context, the ham, too, seems ironic, though of course he eats pork—he eats whatever Leslie cooks for him, is lazy about food and always has been. She asked when they first got together if there were things she should avoid, but he said not to be silly, even in London he ate what he liked so long as his parents weren't looking. "Then why don't you drink?" she asks—has asked at least seven or eight times in their marriage. "If the dietary restrictions don't mean anything to you, why won't you have a glass of wine with me?" Hasnain has no good reason, always says only, "I just don't like the taste."

He pushes his food around on his paper plate. The sandwich contains an excessive amount of mayonnaise.

LESLIE ANSWERED THE phone with a gasp in her voice. She heard his voice and began to cry, voice trembling as she said, "I would die if anything happened to you, I would die, Hasnain," so that he had to blink the tears from his own eyes, even though many of his fellow stranded Americans were weeping openly.

But now he thinks: she would *not* die. She might want to, maybe, but probably not even that. There are the boys to consider. She would go on—she is only thirty-nine—would probably even marry again someday, another man she would clutch in the night in her aerobicized, passionate arms, another man his sons would call Dad instead of Baba. This knowledge of love's transience is not the death of romance exactly, but certainly it is its foe. Every fevered moment of a young man unable to get past security at Heathrow and blindly shouting out the name of his beloved—every weeping declaration of the power to die at will—is both measly and powerful in tandem, and he receives Leslie's words, trying to honor her intentions, trying not to cast himself as wiser somehow just because his own staying power proved so slim.

PEOPLE CRY, EAT, play cards, or watch TV. All around him, life goes on.

"Hasnain!"

It is a woman's voice. At first he does not think she means *him*. He is not in New York. No one here knows his given name.

"Hasnain! My God, someone I know, someone from home in the middle of this nightmare!" And the woman throws her arms around him, pulls back, blinking wildly, taking him in, hungry for something familiar, for recognition.

It is Rebecca Fishman. He used to teach her daughter Susan, who must be ten or eleven now. Susan still plays piano, but she's working with another teacher at the institute now. "Rebecca," he says, standing. "Have you been able to reach your family?"

She starts to cry. She sobs into his shoulder, nodding. "Yes, yes, they're fine. Alan didn't go to work today—can you believe it? He works from home a lot now and he said he was going in—he made me find someone else to pick Susan up from school and everything—but in the end he stayed home. His office is only a block away from the towers, who knows what would have happened?" She sniffs, wipes her nose, he believes, on his shoulder unconsciously. "What about your wife and sons?"

"They're fine," Hasnain assures her. "Safely in Brooklyn." He tries to smile. "Finally, an advantage to not being able to afford housing in Manhattan."

She laughs, almost deliriously. She clutches his arm.

"I just—" she begins, falters, glances around the room like a caged animal. "I just want to see my daughter's face . . ."

"Come on," he says, steering her toward the door. "I hear it's a beautiful town out there. Let's go and have a look around."

HE IS AWARE that he is thinking less of Rebecca and her tears than his own longing to leave this church—of Rebecca's blond hair and fair American skin serving as his bodyguard. He is aware that, while all around him is nothing but small-town hospitality, he has not yet given up a nagging suspicion that he will be killed before he can make it back to New York. He is aware that in some far-off corner of his mind he is relieved he married a white, Christian woman, because if his wife were dark skinned he would be ripping out his own hair in anxiety right now, fearing that, home in New York, she would be dragged away and lynched by a crowd. He is aware that somehow he has come to equate paleness with safety even though the majority of people killed yesterday were probably white, and even though Nicole's skin was virtually translucent and she, too, is dead.

ON THE STAIRS outside his door—his parents' door—stood the American girl from the restaurant. Hasnain recognized her immediately: she came in a few times a week and ordered dry vegetable curry, always take-out. She usually waited for her order by the door, pacing and skittish and always wearing the same black sweater that was no protection from the rain or wind. Sometimes her yellow hair was wet. Hasnain had spoken to her; he took her order sometimes and delivered it back to her waiting, shaking hands. Most of the American girls this age who lived in London were students, yet this girl did not seem like a student. She was striking, but in a raw, desperate way. He thought she lived on his street but didn't know which flat. He suspected she was on drugs.

She stood on his steps. She was wiping her eyes with the back of her knuckles, the motion almost aggressive. He thought for a moment that she must have been attacked, had dashed up the first set of stairs for help, though he saw no assailant. She stood blinking at him and he had the sensation—familiar when among English girls and, he supposed, American girls, too, though he did not know many of the latter—that she recognized him not at all: that she had never really noticed him in the first place, had looked right through his face as though he were a ghost.

She said tentatively, "Are you the piano player?"

He did not know how to answer. Ali was gone, already in class. Hasnain stepped aside in the doorway. "Are you all right?" he asked. "Do you need to come inside?"

She said again, "Are you the one who plays the piano every morning? You play, every morning at nine thirty sharp, right? Why aren't you playing today?"

It had to be a dream. *She* was the ghost, then—her pale, haunted face an apparition. It was as though his music—or its lack—had conjured her.

As though anybody *real* possibly cared.

They stood together in his foyer. The morning was gray but dry, and her long hair seemed full of static. She reached out her arm and Hasnain felt himself recoil slightly, as though she meant to strike him, but instead when she touched him he caught a fleeting glimpse of thin razor marks along her forearm as the loose sleeve of her sweater fell open. But there was no blood on her hand: the cuts must have been old. She chewed her lip. Kohl was smudged under her eyes as though from the night before. She looked terribly young, but he suspected she was not as young as all that. He knew he should call his mother or fiancée — some woman who would know what to do.

"I told myself," she said in that American twang he had never cared for, "that on the first day you didn't play, I would take it as a sign. But I don't want to die today, so I came over instead to see if you would buy me another day. Now."

The day I found out began as a "good day." When I first got here, there were still times I could act normally, conscious of playing a part but confident in my ability to pass undetected. That morning I'd felt strong enough to go to my Women in Literature class, thinking in my idiocy that it might help. A student in the class, English with a fancy English name, has hair like yours, and for the first half of class I sat watching her wind it round and round her fingers, tucking it into the back of her turtleneck sweater, which was too warm for the weather, and I felt for the first time since leaving you in Athens the sharp longing to talk to another girl. I fantasized that she could become my new best friend and I could tell her all the things I'd had to keep from you, and she would be strong enough to bear them. They were discussing Jean Rhys and I'd been staring at the nape of the not-you girl's neck, when suddenly I realized the class discussion was about rape. They were all quite animated, giving their views. "I would rather be murdered than raped," the turtleneck girl proclaimed proudly, and a fat girl began to protest but the turtleneck girl was strident and overtook her, saying, "At least I could die with dignity, I could die without someone else having control over me." The fat girl was so flustered it became immediately clear that the turtleneck girl was saying that girl would be better off dead than living in her own violated skin, and I thought about you and what I had told myself that day. That anything is preferable to death because only death is irrevocable, only death is a condition that cannot be healed. But I didn't trust that anymore, so I walked out of the classroom. That was the day I almost fainted twice on the Tube, even though I'd felt strong enough that morning to eat breakfast and hadn't thrown up the way I usually did. That was the day I finally took the test, because of

*course, like everything else, by the time I faced the situation enough to
act, I already knew the truth.*

To be clear: he could have sent the letters to her family. She left him the Ohio address of her mother, who surely would
know the friend for whom they were intended. But Nicole's mother
knew nothing of the rape, nothing, even, of Hasnain's existence, so the
move seemed potentially cruel. Plus, her family owned her death: her
mother must have claimed her body, presided over her burial. From
all that, he was excluded. *This,* these letters, is all he has left of her
and it is his. He could have sent the letters back but didn't, because
they meant more to him than he could ever imagine them meaning
to anyone else.

The town is what Leslie would call "darling." Hasnain and
Rebecca walk quietly, staring out at the rocky water. The landscape
reminds Hasnain, actually, of seaside English towns. The weather is
crisp, air full of invisible wetness that feels thick in his mouth. When
Rebecca is quiet like this, he can almost pretend he is back in England, he and Ali on holiday collecting rocks their mother would of
course never allow them to bring home. He can pretend that he and
Leslie have taken the boys to Cape Cod, to a world full of white-
shingled beach houses and reeds blowing in the wind and violent wa-
ters that belie a world of peace.

There will never be a world of peace again.

No, no, that is American nonsense: how has he become such an
American? There was never a world of peace to begin with. It is just
a rumor the old like to circulate because they're jealous of the young.

Rebecca turns to face him. She has been staring at the water, hair
whipping around her face like a tattered sail. Hasnain supposes she
must be fifty or so, but in her he can still see the vestiges of an exceptionally beautiful youth: the bone structure, the eyes. If he is perfectly
honest about it, Leslie is not beautiful in this powerful, primal way.
His wife possesses an earthy prettiness, a strong, lanky body as tall
as his, and smile lines around her eyes, which she makes no effort to

cover with creams or makeup. Rebecca Fishman, on the other hand, is a woman whose face could have launched ships, though of course this world granted her no such fate—granted her a husband some ten years her senior, paunchy and with a gruff, condescending manner to servers in restaurants. Hasnain recalls this from the one time he went to lunch with the Fishman family after Susan's piano lesson. He remembers, and is not proud of the memory, amusing himself during that lunch by imagining the beautiful Rebecca staring blankly up at the ceiling while her sweating bear of a husband grunted into her. He does not usually think of himself as that kind of man: the kind to imagine the copulations of other couples he barely knows. But Rebecca is a woman to inspire such musings, even at fiftysomething, even here in Gander amid a world of terror.

"I've lived in or near New York my entire life," she tells him. She is crying a bit again, as everyone here seems to be doing sporadically, in random conversation so that the tears are barely noticeable, just a natural function like breathing and swallowing. "I grew up on Long Island and for a while I lived in Greenwich Village and then I was on Long Island again until I met Alan and we moved to the city. This whole thing feels unfathomable. New York always seemed like a fortress, full of everything exciting and everything ugly, but I thought the ugly things were our *own*—that they came from within and not from the outside. New York seemed totally self-contained. Does . . . does that make any sense?"

He notices his hands are as deep in his pockets as they will go. "I don't know. It makes sense—I think many New Yorkers view their city this way. But to me, it's different, of course."

"Because you didn't grow up here—I mean, there? You said *their* city. You don't think of it as yours, even after all this time?"

He shrugs. "I don't know." Why does he keep saying this? "It's my home, yes, my children's home. What I meant is I don't think of any home as a fortress. In London, when I was growing up, the idea of terrorism was very ingrained, part of the world around us. The IRA, bomb threats on the Underground, that kind of thing. It was something everyone knew could happen, really, part of our subconscious, just the way all living people know that someday we will die. You don't think about it all the time, you don't dwell on it, but the knowledge is always there."

"But on this *scale*," Rebecca protests. "Something this terrible in the United States!"

In his pockets, his hands folding and unfolding. "Yes," he says. "This is a bad one. Very well organized. Usually people who hate, they are not this well organized. But then sometimes they are. Look at the Nazis. It seems preposterous now, to think they were so successful at their campaign of hate in our parents' lifetimes—and yet they were. And if they had been even *slightly* more successful, you would not be here."

She looks at him with something like alarm, but it may just be the wind in her eyes.

"You remember," he continues quietly. "Lockerbie, the explosion, Pan Am Flight 103. December 1988—you remember that happening?"

With Americans he has found you can never assume. They are, many of them, a people without memory. But she nods, yes, yes, of course.

"My fiancée, she was on that plane. She and our unborn child. She was four months pregnant—only just beginning to show. We had told no one yet about the baby. No one knew, so when she died it was only she who was mourned."

"My God!" Rebecca reaches out to grasp his arm the way she did in the basement, but without planning to—without fully knowing he has even done it—Hasnain steps just beyond her reach, so that her arms fall flat back to her sides. "Hasnain! That's terrible! I'm so—so sorry."

"Yes," he says. "Yes."

"She was English?" Rebecca asks, no doubt to have something to say, because really, what does it matter if she was English, *what* she was, when she is gone?

"No. American. A student."

"Oh God, right. So many students died on that plane. I went to Syracuse—well, I didn't graduate, but I went there for a couple of years, and I remember how many Syracuse students were killed.

There's a memorial on campus, I think, and a scholarship or something now."

"She was not a Syracuse student," he says, though of course this, too, means nothing, reveals nothing, and as always he has told an incomplete story, to the extent that he ever tells this story at all.

Rebecca continues to nod, and the movement of her head makes Hasnain feel dizzy. He should have eaten his sandwich, that slippery ham and river of mayonnaise on sticky bread. It is permissible, he remembers, to eat pork during times of starvation if doing so is the only means of staying alive. But what has that to do with him?

"We are all vulnerable," he mumbles. The words feel stuck in his throat. "After she died, I left the UK and went to New York for a fresh start. My parents had been furious at me for planning to marry an American girl, a non-Muslim, and after her death I couldn't stand the sight of them anymore. I didn't see them again for nearly ten years, until my father got ill a few years ago and my brother summoned me. By then I was married with children. By then, it was all from another life."

"Another life." The wind is at her face now, so that her hair blows straight back like a figure at the mast of a ship. "I understand. I lost a child once, too, Hasnain. There's nothing, nothing that ever makes that go away, is there? I gave up my daughter, my baby girl, when she was only a week old, when I was too young and too messed up to take care of her. But I've never stopped thinking of her—never. When we adopted Susan from China, I was terrified—I was sure I'd be killed on the plane over, that God would never allow me to be a mother again. I thought I'd arrive to find Susan dead in her orphanage as some kind of penance for what I'd done. It took me years, *years,* to stop checking on her in the night to make sure she was still breathing, that she hadn't simply disappeared. And then this—when I heard, when they made the announcement on our plane about what had happened, I thought, *Surely my daughter has been killed.* I don't even know how to explain it. The entire thing—the entire scope of the horror—seemed singularly about me, to steal my daughter as punishment for what I'd done."

He watches her eyes, so like Nicole's: that demon guilt biting her heels. It was the way Nicole had felt about the rape in Greece—the way she had believed, almost until the end, that it was all her fault. And yet her story is *nothing* like Nicole's. This woman walked away from her daughter, whereas he and Nicole had chosen to keep the baby she was growing—to love it regardless of its violent origin. *The men were dark like me,* Hasnain remembers telling her as they lay skin to skin under his piano only weeks after meeting, the fetus already sprouting inside her. *The child will look as though she's ours.* It was pure madness. He had a fiancée; he had his studies. Nicole should have been finishing school, should have found a doctor to take care of the pregnancy and gone about her life. Yet from the moment she entered his parents' flat and walked to his piano, sitting on the floor and waiting for him, there had never been any possibility again that they would be apart. The moment was larger than both of them in a way no moment has ever been for Hasnain since: their love immediate, chemical, irrevocable. There is no way to explain it other than madness, other than timing, other than destiny, other than what could have amounted to a terrible, ridiculous mistake that Nicole and the child died too soon ever to have realized they had made.

They spoke of the baby as if it were a girl, always. Still, he thinks of Nicole's child as the daughter he never had, who would have altered the course of his life in ways he can scarcely imagine now.

"You don't look well," Rebecca says, and this time when she reaches out, her hand makes contact with his arm.

"I'm fine," he promises. "I'm only hungry. Perhaps we should go back now."

Like you, I am still alive despite everything. They say that love cannot save anybody, but it's a lie, a specifically American lie, too, I've come to believe. If I hadn't met Hasnain, I might still be lost, but even if someday he's gone I can never go back to being what I was before I knew him. We are not islands, we are not meant to live in isolation, becoming whole only in some self-contained cocoon, but with others, in that kindness and that curiosity and that struggle. We have to stand on each other's shoulders if we ever want to climb.

Two HUNDRED SEVENTY people are not so many in the scheme of things. Not even equal to the number of New York City police officers whose lives were claimed yesterday at Ground Zero. And yet finally, just last year at the Lockerbie trial held at Camp Zeist, a former NATO air base in the Netherlands, it took the prosecuting lawyer an hour to read out the names and addresses of the dead.

HE GOES TO the men's toilet in the church to make *wudu*. He has not done this, not once, in almost thirteen years. The last time he performed any ablution, it was a mockery because he was demonstrating to Nicole what you were supposed to do, the cleansing of every part of the body that was necessary after intercourse, he explained jokingly, or even after wet dreams. *You see,* he told her, making his face somber, *this is why we managed to live side by side in these two flats and not even know it. After seeing you at the restaurant that first time, it was necessary for me to spend my every waking moment in the toilet.*

And she laughed, then pulled her sweater over her head.

He has been waiting for a free moment in the toilet for hours. With so many people here, there has often been a line. But most people have finally retired, sprawled out now on pews cushioned by sleeping bags, or in the basement on cots, and Hasnain has escaped them, stands in the small, paint-and-piss-smelling room, and says quietly to the empty walls, "Bismillah."

Even this takes too long, so he shortcuts. Washes the hands and rinses the mouth once instead of three times, skips the water-sniffing part altogether, merely splashing water onto his face and arms. When he has finally finished, his heart is throbbing in his throat.

What is he doing here? What is he trying to say?

He expresses his intention—*this Isha'a for Allah*—only in his head before beginning Salat.

"Allahu Akbar."

But is it true?

He puts his right hand atop his left. If there is nothing out there, if there is no God, then it is madness, all of it. Love and death and sex and war and terror. It is for nothing. If there are no absolutes, then the men who blew up Pan Am Flight 103 were wrong only according to the sentimental code of other *men,* and a mock trial in the Netherlands is the only trial there will ever be. Hasnain bows into *ruku.* If Allah is watching, perhaps he and Hasnain are not even friends. Hasnain has not followed Allah's laws, has honored nothing he was taught, has not even raised his sons Muslim. Such crimes, were he to die at this instant, are unforgivable. Fine then, fine. Let there *still* be the trial, the judgment. Let him be cast into the pit, too, so long as those animals go with him.

He gets to his knees, touches his head to the jacket he has spread out over the floor to use in the absence of anything else. Even under his thin jacket the tiles feel cold, and for a moment Hasnain rests his pounding head against them. When he met her, Nicole claimed to be an atheist, said religion made no sense to her. But by the end of her time in London, with all the hours she had free since leaving school, she had started studying Buddhism, meditating—or what she called "sitting"—every day, and studying yoga with a guru, modifying the positions for pregnancy. When you are twenty, three months can change your entire worldview; three months can change everything. By the end, Nicole—like Leslie since—urged him not to make light of his heritage and expressed an interest in studying the Koran. *I've been saved by British irreverence,* he tells Leslie now whenever she brings this up. *It all seems a load of rubbish to me.* But what he really wants to ask is how she fails to understand that everything about them would be deemed unacceptable through the lens of the Koran—that Nicole naked under his piano with another man's seed in her belly, and even Leslie, his wife and the mother of his sons, would be a whore through the eyes of Islam.

They were fanatics, those men. Religious and political fanatics. They do not represent truth, but their failure to do so does not mean—cannot mean—that Truth does not exist. Abandoning ritual, head still against the tile, Hasnain prays freestyle like a Christian, the insufferable type who act as though they maintain a standing golf date with Jesus and find him obsessed with all their petty trivialities: *Please be something other than what they think you are, please give me*

a moment of clarity so that I can understand you, reveal yourself to me,
please.

And then, in response, the squeak of the door.

Please don't worry about me, please. I know what I'm telling you
sounds crazy, like I've lost my mind, but I promise I have not. I don't
know how to explain why going back to Skidmore means nothing
to me anymore, why it all just seems like part of something I was
supposed to subscribe to, like worrying my thighs were too fat or
picking up guys in bars. I know there's something that finishing college
has to offer, I do, but right now it feels constrictive, like I can pursue
what I need better on my own, and it's not a giving up or "dropping
out" but exactly the opposite. I want to eat the world. In yoga they talk
a lot about detachment and for a while I tried to learn that, I thought
detachment was what could save me. But I don't want to notice
rather than feel. I don't want to be equal to a tree or a blade of grass,
impassive. I thought detachment would allow me to forgive them, but
I don't want to forgive them, they don't matter anymore, there is too
much else out there, too much to stay stuck in that day. I want to feel
deeply, and if that means at times I have to feel that day, too, it's a
price I am willing to pay for everything else there is still in me to feel.
Do you understand? I need you to understand not even because you
were there with me in Greece but because of the limits your parents
and doctors have set for you, that you're allowing to be set and that I
no longer believe in. You don't have to stay there in fucking Kettering
being who they think you are—who I thought you were. You are more
than that, the world is more than that. I need you to believe me.

The body remembers violence. The shoe in his ribs is no different
from the trainers that kicked him in primary school, only larger, as
his body itself is larger to accommodate the greater violence now,
the greater malice. There is no question of getting to his feet and
fighting back the way he tried to as a boy; since he is already on his
knees, face to the ground, his assailants do not need to topple him
but only, quite literally, to kick him while he's down. Hasnain's arms
have gone up round his head, though it takes all his will to keep them

there—to shield his face, his skull, rather than allow his hands to fly to the areas being attacked. If he leaves his head unprotected, it could be the end of him: one sharp jab, even accidentally misplaced, could be all it takes. He hears grunting noises coming from his throat, feels the jacket under his shoulder sliding on the slippery tiles with each blow. His vision is blocked by his arms, so that he cannot see his attackers, caught only the briefest glimpse when he tried to rise at the door's squeaking, before the first kick landed in his stomach and he doubled over, gone.

Camel-fucking murderer!

String you up and let the families cut off your dick and shove it down your throat!

Other voices, too. The din of a crowd forming: curious and unsure. If he were in Brooklyn he would say to Leslie, *Well, of course they didn't know what to think. A dark-skinned man performing a secret Islamic prayer in a toilet, versus two middle-aged white men in business suits—given the events of the day before, the crowd would not know whose defense to rush to, would they?* Still, some *are* rushing to his—he hears them through the tinny tunnel that has become his consciousness, everything drifting from afar, flickering weakly like Morse code.

Get off him—stop it!

Somebody call security!

I know this man—I know him—leave him alone!

His assailants are being restrained now, restrained not by men who look anything like he does but by other white Americans, by a hefty African American man who, in Brooklyn, Hasnain would probably cross the street to avoid. A gaggle of women led by Rebecca have pushed their way into the bathroom and help him to his feet. The white tile beneath him is stained with splotches of blood that he realizes—to his horror and surprise—he has coughed up. One of the restrained men screams at the others, "Yeah, pat yourselves on the back for your liberal delusions when he slits your throat in your sleep or blows this place sky-high!" and another man shouts at him, "Shut up, asshole, you think this is any way to honor the dead?" Hasnain blinks rapidly at the blackness closing around him, coughs a mouthful of blood onto the floor.

He thinks, *Are there even camels in Kashmir, or only nuclear weapons?*

And then the blackness is everything.

THE DAY HE took Nicole to Heathrow, they had slept not at all. In his brand-new flat, the first he had ever paid for on his own in twenty-four years, they'd stayed up all night, talking, making love. It was a shabby place, cheap, all the way in North Islington, a mainly Afro-Caribbean neighborhood. Nicole had arrived with all her belongings, most of which she would now bring back to Ohio for two weeks before returning to him here, in London, where they would await the baby's birth in early June. After that, who knew? They spoke sometimes of going to India or Morocco, where he had relatives, of finding some kind of humanitarian work, of taking the baby and just disappearing, but even such a plan took money they didn't have.

He was waiting tables at another restaurant, the only work he knew. His parents had never paid him wages—there was no need, since they always bought him everything he needed. Now his mother was not speaking to him at all. His father expressed sympathy, but as in all things, he toed Hasnain's mother's line. She had come to London at sixteen to marry a friend of her uncle's, nearly fifteen years her senior but an educated man of ambition. Though she herself had little formal education and had been brought up merely to serve her man, her upbringing, as is the case with certain irrevocably strong women, simply hadn't *taken*—she had always ruled her husband, their restaurants, and their home with an iron fist wrapped in a silk glove. She was still lovely, often taken for his older sister. She had grown up persecuted among a Hindu majority, so London had paradoxically strengthened her Muslim pride. She had no use for Baba's interest in Western pastimes and predilections—no use for an American girl or, it seemed, for Hasnain now. He had never mentioned Nicole's pregnancy: not their fabricated tale much less the truth. He had been written off even *without* it, dismissed as a fool who was throwing his future away—and who could argue? Here they were in North Islington, among new immigrants, preparing to bring a child he could only barely support into the world. They would marry as soon as possible so that Nicole could work legally, but really, what could she do? And they would have to pay for the baby's care. It was an insurmountable situation, one that he knew rarely ended well in practice.

He had never been happier in his entire life.

They had stayed up all night, talking, making plans, making love, which her doctor insisted was perfectly safe. Nicole was drowsy on the ride to Heathrow but fought to keep her eyes open, clutching his hand so that he drove with only one. "I feel," she said softly, "like when I get home no one will recognize me. I feel like I'm another person now, like all those years I was there I was wearing a mask and it's finally off, but they won't understand that—they'll think this is a mask, now."

It frightened him when she spoke that way. What if what she wore *was* a mask, born of trauma and heady expatriatism and pregnancy hormones and youth? What if she landed on US soil and woke up like one who had been sleepwalking? What if she never came back to him?

"I'm worried about you," he said, kissing her hand. "I shouldn't have let you stay up so long at a stretch—it isn't good for the baby."

"You're good for the baby," she said, and in her smile he saw truth, the only truth he had ever recognized, and knew she would come back—come home to him. "I'll sleep on the plane."

FOR ONE MOMENT then, like students hiding out in the hall-way in the middle of a church dance, these two not-friends, not-lovers, in-New-York-merely-acquaintances will kiss. Hasnain and Rebecca, he just barely conscious again and wandering back from having had his injuries checked out; she waiting for him so as to tell him that the men who jumped him have been relocated and he doesn't need to worry about them now. For one moment, this is all there is: the dark night of a small town invaded by shell-shocked foreigners; the pain in his ribs, his groin, his back; the hunger in her to feel something life-affirming, to remember desire; the crumpled bulk of Nicole's letters stuffed deep into his pocket, and this—this kiss. It doesn't last long. In Hasnain's broken condition it escalates to nothing else, though maybe it would not have anyway: he has never cheated on Leslie and suspects, though he is not sure why, that Rebecca has never cheated on Alan. Still, for the moment there is the taste of her in his mouth intermingled with his blood: her blond hair—streaks of white gray at the temples—inside his hands. Her Jewish American blood as devoid of the history of her people as he is removed from the nuclear stalemate between India and Pakistan, playing itself out on the soil of his father's kin. Yet for that moment he savors in her the taste of another exile for the first time in many years—the taste of another woman who has known irrevocable loss.

Then it is over, and Rebecca turns and walks back into the church basement, where she has a cot, and Hasnain heads back upstairs to his pew and sleeping bag.

HAD SHE SLEPT on the plane? Had she been, then, asleep when it happened—blown to oblivion while under the deep cloak of dreams? He has heard the stories: tornado winds tearing the clothes right off passengers' bodies; lungs expanding to four times their normal size; passengers still alive as they fell from the sky; mothers found clutching their babies' corpses. He has spent the nights writhing in his bed imagining her eyes—her hands reaching out for him, only to come back empty, then rushing to her stomach to shield the child she loved already, the baby she could never possibly protect from this world. *Please, please, let her have been sleeping, let it have been fast.* Let the dream of their improbable, magical future have been the last thing ever to float through her head.

And for lack of anything else left to give him, let us agree that we will leave it at that.

FOR A FEW brief hours, he plans how he will finally send the letters to her mother. He will find out, somehow, if she still lives at that address and deliver these last remains of her daughter, maybe even in person. He will finally explain. He rehearses conversations in his head all day, waiting in the crowded solitude of the church basement or gazing out at the isolated vastness from the town's rocky shore. The baby he planned to raise shared the same blood as that bereaved woman, and only now, thinking of his sons, can he bring himself to face his youthful arrogance in resenting her. Only now can he see that they are partners on an eternal journey: his boys, himself, and the grandmother of his child who never was, the woman whose womb ferried Nicole to life's shores. But by nightfall, already, he has abandoned his plan. He was right, all those years ago—if for the wrong reasons. Nicole's mother is better off unaware. If he could somehow find the Mary of the letters without notifying anyone else first, that would be one thing, but he has no surname or address and the task seems impossible. He was right to bear the burden and the treasure alone all these years. It is too late to find Nicole's long-gone girlhood friend now.

On September 11, 2001, all over the world people went about their ordinary business of being born and dying. Time waits for no media loop. Mere hours before the towers fell, before Hasnain's flight was grounded, in a Johannesburg hospital Joshua's wife, Kaya, gave birth to their third child. At daybreak in Columbus, Eli woke stiff on a plastic couch in Diane's room on the oncology ward, her breasts now part of a long past they shared and would never see again. In the twilight of peacetime America, Kenneth stood on the manicured lawn of an affluent northern Atlanta suburb and summoned the courage to ring a doorbell, unaware that by November his son would be deployed to Afghanistan. In Querétaro, Gabriella raced to help her aging mother to the toilet, while in their new home in Santa Fe, Daniel and Esther slept through a ringing phone, having debated in hushed tones late into the night about whether to comply with Esther's sister's wishes and send their thirteen-year-old son to live with her in Spain. So it happened then that their son was the one to take the call from his middle-aged not quite brother Leo's boyfriend, Sandor, phoning from Marrakech to report that Daniel's biological daughter, Mary Rebecca Grace, had died in the arms of her husband, her mother and brother gathered bedside.

But of course, Hasnain knows nothing of this.

ON THE FLIGHT back to New York, the airline crew will stay out of their way. All the passengers will know one another's names by then, will walk up and down the aisles boldly, drinking and laughing as if on a charter flight to a tropical island. On the flight back to New York, Hasnain will see neither his bathroom assailants nor the three Muslim women, but the two fellows in their Islamic dress and long beards will still be present, smiling through their language barrier, friendlier than before. Over the next days and months, tales will continue to filter in from Gander: how one American family arrived at their Canadian host's home to find a full Thanksgiving dinner prepared for them; how others arrived at an evacuated school to find the high school band playing "God Bless America"; how countless residents of Newfoundland approached the "plane people," as they were called that week, thanking them for—despite anything Leslie believes—all America has "done for the world." Though Hasnain and Rebecca will have seen each other over their remaining days in Gander, they will not have shared another kiss, and now Rebecca is on a different flight entirely. Once they land separately, Hasnain knows that, New York not being Gander, it is entirely possible—probable, even—that they will not cross paths again. Susan's lessons are on a day he no longer teaches, and soon enough she will be a teenager, consumed no doubt by other less beautiful, more urgent pursuits than studying piano. On the flight, Hasnain does not drink the champagne the other passengers have brought on board and dispensed with the help of the crew, but he will meet the eyes of the two men with their long beards and say to them, "Assalamu alaikum," and they will respond in kind without taking him for an imposter or even registering surprise. And in New York, Leslie will be waiting for him with open arms, into which he will all but collapse as she gasps over his limping and his injuries, and his boys will try to hang on to his arms and Leslie will admonish, "No, careful, Baba is hurt, can't you see?" but he will hold his arms out to them and let them swing from them like from the branches of a tree, resolving fruitlessly, pointlessly in a world such as this, never to lose them, never to let them scatter as he did from his parents, his brother, even though if he had it to do over again he would do exactly the same thing. And so here, at last, he is home: my beloved Hasnain standing in the middle of JFK Airport, thirty-seven and twenty-four years old at once, remembering me with the echo of Rebecca still on his lips, and with all the faith and hope he once believed irrevocably stolen from him, holding on to his family and looking ahead.

I'm so sorry I didn't tell you about the baby sooner. But within only a matter of hours you'll see me for yourself and then you will know. Then your hand will touch my stomach, touch her life inside me, and I will begin, if you'll let me, to explain how the worst of all possible fortunes can somehow turn into something beautiful. I will start my campaign to get you to come back here with me and find a beauty of your own—to where these letters are waiting for you, to where the world is scary and huge and without limits. I hope so badly you will come. I can't wait to tell you everything.

Acknowledgments

During the years of writing *A Life in Men* and then waiting for it to come into print, I visited most of the countries where chapters of the book are set, in one instance for the first time (Kenya), and in other instances for my first return in more than a decade (Amsterdam, London). If I were to make a list of all I am grateful for regarding this novel, the list would read something like: the Cyclades, London, Kenya, Querétaro, La Gomera, Amsterdam, Morocco. If I were to try to draw a circle around the places that made this novel possible, it would grow too sprawling to make digestible sense. *A Life in Men* is a book as much about travel as it is about friendship, about the body, about hope; a comprehensive acknowledgments list could go on and on (thank you, Battersea Park Road!) before ever reaching a single *person* with whom I spoke.

But of course that would tell such a lesser story. Our worlds are made up of those with whom we share some manner of intimacy—transient or otherwise—the people who make us *need* to tell stories. And so:

Thank you to my onetime fellow nomads of Arthog House, wherever they may be: Jude, Heath, Terry, Roger, Greg, and especially Anthony Blair and William Milne. When my recurring dream of flying through that upstairs window, like Wendy searching for my Lost

Boys, finally stopped visiting me at night, I guess I knew it was time to commit some version of our old world to the page. Thanks for taking care of me when I needed it badly.

Thank you to the first reader of this novel, Tom Johnson, who saw me through a turbulent creative period mostly intact. To my tribe of trusted readers and collaborators over *A Life in Men*'s many drafts: Rob Roberge, Zoe Zolbrod, Emily Tedrowe, Rachel DeWoskin, Thea Goodman, Betsy Crane, Patrick Somerville, Laura Ruby, Cecelia Downs, Karen Schreck, Allison Amend, and Tom Hernandez. Thanks to my best girls at Other Voices Books and *The Nervous Breakdown*, Stacy Bierlein and Leah Tallon, who somehow prevented our many endeavors from crashing and burning when I was so preoccupied I didn't know my own name. Eternal appreciation for my husband, David Walthour, who, as he has done with every book I have written, welcomed these characters into his life and home, and held down the fort with grace when I was away, either literally or in the wilds of my mind.

Thank you to the editors at *F Magazine,* who ran the very first excerpt of the novel; to Summer Literary Seminars and Mary Gaitskill for sending me to Kenya and changing its course; and to Ellen Levine for her wise guidance in the early stages of *A Life in Men*'s journey. A thrilled shout out to one of my very favorite people on the planet, my agent, Alice Tasman, with whom I fell in blissful literary-love at first sight—Alice, you are never freaking allowed to retire.

It's been my honor to work with one of the greatest editors in the business, Chuck Adams, and to have the whole Algonquin team watching my back. You are all simply an old-school, close-knit, smart-as-hell, dedicated, high-integrity pleasure in a world where not all publishing rides roll this way anymore.

I am in great debt to many people—most of whom I have never met— who have written medical articles, self-help books, blogs, and other resource material on cystic fibrosis. Although I took certain fictional liberties with Mary's condition, it would have been wholly impossible to write this novel without these knowledgeable guides, who enabled me to form a picture of the world of someone with CF. Part of the proceeds of the book will be donated to the Cystic Fibrosis Foundation, and anyone who wishes to learn more about global organizations working with CF can find a list at en.wikipedia.org/wiki /List_of_cystic_fibrosis_organizations.

Finally, I have been fortunate to know a handful of astounding, courageous people who inspired this novel—and *me*—in ways impossible to quite pin down. *A Life in Men* is, above everything, an exploration of the human drive to live as large as possible despite limitations that may be imposed by the body or from the outside. And so, to the fighters and dreamers and questers in my life, who have not had an easy run of it but whose unstoppable hope, heart, and will could power planets, in particular Amy Sue Chandler, Jennifer Nix, Emily Rapp, and Rob Roberge. In different ways, each one of you has taught me the vital difference between "surviving" and "living," and has changed me, as a writer and a person.

A LIFE IN MEN

Life Imitates Art: Notes on (Not) Writing the Dead

*

Questions for Discussion

Life Imitates Art:
Notes on (Not) Writing the Dead

BY GINA FRANGELLO

A year ago, my lifelong friend and surrogate sister, Kathy, was found dead in her apartment by her fiancé. She had metastatic ovarian cancer, and we knew that her chances of ever reaching old age were slim. At the time of her death, however, she was almost finished with her first round of chemo and was on the verge of remission, which could have bought her healthy, symptom-free years. Then, while getting ready for work, she threw a blood clot—a side effect of cancer, which is a thrombotic disease—and died, hopefully instantly. We'd been friends since we were sixteen—since she cornered me in a bathroom at school and confessed her passionate, unrequited love for the guy who sat behind me in Physics. In the nearly thirty years that followed, I had remained her confidante—a kind of emotional big sister, although to describe it that way would be reductive. We were also partners in crime, sneaking flasks of Jameson into booze-free events, or wearing our leather pants to children's birthday parties. She was also the first "nanny" my twin daughters ever had, and ten years later, the loss of her hit my three children almost as hard as it did me. She had visited me in every country I'd ever lived in, including several that appear in my new novel, *A Life in Men*. After her death, there was not a bar, a restaurant, a bookstore, a vintage clothing shop, a nail salon, or even a European city I seemed able to enter without her ghost accompanying me. We had been *everywhere* together. We had lived a sprawling, messy, intertwined life, and now I was set with the task of navigating this ghost town alone.

Kathy was not the inspiration for the character Mary. The novel sold, in fact, just weeks before her shocking cancer diagnosis. Prior to that she had no symptoms of illness, and I had never known her to be sick. In fact, *I* was the one always being hospitalized for one thing or another, and before she met her fiancé, she often joked that she would marry my husband when I kicked the bucket.

Tragedy is hard—maybe impossible—to define. Kathy was forty-three at the time of her death. She had traveled the world, had many friends, had worked and lived independently for years, and was madly in love. Surely her death was premature, and devastating to those who loved her. To call it "tragic" might be a stretch in light of so many who, like Mary in *A Life in Men,* live daily with the reality of terminal illnesses, or who, like Mary's best friend, Nix, meet chilling fates born of human violence. Still, like Mary and Nix in the novel, I have found myself quite literally haunted by the absent presence of my friend, speaking aloud to Kathy on empty streets late at night, trying to figure out what it means to be, as Faulkner wrote, "one of those who is doomed to live," with all the privileges and burdens it entails to carry the dead with us, to live for ourselves as well as them.

When I was twenty years old, I arrived in London for a semester abroad only weeks after the Lockerbie disaster of 1988. Many of my new friends in London had lost friends in the plane explosion, but it had not touched me directly. I did, however, find myself living that semester with a beautiful, whip-smart, fearless woman named Sarah who read Updike and worshipped the band Miracle Legion. We traveled together; we picked up guys together; we swapped our sometimes-boyfriends' ripped jeans. Sarah had cystic fibrosis. The man she fell in love with in London, in fact, called her "Cystic" as a pet name, which I found so irreverently tender that it may be the only direct detail about Sarah to have survived in the pages of my novel. After our semester ended, we didn't keep in close touch, but some five years later I saw her again in Boston. Her health had deteriorated, but she had continued to travel, as had I. Five years after that reunion, Sarah died, at age thirty, while living in Jordan among the Bedouin people. She had been pursuing a degree in cultural anthropology. Considering that I had seen Sarah only once in the past decade, her death hit me perhaps bizarrely hard. I am a hard sell about admiring people, but I had admired the hell out of her. She was, in the least cheesy possible application of the word, *inspirational.* She lived large and hard, often against the counsel of doctors and friends. She never let her illness define or confine her. She also loved as hard and recklessly as she had lived. In a fit of nostalgia and sadness, I wrote to Sarah's mother, whom I did not even know, and asked if I might write her biography. I never heard back from her, which does not, in retrospect, surprise me. Likely this grieving woman had never even heard of me. Sarah's story was not mine to tell.

It would be ten years before I would begin *A Life in Men*—a fictional novel centered around a woman traveler with cystic fibrosis. I purposely gave Mary an unusual genetic mutation of the disease, because I did not want this to be a novel about CF, a condition I don't personally have, so much as about what it is to struggle to live on a large canvas despite physical—and psychological—limitations. The countries Mary travels to are not based on Sarah's life but my own; in all cases except for Gander, Newfoundland, the book became autobiographical when it comes to geography, and in other, more unexpected, ways, too. I wrote the novel to honor Sarah's memory, but in many senses the more I wrote, the more anything based on her receded from its pages. By the time it sold to Algonquin, it had become the most deeply personal work of fiction I've ever written.

It would be fair to say then that losing my own best high school girlfriend five months after selling the book was one of those instances of Life Imitating Art—in this case, in a most unwelcome way. In the months leading up to the novel's publication, I have found myself walking in Mary's shoes, trying to relearn life without Kathy much as Mary has to without Nix. Who are we without the audience, company, and conspiracy of our closest friends? What do we want to do with the time we have left, however long that may be? What do those who are gone continue to teach us?

A *Life in Men* was inspired by one courageous woman, whose life was ultimately very separate from my own. And yet ironically, after my own childhood friend's death, the book became *my* inspiration and template for how to go on from there, as I found myself living its pages in ways I had never expected. As I had once learned things about bravery from Sarah, so my own novel has strangely instructed me in the ways of grief and memory as I mourn Kathy. The book is dedicated to two very different women, both of whom taught me difficult, sometimes frightening, and ultimately freeing things about how to live.

Questions for Discussion

1. Mary longs at one point for Geoff to forgive her for being "weak and selfish when the ill were supposed to be strong and heroic" (page 310). Where do our notions of the terminally ill as noble, pure, and heroic come from? Which popular films and novels support these ideas? Why might it be comforting to the survivors to think of the dying as somehow "stronger"?

2. Although Nix's death takes place between the first and second chapter of the novel, the reader does not learn the specifics of how she died until late in the third chapter, when Mary reveals the details of Nix's death on Pan Am Flight 103 to Kathleen, a virtual stranger (page 102). Why is Mary able to speak openly about Nix for the first time to a woman she barely knows when she has withheld these details from the men close to her, like Joshua and Yank? What impact did it have on you to learn of Nix's death this way? Did it prompt you to think differently about Mary's behavior in London? Why do you think the author chose to withhold this information from the reader until Mary was ready to talk about it?

3. The body plays an intense role in this novel. In particular, the gritty realities of a life-shortening lung condition are juxtaposed against the strong and burgeoning sexuality of a young, attractive woman. Reflect on some of the struggles Mary endures to identify

as a sexual being despite her condition. What does sex represent to Mary? Is our society's construction of young women's sexuality compatible with Mary's life experiences?

4. Mary and Nix both strongly react against their mothers' lives, wanting something different and "larger" for themselves. Yet Mary ends up understanding her adoptive mother better as she faces infertility, and Nix ends up—like her mother—choosing to keep an unplanned pregnancy that might limit her opportunities. How do you think we begin to see our parents' choices differently as we age and face similar challenges? Although neither Mary's nor Nix's mother makes a concrete appearance on the page, did you as the reader think these women were likely as "simple" as their brash, college-age daughters made them out to be? What might your own mother's story "look like" in a novel versus the way you thought of it when you were younger?

5. At the beginning of the novel, Mary and Nix assume that Nix will long outlive Mary, and Nix's untimely death serves as a catalyst for Mary to begin a more adventurous life. How does the tragedy of Nix's death ultimately serve to make Mary live more fully? How conscious do you think most of us are in our daily lives that life is precarious, not only for those who are ill, but for everyone? What does it mean to live each day as though it may be your last? If you were suddenly to find out that your life expectancy was much shorter than the norm, would you make any changes? What would they be?

6. Discuss the role of "survivor's guilt" in the novel. First, Nix's feelings of guilt regarding Mary's illness (and her behavior with Mary's first boyfriend, Bobby Kenner) prompt her to make a sacrifice that is much greater than she could have understood going in. Later, Mary struggles with the guilt of being the one still living when she was supposed to be the one to die young. Still later, Mary's guilt is complicated further as she begins to realize the truth of what Nix did for her in Greece. Why are we so often haunted by guilt over things we cannot control?

7. A Life in Men is written in a style that permits readers to uncover certain mysteries at their own pace. At what point in the novel did you

realize that Nix was dead? That she had been raped in Greece? How do the various stages at which the different characters learn things add to your cumulative understanding of events?

8. *A Life in Men* tells us that there is never only one truth, but rather, "there is only one truth at a time" (page 339). How does that play out in the story? How does that play out in real life?

9. The author shows you Mary's life from several angles by getting into the minds of numerous characters, including Geoff, Kenneth, Daniel, Eli, and Leo. What are some of the insights you gained from those points of view that you might have missed out on if the novel had relayed only Mary's perspective? The story ends not with Mary's death but with Hasnain—a character the reader has never met before—as he revisits his relationship with Nix after his flight is grounded in Gander on 9/11 (page 376). How does this final installment of Mary and Nix's story add to your understanding of the whole? What is revealed, and how does it change things? Whose novel, ultimately, is this?

10. The characters in *A Life in Men* are not "religious," and yet spiritual identity plays a key role in several characters' journeys. Mary is surprised to learn, as an adult, that she is of Jewish descent; Hasnain struggles with his identity as a Muslim man in a world torn by stereotypes and violence; Nix seeks to find peace through yoga and Buddhism. In a contemporary, global world, how does our access to the smorgasbord of world religions impact us? What do you think the novel's overall sensibility is in terms of the role religion plays in human connection and fragmentation?

11. Very close to her death, Mary refers to Geoff as the "man of my life" (page 339). And yet in many ways, she appears to be more intimate with Kenneth, with whom she feels an unsurpassed "recognition" and kinship, and whose acceptance she sees as unconditional and unflinching. What characterizes Mary's relationships with these two very different men? What are the differences and overlaps of romantic love, sexual attraction, and friendship she feels with each? Do you think Mary's relationship with Kenneth

is "immoral"? Is their bond a betrayal of Geoff? Is it possible to love two people at the same time? Does Mary's illness have an impact on what she is "entitled" to in this regard?

12. What did you think of the appearance of the character Rebecca at the end of the novel? Does it matter, in the end, whether this is the same Rebecca that Daniel has mentioned as Mary's biological mother or is simply another woman by the same name who has given up a child?

13. *A Life in Men* is full of six-degrees-of-separation "coincidences," such as Geoff's walking into Mary's hospital room in Cincinnati and Mary and Leo's encountering Sandor at the gallery party mere weeks after he has seen Yank playing saxophone. The author sets up these coincidences — Geoff is, after all, a doctor, and Leo and Sandor are both artists, living in the country where Sandor was born — but even so, are such coincidences believable? Have you ever had an implausible coincidence in your own life that led to other important developments?

14. The author writes, in the essay that follows the novel, that she initially wanted to write a biography of her college roommate who had cystic fibrosis but that the story was not hers to tell. She goes on to speak of the ways *A Life in Men* became instead infused with her own travel experiences, and then — when her high school girlfriend met an untimely death — became a template for teaching herself about grief. Talk about the differences between fiction and nonfiction in terms of accessing "emotional truths." What freedoms do our imaginations grant us, and how might they work to dig deeper than "facts"?

BLAIR HOLMES

GINA FRANGELLO is a cofounder of Other Voices Books and the editor of the fiction section at *The Nervous Breakdown*. She is also the author of one previous novel and a collection of short stories. She lives in Chicago. Her website is www.ginafrangello.com.